DIVER'S HEART

ALSO BY K.A. KNIGHT

COURTS AND KINGS
Court of Nightmares
Court of Death
Court of Beasts
Court of Heathens

DAWNBREAKER
Voyage to Ayama
Dreaming of Ayama

DEADLY LOVE (with Ivy Fox)
Deadly Affair
Deadly Match
Deadly Encounter

THE FALLEN GODS
Pretty Painful
Pretty Bloody
Pretty Stormy
Pretty Wild
Pretty Hot
Pretty Faces
Pretty Spelled

FORGOTTEN CITY
Monstrous Lies
Monstrous Truths
Monstrous Ends

THE FORSAKEN (with Loxley Savage)
Capturing Carmen
Stealing Shiloh
Harboring Harlow

HER FREAKS (with Erin O'Kane)
Circus Save Me
Taming the Ringmaster
Walking the Tightrope

HER MONSTERS
Rage
Hate

LEGENDS AND LOVE
Revolt
Rebel
Riot

THE LOST COVEN
Aurora's Coven
Aurora's Betrayal

PINE VALLEY COLLEGE
Racing Hearts

PRETTY LIARS
Unstoppable
Unbreakable

THEIR CHAMPION
The Wasteland
The Summit
The Cities
The Nations
The Forgotten
The Lost
The Damned

THE WILD BOYS
The Wild Interview
The Wild Tour
The Wild Finale

Alena's Revenge
Burn Me (with Kendra Moreno)
Cirque Obscurum (with Kendra Moreno)
Crown of Stars
Daddy's Angel
Dark Temptations Volume I (with Erin O'Kane)
Den of Vipers
Gangsters and Guns (with Loxley Savage)
Fractured Shadows (with Kendra Moreno)
The Hero Complex (with Erin O'Kane)
The Horror Emporium (with Kendra Moreno and Poppy Woods)
Nadia's Salvation
Scarlett Limerence
Shadowed Heart (with Kendra Moreno)
Shipwreck Souls (with Kendra Moreno and Poppy Woods)
The Standby
Stepbrothers' Darling
Stolen Trophy (with Kendra Moreno)

DIVER'S HEART

K.A. KNIGHT

Cover design by Dawn Adams

ISBN: 979-8-3470-2102-4

Published in 2026 by Podium Publishing
www.podiumentertainment.com

For my family, both blood and found, this one's for you.
Thank you for putting up with my weird research and crazed mumblings.

My fellow thrill seekers,

I know *Diver's Heart* stole many, well, hearts when it was first released, and mine was no different. Threaded throughout the adventure and action is a love story that has stuck with me for years.

As with everyone, I think finding your family and the people who would stand with you in the face of danger is all we can hope for, and Peyton and her guys did that within these pages.

This isn't your typical love story, however. While it's filled with second chances and raw, honest truths that tore their worlds apart, it also shows the hidden, inner strength of this little family and what they are willing to do for the ones they love.

I couldn't sum this book up better than the characters themselves, so I won't even try. "Don't fear the dark, Minnow. You find out what you're made of in oblivion."

I hope you enjoy this brand-new edition, featuring bonus scenes and custom art, as much as I do.

Are you ready for the adventure of a lifetime, Minnow?

Katie Knight ♡

CONTENT WARNING

Diver's Heart is a dark romance featuring a polyamorous relationship dynamic that includes explicit sexual encounters, including scenes with multiple partners and forceful penetration. Additional themes that readers may find triggering include controlling behavior, verbal degradation, and emotional distress.

DIVER'S HEART

Some places should never be explored . . .

PROLOGUE

The first time I met Tyler Lucas, my heart skipped a beat. I was seventeen years old. He was twenty-three, six foot five, and two hundred and thirty pounds of sex personified. His sun-bronzed skin glistened with water as he heaved himself over the side of my dad's boat. When he flashed those pearly white teeth at me in an arrogant smirk, I fell. I fell hard.

It took only one summer for me to fall in love with him, completely head over heels in love. The kind even my dad said you never find anymore. We spent the summer exploring the world with my father, learning everything. Tyler was an experienced diver, but he wanted advice on starting his own company with his brother and friends, and my dad was happy to oblige. We spent our days in the water, and our nights curled up in the tiny beds below deck. Time passed so quickly, and soon, summer was over, and he was ready to leave . . . to start his future. But he took me with him, much to my dad's delight and sadness.

He looked me in the eyes and told me it was time to have my own adventures.

I was so excited . . . But when I met Tyler's brother, my stomach sunk, and my heart pounded at his proximity.

And when I met their two friends? I hated myself. I had to hide it. I loved Tyler . . . only Tyler, right? So why did my heart skip a beat around them? The more time we spent together, only growing closer, I realised I had a problem.

Our lives were a constant adventure with twists and turns just like the caves we explored, but when push came to shove . . .

I did the very thing I thought I would never do. I walked away. I left my family behind to protect them, to save them. I left my heart on our boat and lost myself in the deep blue ocean of this world.

Searching for myself once again.

This is our story.

This is my diver's heart.

ONE

Four years later . . .

Peyton

Tyler is up to something. I know it.

As I resurface and pull off my mask, I look around at the almost empty boat. Where is everyone? I heave myself up onto the freeboard, push my hair back, and clear my nose and eyes of water as I pull my tired feet up and strip off my fins. Standing on aching legs, I drag myself and my equipment up onto the deck, sit on the edge, and undo the tanks and empty cylinders. I store it all, ready to check it over later, and pull down the zipper on my wet suit, folding it until it's at my waist. I wring out my wet hair as the Mediterranean sun starts to set, but it's still no colder. Water trails down my skin as I step farther onto the borrowed boat's deck.

Just another rich man looking for a purpose. That's who's funding us now.

It works for us though, and this time, it's treasure hunting. We have been looking for almost three years, and today? Today we fucking found it, so we should be celebrating . . . happy.

So where is everyone?

"Ty?" I call, looking around. Maybe they are inside or down below?

"Kalen?" I shout, my tongue tripping over the name of the one man I probably shouldn't call for. "Riggs? Fin?"

It's silent. Even the waves crashing into the boat are quiet from where we're anchored off the coast of some undiscovered island. The treasure lies below the surface of it, only accessible by the cave system we found, mapped, and yesterday, broke through into the treasure room.

Biting my lip, I furrow my brows as I poke my head through the sliding glass door into the galley of the yacht we're on. Seriously, where are they? Usually, Riggs is sitting at his computers in here, working on his software for mapping, but even they are dark. Fin isn't at the helm, I don't see Kalen lurking anywhere, and where the hell is Tyler? He was supposed to meet me back on deck after he went up first, starting his decomp stops before I did.

I panic then. Shit, what if something went wrong? I took the long way back, exploring the reef when I saw him nearing the boat. "Ty?" I almost scream. "Ty?"

I hear a noise up top, so I grab the metal pole next to the ladder and I quickly yank myself up onto the deck, almost falling onto the floor. But when I get there, I freeze, my eyes wide and chest squeezing tight.

A sick feeling starts in my stomach as I struggle to breathe. He smiles at me, thinking it's just shock . . . not guilt and panic.

He's down on one knee surrounded by a heart made from shells. Shells we have found all over the world together. His black hair is swept back, still damp. His blue eyes are wide and happy, and those lips I love so much are parted in a trembling smile. His chest is exposed like always, showing his impressive muscles, his bottom is covered with shorts, and his feet are bare.

In his hand is a ring.

"Peyton Andrews, I have loved you since the first moment I met you, and every day since, I have only fallen deeper." I swallow as tears come to my eyes. I want to run, I want to pretend this isn't happening. "You're my best friend, you're my family . . . So why not make it official? Baby, living without you is like diving without a tank—useless and without air."

"Ty—" I start, trying to stop him.

How could Kalen let this happen?

How could I?

Oh God! Everything comes back, everything I've tried to bury so deep, and I have to swallow bile. I feel weak and lightheaded, like I might fall overboard—at least that would be easier.

"Peyton . . . I asked your father before . . . before he died, because I knew you were the one I want to spend the rest of my life with, exploring the world. Will you marry me?"

I can't speak.

His lips dip as concern enters his eyes. "Baby, you okay?"

"I—" I swallow hard, and tears fall freely down my face as I try not to scream from the unfairness of it. I love this man, and once upon a time, this was my dream . . . But I can't. I can't do this. I can't hurt him like this, because he would find out eventually, and he would hate me. I couldn't bear that.

It would tear our family apart.

I can't do this, even if it means crushing his heart now. Even if it means walking away from the best thing to ever happen to me. "I— Ty, I can't."

He blinks, dropping his hand slightly. "What? Peyton, are you saying no?" he asks incredulously.

I nod my head and shake it, and he gets to his feet before rushing to me. He holds my cheeks as he searches my eyes. "Baby, what's wrong? I thought . . . I thought you loved me?" He sounds so confused. God, I wish I could take that away. He's put so much effort into this . . . Fuck, I'm a horrible person.

"I do," I gasp, sobs racking my body. "I do, Ty, I really do, but I can't. I'm sorry, I can't do this—"

He stumbles back, looking away, and I spot the sheen in his eyes and the tremble in his limbs as the sun sets. "Okay. I— Yeah, okay. It's not time, you're not ready. I get that—"

Oh God, even now he's trying to protect me and make it okay for me, like always. It's like the time we found ourselves surrounded by sharks and he went under to save me. Or when my tank ran out of air and we got caught in a sump, and he buddy breathed with me, putting his life at risk. He's always protecting me, loving me. God, he deserves so much better than a woman who lusts after others . . . after his family.

I know what I have to do. For once, I need to save him—from me.

"Tyler, no, I can't do this anymore."

He turns to me, confused. "Baby, what do you—"

"It's over," I blurt out. "I'm sorry, I can't be with you anymore." I feel the words tumbling from my lips as he falls back like I've struck him. His heart is breaking right before my eyes. He tries to reach for me, the bracelets I made him wrapped around his wrist all the way to his forearm, one for each cave we have been in.

"Pey—"

I shake my head and back away, hitting the stairs. "I'm sorry, Ty. It's over, I can't do this. Please, let me go." Then I turn like a chicken, not being able to stand the confusion and heartbreak written across every beautiful plane of his face and crushed body. I slide down the stairs, wandering inside in a haze. I hear him yell and then start to cry, and my tears fall harder.

I make it back to my cabin and stare around at the space we share. Turning, I grab a pack and shove my clothes and possessions inside, hesitating at the picture tacked to the wall of my dad and me. We're both in our gear and smiling with the sun behind us. It was our first exploration together . . . the one where I met Tyler.

I kiss it. "I'm sorry, Daddy. I messed up so badly this time. Breathing isn't going to help. I don't think this one is fixable." I can almost hear his sigh as he tells me everything is. But not this.

Not his heart.

Not mine.

I zip my pack, and when I turn, Kalen is standing at the door. His dark eyes are locked on me, and the worst part? It's the knowing there, the disappointment. He knows what I'm doing and why, and he's going to hate me for it.

They all will.

He opens his mouth and then shakes his head and steps back, not blocking the door. Not stopping me. I rush past, and with each step, my heart breaks further.

"I hope you know what you just threw away," he whispers behind me.

I do, but that was never the issue. I threw my life away, and the only man who ever loved me. My whole family. I'm cracking it, but it's better than breaking it completely.

It's better than me ruining it.

Better they hate me and not each other.

I can hear Riggs and Fin trying to calm Ty down, asking what happened as I make it out back and grab my shoes. I throw my bag onto the rip. I don't look up or back—I can't, or I'll fall to my knees and beg them to understand. To not hate me.

I untie the boat with shaky, clumsy fingers and leap onto it. That's when I hear it. "Peyton!" Ty screams.

I look up, meeting those heartbroken blue eyes from where he stands at the ladder, chest heaving. I see it in his face; he's begging me not to do this. Not to leave him.

To leave them.

To not crush his heart into a thousand pieces and sink it to the depths below.

I stare at him, memorising him. Those hands that held me through my nightmares, those eyes that contained all our hopes and dreams, those lips that whispered such loving words to me when I thought I couldn't go on anymore. His heart where he kept mine with his, that he gave me so easily. Selfishly. I know every inch of that man, I know his dreams. His hopes.

His pain and fears.

And I still turn and start the engine, sitting on the bench, and look away from him. I'm unable to take it, unable to take the crushed look on his face as I rip out his heart, shred it in my hands, and leave it up there on the deck where, not hours before, we were laughing and kissing.

I speed away, leaping over the waves, the sobs cracking open my chest as tears blur my eyes. But I'm weak, so fucking weak. I look back, and they are there, all four of them. Their silhouettes lit by the dim sun, all standing on the deck watching me flee, watching me run away from everything we are.

Watching me leave them.

It's for the best, I want to scream, but I don't. Instead, I turn around and leave my heart back there with the four men who claimed it without even knowing.

It's done.

It's over . . .

TWO

Three years later . . .

"You hear me, Minnow?"

I shake off the memories, tuck the pearl necklace back into my suit, and zip it up farther. Michael's voice crackles through my mask. Usually, I would just wear a smaller black one, but this makes it easier to communicate when he stays up on the boat while I dive.

"I hear you," I tell him. "I'm coming back. It's all mapped and ready for the excavations tomorrow."

"About time. I can't wait to be done with this one, it's a hell of a fucking cave. I'll have nightmares about it." The sun doesn't reach down here, the light on my helmet the only way to see, illuminating the dark depths.

Something about being down here, the first person to ever explore the cave, makes me giddy, it always does. I love seeing the wondrous nature of this planet and what it has to offer, and there is so much left uncharted. When I'm diving, when I find myself alone in the dark water seeing things that have never been seen by the human eye, I feel whole.

It's the only time I ever do.

I laugh, blowing bubbles back as I softly frog-kick my legs and push myself from the opening of the shadowy cave and into the dark blue of the open water. Gradually, I begin to swim up. It's not too deep, so there's no need to decompress or worry about the bends, but there is silt everywhere making it hard to see, even with my small kicks.

The higher I get, the clearer and brighter the water becomes, the sun penetrating it. I spot the base of the boat and aim for the back. When I break the surface, I yank off my mask and blink my eyes clear, pushing my hair back as I grin at Michael. He's crouched on the freeboard with his shades on, his grey hat pulled on backwards, strands of blond and grey hair escaping it. His muscular body is slightly pudgy in his old age, not that I'll ever tell him that, and his skin is dark from the sun and the hours we have spent in it recently.

His navy tattoo is on display from his cutoff tank, which is tucked into his khaki-coloured shorts, and his feet are bare. His gold chain hangs around his neck and catches the sun. He offers his scarred hand to me, and I clasp it as he yanks me up.

Sitting on the deck, I let him help me pull my gear off. When it's all removed, I strip from my suit and grab the towel he throws at me midair, running it through my hair before wrapping it around my shoulders. "So, the beast is finally done?" He laughs, popping open a beer and passing it to me.

I chug it, burping before wiping my mouth. No need to be ladylike around him. Plus, after living with men in close quarters all my life, I have bad habits. "Thank fuck," I reply, rubbing my hair again as the condensation from the cooler we store the bottles in drips down and onto my hand. "Let them know over the radio. Tonight, we dock, and tomorrow, we get the hell out of here. I can't wait to see the back of this place."

"You and me both, kid." He smacks my shoulder, sending me lurching forward as he laughs. "On to the next adventure."

"Always." I nod as I sit back and close my eyes, letting the sun heat my skin and dry me. Sipping my beer, I relax my tired muscles. I've been doing too many hours underwater, and it's taken its toll, but I wanted this beast done. Michael is right—it's been a bitch of a dive, and I couldn't wait to get it done.

I hear him on the radio as the boat purrs to life, making me crack open my eyes and sit up with a sigh. My abs clench with the movement, showing off my six-pack. It's hard-fucking-earned, but being a diver and exploring means you have to be strong. Hell, I have some arm muscles that even men don't. I can deadlift two hundred and forty pounds from years of hauling tanks and equipment.

My long blond hair sticks to my back, making me sigh. I need to get it cut, but that means taking a break from work to go to get it done. I have the same eyes as my daddy, bright green—emerald, he used to tell me. Hell, he even once held an emerald we found up next to them to prove it.

I also got his height, all five feet nine inches of it, but I got my mum's curves. No amount of working out or training gets rid of those. My left leg is covered in tattoos from hip to ankle. Of boats, treasure, skulls, the sea, and everything in between. On my right hip, I trace a faded white shark bite, smiling as I remember the day it happened.

I'm pulled from my recollections though when Michael calls me. "What?" I snap, standing and ducking into the tiny galley where he's standing at the helm. "What's up, old man?"

"Call." He holds out the phone, and I take a sip of my beer as I grab it.

"Yeah?"

"Peyton, it's Mr. Rogers." I blink and smile for real, my beer dangling from one hand, which Michael feigns trying to steal, so I kick out at him.

"Steve, how are you?" I ask casually. As one of the only rich men I like, I make a genuine effort with him, rather than playing nice for the sake of a dive or funding.

He laughs, knowing I hate small talk. "I am very well, and yourself, Peyton?"

"Good."

"I know you're on a job . . ." He trails off, rustling papers as I lean against the cabin wall.

"Just finished actually," I reply.

"Wonderful! I have one for you, if you're interested. Double pay."

"Why double?" That usually means it's more dangerous . . . or I'm not going to like it.

"I have a team already in place, and they have been ready for a while, but I need someone I can trust to monitor and report back. Not to mention . . . you are the best."

"Second best," I correct automatically. There is only one person who is better at what we do than me, mainly because my dad trained him—Tyler. I shake that off and drop my hand when I realise I was playing with my necklace. "What's the exploration?"

"A new cave system deep in the jungle off the coast of South America. You know I like to be the first person to step foot in those types of places. I have a documentary crew coming out in the next few months, and I need the place mapped and made as safe as possible by then."

"Got it." I nod. "You think there's anything of interest there?"

"I don't know, it was stumbled upon after a hurricane and, well, it got my interest piqued."

Oh, I bet. Steve is a man with money to burn, and he does. Not that I complain, since he keeps me in business and exploring the world, where most others have stopped. Others aim for the stars, while I aim for the deep unknown in the crust of our planet. It does sound interesting. Untapped caves are fun, lots of diving and mapping, which is my favourite part, not the treasure hunting I'm doing now. I genuinely enjoy discovering and working for the good.

"I'm in. I can be there in two weeks."

"Good, they will be ready by then. I'll inform them of your presence."

"They might not like it."

"Maybe not, but it's my money, so they will do it."

I hum, peering down at the watch on the controls. Damn, it's getting late. If we want to get back and restocked before morning and get going to meet in two weeks, we need to go now.

"I can tell you're eager to get ready. I'll see you in two weeks to brief at the site."

"Oh, do I know them, the team?" I inquire curiously. There are only so many of us left, and I know some of them. Some are swindlers and shit, and I need to make sure these aren't.

"I don't think so, but I'll introduce you. I'm also sending across the information and coordinates, liaise with Mary like always," he offers evasively. "See you there! Safe trip," he says before hanging up.

Shrugging, I look at Michael. "Yo, we got a gig. Let's get back and return the boat and restock. We're on the next plane out."

Time for another adventure.

Another day, another dive.

THREE

We don't have to wait too long to fly, only twelve hours, seeing as our last dive was only into sea caves with no decompression stops. It gives us time to return the boat and conclude our current job with a satisfied customer. He informs us he will be putting the treasures in a museum, which makes me smile. It's where they should be, not kept as relics by the rich.

After that, we eat and chill, calling companies to order the gear we're going to need. We always sort it ourselves—never let another handle your gear, trust yourself. I liaise with Mary on it and locations, getting some gear sent ahead for us as well as making sure they have everything we'll need. They do, even some fancy equipment like sonar guns. It seems they spared no expense.

I don't worry too much about equipment, since Michael sorts it out to make sure we get the correct kind—the best computers and gear—from some of the companies we trust. Every diver has a particular kind they prefer, and I'm no different. I do bring my trusty compass that my dad gave me on my first dive though.

We also grab some sleep before heading to the tiny airport on the island. The flight is long, but I'm used to them by now, and I sleep most of the way before looking over the printouts of the emails sent about what we're going into.

It's exciting. It looks like a deep underwater cave with sumps and unexplored passages. The first team has barely gone down yet, and we're going to be the first. It fills me with the adrenaline and excitement I crave.

The only things I feel anymore.

Each dive is harder than the last as I push myself to feel alive. I realise I'm fiddling with my necklace and drop it, forcing myself to relax. We have a lot of work ahead, so this might be the last time I get to for a while.

But the exhaustion is part of the job, and at the end, it only makes it all worthwhile.

When we land, our gear is waiting at the hotel. I check it out to make sure it's all correct and accounted for. Your gear is your life in cave dives, and you treat it with respect and check it often. My paddle fins look new and good quality, as do the wet and dry suits. The full face masks are state of the art, with comms and lights built in. I have my tanks, harness, and primary and secondary lights. My knife, computers, BCD, regulators, tanks, and climbing gear have already been sent to the site, as well as some deco, safe bottles, and my backup gear. We can't take all of it with us, so cave divers learn to pack light on the stuff we don't need, but we always bring extra gear. Down there, anything could go wrong, so you have to be prepared for the unexpected.

I have my thermals to wear under my suit and a couple changes of clothes and essentials in my backpack. I grab my bandanna and bag, and we're ready to go. That night, we eat at the hotel before taking another plane out, and then fly on a seaplane until we reach the dive boat.

We are both tired, so we sleep for a few hours while the sun is still down and we are cutting through the waves on the way to the island. It's only accessible by boat or a helicopter from a ship. This boat is bringing in the last of the gear, the storage filled with tanks, ropes, food supplies, water, lights, DPVs, and so much more. It's impressive.

I can't wait to play with all the equipment.

When the sun comes up, I'm awake and standing on the deck, nursing a mug of coffee. The bright blue water crashes into the side of the boat, and I notice the tides are strong today, making me grin.

Then we come upon the island, and I gape in awe. Fuck, I love exploring new places. Seeing them, wondering what other secrets they have hidden. It rises from the ocean like an untamed beast, daring us to explore and conquer it.

The side we're facing has huge cliffs reaching into the sky, filled with trees and foliage. Michael joins me on deck as we stare at it. "Cap says we moor near the cliff edges, and then we have to climb up the cliff. It's a two-mile trek to base camp. When you're there, let them know the boat is waiting so they can haul the gear up."

"Hell yes," I mutter, downing my coffee and rushing inside to put my wet suit over my shorts and tank top. I tuck my necklace in and brush my hair back into a ponytail before grabbing my mask. "We're going to free-dive this shit," I tell him as he swears and gets into his suit. I grab my backpack and thread my arms through as I wait at the back of the boat.

When the engine cuts and the anchor drops, I look back and thumbs-up the captain as Michael steps up next to me. "Race ya, old man."

"Fucking Minnow, you know you'll win," he mutters as I turn and step onto the freeboard.

"Not my fault I hold the record for being able to hold my breath for eleven minutes," I tease, and with a turn, I dive into the cool water.

I reach the cliff first and heave myself up onto the ledge at the bottom. Yanking off my mask, I tie it at my hip and grab my chalk, dusting my hands to make it easier to climb. There is already a rappel and belay, and ropes with crampons in place. I grab one of the helmets waiting on top of the supply box and tug it on.

Safety first.

I attach myself onto the rope, but instead of using it to pull myself up, I start to climb. Using the small rocks and ledges, I wedge my toes and hands in, pulling myself up and pushing with my legs. I'm halfway up the wall when I hear Michael below me. Grinning, I search for the next handhold and find one across the wall. I leap for it, swinging as I connect with it, and scramble to find some footholds.

I hear Michael yell, and when I'm secure, I look down to see him glaring at me. "Come on, old man, what's life without a bit of risk?" Winking, I start back up the cliff edge, moving quickly and easily, yanking myself over the top before tying off and looking down at Michael, who's moving slowly but surely. Pulling off the helmet, I strip from my suit, fold it, and put it into the wet bag as I grab my shades and look around at the forest before me.

There is a cleared path heading to the site, and I can't wait to get there and get started. Excitement fills me until I'm almost bouncing on the spot, waiting for Michael. I look back out at the ocean, seeing the boat, which is just a dot from up here, and the vast blueness stretching out as far as I can see.

This world still has so much to offer—places never before seen, paths never traversed, rocks never climbed, or caves never dived . . . and I plan to find them all. Starting here. This dive is the one that will properly kick off the rest of my career, I can feel it.

When Michael is at the top, I turn back to the path with a smile. "Let's do this." I grin over at him, and he smiles, shaking his head.

"To the next adventure."

"Always," I agree as we start off into the forest.

FOUR

My legs burn, and sweat drips down my forehead and back. I love it, the pain only makes me push harder. It's not a long trek, but pushing through a rainforest after two weeks of constant dives means it's not easy either. The terrain is rough and raised, and though they carved through the foliage, we still have to climb, duck, tramp through water, and scale a small mountain and rappel down.

Michael is panting behind me when we reach the bottom and cover the last mile between us and the camp. One second, we are in the forest, with the monkeys grunting above us and the snakes slithering about, and the next, we're breaking into the clearing.

Into the camp.

It's amazing, and you can definitely tell Steve is rich. The tents are erected around the perimeter with alerts for predators. The dive site is closed off with supplies waiting to go down next to it. There are fires ready to burn, a helicopter landing pad with one sitting right there, and it's bustling with people carrying equipment, coming up from the cave, and helping get set up.

It's incredible, one of the best I have been on.

"Jesus, kid, would you look at this? Our last boat was held together by duct tape compared to this." Michael laughs as he wraps his arm around my shoulders. "We are finally making it, kid, like you deserve."

"Don't get soft on me, old man. Let's go introduce ourselves and get started." I grin, pulling away.

"Just can't wait to get down there, can ya?" he calls and laughs, following me. I get smiles and quick hellos as I wind through the camp. I spot Steve talking to a huge fierce-looking Black man, but when he notices me, he dismisses him and turns with a grin, his arms wide to showcase the camp.

"You're here!" I meet him halfway for a hug. When he releases me, I drop my gear on the ground and look around.

"This is impressive," I tell him, and he grins wider.

"It is, isn't it? I can't wait for you to see the cave itself. We haven't mapped much, just been planning our attack, but we can discuss that later during the briefing. I'm sure you're tired. Let me show you to your tent before you meet the team."

"Thanks." I nod, grabbing my pack and hauling it over my shoulder. "Also, let them know the boat is here and waiting to unload."

He nods and calls out to someone as I look around again, noticing the huge hole in the ground the camp is built around. It's obviously the way down into the cave and the entrance chamber. I can't fucking wait to rappel down it and see just what Mother Nature has in store for us.

Steve turns back and leads us through the camp as he talks, his voice rushed and excited. That's another thing I like about him—he has an adventurer's soul, he just got into the game too late to actually dive and explore. Instead, he funds others so everyone can see what the world has to offer.

He could spend his immense wealth on anything, but he chose this, and he has my respect for that. He doesn't do it for the credit, though it helps; he does it because he wants to inspire and prove our world is incredible and still so unexplored.

"We'll have a team up here at all times, including a crew bringing down more equipment and rations if you need them, and of course emergency help. There's a comms unit and relay up here so you can send what you find at the end of each day. We have medics and professionals, but this will be yours and my teams' mission. You're in joint charge with another team, with you lot staying down there while we come up."

I nod as he explains the parameters.

"Oh, and this is you." He points at a smallish single tent. I drop my bags inside and stretch my muscles as he grins. "So, are you ready to see it?"

"Hell yes! I thought you would never ask."

He grins and leads me back to the hole. I walk around the edge, staying a safe distance away and peering down. But it's black—pitch black—and deep.

"How far down?"

"Forty metres," he answers, making me whistle.

"And nothing mapped yet?" I ask as we wander back into the camp.

"Not really, only the first tunnel since we started bringing the equipment down." I nod as Michael meanders away to check on our equipment, which should be here by now.

"What about your team?" I query, looking around, curious to meet them. They have to be good to be diving in this and sorting all this out already. I can't wait to get started with them. I just hope they aren't pissed Steve has brought me on, but we are all adults.

"Down there— Oh wait, I think they're coming up," he tells me, and I nod and look farther into the forest surrounding us, wondering what else is hiding out there and how far the cave system stretches under the surface. Fuck, I wonder if it goes to the ocean . . . Wouldn't that be great?

"Peyton, let me introduce you to the team. They have just come back up from taking more equipment down," Steve explains, and I turn with a polite smile on my face but freeze. My heart stops, my lungs scream, and my stomach drops.

"Peyton, this is . . ."

But his words fade as I stare at the men unclipping from the ropes and talking among themselves, completely oblivious to my presence in the bustling camp.

It's them.

Tyler.

Kalen.

Riggs.

Fin.

All four of the men I loved . . . and left.

I stand immobile, unsure what to do. Panic winds through me, rooting me in place. Oh fuck, oh fuck.

But then Steve whistles and draws Tyler's eyes. He blocks them from the sun with his hand and looks over. "Tyler, meet Peyton, the diver I was telling you about!" he calls.

Tyler freezes, his gaze swinging to me. Our eyes clash and stay locked from feet apart, neither of us speaking nor moving. I drink him in, unable to help myself. Even after all this time, he still has my heart racing and stomach clenching.

He's more beautiful than ever.

He's changed. He's bigger, more muscular, and has darker skin. He also has more tattoos from what I can see, but it's his face that has me wincing—harsher, colder, and darker.

The Tyler I knew was sweet and kind, compassionate, and could make me laugh for hours. He had hopes and dreams and the spirit of an adventurer. This isn't my Tyler. I don't know this stone-faced man who so easily barked commands. I knew when I left him it would kill a part of him . . . break his heart. I thought I could handle it if it meant he never found out the truth. Seeing him now, how much I changed him, I know I was wrong . . . It makes me question if it was worth it at all.

After all those years and distance between us, not speaking or seeing each other, the wound is still fresh and easily ripped open. And, not for the first time,

I regret my decision to leave. For a moment, I think he feels the same, the stone façade dropping and revealing the man I used to love underneath.

But then it disappears.

Like he wasn't my world.

Now he looks at me like there was nothing between us, like I wasn't the girl who broke his heart and ruined her own. His eyes are cold, unforgiving, and without a word, he turns away to shout orders at someone, releasing me from the trap of his gaze, but it's too late.

The others look over.

They all freeze.

Riggs's jaw drops in shock, his expression flashing with hope before fading to sadness, and I wince. Out of all of us, he was always the softest. He felt too much, trusted too easily . . . It makes my heart crack to see my usually happy friend not even able to meet my eyes. He turns away as well, his shoulders slumped. His short, styled blond hair catches the sun, and I notice he's filled out too. He used to be lanky and skinny, but now he's built, even rivalling Tyler, his muscles bulging as he moves.

Fin is standing next to him, and my eyes drift his way. He glares at me for a moment, but a smile pulls at his lips as he runs his gaze down my body, being flirty like always. He's taller, wider too. His hair is longer, down to his shoulders, with half of it pulled back and curling from the humidity. His bright blue eyes are cold where they used to be filled with such heat. I drag my eyes away from his, not liking the mocking expression on his face, and lock with those dark orbs I used to hate and love.

Kalen.

Fuck.

And Kalen?

Fuck, Kalen looks angry—no, not angry, furious.

Tyler's brother was always different, angry at the world. We used to wonder if he had a death wish since he got back from his tours overseas. The broken part of him called to the broken parts of me. The girl who lost her mum . . . and her father. I hated that part that thrived in his anger, that fed on our fights. I wished I could be the girl Tyler thought I was back then, that I pretended to be all the time—happy and perfect. But I simply wasn't, and Kalen knew that. He brought out the worst in me . . . and I in him.

He's big, wide as hell, and taller than Tyler. His impressive ink is on display. His black hair is styled back, longer on the top and shorter on the sides. His dark eyes pierce me with such hate and disgust, I almost recoil. His body vibrates from his rage before he slams down his equipment and storms away.

Some reunion.

I almost shake from my swinging emotions, but I'm not that same girl anymore. I was seventeen when I fell in love with Tyler. Twenty-one when I realised I loved them all and left. The three years since, I've grown up a lot. I've picked myself up off rock bottom after almost drinking myself to death. I started my own business when I was so broke, I had to sleep on the leaking boat. I took every dive, dangerous and rubbish. I almost died so many times and broke down repeatedly until it got easier.

Until I started to set records and smash others'.

Until I got noticed and started to make money. Now? Now I'm one of the best in the world. I'm a fucking explorer . . . a strong-ass woman . . . right?

I thought I'd fixed myself like my daddy always told me to . . . but now I'm realising I simply fixed my mind, not my heart. That part of me is still broken, still theirs.

Shit, I should leave . . . but this was a favour, and we already took the money . . . and, fuck, it's such a big exploration. This could be it for me, the thing that I'm known for. I can't leave, not now, not even because they are here and looking at them again brings it all to the surface.

All the pain, heartache, and grief . . . everything I've been swimming so hard to avoid since I left all those years ago.

It's been three years, four days, and twelve hours since I last saw them.

Not one spark of how I feel has dimmed, and watching them now, I realise it never will.

FIVE

Tyler

I have to turn away to gather my composure so I don't cover the distance between us and kiss her— No! Fuck.

She's not mine to kiss anymore. Maybe she never really was.

I loved her more than anything in this world; I would have done anything for her. I wanted to spend the rest of my life with her . . . I knew from the moment I met her I loved her.

Then she crushed my fucking heart.

Ripped it right out of my chest like it was nothing and tossed it away.

I still remember watching her speed away across the ocean as I stood side by side with my family, the ring I bought held in one hand. Losing her destroyed me.

And now she's back.

Like nothing happened. She's standing there as beautiful as always with that same smile, those same green eyes I used to stare into for hours on end, the same curves I worshipped, the same person I loved.

But I'm not the same man anymore.

I grind my teeth as I hear Kalen storm away and lock the trunk with the computers. I should go over there, be polite, but fuck if I don't want to yell for her to fuck off right back onto that boat that she came in on.

This is our find.

Our fucking find. We have worked our asses off to get here, to be able to explore places like this, and she doesn't get to come and take it away. Turning, I head right up to her, making my face cool and easy, hard, even though my heart slams as I meet those emerald eyes I love—loved so much.

I become the leader my people depend on. "So you're the diver?"

"Last I checked," she teases, making me want to wring her fucking neck. I have to clench my fists at my sides to stop myself from grabbing her, dragging her to me, and demanding her obedience, something I never did before . . . something I was always scared to show her.

Fuck that.

How dare she tease me and stand here before me like she didn't kill me when she left?

"We can't have people down there who we don't know or trust," I snarl, looking her over. "You will slow us down." I look at Steve. "I told you we didn't need another diver."

"And I told you that was my condition, having someone I trust here."

I snort at that, wondering if you could ever trust a snake like Peyton. She winces at the sound.

"Ty—"

I swing my eyes to hers and narrow them, stepping up to her and craning my head down. She doesn't shrink back, that's not Peyton's style. She stands taller, narrowing her own eyes, which are flashing with anger now, and fuck if that doesn't make me hard.

I used to love fighting with her and then making up.

My body doesn't seem to have received the fucking memo that that will never happen again. "My name is Tyler. I don't give a fuck if you talked or bought your way onto the expedition." Fucking lie. I want to know how she's been . . . how she got here. I know she's one of the best. Shit, she always was, not that I've been tracking her career. "But this is my dive. You do as you're told or you're out of here, understood?"

She smirks at me and steps closer, her chest pressed against mine, and it's my turn to step back, unable to have her body against me. I don't want her to feel just how hard I am for her, how much my muscles are screaming at me to touch her. Grab her. Kiss that cocky smile right off her face until she's screaming my name. "No problem with me, Tyler." She rolls her tongue around my name the same way she always did. It drove me crazy then, and it still does now. "But I'm here to stay, better get used to it."

"They don't like it," I snap. "This won't be easy for you."

"Nothing worth doing ever is." She winks, throwing my own goddamn words back at me. I said them to her about trying to date her when I first met her, knowing her dad would hate me for it. She turns to Steve then. "I'm going to get a few hours of sleep. We came almost straight from another dive, wake me in time for briefing."

Then, like a fucking princess, she turns and, without a goddamn word, strolls away like she owns the camp.

I hate that my eyes drop to her perky ass, the tight khaki shorts covering it lovingly. I still remember the way she tasted on my tongue, remember those long, lean legs wrapped around my waist as I fucked her like I owned her.

Possessed her.

"Is this going to be a problem?" Steve questions, confused.

"No, no fucking problem," I snarl.

"Do you know each other?" he asks, swinging his gaze to me as I drag my own from her retreating back.

"No, she's just a stranger."

Kalen

Three years.

Three fucking years of hell since she left.

Of watching my brother break and struggle to go on every fucking day without the love of his life. Seeing him pale, tired, and not himself. Of watching him barely eating or sleeping until he threw himself into the job.

Taking stupid risks, crazy dives . . . just to stop the pain.

When did I become the one protecting him? All my life, it's been the other way around, even though I'm older by four years. I was always more reckless, stupid. He's the smart, careful one.

But that was before Peyton fucking Andrews.

After . . . after her, he became nothing but a shell of the man who used to exist, a shell filled with anger and pain. Pain she gave him. I turn away from her in disgust, unable to look at her anymore, incapable of seeing those green eyes screaming something at me.

Screaming for forgiveness.

She stands there all alone, so small and so fucking perfect like always. I won't say weak, Peyton is never weak. It's one of the things— Fuck, no, not going back down that road.

How— How can she be here?

Why now, after all this time?

Peyton was ours . . . to tease, to torment, to care for. Not that I ever did that; we never saw eye to eye. We were always clashing and arguing, but honestly, it's the only way I knew how to communicate with her.

Tyler always says if I'm not arguing with you, I don't care about you.

Ain't that the fucking truth? His words still haunt me, because in his eyes, there was a knowing. We never spoke about it, nor the fact that I argued with her more than anyone, that I purposely went out of my way to start shit with her.

To piss her off and rile her up.

And fuck, when she exploded . . . it was goddamn breathtaking.

Nothing compared to the heat of our fights, of the breathless anticipation, the anger, the need. The snarled threats and insults, the look she would get in her eyes as she went toe-to-toe with me. Our bodies vibrating from the force of it.

All I ever wanted to do after was grab her and kiss her, but I never did. She was never mine and never will be. She's just a blast from the past that, once this is through, will disappear into the fog again.

I want to fucking strangle her, kill her for what she did to my family. I've never hated someone as much as I do her.

She is nothing.

I storm away, leaving her there staring after me as I repeat it in my head.

She is nothing, she is nothing . . .

SIX

Riggs

I heard her name, but I didn't believe it until I turned. Peyton. Standing here at the dive site. It's been three years, yet that time when faced with her floats away to nothing, until it feels like only yesterday we were diving together, watching movies, and giggling like teenagers.

But it hasn't, it's been three years.

Everybody leaves, they always do. She did, and now she's back, standing there like no time has passed. She's just as beautiful as ever. It cracks my heart, and I suck in a wobbly breath before turning again, unable to stare into those emerald eyes.

I pretend to be checking the equipment as Fin claps me on the shoulder. "Breathe," he whispers as I suck in a desperate breath. He's the only one who ever knew how I felt about Pey . . . not that I would have ever done anything.

She's Tyler's girl.

But—but that didn't stop me from falling in love with her and wishing she were mine. Lying awake at night, hearing their giggles and moans and wishing it was me with her, waking up with her in my arms.

Every smile she ever sent me, every stolen moment, every time she was proud of me . . . all accumulated until I couldn't deny my feelings.

And then she left.

Like we were nothing.

Like she wasn't our entire world, our heart . . .

Like she never really loved us at all.

Fin

Peyton Andrews.

The flaxen-haired beauty who was once my best friend stares at me. She looks good, amazing actually. The years have been kind to her. When we met her, she was young, so young, but now she's all fucking woman. Her curves have my mouth watering, her breasts are almost spilling from her tank, and those same long, lean legs are tanned and covered in tattoos now. Her hair is pulled back and messy, and her face is sweaty and tired.

Yet no one ever compares to her beauty. Ever. Trust me, I've tried.

I never told anyone how I felt about that troublemaker, not even myself, and it worked for so long, but when she left . . .

It devastated me.

I struggled to understand why, while I held my family together with pure fucking grit. Tyler was broken, Riggs withdrew, Kalen was angry . . . and me? I was trying my fucking hardest, not able to comprehend why my heart was breaking with each passing day she didn't come back.

I really thought she would.

I should have known better. Love is a fucking lie. Just something we use to make ourselves feel better, a chemical reaction in our brains. I spent my life discarding the notion of it, too busy with studying and then exploring. But Peyton? Peyton was a fucking surprise. She turned up one day . . .

And each day that passed, everything I thought I knew about love disappeared into a cloud of smoke.

Fucking typical I would only realise I loved her after she left . . . Fuck, it was okay then. I didn't need to tell anyone, especially Tyler, but now she's back. And all four of our hearts are on the line.

This girl broke them once. She won't ever again.

They aren't hers anymore.

Our hearts belong to the bottom of the ocean, where we let them all sink to after she broke them.

SEVEN

Peyton

When I reach my tent, I cover my slamming heart with my hand and struggle to breathe. All four of them. And Tyler, God, he was so angry, so filled with hate. I've never seen him like that, so fucking . . . cold. Is that what he's like now, or is that just for me? I don't blame him if it is. But Christ, my panties are damp from that harsh, dominant tone and the way he watched me.

We never had a problem with wanting each other, but it seems the years apart have only made me want him more. This new, twisted, dark Tyler is getting me all riled up in ways that sweet, loving Tyler just never could.

God, I'm a bitch.

And Kalen? Fuck, I wouldn't be surprised if he tried to kill me.

Riggs, shit, the heartbreak on his face was too clear to see. My sweet boy always did wear it on his sleeve, and he couldn't even look at me. Fin, well, was Fin. Charming, sexual, hiding all that lurks below his depths. The man was my best friend once, and I still never felt like I really knew him. Just when I discovered another side of him, he would change again.

A bit like a cave system, his depths unexplored.

But shit . . . if I didn't want to explore them.

No.

Concentrate.

I'm not here for a reunion, I have a job to do, and no amount of memories or pain can stop the excitement of the dive that's to come. And knowing it's with them . . . well, shit. Tyler is right—you have to trust your buddy down there in the caves, and I was worried about working with people I didn't know having my back.

I know these guys, and even if they hate me and don't want me here, they are amazing divers, the best. It's going to be incredible down there, even if I'm scared of working together.

I'm worried I might say the wrong thing or let some of my secrets slip. I can't. I made my choice, they—he isn't mine anymore. This is business, and the sooner we get down to it, the better I can focus and stop thinking about all those abs on display.

About the way Tyler used to fuck me, all hard and fast. He was such a softie normally, but in the bedroom . . . fuck, it was like something came over him. He would have me screaming in minutes, his fist in my hair, his cock slamming into me with wild abandon.

I trace my lips, remembering the way Kalen tasted that drunken night. Fuck. I drop my hand and unpack and repack my bag with the equipment, which is in my tent, thanks to Michael. Then I do as I said and try to grab a few hours of sleep.

But knowing they are only a few feet away makes it hard, and when I do finally fall into that abyss, it's with their names on my mind.

I wake up to my tent shaking. "Get up, kid, briefing in ten."

I get to my feet and stretch, having slept in my clothes. I debate changing but then sigh. I wouldn't if they weren't here, and they have seen me in a lot worse, so I put on my bandanna and sunglasses and head out. I stop at the toilet before grabbing some water and an apple, then head to the briefing tent.

They are already here when I arrive, and as soon as I step into the room, they all go quiet and angry. I slip into a chair next to Michael, pull my knife from my ankle, and start to cut chunks of the apple, eating it from the blade as I wait.

Fin watches me with a smirk, while the others purposely don't look at me. I don't know the additional people in the room. Michael leans in. "Minnow, you pissing people off already? You usually save that for day two at least." His voice rumbles through the space as I laugh.

"Nah, there was that one time we were saving those whales. I pissed off those hunters in two hours. But this might be a record for me." He grins as I finish my apple, clean my knife, and slip it back into my side before drinking my water.

"Whalers?" Fin asks.

Well, at least one of them is talking to me. Riggs is typing away, concentrating on his computer, which is hooked up to a projector on the rickety metal table. Tyler is hunched over some maps, wearing nothing but some cutoff shorts. Kalen is sitting at the end, his arms crossed as he silently fumes.

Fun times.

Michael chuckles. "Yeah, you should have seen her. Christ, she leapt onto their boat and poured booze right into the engine. You have never seen so many angry rich people."

"I remember that." Steve laughs as he comes in. "That's how I met you! You were this tiny thing in this little bikini, standing off against six men."

"Even odds." I shrug, making him chuckle as he sits.

"I remember thinking anyone crazy enough to do that is crazy enough to work for me," he offers, making me smile wider.

"Beautiful fucking story," Kalen snarls, and I raise my eyebrow at him as he turns away again.

"Enough. Now that we're all here, let's begin," Tyler snaps, throwing me a narrow-eyed glare. I salute him and put my legs up on the table, leaning back to watch. His eyes twitch, but he turns away without saying anything further.

"We have only mapped a tiny portion of the cave." The projector comes on, showing his mapping system. I want to congratulate him on getting it finished finally, but I don't think it would be welcome . . . although I know how hard he worked on it.

I'm proud of him, I always knew he could do it.

"The entrance chamber has two passes going from it—one is too narrow for even our cameras to get through. The other we explored a tiny amount, and it seems to slope down. That looks like our way in." I nod, following the incomplete map on the screen before it changes to pictures. "We are taking equipment down as we speak. Comms will be set up in that tunnel, and in forward and advanced bases, with guidelines back with stores of deco bottles. We take more kit than we need with enough tanks to last us a month."

"How long are we staying down for?" I question, allowing him to take control, as he's been here longer . . . and he might think I'm playing nice then.

I see him not wanting to answer me, but he knows we have to work together. "Fourteen days in total, then we regroup and rest up here. We go back down if need be, but I would like it mapped in those fourteen."

I whistle at that, and he narrows his eyes. "We dive and map in shifts. Kalen is first scout, and Riggs is in charge of the map, cameras, and equipment. We will assign dive buddies. No one exceeds five times, and no one goes alone unless ordered. Let's not forget this is an unexplored cave, so Mother Nature is sure to have some tricks up her sleeve."

Fuck, I almost break then. My dad used to say that.

"We go in smart and work hard. It's going to be exhausting, it's going to be long, but we work together to get it done." He looks at Michael then. "You dive, I assume?"

"He does, but he's better staying at base for communication and helping with equipment and hauling," I inform him, not disclosing his lung issues.

Tyler frowns at me, and I narrow my eyes.

"He stays at base," I state.

"Fine," Tyler snaps. "But if you're here to work, you will dive and do your part, nothing more. I will expect no drama or complaints on this."

"Not a problem; same goes for you. I'm not your employee, I'm here on behalf of my friend to ensure this runs smoothly. I'm joint lead. Do your job, and we'll have no issues," I retort, speaking the same way I would to anyone. I'm trying to keep it fair and not personal, because that's what he seems to want.

Kalen snorts, and it's a harsh, angry sound. "No issues?"

Tyler glares at him. "Don't." He looks at me then. "Same goes for you. I'll be honest, I don't want you down there, I don't want you here at all. But we have to work together, so be it."

"Ouch." Michael laughs. "Harsh."

I struggle to contain my anger . . . and yes, pain. Fuck, in those blue eyes, I see an ocean of it. "Understood, when do we go in?"

"Tomorrow, five a.m. sharp. Everyone is to get some sleep and be prepared. Your equipment is your own, so make sure you check and double-check it. I will not babysit anyone."

Then he turns away, dismissing us all.

EIGHT

That night, there will be a celebration for opening the dive tomorrow. We all work together throughout the afternoon, getting the equipment down into the opening chamber, though I'm not allowed to go down yet. I just have to carry it to the edge, which I do without complaint, especially when I see Tyler watching me.

He's waiting for any excuse to get rid of me.

I won't make it easy for him.

When it's all done, we sit down to eat and drink. They stay as far away from me as they can, and as soon as they are finished eating, Tyler is back in the command tent, staring at maps and planning for every possibility. I know because we used to do it together. The night before a dive, we would sit with a bottle and come up with everything that could go wrong and what we could do to prevent or help if it did. Now he does it alone.

Kalen disappears into his tent.

Riggs rushes away, back to his computers, and Fin climbs the mountain and lies on the top of it, under the stars. Everyone has their own method for preparing for the next day.

Mine used to be them, just being at their sides.

Now, I grab the bottle of beer and go sit on the edge of the hole, my legs hanging down into the dark as I sip my drink alone. I let myself relax and prepare for tomorrow as I stare down at my next adventure.

I can hear the laughter and talking behind me, but I don't look back, feeling completely alone. It's something I've found I hate, being alone. I was always surrounded by my guys, since we lived and worked in tiny boats and spaces. I got used to being with people. When I left, I had nobody until I found Michael. But even then, we like our own space from each other.

It's one of the things I miss.

The laughter, the friendship.

Now? I usually work until I pass out, so I don't think about the bone crushing loneliness, or I find it in the arms of strangers and at the bottom of a bottle.

I hear him before he sits as he sighs and groans. "Fuck, I'm getting old. My muscles are as stiff as a cock."

I snort and swig my beer as I tip my head back and look at the stars. "That you are, old man."

"Less of the old, you cheeky bugger," Michael retorts as he looks at the hole and sips his own beer. "Why didn't you tell them?"

I know what he means—why didn't I mention his lung damage from the bends? They wouldn't let him down there if they knew, and Michael lives for adventure like us. When it happened, he tried to kill himself because he knew he would never dive again. This was before I met him. When I did, he was a drunk in Thailand. After I learned his story, I hired him on the spot, needing a captain and someone to watch my back. He knew the ropes, so I offered him the job with the condition that he get sober. I don't mind a few sips, even the occasional beer, but he hasn't touched anything since that day. And for the last three years, he's been sober, keeping his promise.

He's turned his life around, but without our jobs, I know he'll spiral again. So no, I didn't tell them. "None of their business."

He sighs, running the bottle through his hands, feeling it in a nervous gesture, since he won't take a sip. "Kid . . . are they them?"

"Them what?" I query, looking at him. I've never mentioned my past to Michael, and he never asked. Both of us have our own demons to conquer.

"The ones who broke your heart so badly, you race across the world jumping from one high to the next?" he offers.

I turn away from his knowing eyes as I peer back into the black hole. "No . . . I broke theirs." I down my beer and stand, looking back down at Michael. "It won't be an issue; this is just another dive."

"Another day." He nods, and I start to walk away. "But what if it's not?"

I don't know what to say, so I don't. Instead, I keep moving.

I head back to my tent and get into the sleeping bag, staring at the tent's fabric ceiling. I need to sleep, I need the energy for what's to come, but I just keep rerunning the initial conversation in my head and the looks in their eyes.

After everyone has settled down to sleep, I'm drifting in and out of it when I see a shadow outside my tent in the shape of a person. They hesitate, and I sit up, frowning. The person is big . . .

One of the guys?

They hesitate for a moment longer before disappearing again like nothing happened. I can't help but wonder who it was. Michael is asleep, I can hear his snoring from here, and no one else in the camp knows me that well . . .

It had to be one of them.

The question is, which one?

And why?

I'm up before anyone else, I always am on dive day. My nerves and excitement are too much to allow me to sleep. I used to be the same as a child on Christmas and my birthday, and when my mum died and I went to live with my dad, I was awake early every morning when I knew he was taking me to work with him.

I think my grief was why I fell in love with the ocean. It was so vast and easy to lose myself in. I could be anything down there, be anyone, and it didn't care . . . Maybe that was why when I was broken once again, I retreated to the water.

I put on my trousers and my vest. My thermal fleece is ready to go down in, so is my suit. I double-check my equipment and take it to the edge of the hole, prepared to don and take down. Then I stretch and warm up, and head over for breakfast, which I can smell cooking.

Everyone is there, so I sit down and drink some water before accepting a plate and digging in. This will be one of the last proper meals we will have for almost two weeks, so I devour it.

After we have eaten, I pack my bags and get into the rest of my gear and my fleece. I pull on my helmet and have my suit and equipment ready to change into. They mention the first part is passable, but after that, we might be submerged. Hauling everything to the edge, I wait for the others there. I tilt my head back to look at the sky one last time, memorising the warmth of the sun on my face, heating my skin.

"Ready for this?" Steve inquires, coming up next to me.

I smile over at him and wink. "Born ready. We'll message you when you can come down."

He nods and looks around at the activity, everyone preparing to get started. "Are you sure? I know I have no place to ask a—"

I snort and nudge him with my arm. "Liar, you knew I knew them. I saw it in your face. Real sneaky, old man."

He laughs as Michael comes up with his bags in tow. "Right, let's get this party started!"

The others join us then, and the mood sobers at the glare Tyler throws my way. "Kalen, you go first, then you." He nods at me. Wow, I only get a *you* now, not even a Peyton. But I move over and start to get into the harness. "The rest follow. We get all the equipment down to the entrance chamber and set up comms before I send out the first scouts. It's going to be slow going and long days; I hope you're already. If not, now is the time to turn and leave." He purposely looks at me, so I smile sweetly. "I won't accept anything less than your best down there."

Grunting, I strap onto the belay as Kalen does the same, and I begin to walk backwards. "You know I never give less than my best . . . especially since I am the best." I wink at him. "See you down there." With those parting words, I throw myself backwards.

I hear the swears and gasps as I laugh and free-fall.

This is going to be amazing; I can feel it.

NINE

Kalen

I watch her plummet over the edge, and with a curse, I pitch myself after her, worry making my heart slam as I hear her laughter. Her light swirls around the cavern wall as she descends below me. She jolts to a stop on the rope, and I do the same beside her, my eyes narrowed as my light shines on her face. "That was reckless and stupid. Don't pull shit like that again, or you're gone."

She smirks at me like she used to, giving me the one that would signal she was getting ready to fight back. My cock hardens, even in the harness, at that one simple expression, remembering just how much I loved our arguments. "Whatever you say, Kay, but you should learn to have some fun. If you're not careful, your face might freeze like that."

Then, with a grin, she starts to lower herself, and I do the same. Both of us descend side by side down the hole. It's huge, almost sixty metres in diameter. The cavern is dark, and the grey-coloured walls are wet from condensation. It's close to forty metres down, and luckily, Peyton goes at a normal pace, not showing off. She's confident in her actions as we hit the floor, and she disentangles herself from the harness before tugging to send it back up. I follow and watch her as she looks around with a whistle.

There is something so attractive about a woman as self-assured as her. It used to kill me watching her dive, the way her body would move in the water . . . the way she handled pressure and her excitement.

"Impressive," she calls, her voice echoing around us.

I force my gaze from her to the entrance chamber we are in. We set up lights in here yesterday and started the guidelines down the passages. The floor underneath us is dry, hard rock. She walks around, examining each and every inch of the space, looking at the one other exit we can't fit through.

"Don't even think about it," I snarl, knowing exactly what she's thinking of doing.

"About what?" She chuckles.

"Going through there. You're small enough, but we aren't. It's a stupid fucking risk. We stick to the plan," I order.

For once, she listens to me. She never used to. We were frequently dive buddies, working together as first scouts. It meant long hours in caves and underwater together, cut off from the others. She was reckless, crazy, and daring, pushing herself and her body to the limit. It seems she still is—I just hope this time, it doesn't get her hurt . . . or worse.

"Fine, are you going to be like this the whole time?" she asks, treading closer as we see some of the equipment coming down.

"Like what?" I snap, purposely not looking at her. When I do, I get angry. My body still wants her, but inside, I'm as cold as ice where she's concerned. She broke my brother's heart; she doesn't get to stroll back in like everything is okay. If I had my way, I would rip her apart and leave her up there to pick up the pieces.

The cold bitch.

"An ass." She laughs before wiggling her eyebrows at me. "Or will getting into the water chill you out like always?"

I don't know if it's how well she knows me, or the fact that every time I look at her, everything from the last three years comes back—the betrayal, the pain, the anger—but I'm pissed.

Really fucking pissed.

I want revenge, I want her to know how much we all hate her. I want to see her flinch in pain and feel even a fucking ounce of what we did when she left.

Stepping closer, I tilt my head down, almost pressing my lips to hers. I watch her inhale, her eyes widening and tongue darting out to lick her lips as she clearly remembers the last time we were this close.

Which was a fucking mistake, the biggest of my life.

She's my fucking mistake, and now she's before me, looking like a sheep led to slaughter. I don't think she even realises she's leaning into me. "I don't want you here, none of us want you here, so get that through your selfish skull, Andrews. We aren't going to be friends, or family, or even get along. So keep your mouth shut for once and just do your job," I growl out and step back. A grin finally curves my lips when she flinches like I physically struck her. Good. I watch as her face drops before contorting in anger.

She steps forward and stabs her finger into my chest, making me glare down at it in contempt. "Fuck you, Kalen. I didn't even know you guys were here, but

I'm not going back on my word because you're an asshole who can't deal with emotions. You hate me? Fine, I fucking hate you too, but we'll have to work together, so get the fuck over it and remove whatever stick is in your ass. If not, I will and I'll beat you with it, fucking wanker."

Just then, the equipment drops next to us, and without a word, she turns and begins to unhook it and haul it away. We've said what we need to say, but she's wrong—I don't hate her . . . not completely.

And that's the problem.

I wish I hated her; it would make this much easier. Instead, my emotions are swirling and confusing, so I take them out on her, just like always.

I guess things never change.

TEN

Peyton

I want to punch his smug face . . . and then kiss it better.

No, fuck, just punch him. No kissing.

Fucking asshole, distracting me with those kissable lips and pressing his hard body against mine, making me think all sorts of dirty thoughts only to rip out my beating heart and crush it in his fist. I almost staggered back, but I refuse to let him see that his hits landed. Instead, I lift a crate and carry it over to the storage area, forcing the tears away.

I knew they hated me, but I didn't realise how much it would kill me to actually see it.

Kalen was always angry, and we always argued, but despite that, we were friends. Family. He would have done anything for me. It took me a long time to get past his barriers and earn his trust. And in one moment, I destroyed that. Now all that's left is an angry, vengeful man. Our arguments are no longer foreplay or teasing, they are cruel.

Mean.

Is this what the next fourteen days will be like?

No, I refuse to let them ruin this for me. They don't want to talk or get along? Fine, I will be professional and cold, and I won't let them land another blow no matter what they say or do. I might have left, but they never followed either.

By the time we've unloaded the next batch of equipment, Fin is descending. We don't speak as we unpack everything, causing Fin to throw us knowing glances. Then Riggs and Tyler are down, followed by Michael and one of Tyler's new hires, whose name I don't know yet.

We all continue to work in silence, and once we're done, we gather at the passage leading down. Tyler peers into the darkened entrance before looking back at us. "Suits on, but no masks yet. It's too tight down there to get into gear, so always do it when you can. I want four extra bottles on everyone's hip. Kalen, take more deco with you and tie it onto the guideline as you go."

"I'm going first," he concludes.

Tyler nods and grinds his teeth, knowing he has no choice but to send me too. Riggs is better with computers. He's a great diver, but he can be overly cautious, while Fin is too reckless. I'm the perfect mix, and he knows it. Even with as much as he hates me, I'm the best choice. "Peyton, you go with him. Let us know when you've reached an area where we can set up the forward base and how far it is. If you pass three miles and there's still nothing, radio in."

"Got it." I nod, being nice for once as I slip into my gear. He's right—it will be too tight down there to do it. I secure my main and extra masks to my side. Michael helps strap on my extra tanks and ropes as well as checks that everything is tied down securely. It can't move, all it would take is one string getting caught on a jagged rock and I would be dead.

Down here, everything is a game of life and death, and every time we do this, we roll the dice.

Kalen is ready and waiting while I grin at Michael. "See you soon, old man."

He claps my head and drags me closer, pressing his forehead to mine for a moment—a ritual. "Stay safe, Minnow." I nod, staring into those fatherly eyes. He releases me, and I step back, and then he looks to Kalen.

"I don't give a fuck what your problem is, you watch her back or I'll kill you," he warns. Chuckling, I pat him on his arm as I pass by.

"Kalen might be an asshole, but he's not stupid enough to let me die." I look at Kalen. "There is no room for your bullshit down there. Get it together and let's do this."

After all, anything can happen down here in the dark. As much as I hate him right now and he me, we have to depend on each other. We have to keep each other safe and alive.

He grinds his teeth and turns away without a word. Tyler glares at me and steps up next to his brother. He whispers something, making Kalen nod, and then Tyler moves back. "I want constant updates; that's an order," he demands.

Kalen ducks through the opening first, and I follow him. I stay a few steps behind him as he switches on his head torch. I do the same, leaving my primary and secondary diving lights off until we go underwater.

I keep my steps unhurried and measured like his, knowing the cave could drop off at any point, so we need to go slow. The tunnel is small, barely big enough to stand in, and as we move deeper, the light from the entrance chamber slowly fades away until we're plunged into darkness. Our lights are the only sources of illumination down here.

Our breathing is even but loud as we carry on walking, the drip of water occasionally reaching us. We don't talk, and it saddens me. This used to be when we teased, chatted, and shared. Our nerves and excitement bonded us—hell, it was the only time he was really nice to me.

The only time I got to see below that angry, war-hardened exterior to the man beneath. The man I fell in love with.

I watch his back as we walk. His wide shoulders almost scrape along the wall, and he even has to turn at one point. I press my talk button, which is built into my mask, but when we aren't wearing them, we have to use a version of walkie-talkies. "First tunnel is tall enough to walk in, barely wide enough to fit through, sloping down and dark, will need lights throughout. Still going," I report before letting go.

Kalen doesn't talk. He's the one who's supposed to spot any issues while I report them. We fall into the routine easily, but this time, it's filled with tense silence and shared pain. The tunnel begins to slope down at a steeper angle, so I bend my legs slightly and watch my footing, ensuring I don't slip.

"Gets darker up ahead, can hear water," he calls back. A moment later, I hear it too. It's faint but definitely there—rushing water. It could be a current or a rapid in a syphon or something else entirely. Excitement fills me, and I find myself smiling, knowing Kalen will be doing the same.

This is why I do it—for the unknown, the thrill that at any moment, the tunnel could change. We might have to dive, climb, scale, or stop. The twists and turns always keep us guessing, on our toes, and feeling alive.

"We can hear water. At mark ten, the incline is steeper," I report.

"Understood," Tyler replies sharply.

Kalen snorts, and I roll my eyes. "What?" I ask, unable to help it.

"Nothing, princess, nothing at all." We both freeze at the use of his nickname for me, but this time, it sounds bitter and filled with hate. It's not like the tender way he used to say it. It was the only weakness he ever showed towards me, even in front of others . . . Now it's filled with regret and pain and a whole lot of anger.

"Stop," I snap, and he sighs and glances back at me, his light blinding me for a moment.

"Being an asshole?" He moves closer, almost touching me, our breaths mixing between us. We're alone in the dark, which only heightens all our emotions. "Don't like it, then fucking head back."

I roll my eyes again. "I meant stop, I felt something," I retort sharply, and he freezes. His eyes narrow, he knows to trust me on this. There's a reason I was always first scout, I have a sense for things.

Closing my eyes, I press my hand to the wall and just listen and feel, ignoring his weighted stare. "There," I murmur. "The air is changing, less stale. It's blowing back, and the wall is vibrating slightly." I pop my eyes open, and I can't help the grin that curves my lips. "I think there's a fall up ahead."

He grins back, his excitement filling his eyes before he remembers he hates me, and it fades to a scowl. "Fine, we go slow, stay close."

He turns and starts walking again, sliding his feet forward in case of a sudden drop. His guideline drags behind him until we find a place to clip it to at the end of this section.

"We think we can hear a fall up ahead, might be the source of water, proceeding with caution, about thirty metres in," I tell Tyler, and he acknowledges me.

We keep walking. It's slow going, and my heart speeds up with each step we take. The sound of flowing water grows louder and louder until it's almost a roar.

It's so close, I can taste the spray. Kalen freezes and whistles, so I step up next to him, and my mouth drops open. We are on the lip of a ledge.

It's a fucking waterfall.

I let out a laugh, and it echoes out over the sound of crashing water, so I cup my hands around my mouth and let out a whoop, listening to it resound.

I turn and spot Kalen watching me. His eyes are lost and confused, and his mouth is tilted up slightly. I suck in a breath, rolling my lips in as his dark gaze drops to them hungrily. The air sparks between us as the electric connection that was always there returns with a vengeance until we're both nearly panting. His hands are curled at his sides to stop from, what? Reaching out?

Grabbing me?

Fuck. I swallow again and watch as he does the same, his Adam's apple bobbing before he turns away. "Let's clip the rope back there." His voice is hoarse and low.

"Sure," I concede, blinking at his sudden change in demeanour.

Maybe being here is stirring up memories for him too?

Maybe about that night . . . that night I admitted how I felt and kissed him?

Mouth tasting sour, I work silently to help him secure the guideline, my own regrets and pain making me quiet. Fuck, this is going to be a hard fourteen days.

ELEVEN

Kalen

"Sixty feet in, waterfall with natural flowing water. Guideline is secured just before it, rock is slippery. We're going to clip in and see if there's a way down or up, and then look for the next tunnel," Peyton relays.

"Understood . . . Be careful," Tyler calls back.

She drops the button and checks the harness with a tug before slipping on her helmet, fumbling in the dark to fasten it. I sigh but step forward. "Let me," I growl.

I don't want to be anywhere near her, but here I am. Close enough to touch . . . to taste.

She nods and lifts her chin, her green eyes focused on the top of the cave. Her lips are so close, I can almost taste the sweetness of them. The memory of the plump flesh against my own makes me rush to secure and check her helmet before stepping back.

She wiggles it and turns on her light before peeking over the edge, totally unaware of my dirty, traitorous thoughts. Just like when we found it, I'd been so tempted to get it all out in her—in her lips and body, but we both know that's not going to happen.

Not ever again.

It can't. Peyton is an obsession, and every taste only makes me want more. I can't let that occur again. As soon as this dive is over, she'll disappear, and I can't let that wreck me anew.

Not when she destroyed us before.

I've faced a lot of hard times in my life, especially during my tours overseas, but none were as hard as watching her leave. I can't let her get close to me again.

Not this time. This time, I'm hardened against her. We are nothing but ghosts to each other. I step up to her side, ignoring the awareness that always comes when I'm near her. An aching knowledge of where she is, of each breath she takes, each tic and smile.

I hate that I'm still so in tune with her. It helps for dive buddies, but right now, it makes me despise her more.

She grabs on to the wall and sticks her head out of the opening, making me bark a warning at her, which she ignores as always. She swivels her head, searching above us before looking down. "Okay, no tunnels or signs of entrances up top, but I can see one down below, maybe twenty feet. We could climb down the side—it'll be slippery but possible—and then tether a rope for the others."

She looks back at me with a grin. "Shotgun."

"Peyton, just let me go," I demand, but she laughs, and I know she won't; she never does. She's reckless, strong, and infuriating. She can do anything I can do and usually better.

"Anchor me. You have a better shot of keeping me upright if I fall than I do with your big-ass body," she teases, making me grunt in response as she steps back. Grinding my teeth once again, I strap her to me and anchor us as she slips on her gloves and cracks her neck.

"Ready?" I ask.

"Ready," she replies. "Don't let me fall." She grins at me.

"Never," I counter automatically, the word falling like a stone between us, and she winces and looks away.

She walks backwards towards the ledge, and I spread my legs, keeping the rope in my hand as she moves to the left side of the wall and, with a deep breath, reaches out across it to grab some handholds. When she has them, she swings out onto the wall, hitting it with a smack, eliciting a grunt from me at the tug as I keep the line taut. "You okay?"

"Yup, sharp rocks though; keep the line tight so it doesn't snag and rip," she murmurs. Her tone is even and unaffected despite the strain on her body, so used to relaying everything to me as we work together. Our actions are always in sync.

I hear her breathing and the crumbling of the wall as she descends it, moving quickly as usual as she finds footholds and handholds and swings herself down. She was always the fastest of our group. In the water, she's like a fucking fish, but she's an amazing climber too.

It's annoying. Is there anything she can't do?

I loved that about her once, how easily she could keep up with all of us. When I first met her, I hated that she was working with us, thought she would hold us back, slow us down. It was the opposite. She could fit in spaces we couldn't, climb what we couldn't, and it made us unstoppable.

After she left, we had to change how we worked and even turn down some jobs—the reminder of that has me snarling, "Fucking be careful!"

"Calm down, Kal," she replies, and I peek around to see her more than halfway down. The slip of my name doesn't even faze her. I don't think she even realised she did it. It's what she always called me, even at the beginning, when I told her to her face she wouldn't last a week.

She proved me wrong then.

She will now.

It makes my anger ease a little, but all it takes is for her to glance up at me with a grin for my rage to return. She's acting like this is so easy, like she isn't upset to work with me again, like this doesn't hurt.

Like she doesn't miss this.

Did we mean so little to her?

Did I?

She goes quiet, but the movement of the rope tells me she's okay, and two minutes later she calls, "I'm down! Going to secure the rope."

Stepping back, I wait for the big tug on the line. "Secured!" she shouts.

I release my hold and strap myself in. Time to test it. It's better if I get hurt than the others. That's the job of a first scout, to find and secure. I just wish it didn't come so easily to me.

But when I came back from the military, Tyler knew I needed this, needed a way to feel alive, to express the death wish I had. At least this way, I'm rolling the dice, but it's with my own life to protect theirs.

And hers.

TWELVE

Peyton

I made it! I crane my neck back with a smile and look at the wall I free-climbed down, my belay in place to secure the rope. I watch Kalen walk backwards to the edge and easily push off and descend the wall like this is second nature. Which, for us, it is.

He makes it look easy.

His ass also looks amazing, so I turn away to stop myself from staring at it, knowing if he catches me, he'll probably spit more threats my way.

Out of breath, I relax for a moment as I shine my torch into the tunnel we're likely going to take next. I listen to him coming down, although the water is louder down here and splashing my arm and legs. When I hear him land behind me, I turn back to see him unclipping and securing the line, as well as some tanks.

"At the bottom of the waterfall, a belay is in place to descend, tanks are secured at the base, and a new opening is to the left. It's big enough to walk through, so we're going in," I say.

A moment later, Tyler's voice fills the cavern. They are undoubtedly all listening in as Riggs takes notes and forms a map for us to follow. "Understood, no farther than three miles," he reminds me.

Yeah, yeah. I don't answer him as I look back at the tunnel, wondering what awaits us down there. I hear Kalen stepping up next to me, ready to move on.

He stops by my side, and I glance up to see him staring at my chest with laser eyes. Following his gaze, I look down and wince—my necklace has come free. I quickly tuck it away and turn away from him, not wanting to see his expression at my having kept it all these years.

They have clearly moved on, forgotten about me, and hate me . . . but I was stuck between the past and the present, and my necklace is a reminder.

"I'll go first, seems smaller than the last." I tie on my guideline, linking it to the other, and without looking back at him, I duck into the tunnel. I don't want to see his reaction, his anger, or worse . . . his pity.

This tunnel is darker than the last, and they will gradually be more so the farther into the earth we go. Some will be pitch black, which is why we always have so many lights. Nobody wants to get caught below water or in a dark cavern without light, it could mean the difference between life and death.

Mine shines around now as we slowly make our way through it. The shaft seems to be straight, with only a few twists and curves and some sharp edges we have to duck and squeeze through. Kalen reports them all while tying off the guideline as we go.

The sound of rushing water fades the farther we venture in, and I spot something up ahead, making me squint as I still. Only years of practice keeps Kalen from ramming into my back, but I feel how close he is. The heat of his hard body and his breath blowing over my neck makes me shiver. "What?" he murmurs.

"Looks like a crawl space," I tell him as we tread closer. Sure enough, the obstacle before us is an almost full rock wall we'll have to crawl through. The space is wide enough for equipment and people though, which is good since none of this would make a good forward base.

"I'll go first." I slip from my equipment and place it in ahead of me as Kalen helps boost me into the hole, his hand on my ass. I hesitate at his touch, but then I ignore it and shuffle in, my legs kicking behind me. I still have my helmet on, and my light shines brightly as I use my elbows and knees to propel me and my bag forward.

My breathing is loud as I wiggle and move through the crawl space. "Okay?" he calls.

"Fine," I reply instantly. It's only about a two-minute crawl until it opens up. I pause at the end, and with a grin, push my bag through and climb from the hole, shining my torch around.

"I'm through!" I yell, and look back through the crawl space, seeing him waiting. "You've gotta see this, it looks like we've found our forward base."

THIRTEEN

"Coming through," he calls.

I step farther into the room, a smile curling my lips at the immensity of this opening in the cave system. I'm betting this is going to be a huge network, and I can't wait to explore the rest of it.

"A short fifty-metre walk to a crawl passage, wide enough for equipment and others, out the other side into a potential forward base. Waiting on Kalen, then we will ensure safety and sustainability," I inform Tyler.

"Good job," he replies, and there's a warmth in his voice that has me standing taller.

I hear a few grunts, and then Kalen is through and standing next to me. "Fuck, you weren't kidding. Those ceilings have to be forty metres up. Look at the water over there."

"And the stalactites and stalagmites are huge." I nod as we start off in opposite directions.

"I have water over here, a potential through passage!" Kalen calls.

"I have a place for base!" I shout back, and I hear him hurry over, winding through the cave to the large flat area I'm on. It's raised slightly above the others, which will be good in case of flooding or rising water. There aren't many rocks or boulders, and there is plenty of room to set up. It also has a few columns to support the area as well.

"Looks good to me," Kalen agrees, and I begin to wander again.

"Another entrance," I yell as I peer up at the hole. "About ten feet up."

We explore the rest of the room, not finding any more tunnels branching out from it.

"Tyler, forward base located. Plenty of room to set up, good signal, two exits. One submerged, one a ten-foot climb. About two miles from the entrance chamber. Bring your gear, we're going to get wet," I tease.

I hear his excitement when he radios back. "Good job, guys. We'll start prepping to bring the equipment down there. Ensure the guideline is tied and have a rest."

"Sure thing," I reply, already looking at the entrance and the wall leading up to it.

Kalen snorts behind me as he swigs his water. "You're going up, aren't you?"

"Yup." I grin, looking back. "He should know better." I laugh as I drop my gear and strip from my suit.

"Why? He doesn't know you," he snaps, and I sigh at the venom in his tone. So we're back to hating each other? I swear this guy's emotions are giving me whiplash.

Once I'm in my fleece, I keep my helmet on and chalk my hands. "I'm going to free-climb and secure a rope," I tell him tersely as I begin to the wall, running my hands over the slightly wet, sharp surface.

Digging my foot in, I reach above me to some shallow shelves and start to climb slowly. I focus on finding my foot- and handholds, and soon enough, I'm at the opening. I haul myself up and in, crouching in the somewhat cramped cavity as I shine my light down it. "It's small, looks to go up at the end though, not down," I call out as I secure a rope just in case. "I think we should try the submerged one first," I suggest, peering over the edge to see him waiting at the bottom.

"Fine, now get down," he barks.

"Asshole," I mutter.

"What was that, princess?" he shouts, his voice harsh.

"Nothing!" I reply quickly as I begin to descend. As soon as my feet hit the floor, he passes me my water bottle.

"Drink and rest until the others get here. This isn't a fucking sprint, it's a marathon, and we're a team. No fucking solo missions. If you can't handle that, you'll be pulled from this exploration," he threatens with narrowed eyes before he storms away.

Something needs pulling, but it ain't me. What a jerk.

He always used to be the first to cheer me on and nudge me to explore further, even against orders. When did he become such a stickler for directives? Is it just because it's me, and he's doing whatever he can to get back at me? Or has he really changed that much?

Three years is a long time, I remind myself.

I changed, and they have too. If I'm going to work with them, we all need to adapt, and if that means reining in my adventurous nature, then so be it. Sipping my water, I meander around the cave until I reach the water area. I crouch down at the cave sump and dip my finger in. It seems stagnant, and there isn't much of a current, but that doesn't mean anything. This is definitely a wet cave and not an end point.

We won't know until we explore.

FOURTEEN

Riggs

"All right, you heard them. We have a forward base, so let's get the equipment down to them!" Tyler instructs as everyone starts to move gear to the entrance of the tunnel. I pack up my computers as he heads my way. "You ready for this?" Ty asks.

"Sure," I reply as I zip up my waterproof bag. "I'll set up comms before the base of the waterfall and in the forward base, as well as doing mapping and all this," I tell him, indicating my computers.

He nods and then hesitates, so I look up at him, stilling at his expression. He seems to be debating saying something, which isn't like Tyler, especially not over the last few years. He's short-tempered and doesn't care whether or not what he says hurts. "Are you okay . . . with her here? I know you were close." He scrubs his face. "If it's too much for you . . ."

"It's fine." I shrug, trying to paste on a smile for his benefit. "But what about you?"

He snorts as he averts his gaze, glancing to the others. "She's nothing; just wanted to check in with my team."

I nod and watch sadly as he wanders away. That poor man. He doesn't even realise how broken he is or how he still stares at her, but now it's with a mixture of hatred and love. He's darker, angrier, and he reminds me a lot of Kalen when he first got back from overseas. We all handled her departure differently, but Ty . . . Ty lost it. This job is so important to him, so even though my heart aches at seeing her again, I push it away. For him, for my family.

We need this.

Peyton's presence can't change our dedication and goals. She's already destroyed everything else, she can't destroy this too. I won't let her. They may not think I'm strong enough, but I am when it comes to my family. She hurt them, and yes, me, and I wish I could hate her like the others, but the truth is I understand why she left. I really do.

But even that understanding doesn't allow her any leniency. She chose to leave and now she's back, so she better keep her head down and just get on with the job, or she'll have four angry divers after her.

"All right! Let's get moving!" Tyler calls. I shake off my depressing thoughts, haul my equipment onto my shoulders, and head his way. He claps me on the shoulder as I pass, and when I join Fin, who's waiting at the tunnel entrance, I notice he's wearing a cocky grin on his face.

"Ready for this?" He's jumping up and down with excitement, his eyes alight with the thought of getting in there. "I can't wait for the waterfall. Come on, nerd!" He drags me after him, making me chuckle like he knew it would. I'm betting that's why he did it, although I don't think he even realises he's still always trying to lighten the mood.

It started right after Pey left. He found ways to make us all smile, to keep us going, and even now, he's attuned to all our feelings. He must have seen my heavy thoughts and tried to bring me out of it.

But he's right—this is going to be amazing . . . with or without Peyton.

I know Fin will keep his eyes on Tyler as well, but we need to watch Kalen. I don't think Fin even realises just how deeply Kalen was in love with her, but I did. I saw the way he watched her, gravitated towards her, and followed her everywhere. I'm even assuming if she'd asked, he would have gone with her when she left.

Not that she will ever find that out.

I follow Fin down the tunnel. The lights are being set up ahead as we go. I make sure to keep my footing on the rough rock and duck when he ducks. Soon, we are at the waterfall with the others already at the bottom, hauling down equipment under Michael's leadership. Tyler is behind us, always taking up the rear. He says it's his job as dive leader in case anything goes wrong.

I retreat a few steps, finding a position that's a safe distance from the water, and then I begin to set up communications. It will allow us to talk to base up top as well as each other in the cave system. It's a vital part of such a long exploration. We can keep Steve updated as well.

It's why they call me Riggs, after all. I rig all the equipment. Peyton actually gave me the name, and it stuck. Fuck, I have to stop thinking about her. For three whole years, I've managed to go without being a stupid shy wreck pining after a girl I could never have. I thought about her, of course I did. I even kept track of her, watching her grow as a person and even more as a diver.

She's legendary, not that I ever doubted she would be. She has a natural talent in the water. I know Kalen never wanted to hear what she was up to, neither did Fin, but I caught Tyler reading my notes once or twice. It was easier then, loving her from a distance. She was just a fantasy, a memory, a ghost . . .

But now she's back in full technicolour and once again consuming my every thought.

Fin jogs over and grabs the wire for me. "I'll take this back and get it connected for you."

I nod my silent thanks, consumed by the comms process, and he laughs.

"Yes, Fin, you magnificent creature, thank you so much," he mocks before kissing my cheek with a loud smack. I push him away with a chuckle, and he jogs back to the entrance chamber. By the time he's plugged in, I'm set up and ready. I wait as it powers up, meaning it's correctly installed.

Next, I press the button, testing it. "Top base, can you hear me?"

"Loud and clear," comes the quick response.

"First line of comms is established!" I yell to Tyler as I pull my bag on and head to the waterfall. I quickly clip my bag onto the line and lower it before securing myself and rappelling down. The feeling of free-falling makes me grin. I might like computers, but being free like this, being in the water or climbing? It's my element, it's how I escape the chaos, the numbers, and the constant stream of information in my head.

I hear a whoop as I unclip at the bottom and look up to see Fin leaping onto the rock wall. Tyler shouts, but I can't help but laugh as he quickly descends and shows off, flipping from the wall and landing on his feet near us.

"Fin!" Tyler snaps. "No fucking showboating!"

"Sorry, boss man, couldn't help it." He winks and saunters between us. "Now let's go find this forward base. I can't wait to get into the water and get all wet." He wiggles his eyebrows at us, making Ty snort, even as he grins slightly.

"You know he's only going to get worse the longer we're down here. He's like a kid on sugar," I tease as Tyler walks behind me.

"Yeah, yeah, I swear he gets worse on every dive," he mutters.

He's not wrong. I noticed it a while ago, mainly after Peyton left, but in all honesty, it began somewhat before, so we can't totally blame her. He's getting more and more reckless, pushing his body. He doesn't have a death wish, I know that—I read some books on psychology to make sure. I think he's just an adrenaline junkie, and since he's done a lot of things already, he needs to do crazier and crazier stunts to get that high. He has an addictive personality, which I figured out as well.

Tyler taps my back. "Get out of that big head of yours, Riggs, and concentrate. That's how we make mistakes," he cautions.

I nod, wincing. He's right—I often get lost in my own thoughts and lose any sense of time and my location. Once I was so consumed by how to improve my new computer system I was developing for mapping that I almost walked right off a cliff. I was only saved from plummeting to my death by Kalen, who reached out and grabbed me, halting my steps.

I guess we all have our flaws.

There's a slight queue as we head through the crawl pass, carefully making sure the equipment gets to the other side. I wait patiently with Tyler behind me. "Riggs, seriously, if you're not okay with her being here . . ." His voice is almost a whisper in the dark so as not to carry to the others.

I turn with a sigh. "I'm fine. Yes, she hurt me. She was my friend." He winces at that. "But she hurt you more, Ty. No, I'm not happy she's here, but it's not for me, it's for you, because I saw the way it killed you. The way you beat yourself up over it. However, we have no choice but to work with her. It's just another job. Fourteen days, and then we'll be gone."

Technically, thirteen days, nine hours, and forty-seven seconds, but who's counting?

He searches my face and nods. "Okay, fourteen days."

I don't know who he's reassuring more, him or me, because when it comes to Peyton, it's clear we can't control ourselves and our emotions, both good and bad.

We discuss the dive as we wait, deliberating splitting teams and dive times. He asks me to ensure I can calculate the times correctly until everyone has had enough rest and sleep. We've already been over most of it, but I know he's nervous, and like me, he likes to focus on what he can control to calm himself.

When it's my turn to go through, he quietens, and when I reach the other side, I gawk. I've never seen such a massive chamber. I blink as I try to quickly categorise everything—entrances, exits, obstacles, potential hazards, and plant and natural life. All in a flash, my mind is whirring a hundred miles a minute, and then Peyton's there before me, smiling, and my mind calms just like it used to.

All the numbers and statistics fade until I can breathe. Her smile widens, and her eyes sparkle with excitement. "About time!" she says eagerly. "Come on! Let's get set up so we can start exploring."

She automatically reaches for my hand and tugs me along like she used to when I got caught up in my own head, but then her smile fades, and she drops my hand and steps back as she seems to remember herself.

"Sorry," she mumbles, and then turns away and begins to walk back to the others, mainly her friend, Michael.

I want to call out to her, but my tongue is tangled. My hand tingles from her slight touch, and I ache for the peace she brings as all those numbers come back with a roar.

FIFTEEN

Fin

When I first stoop into the cavern where we're going to establish the forward base, I can't help but grin. It's fucking massive. At least we have plenty of space for fourteen days and we won't be trapped in an area barely big enough for two grown adults like last time. Let me tell you, sleeping with three big guys in tiny, underground spaces tends to get annoying.

Not this time.

I explore while the others bring equipment through the tunnel, coming upon Peyton and Kalen. They are glaring at each other. Kalen's arms are crossed, meaning he's pissed and trying not to strangle her, and his body is tense. From here, I can see his stone-cold expression. She looks equally pissed, her beautiful face creased in anger when she throws her hands in the air at something he says. I can't hear, so I sneak closer, ducking behind a rock to listen.

Their arguments are legendary. Hell, I used to sit and watch them while I ate snacks, but this feels different. He genuinely hates her right now, and I don't want him to do something he'll regret . . . and, okay, yes, I like seeing her argue. She gets all riled up, her breasts heaving, her eyes mean. Fuck. I shift my hard cock and zone in on them and not my dirty thoughts about my ex–best friend.

"Shut the fuck up for once, Andrews," Kalen snarls, making me grin. "I swear you talk more than Fin." I want to protest as I narrow my eyes. "Just shut the fuck up and stand there and look pretty. You're useless for anything else."

"Oh, take a fucking hike, you condescending wanker. We both know I can outswim, -climb, and -explore you. You're just pissed Steve knows I'm the best and doesn't trust you guys, but you're going to have to fucking get over it."

"Or what?" he demands, his tone low and threatening. Shit, he's reaching the point of no return. He's going to explode. I hear the others entering the cavern, and I know I need to break this up. "Going to leave again, princess? Have a tantrum and storm away?"

Ah fuck.

I step out, but neither of them sees me. They are standing toe-to-toe now, and his head is lowered while hers is craned back. She raises her hand, no doubt to slap him, so I slide between them and grab it midair, softly. If she hits him, he might actually kill her, or fuck her, and neither of those options would be good, though both would be highly amusing to watch.

Kalen is nearly pressed against my back before he steps away. I look over at him. "Go cool off before Tyler catches you," I warn, glaring at him. He grinds his teeth but stomps off to do just that. When I turn back to Peyton, I almost groan at how close we are, her enticing sweet scent filling my nostrils. Her soft, curvy body is so close to mine, I can feel her heat. So close, I would only need to lean in to taste those frowning lips.

I've been tempted more than once.

I step back now and release her. She drops her hand and looks away for a moment. "You two are going to have to find a way to work together," I comment conversationally.

"Yeah, no shit, Sherlock," she retorts.

I smirk, and she winces when she looks back at me. "Hey, don't get all pissy on me, baby cakes." The old name slips out, and I falter for a moment before I turn the charm on, which is my way of keeping her at a distance. "Now get your beautiful ass over there and help us unload. The faster we do, the faster you can get wet." I wink at her and purposely drag my gaze down her body. Unlike before, when we used to flirt and tease each other but never cross the line, it feels different this time. Like there is a promise there, like it could actually happen. Before it was harmless . . . right? "I remember how wet you used to get."

She gasps but laughs. "Not for you, babe, never for you." She grins and steps closer, both of us easily falling back into this routine, but in her eyes, I see it too—the knowledge that this is different, that this time, there is nothing holding us back, other than the emotions clouding our team and our past. "But I'm sure if you put in the work, I could get there," she purrs, trailing her hand down my chest. Her touch makes me shiver. She used to do that a lot when we teased before, both of us toeing the edge, but this time, I want her to carry on, damn the consequences. I have no friends holding me back.

I want her.

Always have.

She turns and sashays away, and like she knew I would, I drop my eyes to her ass as I watch her go. She's so fucking hot, I almost bite my knuckle to stifle my groan as my cock throbs. Damn. I really shouldn't have restarted that shit. It might kill me this time. After being down here with her for fourteen days, looking like she does and making dirty jokes, I'm going to have a serious case of blue balls.

Fuck.

It was bad enough when we were stuck on our boat together, but Tyler's presence was always between us, stopping us from crossing the line, even though we flirted a lot. Now? Now I don't know if I would stop. Would she?

I understand we shouldn't—she broke our hearts—but my body doesn't care. It wants her, and it seems like my stupid heart still beats just for her too. I drop my head back and try to think of anything other than her touch, her scent, her lips, her curves, until I can finally walk without a third leg.

I hear them call me, so I suck in a breath, plaster a smile on my face, and head back to help establish base camp.

Riggs is finishing assembling his computers, and the others have sorted out the tents. We have all the rest of the equipment ready to go. Tyler releases a diver propulsion vehicle into the water with a camera attached, and we all crowd around Riggs's screen to see if we can get through that way. It lights up a dark opening, which is big enough to get through. He pulls it back now that we know it's passable, so we don't drain its battery.

"All right, let's get in the water, no time to waste." Tyler sighs and stands, looking us over as he considers his next move. I already know the names he's going to call though. "Kalen, Peyton, suit up. You two are going down, but only for two hours while we set up. See how far you can get and tie a guideline," he orders.

"Got it," Kalen replies.

"Sure thing," Peyton offers, and they both go off to get ready.

Fuck, I wanted to go, but it makes sense. Even when they hate each other, they are the best. They work together so seamlessly, and their individual weaknesses and strengths make up for the other's. I turn and observe Tyler as he watches them go. He has a strange look in his eyes, and when he turns and catches me staring, he coughs and quickly turns away.

What does he know?

"Check their gear before they go down. Give them the DPVs," he tells me as he storms away.

I make a quick toilet stop before I head over to where they're crouched on the edge of the pool. Their fins are already in place, and they're in their suits with their harnesses on and tanks ready. I check Kalen over, making sure everything is tied down, his tanks work, his computer is on, and he has all his equipment before crouching behind Peyton to do the same.

"Stop staring at my ass," she teases as she checks her air on her end and ties back her hair.

"Darling, I'm always staring at your ass. That ain't gonna change," I joke, even as I finish checking her over. I hear Kalen snort in disgust as he slips into the water and dons his mask.

She does the same, and they both peer up at me. I slide their DPVs into the water, and they both grab them. "Be careful, don't do anything I wouldn't."

"So, nothing," she murmurs, and with a wink, she turns and goes under, pulled by the DPV. With a swear, Kalen follows.

I laugh as I walk back to Riggs to see he has the cameras ready. They're already broadcasting, and when the lights flicker on, I can see everything they can. "Comms check," Riggs calls.

"Peyton on," she responds.

"Kalen working."

"Good, now go slow, visibility looks pretty low from up here, and keep us updated on what you find," Tyler advises. He moves closer as well, leaving the others to organise our sleeping arrangements.

This is the first glimpse we're going to get into the belly of the beast we are exploring.

SIXTEEN

Peyton

Riggs is right—visibility is low. Even with our primary lights and the DPVs' lights on, it's still nearly black. I keep my kicks low and slow so as not to disturb the silt too much and make it harder to see. I feel Kalen behind me, both of us tied onto the same guideline as we swim one by one. I head farther down, letting the DPV do most of the work to keep my strength up.

The passage tilts down nearly at a direct angle and narrows farther, so I go slower then and warn Kalen. He grunts his affirmation, but after about ten metres, it opens and curves up to the left with another shaft straight forward. I take the left first. "It's a sump," I murmur. The water gets clearer the higher we go, and I can almost see clearly now.

It widens even more until we're in a pool. "You seeing this?" I say into the mic. "It seems to open into a small pool. We'll explore farther." I pause for a moment, looking around and letting Kalen set an anchor for the rope. "There's another passage leading from the north. Going up first."

"Behind you," Kalen calls.

I start moving again, and just like I thought would happen, I break the surface of the water. "Surface broke." I glance around with a smile as I pull my regulator from my mouth. "At least thirty metres tall with what looks like climbable surfaces, and there's a ledge running around the pool wide enough for us to sleep on if needed. No obvious routes."

Kalen surfaces next to me as I pull off my mask and shut down my DPV. Grabbing the ledge, I haul myself up and spin so that my feet are dangling in the water as I look around. The cavern is curved and tall and not too wide, but wide enough for us all to sleep in if need be on dive trips. Standing, I tread the perimeter, testing the wall before I glance at Kalen, who's watching me. "I think I can see an opening up there, but we're probably better off carrying on through the other passage for now. Thoughts?"

He pulls off his mask, looking around. "I agree. Let's see where this fucker goes." I nod and slip my mask back on before sitting on the edge and sliding into the water.

"Advise, we are heading to the next opening," Kalen calls as he goes under. I grab my DPV and follow, this time with him going first.

"Understood," Riggs replies.

Both of us move slowly, unsure where this beast is going to take us. I have a feeling this is going to be an intricate web of tunnels, caverns, and dead ends, but I'm hoping it leads us to the ocean or a significant find, which would be amazing.

"See anything?" I inquire. He ignores me, and I grind my teeth. "Kalen, this is not us anymore, this is business. See anything?" I snap.

"It's going to get tight, so slow down and give me room to manoeuvre," he retorts sharply.

I hold back as he heads into the murky opening. "Okay," he calls, so I follow. He's right—it's tight. My tanks almost scrape along the walls as I swim slowly, pulled by my DPV. It twists and turns, our lights refracting in the water, barely penetrating the space right in front of us. We bank left, right, up, and down for around fifteen minutes before we swim into another opening.

The difference is that this one is completely underwater. I head up, and Kalen follows, but the ceiling is a light brown rock with no air, just a few rogue pockets. They would do in an emergency, but there is no telling how long the air has been down here. It could be filled with carbon dioxide, so that's a last resort.

We swim down again. The bottom is deep and dark as hell, filled with rocks and debris. We even find a skeleton, which gives us pause, before we carry on. There is a slight current here, but nothing too strong. We relay everything, and I know Riggs is mapping it.

The cavern itself is wide, really wide, and oval. We find at least three tunnels leading off before we regroup in the middle, secure an anchor line, and drop some emergency bottles. "What do you think?" Kalen asks me.

"I think we could take any, but we don't know how long they go on for, and I'm betting we have nearly reached our dive time."

"You have," Tyler barks and then sighs. "Come back, that's enough for now. Fin and I will suit up and take the next shift. We'll drop anchors and emergency bottles and take equipment to the breathable cavern you found just in case. Tomorrow, we start fresh."

I groan, wanting to carry on but also not wanting to push him. I don't want to give him a reason to pull me from the dive, plus we still have thirteen more days to explore, this was just to get a feel for the place first. "Understood," I reply.

Kalen nods, flashing me the okay symbol. As I turn back, I blink as something dark darts across my line of sight. Narrowing my eyes, I swim closer, shining my light in the direction where I saw it.

"Andrews," Kalen snaps, "you heard him."

"Yeah, one sec, thought I saw something—"

"Like what? Christ, come on, let's get back before he has a shit fit," he snarls but follows me anyway.

"Shut up," I mutter as I swim closer. Something dark swims by again, this time to my left, making me turn slightly. Down below, you can see things, it happens. It can be rocks, shadows, anything. I just want to make sure nothing's falling so we don't get hurt, but when I can't spot anything and Kalen's bitching gets to be too much, I turn back and follow him from the room.

Using the guideline, I shadow him into the tunnel, being careful in case anything is falling. My legs begin to ache, mainly due to the lack of rest I've had recently, but I ignore it and keep going.

Luckily, we don't need to do decomp stops, so we just head straight back quickly and quietly. When we reach the pool and surface, I yank off my mask, and Fin helps me up onto the ledge and out of my gear before assisting Kalen. "So how was it?" he questions eagerly. I know he's aching to get down there.

"Good, has potential. I really think we got something." Kalen grins at him the way he used to at me after a dive. Fin whoops, and then Kalen looks at me. "When he says come back, we come back. Get your gear stowed and eat," he demands before standing and striding away as he strips.

Fin winces but follows after him, leaving me alone. As I watch them join Tyler and Riggs to discuss today, aching loneliness crushes me for a moment. I wish I could be over there grinning with them. I can feel their excitement. But instead, I turn away, check my gear before standing, and strip down to my sports bra and knickers.

Michael heads my way with a grin, and it makes me smile. At least someone is happy to see me.

"You did great, kid. Come on, let's get you dry and find you something to eat." He wraps his arm around my shoulders and leads me away.

I'm unpacking and helping establish the rest of forward base. Tyler is emptying some crates near me, though he refuses to talk to me. The radio plays softly in the background, rock music pouring from the speakers and filling the space. After we finish, I need to get some sleep, since Kalen and I are up early for the next dive at four a.m. Time doesn't really have much meaning down here in terms of day or night.

Ty and Fin are going in next while we sleep. We're taking it in shifts, with Riggs and Michael watching for safety.

When Ty leans farther down, I spot something sparkling on his neck. Frowning, I watch as it slips out of his wet tank. It's a silver chain, and at the end is . . . my ring.

Fuck.

I can't even breathe. My heart clenches painfully, and tears try to fill my eyes. Has he worn it this whole time? What does it mean? I can't look away, and he must feel my regard. He lifts his eyes, meeting my undoubtedly shocked and pained ones, and frowns. Following my gaze, he sees the necklace and grits his teeth, tucking it into his shirt before he looks back up at me.

There is a whirlwind of emotions in his eyes, and they batter against me accusingly. I did this. I see my own regret and love in his gaze before it shuts down, turning cold once again.

"I can finish this; get some rest," he snaps.

"Ty—"

"That's an order. You need to be able to keep up tomorrow morning—you're exhausted. Sleep," he snarls and then storms away, leaving me staring after him, my heart broken once more.

I stand there, alone and lost, unsure what to say or do. Dashing the tears away, I take in a deep breath to repress the pain, not wanting anyone to think I'm weak and letting my past cloud my judgement, but fuck, it's hard.

Does . . . does Tyler still care for me? Could it be possible? Or is it just a wish . . . a wish that he could still love me the way I still love them?

SEVENTEEN

Tyler

I storm into my tent, smashing back the flap before I begin to pace. I tug on my hair, wanting to scream. She saw it! She fucking saw the ring I bought for her. I don't know why I couldn't sell it or throw it away. Instead I kept it, and like an idiot, I wore it on a chain above my heart. And she saw it.

Fuck!

As if she didn't think I was pathetic enough, now she knows exactly how much I missed her. Ripping open my bag, I yank my shirt off and rummage around for a clean one, pausing at the tangle of bracelets there. I stroke my fingers across the worn leather.

I took them off when we got here, not wanting to lose them. They're getting loose with the years. She gave them to me, and I couldn't bear to part with them, each strand signifying another part of our journey together. It's my past, she's my past . . .

So why does she feel like my future?

I hate her, I really fucking do. I hate that she still has power over me. That she can reduce me to nothing but an obsessed, lovestruck man with just one look. I used to love it, love how easily she made everything else disappear. I fell so hard for her, I thought we were meant to be together, but I was wrong.

Her father was wrong.

Lifting the ring from my shirt, I finger the stone, remembering how he grinned when I asked for his permission. It was only days before he died. He was so full of life and so happy for us both. He welcomed me as his family years before, but our marriage would have made it official. All he asked was that I'd make her happy, that I'd protect her for him.

I failed both requests.

I can't love her, not anymore, not after what she did, and I certainly can't protect her any longer.

Especially from me.

From us.

It's becoming painfully obvious we are all still susceptible to Peyton Andrews. She was family once, a friend, a lover. I see the way my brother and friends look at her, I always did. It used to make me happy, knowing she was mine. Now it makes me scared, scared of the damage she could do to them once again. Even heartbroken, angry, and hateful, they still want her.

But this time, I think they might break her in return.

We aren't the same sweet boys she once knew. We are hard, dominant men who know what they want, and for some fucking reason, it's still her.

Scrubbing at my face, I push away all thoughts of Peyton Andrews. I have too much to do to keep obsessing over her being here. This is our time to shine, to get our name recognised and our business back on track after she left. Slipping into my wet suit, I leave my tent to meet Fin, ready to check the guideline, add lights, and leave emergency bottles.

I hesitate outside Peyton's tent like I did the night before, and then I drag myself away and over to the pool. It's my turn to see what this cave has to offer. Kalen may be first scout because I'm in charge, but everyone here knows I'm the best diver.

It's time I showed them why, and that includes Ms. Andrews.

EIGHTEEN

Peyton

I get a few hours of sleep, and then I'm up and dressed, ready to dive again. I eat and drink first, then use the toilet before zipping up my suit. Tyler is gone, as is Fin, so I'm guessing they're asleep, but Riggs is still awake. I head over and lean against his stool. "You gotta sleep sometime," I tease.

"I will." He yawns. "Ready to go again?"

"Always. Did they find anything?" I ask as I sip from my water bottle, peering over his shoulder at the map he's drawing. It's 3D and adaptable to move around, with additional information when you click on certain sections. It's really impressive. "Damn, babe, this is amazing. I forgot to tell you yesterday how proud of you I am for getting it working!" I gush.

He turns his head and opens his mouth to speak before he slams it shut when he suddenly realises how close we are. Our heads are almost touching, and our breath mingles between us. I should pull away, but I don't want to. His eyes widen, flicking between mine, and his mouth parts again.

Electricity zings between us, stronger than ever before, as if it's been building all these years and is now trying to drag us along. I'm suddenly aware of each of his breaths, of the shifting of his clothes, and the clenching of his hands on the keyboard, making his arms bulge with muscle that wasn't there before.

Riggs always was a sweetheart, and yes, I was attracted to him. He was kind, loving, smart, and sexy as hell, but this new Riggs? Covered in muscles? He intimidates me. I don't know who he is now, but in his eyes, I see the same man I used to love.

He's just not as shy, if the desire blooming there is anything to go by.

My own lips part as my breath hitches, and my pussy clenches from that one look, from the promise in his eyes, which dip to my lips hungrily, tracing them until I can almost feel him touching me. I ache to reach out and grab him, to kiss him and see if he tastes as good as he looks.

I yearn to find out once and for all if I could really love and want four men at the same time. Four men who are very, very different. But right now, my body doesn't care. It's screaming for us to close the gap, to be brave and take what I want.

Him.

A noise has us jumping apart, and reality crashes down around us. The many people who are milling around come back into focus, reminding me they could have just seen how close we were to kissing. What the hell came over me? I've never struggled this much before. I mean, there were moments, but I fell in love with him slowly, as a friend at first and then more. It was never this instantaneous, like I *had* to have him, had to taste his lips or I might scream. Maybe it's because I'm done fighting it, or maybe it's due to time and age.

I want him.

Badly.

And from his expression, I know he still wants me too. He used to look at me with similar eyes, but he would always turn away when I caught him staring. He was always too shy, even when I walked in on him in the shower and all I could do was gawk, even though I'd come to clean up after fucking Tyler. He'd been wanking, and when he saw me, he didn't stop straight away. But for the next few days, he couldn't even look at me.

Could Riggs really have changed that much? Gained so much confidence? And why is the thought so appealing?

"I, erm, thank you. It took a while, but I got there," he rasps before clearing his throat. "Yeah, they went farther into the second submerged cavern you found." He spins then and brings up the map. I make sure not to lean in too close, but it doesn't stop the musky, male scent that's all Riggs from wrapping around me with comforting familiarity. It's almost whispering for me to lean into him, accepting his warmth and comfort like I used to, even though now it's morphed into a hunger so strong, I don't think either of us will be able to control it. I drag my gaze from his profile to the map and watch as he spins it for me to see. I'm not surprised Tyler went and explored more. First and foremost, he's a diver. He would have been dying to get down there.

I miss diving with him. Not so much in caves, but out in the open water. He was something to behold, the way he would move through it. How easily he understood the ocean and the animals that called it home. He was born with an affinity for water. He loved it, and I loved him. I loved him so fucking much, and not just because of who he was, but because he shared my dreams and love of this world. It was there, in the water, where we fell in love, working side by side, day after day. I miss the simplicity of that back then.

We were younger, more idealistic, and still dreamers.

Now I know how hard the world can be, how unfair and jaded. How easily trust and love can be broken, and just how fucking quickly you can lose the ones you love. Like my mother. Like my father. Like them.

"How far did he get?" I murmur, ignoring my depressing thoughts.

"He explored the tunnel to the left. It goes into a partial sump, but it seems to rise. He thinks we would need to climb it." He shows it to me on the map. "He also went into the second for about twenty metres, and it seemed to head pretty much straight. He only went into the third for like a minute or two; it appeared to curve down. Unsure about the fourth."

"Hmm, okay, which one does he want to hit first? I would say the second if it seems to head straight—that would be leading us to the ocean," I muse.

Riggs laughs, making me smile at the happy sound.

"What?" I ask.

"He said the exact same thing. You two really are the bloody same. So yeah, you and Kalen hit the second, keep going until he gets up and calls dive time."

"Got it." I tap his shoulder and turn to go get ready.

"Peyton?" Riggs calls, I stop and look at him with a smile.

"Yeah?"

He hesitates, licking his lips as he seems to debate something. "Just be careful, okay?" We both know that wasn't what he was going to say, but I nod anyway.

"Okay, and make sure to get some sleep. Michael can take over. Promise me," I urge, the familiar words leaving my lips. I used to have to force him to sleep. He would work on his systems and maps for days, staying awake and almost killing himself. He would never listen to the others, only me.

"Sure." He smiles, and it settles something deep inside me. It feels like a peace offering. Is Riggs forgiving me? Could we be friends again? I guess only time will tell, and we have two weeks down here to figure that out.

Below ground, in the dark, in the water, life has a funny way of showing you exactly what you want.

Then it gives it to you, just not always in the way you would hope.

We are back in the water. I found Kalen waiting for me after my talk with Riggs. When Michael finished checking us over and helping us into the water, we got straight to it, not wanting to waste any time and, okay, maybe to out-map Tyler too. What can I say? Divers are competitive.

We know the way this time, so we are more confident through the first section, but we slow when we reach the submerged cavern with the four tunnels. "We're taking the second. Want me to go first in case it gets tight?"

"Sure, princess, but go slow," Kalen calls through his mask, the old nickname making me grin. Did he even realise he used it? "Andrews, I mean, fucking Andrews." Yep, he did, and now he's pissed.

"Calm down, Kay, I'm not going to tease you for still wanting to rescue me." I chuckle. After all, that's how the nickname came about. On a dive in a partially submerged sea cave, there was a quick tide that almost pulled me free and spat me from a blowhole. He hooked and anchored me with him, saving me. After that, I teased him that he was always trying to save me, hence the princess moniker. But now it feels bitter, filled with memories and hate. Andrews is probably better. It's cleaner, distant, and it's from the current Kalen, not the man I built up in my memories.

The man I craved, hungered for so much that I used to ache from the thoughts.

I head to the second tunnel, Riggs's voice filling my mask. "Okay, it tilts down slightly as you enter. After that, it straightens out until the guideline ends. After that, you're setting out on your own, Pey."

"Got it, babe," I reply without thinking.

"Don't fucking call him that," Kalen snaps. "We aren't your babes or your loves; use our fucking names."

Rolling my eyes, I clip onto the guideline and head down like Riggs advised. He's right—it straightens out, allowing me to swim a tiny bit faster, especially knowing Tyler has already been through this part. He knows what he's doing, so if there were any issues, we wouldn't be here.

"Ignore him, Riggs. He's just jealous I never call him any of those things. He gets asshole, wanker, cunt . . ."

"He gets them from most people," Riggs teases, making me laugh. Kalen, clearly angry with the familiar banter, loses it.

"Shut the fuck up and focus on the job. I mean it, Andrews, or I will pull you."

"Wanker," I mutter.

"I heard that."

"You were meant to." I grin but focus on the space in front of me as I come to the end of the guideline. Now it's my turn to set it, and from here on out, no one has explored. It could be a dead end. It could go up or down. There could be ice walls, rock walls, chasms . . . anything.

A lot of people call cave divers crazy because we take insane risks. We put our bodies through hell with long, torturous hours just for a taste, a hint of what's left to be discovered in this world. Hell, maybe we are insane. The definition of crazy is doing the same thing over and over again and expecting different results, and we do. Day after day.

And we enjoy it.

The pain, the exhaustion, the risks. We live for it. Even now, adrenaline fuels me at what is to come, at what challenges are lying in wait in the darkness before me, causing my heart to pound as I grin without meaning to.

The tunnel around us is fairly wide, so we could swim side by side if we wanted, but you never know when you will come to a bend or a twist. And down here, one mistake is all it takes.

So you play it smart.

Work smart.

"You remember that cave in Mexico?" I ask, filling the silence as we swim. It's still dark, and we are still heading forward. I keep an eye on my computer stats as we go.

"Oh, the one with the tide at the bottom of the chasm?" he eventually murmurs.

"Yep, fuck, that was an amazing cave. You reckon we'll find anything like that here?"

"I don't know, Andrews, maybe. It's been too easy so far, too fucking easy. Something has to be waiting for us." He laughs.

"Yeah, too easy," I reply.

Just then, my primary light fails—not a shock, they always seem to—so I change to my secondary and carry on. It flickers on as I swim in place, the light shining through the water in front of me, and something dark darts across it. "What the fuck was that?" I exclaim.

"What?" Kalen calls, and I peer harder into the darkness, swinging my light around. "Princess, you answer me this fucking instant!"

"Pey?" Riggs says worriedly.

"Sorry, shit, did you see that?" I ask Riggs.

"I didn't see anything; it was too dark when you switched lights. You guys okay? You need to come back?" he questions anxiously.

Steadying my heart, I peer around the murky water once again. Fuck, it was probably some rocks in the tide. "Nah, we're good, sorry. Going to keep going, note at marker five."

"You good?" Kalen calls.

"Yeah, sorry, shifting rocks. Fucking primary failed."

He snorts. "When don't they? Let's keep going before Ty gets up and calls us back. See if we can find something exciting."

I keep going, loving that we're not arguing anymore. It feels like old times. I don't see any other shadows or rocks, so I relax as the tunnel branches out. Along the way, we've seen small holes and pockets, which aren't big enough to get through, but now it branches off into two separate tunnels.

"Branch, left or right?" I call, letting him pick.

"Let's go left."

"Riggs, we're going left," I note, and turn and swim that way. The tunnel is bigger here, widening the farther we go. I stop to let Kalen place more rope and tanks for emergencies, and then we start again.

We only swim for around fifteen minutes before light penetrates the water, and we head towards it. We break the surface at the very edge of a cavern. Pulling off my mask, I look around and turn to Kalen. "Let's explore."

I wade from the pool and look around in awe. High up in the ceiling is a hole that opens into the jungle. The sun shines brightly onto us, and the whistle of the trees and the sounds of animals reach us even here. It's too high to climb with the ceiling curving up into the small hole, so we split up and walk the perimeter, seeing if the cavern carries on anywhere. We leave our gear at the edge of the water so we don't have to carry it, and we work in silence, knowing we could be called back any minute.

The walls would be hard to climb but not impossible, but I find no other entrances or exits, and when I meet Kalen in the middle, he hasn't either. "Want to try for the right tunnel?"

He nods, looking around with his hands on his hips. "Yeah, let's do it, Andrews. I think Ty is still asleep."

We slip back into our gear and update Riggs before diving. This time, Kalen leads, but just as we get back to the intersection, our comms come on. "Time," Ty calls.

Fuck.

"You can explore the right side later. Come back for a meeting. We're looking at what we've found and where we think we should go next."

Kalen and I share a look, both of us debating carrying on anyway. "Now," Tyler orders.

"Got it, bro, coming back," Kalen grumbles, just as annoyed as I am that we haven't really found anything yet.

"There's always later," I offer, and he nods before we begin the journey back. It's both good and bad. The system is so extensive and takes time to explore, which means there are more possibilities for reaching the ocean and the chances are greater for a serious find, or it could all be dead ends. Only time will tell.

NINETEEN

"Could that location be used as an advanced base?" Tyler asks, leaning over Riggs's shoulder and looking at the footage.

"It could, but there are no real exits, so I would suggest we keep looking," I advise as I tie back my hair and tuck in my shirt now that I'm dry from the dive. I have no clue what time it is, but down here, it doesn't really matter.

He peers at me over his shoulder, wearing a frown, and then looks to Kalen to confirm. It makes me grind my teeth, but I bite my tongue. "I agree. We still have a lot to explore, so chances are we'll find something better. We have stopping points and storage areas now though. I would like to explore the tunnel on the right."

Tyler nods. "Then we'll explore one of the others from the submerged cavern while you rest." He looks back at the map, which now has a small countdown in the corner. "We're doing good on time, but the dives are only going to get harder and longer, and you will be exhausted. Keep up your spirits, and if you're struggling, speak up—remember why we're doing this." He raises his eyes and meets all our gazes.

"For the girls!" Fin shouts, making everyone laugh, including me.

"Glory." Kalen smirks.

"To say we can," I add, my dad's words flowing from my mouth. They all freeze, especially Tyler, who was used to hearing them. They all watch me with a mixture of emotions—longing, regret, love, and hate—and then Tyler's eyes narrow.

"When I say time, you come back, understood?" he snarls at me, calling me out in front of everyone. They are all staring at me, but I refuse to back down or be intimidated. He wants to show me up, to hurt me . . . to make me leave.

He needs to realise that it's not fucking happening.

"Understood, if you can comprehend I know what I'm doing," I retort, crossing my arms and stepping closer.

His nostrils flare as he glares, and he looks to everyone before his eyes land on me. "And this is why I didn't want you here. You're not a team player. One way or another, Peyton, you will be leaving this dive if you keep this up."

"Fuck you, Tyler. I'm here because of my talent, same as you. This is my dive as well, so get the fuck over it or keep your mouth shut for once," I snap, tired of being beaten down by them. I'm not the type to sit back and take it, and the only reason I have so far is because I felt guilty for leaving. Guilty for hurting them. I understand their anger and hatred, I do, but I can't take it anymore.

They want to fight? We'll fight.

I'm not their punching bag, and they are not my guys anymore.

He narrows his eyes on me after the outburst, and without looking away, he barks, "Dismissed," before stalking away.

Oh, hell no!

Ever since we were reunited, this inner turmoil has been stirring, building, and I'm about to set a match to it and blow that shit up. I'm tired of the snarky remarks and dirty looks. We need to work together, and for that to happen, we need to clear the air.

As everyone starts to disperse and he looks back at the map, ignoring me, I tap his shoulder. He disregards it, talking to Riggs, so I do it harder. He sighs and turns. "What?" he snaps.

"We need to talk," I growl.

Tyler's lips press into a flat line before he looks back at Riggs. "Good work, I agree. See if you can add water depth." He completely turns his back on me, almost causing me to fall to the floor, and begins to storm away.

This motherfucker.

I chase after him, matching his long strides as he walks through the camp. "Tyler, don't fucking ignore me, we need to talk. You can't keep shitting on me in front of everyone because of your issues with me. This is business, you need to—"

"I don't need to do anything," he snarls and speeds up.

It's my turn to get angry now, my eyes narrowing on his retreating form until my irritation just explodes out of me.

"Don't you fucking walk away from me!" I nearly scream, stopping as he spins. He's enraged, his nostrils flaring and muscles shaking in anger. Those once bright eyes are dark, gleaming with pain and animosity. Tyler squares up, getting right in my face.

"That's rich coming from you, baby. I thought you were the one used to walking away," he growls out harshly, true fury leaking through his tone. The dark, hateful way he says *baby* sends a shiver through me, and not just from anger. Fuck, why is that so hot? Why do I want to taste that explosive mix on his lips and feel his hatred in his hands while he fucks me?

Ouch.

I swallow, about to retort, when he lifts his head and looks around. I realise everyone is watching us, and so does he. He grabs my arm and none too kindly yanks me into his tent, shoving me away as soon as we're inside as if not to touch me any longer than necessary.

I stumble but turn, glaring at him. I open my mouth to snap at him when he advances, backing me into the wall of the tent. I slip and almost fall as his arms come up, one on either side of my head, and bracket me in place. His tall, ripped body almost touches mine, and our breaths mingle as he lowers his head. "You will stop being such a brat and causing a scene. You will act like a diver, a professional, or you will be gone so fast, you won't even have time to pack," he whispers dangerously, each word hammered into me with those intense eyes.

He starts to move away, and each step he takes unlocks me from his gaze, but I find myself wanting to be captured. I want to be here, right before him. I want to feel the emotions pouring from his body, even if they are all tinged with anger.

Because . . . I still want him.

And I think he still wants me, but we still have those glaring issues hanging over our heads. Like the fact I kissed his brother. Like the fact I love his two best friends.

I'm tired of being alone, I'm tired of missing them every single day. I made the biggest mistake of my life when I walked away from them, and every day since, I've just been trying to survive. But here they are, here we are, and I can't help it. I'm falling back into the same patterns and routines, falling back in love with them.

Except we are all different, and even though it's selfish, I need him to understand why I did it. Why I left.

"Tyler," I start.

He freezes with his back facing me, his fists clenched at his sides. I want to slide my hands over his shoulders and pull him into my arms, to kiss him and make it all better, but he's not mine to do that with anymore, and I know he would push me away. He would be disgusted by my touch.

"Don't," he begs, his voice hoarse.

"I have to," I whisper. "I'm sorry I left, I am. I did it to protect you, because I loved you so—"

He whirls, and I see tears in his eyes, but he's still angry. "Don't stand there and say you left because you loved me! You left because you were scared, too fucking scared, so you ran, and now you feel bad. Well, don't. It's over. It's done."

"It's done?" I repeat.

"Yes, it's done, I'm over you," he snarls.

"Over me? Then why do you still carry the ring? Why do you still have my bracelets?" I yell, having already noticed them peeking from his bag. He freezes, and I scrub at my face. "That doesn't matter. Ty, I am really sorry. If it helps, it's the biggest mistake of my life. I regret it every single day. I never wanted to hurt you. God, Tyler, I loved you so much, but when you proposed—" I dash my own tears away and look at him. "I wanted to say yes," I admit, "but I couldn't."

"Why?" he whispers brokenly.

Because I was never just his. The confession almost slips out.

"Because you didn't know the truth," I reply. Fear winds through me at my admission, at sharing just how fucked up I am, at seeing that last flicker of love in his eyes fade to anger and disgust, but it's now or never. He's right here before me, and I can finally divulge the truth and see what happens—or I can watch him walk away and know I've truly lost him forever.

I can't handle that though, because no matter what I did or how I feel, Tyler was and always will be my forever. I can't help loving the others, but it never stopped me from loving him just as much, maybe even more. Tyler was there when my dad died. He was there to hold me when I admitted how messed up I was over my mum's death. He was with me when I was excited and starting out into the world.

He's woven into my past in an intricate web. All my memories have Tyler in them, and I don't want to be free of that. I want him in my future, and I want to be so wrapped up in him that I can never escape. I want this back—being with them, working with them. I realise that now, and I'm tired of fighting it, of pretending I don't, because if being down here with them has taught me anything, it's that I still love them.

"I kissed your brother," I blurt out. It hangs between us for a moment as we both stare at each other, but all that weight goes with it, all that self-hatred and guilt as I watch him. "I kissed Kalen," I reiterate, my voice low and quiet as I wait for him to explode.

I expect him to kick me, hit me, and throw his vile words at me, because I deserve it. Not only did I break his heart, but I cheated on him with his brother. I wait for the blows to come, so when he sighs, I flinch.

"Baby—Peyton, I know you kissed him." He scrubs at his face as I blink in shock.

"Wait, what?" I ask dumbly. "You knew? You knew the night of my father's funeral I kissed your brother?" When he doesn't talk, I move closer, and words rush from me. I need him to understand, even if they aren't excuses, because no one can excuse what I did. "I was drunk and foolish, but the worst bit? I wanted to do it again, and it killed me. I hated myself and I pulled away, and when you proposed, all I could do was think . . . think that you deserved someone better.

Someone who could love you wholly, fully. You deserved a woman who didn't lust after your family." There, it's out. I feel like I can breathe again.

"I know you kissed him, but your dad had just died and you were hurting," he begins, making excuses for me. He didn't listen to what I said.

"Stop justifying my actions! Be angry! Hate me! Tell me I'm a terrible person, that I cheated and I'm a sick fucking bitch!" I scream, needing him to tell me off, to despise me for it the way I despise myself.

He stares at me for a moment, his expression hard as I brace myself for his anger. "But here's the thing, Peyton, you don't get to choose what I deserve, only I do. I knew about the kiss. He told me that night when you fell asleep. Of course he told me, baby, he's my brother. I was so angry, I punched him, and you know what?"

He shakes his head with a bitter laugh.

"He didn't even defend himself. Not even when I tackled him and pummelled him for trying to steal you . . . or even when he told me he loved you and I broke his nose."

I gasp at his confession. Kalen loves me . . . loved me? But Tyler is still talking.

"I knew he loved you, baby, I did, and I tried to steal you and keep you to myself, to make you all mine because I was scared you would fall for him and leave me." He laughs bitterly again, and I dash my tears away as he stares at me. I expected his anger, not this truthful, raw discussion. "But then I lost you anyway, and I lost him too. When you left, you took whatever was still alive in him. He died, and I couldn't do anything because I was too blinded by my own pain . . . so I thought if I ever saw you again, if you ever came back, that if it was all of us or none of us . . . I'd do it, because I can't live without you again. I tried, and I hated it."

I gasp, hope blooming in my chest as I move closer, but he shakes his head and steps back.

"But three years is a long time, Peyton. Three years of you being gone. I don't know if I can be this with you anymore, if I can do this . . . if I want to do it. Fuck, I still want you, but I'm also still mad. I've finally moved on, Peyton. I can't go back to that place, not even for another chance with you. I thought I would give anything, but my family is finally healing, and I can't break it again. I'm not angry with you for kissing him. I don't even hate you as much as I want to."

God, my heart is breaking all over again, ripping from my chest and bleeding in his hands as he admits just how much he wants me still . . . and can't have me. But I need him, I need to be forgiven, and I need to be punished for what I did, so I step closer and push him slightly.

"Do something; be mad at me!" I nearly scream. "Hate me for what I did! Tell me I'm a terrible person!"

"I was—am mad at you, Peyton, but I'm also tired. For years, I saw us having this fight, of me telling you where to fucking stick it, but I never imagined how sad it would make me feel." His disappointment is palpable and worse than the anger and hurt still lurking in his eyes.

It staggers me. We just stare at each other, with a chasm between us as all our hopes and dreams fall to the bottom. This feels like the end, the true end. We are too broken to fix, but fuck, I can't. I can't lose this. Even when we were apart, there was still a chance we could be together again, but now hearing that there isn't one? That he doesn't think he could ever trust and love me again?

I'm bleeding from a thousand cuts created by each word.

"Tyler," I whisper haltingly, "I still love you."

"I know." He sighs. "But I can't do this—" He stops to turn, but I can't let him walk away. I can't.

I do the only thing I can think of—I hurt him. I'll make him angry so he'll stay, even if it's just to hurt me back. It's better than nothing; it's better than being cold and alone.

His hate is better than naught.

"Yeah, well, fuck you, Ty, your brother was a better kisser anyway." Fuck. As soon as the words leave my lips, I know they were a mistake.

I'm getting whiplash from this conversation, from the emotions flowing between us, but I'm willing to hurt myself and him if it means he'll stay. If it means he'll still focus on me just to hurt me. I'll take all his hate and pain, because I mean it, I still love him, and yes, I'm angry too. I hate that this is what we have become, but hearing him admit it's over breaks down all the walls I've erected over the last several years until I'm just a girl who loves a boy.

Nothing more, nothing less.

He freezes and turns, his eyes turning cold and angry. The new Tyler is back to play, not the sweet man who forgave me for kissing his brother. "What did you say?"

I lift my chin and smile cruelly at him. "I said your brother kissed better anyway."

We are both breathing heavily and glaring at each other from metres away. All the years of lying and hiding how I truly felt, all the days of him missing me, loving me, and eventually hating me, and all the new emotions entangled with the old ones . . . it all explodes. One second, we're standing apart, and the next, I'm in his arms. His hands drop to my ass and yank me closer, straight into his hard body, and his cock presses against my stomach. One of his hands tangles in my hair, pulling back my head as he smashes his lips onto mine.

It's a hard, brutal kiss.

Raw and angry.

On his lips, which I have kissed a million times, I taste the difference. I taste the mix of emotions he hides so deeply, even from himself. I taste his longing, his love, and his hate too. This kiss is filled with everything we can't say to each other. He bites my lips, no doubt drawing blood, and he forces his tongue into my mouth, dominating it. I whimper, and the sound seems to shock him. Tyler rips himself away and stumbles back, his eyes wide, lips parted and red, chest heaving. He stares at me with surprise and hunger before he covers it with that icy exterior, spins on his heel, and stalks from the tent.

I stand alone, observing his retreating form with my fingers touching my bruised, bleeding lips, my hair a mess from his hands, and my pussy aching from the hunger that exploded between us.

I watch him walk away, and it's the first time I realise just how he felt seeing me go. I know just what I gave up that day, something I don't think I will ever really get back—him.

I've lost Tyler.

I've lost them all.

It's finally starting to sink in.

TWENTY

Fin

I see Tyler storm from his tent, his hands in his hair, his eyes wild and lost, his lips red and swollen. Looks like he finally gave in to those desires we all know he still has for Peyton. It makes me smirk. I want to take bets on how long it will be before those two are back together. In my opinion, them butting heads and snapping at each other is just foreplay, a way for them to show how much they still care, even though they are angry.

But then Peyton leaves the tent with tears in her eyes as she pulls back her hair. She looks around, not meeting anyone's eyes, and then slides away. I watch as she slips through camp back to the crawl section, and quickly and deftly moves through it. No one should go anywhere alone, at least that's the excuse I give myself as I follow after her.

I silently move through camp to the entrance of the small tunnel, manoeuvring through on my knees until I find her on the other side. She's sitting at the entrance to the waterfall chamber, her side pressed against the wall as she stares into the water. She looks so small and alone, it sends a pang through my heart. Fuck, I should turn around, but I can't help myself.

I still care for her. I don't even hate her as much as everyone else seems to because I know why she did it. I know how much she hurt herself when she left. So I step closer. I know she hears the crunch of the stones under my feet when she hunches slightly. She hates being vulnerable in front of people, always has. I think one of the only times I ever saw her cry was when her father died. She was a wreck, and all our rules went out of the window. We slept in big puppy piles. We held her and pulled her back together until she could function again.

Riggs washed her hair, Tyler helped her shower, and Kalen twisted and pulled until she came back from the brink of darkness. We almost lost her, but I never realised how much it would kill me when we actually did. But now she's here, she's back, and all that anger I held on to, anger at myself and her for making me love her and then leaving, is disappearing.

Because she's back.

If we lose this chance, she will disappear again. Can we live with that?

Sitting down next to her, I look at her tear-stained face and red lips. It seems she's met Tyler's anger, the one she created in him when she left. I've had it aimed at me, in a different way of course, but it's not nice. He can be cruel when he wants to be, using it as a mechanism to keep people away, to stop them from hurting him.

She sniffs loudly and turns her head, wiping her face on her arm as she drags her legs closer to her chest. She's almost curled into a ball, as if she's expecting me to physically hurt her. That makes me pissed at Tyler. We would never do that. Yeah, he may be an asshole and rip her a new one . . . Okay, Kalen may be a cruel fucker too, but we would never hurt her physically. Ever.

Right now, she needs a friend, and despite everything that's happened, that's what I once was, and I can't stand to see her hurting.

"If you're here to hate on me some more, to tell me I'm a horrible person and kick me while I'm down, please just don't," she implores, her voice hoarse.

I wrap my arm around her stiff shoulders. "I'm not, darling, I promise. I'm here to see if you're okay."

She lifts her flushed face. "Why?"

"Because you're still family. Family fucks up sometimes, they make mistakes." I wince. "Yes, it hurt, and I'm angry and missed you like crazy. I should have seen it coming. You were my best friend. I should have seen you struggling, should have noticed you pulling away. You were lost and alone and thought the only way out was to run, and I will never forgive myself for not stopping you, for not being there for you." She shakes her head and gets to her knees, covering my mouth quickly with her hand. She searches my eyes desperately.

"No, there was nothing you could have done, Fin. Nothing, okay? Please don't blame yourself. Blame me, hate me," she pleads, her tear-filled gaze locked on mine.

I pull her hand away, staring into those eyes I love so much. The darkened cavern is small and isolated, and no one else is here . . . I fight it. I fight the words that want to escape, but I can't. I finally admit it aloud. "I don't want to hate you," I murmur.

The sound of the waterfall resonates around us as we stare into each other's eyes from inches away. I see the same interest in hers, the same lust. I struggle against it, my body rebelling, and she stills, not moving either. Both of us just watch the other until we clash. I don't know who moves first, but suddenly, we're kissing. My fingers thread through the back of her hair, pulling her towards me.

Our lips meet, our teeth clacking in our haste. The taste of her explodes on my tongue, making me groan as my cock pulses. The kiss deepens and slows, becoming less feral. We explore, each of us fighting against the past, using this moment just to give in and be weak.

She tastes amazing, and her lips are so soft, I could kiss her forever. I ache to drag her closer, to show her just how much I care, but I can't. I pull away and press my forehead to hers. Cupping her cheek, I watch her eyes close for a second before they open and lock on me with a knowing expression.

This is wrong.

It feels right, but it's wrong.

It doesn't stop my cock from hardening and demanding my attention like always when I'm with her though.

"I never believed in love, Pey, until you walked into my life." I drop a kiss onto her lips once more, unable to help myself as I press my forehead harder against hers.

My gaze flickers back down to her lips hungrily as I imagine throwing her to the floor and covering her in kisses, tasting all of her like I've wanted to for years. I want to see if I can make her scream louder than she did with Tyler . . . to see if she is everything I made her out to be in my fantasies.

"But we can't do this. I can't do this to them, to Tyler, even as much as I want to. I thought—I thought I made it all up, that I couldn't possibly want someone this much, but I do. I have always wanted you, Peyton. Even when you were in love with my brothers. But I can't hurt him again. I'm sorry." I give her one last lingering kiss, tasting her tears on her lips and the sweetness of her regret, regret that pulls at me. I wish I could stay, I wish I could kiss her forever, but this will be the final time. This is a goodbye, both to her and the feelings I have, because one thing is clear—Tyler isn't over her, and she isn't over him.

They belong together, so I'm backing down. I'll be the best friend I can be to them and have her in my life however I can, even if it means her loving another. Even if it means watching her marry and be happy with Tyler. At least I will still see her, still be in her orbit.

She nods and curls back into my side, her head on my shoulder. I'm kicking myself, but it's the right thing to do, and right now, she's lost and hurting. She needs a friend, not a guy pawing at her and taking advantage.

She needs family.

And despite everything, we are family.

We sit in silence. I hold her as she puts herself back together again. She needs to get some rest after her dive, but I will sit here with her all night if I have to. She would do the same for me. "Aren't you up soon?" she questions, her voice raspy.

"Soon," I answer.

She sighs and lifts her head. "Sorry to cry on your shoulder. I shouldn't have done that. I'm sorry, Fin."

"Pey, look at me." She does, and I grin. "I don't hate you, okay? None of us do . . . Okay, Kalen might a bit. And Tyler. But only because they loved you so much." I don't bullshit her on this. She needs to know, because if she wants to be part of this family again, she needs to earn our trust. "I don't know if you even want to rejoin us, but they will come around. Just keep pushing, keep being you. It's not been the same without you, darling."

"What if I don't want to come back?" she inquires.

It sends agony through me, but I smile through it. "Then that's your choice. When it comes down to it, Peyton, you need to figure out what you want. No one else can choose for you, but stop living in limbo. You're either in or you're out. But if you're out, you need to be completely out so we can move on and get over you, because it's not fair otherwise."

She nods as I get to my feet. I lean down and offer her my hand. She stares at it for a moment before placing her smaller one in mine. I yank her to her feet, and she stumbles into my chest, and of course just then, when I'm steadying her, Kalen finds us.

Fuck.

I know how much he loves her, even if he will never admit it.

When he sees us this close, alone in the dark, his eyes narrow. I see the flash of pain and then hate in his gaze as he glances between us. We step away from each other quickly, making us look guiltier. Thank fuck he didn't see us kissing. He would have throttled me, and I would have deserved it, because even though he loves her, he will never make a move. He loves his brother more, and he thinks only Tyler deserves happiness, not him. He's still trying to atone for perceived sins from the tours.

"Tyler is waiting for you. You're up," he snarls and then turns away.

"Kal," she calls, but he ignores her and crawls back through. She sighs and drops her head back. "Fuck, I need to stop messing things up."

"He'll get over it, babe. He's seen us in worse positions." I wink, making her smile slightly. "Now I'm off to get wet . . . unless you're willing to join me." I wiggle my eyebrows, and she laughs, smacking me on the arm.

"Dirty bastard."

"You love it," I tease as I start to walk backwards, swinging my hips as I wink at her again. "What can I say, I make everyone wet."

"Oh God, stop." She sniggers and follows after me, spanking me as I bend down to crawl.

"Hey, hands off the goods, darling, unless you've got some singles for me," I mutter as I clamber through the tunnel.

"Pfft, you only take twenties—you're an expensive hottie." She giggles behind me. The sound of her laughter makes my smile widen. I love that I can always bring her from the dark and make her laugh. It makes me feel like I have achieved something and fills me with a sense of purpose.

We laugh and joke as we head to the pool's edge, where Tyler is waiting, already in his gear. He groans when he sees us, and I sigh when he turns away in pain. Why is this so hard?

"I better get some sleep," she calls and then glances at Ty. "Be safe," she murmurs. He nods and watches her go as she spins and walks away. His eyes remain locked on her in confusion. Poor man. If he's not careful, he's going to lose her. He needs to figure it out as well, figure out if he can forgive her for leaving.

I quickly get ready, and once I'm in the water, I broach the subject, knowing Kalen and Pey are in their tents and only Riggs is around. Tyler won't listen to Riggs or his brother, but maybe he'll listen to me. He's in front of me, as usual, always controlling the situation—not that he can ever control us entirely.

"So, are you going to forgive her or keep acting like an ass while watching her like a lost puppy?" I laugh into my mask, getting straight to the point. There's no bullshitting with us; he needs someone to call him on his shit.

"Shut up," he snarls. "It's time to work, not gossip."

"Uh-huh. You made her cry, you know." I hear his inhale and then carry on. "It's okay, I made her laugh."

"Course you did," he mutters jealously.

"You could have been the one if you weren't so fucking adamant about keeping her at a distance."

"It's none of your business, Fin," he almost yells.

Oh, now I'm getting somewhere. "Yeah, see, it is. 'Cause you're my brother, and I love you, and I'm tired of watching you hurt yourself. I want you to be happy."

"I'm happy," he grumbles, flicking his fins in front of my face as we dive deeper.

"No, you're not, Ty. She's back. She's here. That has to count for something. Okay, so I bet it's not how you imagined it, but if you let her go again, you'll regret it for the rest of your life, because someone else will fall in love with her. They will marry her and make a life with her, and you will lose your chance at the best thing that ever happened to you," I caution as we slip through the tunnel, ready to explore another passage.

"He's right, Tyler. We love you, but you have been so unhappy since she left, and life is too short for that. Why not give it a shot?" Riggs offers, making me chuckle.

"Did you forget the part where she left?" he growls out. "Left us all? She isn't back, she's just here to work. She'll leave again, we all know that. And I *am* happy, I'm over her . . . We all are."

"Sure," I reply. "Keep telling yourself that, but when she leaves again and you don't stop her, can you live with that? Can you live knowing it will be someone else exploring with her, loving her? Making her laugh and watching her scream at horror movies? Holding her as she cries when an animal dies, seeing her bravery as she tries to rescue and save everyone?"

"Stop," he begs.

"I can't. I've let you wallow for too long. I thought it was how you needed to cope, but I can't let you anymore, not if it means you wreck the best thing to happen in three years 'cause you're blinded by your own anger," I retort, anger lacing my tone. Can't he see what he's giving up? The very thing the rest of us would do anything to have—her. "You've found something we're all searching for, that all of us want."

He goes quiet then as we pass the first cavern, and I wince. Shit, that sounded bad, like I meant with her . . . which maybe I did, but fuck, I didn't mean for him to take it like that.

"Yeah, I know what you all want," he snaps bitterly, and then we both go quiet as we focus on swimming. When we're in the opening of the second cavern, I stop before him. Staring at him through the mask, I will him to see how serious I am.

"Tyler, don't be an idiot. You have your whole life to work through your issues, but at least actively work through them. Don't just throw everything away 'cause you're scared. That girl still loves you. Fuck, she loved you so much, she left because she was scared of hurting you. You don't find a girl like that ever—trust me, I know. She's one in a million, and she's here. For once, take a chance. If it goes wrong, have you really lost anything? She will still leave, and you will be alone, but at least you'll know."

He looks at me through the goggles, searching my eyes. Riggs is quiet, letting our words sink in. We're both hoping he understands and thinks on what we have said, even if we're jealous, even if we both wish it was one of us who met her first and fell in love with her. But it wasn't, and at least this way, she is still in our lives.

"We're heading to the third tunnel," he murmurs distractedly.

Sighing, I give him the *okay* signal and follow him, knowing he will at least have to think about what we said. I just hope he makes the right choice and that Kalen won't stand in the way.

We're cautious as we move through the tunnel, unsure where it will take us. It seems to spin around on itself, heading upwards. We keep swimming until we break the surface around an hour later.

It's dark, really dark. We can barely see anything, even with our lights. I pull off my mask, and Ty does the same and sparks a flare, holding it above the water as we look around. I break another and toss it away, trying to see how wide and deep this cavern is.

"Fuck." I whistle, and it echoes. We can't even see the ceiling, it's so tall, or even the sides of the space. The water is pulling slightly with a small tide, which is promising.

"Let's see if we can find an end," Tyler murmurs. I turn to him, about to swim closer, when something catches my eye.

A dash of black breaks the surface, but when I blink, it's gone, so I dismiss it and focus on swimming alongside Tyler. The paddling of our arms and legs is loud in the quiet cavern, apart from the swish of the water. It smells fresh in here, and it feels large. We swim until we finally come upon a wall, but it's not the end of the room. The water carries on between it, and when we turn and manage to spot the other wall, we groan.

It's a fucking crevice.

The walls are really high, with a massive gap between them. We can't see the top. It could lead to a different part of the cave system entirely, and we need to map it, but we don't have climbing gear with us. Tyler swims to the other side as I paddle alongside this one, looking for a way up, or around, hell, even under it, wondering where this leads to. This whole cave system is a series of twists and turns, with no direct route anywhere.

It's normal to have dead ends and closed rooms, but shit here has been more expansive than we ever imagined, and we need to find a way through this and onto the next part of the system, or our fourteen-day aim will be doubled—fuck, even tripled—which wouldn't look good, and we don't want Steve to lose confidence in us.

"Anything?" I call.

"Nothing. Seems like the only way is up. It will take too long to go back and grab the climbing equipment. Leave it to Kalen and Peyton. We'll check out the other tunnel. Let's go back," he replies loudly.

Sighing, I start to swim his way when a noise, like someone breaking the surface, comes from right behind me in the dark. I spin, causing water to erupt around me as I shine my light into the darkness, squinting as a sudden burst of irrational fear surges through me. I tell myself it could be anything, but my heart is still racing as I shine the light across the seemingly still water. Only ripples along the surface alert me to the fact I'm not going crazy. Taking a deep breath, I duck under the surface and swing my light around.

The water is so dull and dark, it's hard to see. It's almost black as I dive a little deeper to check if it was just a rock dropping. The fear is still flowing through me, but I'm starting to think I was just being stupid. When I find nothing, I resurface, blow out my nose, and slick back my hair. I'm bloody losing it.

I look around and notice Tyler has nearly reached me when something suddenly wraps around my leg and yanks me under the water. I go down with a sputter, but my training kicks in, and I flip, reaching down and stabbing whatever it is. It abruptly releases me, and I swim to the surface. When I break it, Tyler is there.

"Fin, what the fuck?" he yells.

"Something grabbed me!" I shout as I spit out water and suck in air.

Instantly, we both duck under the water, lights shining, Tyler ready with his knife. We've faced octopuses, sharks, and other water predators before, but never this deep into a cave. How could it even survive down here? Yet there's nothing, just the dark, still water and the floating end of a rope.

Fuck.

We break the surface again, and he frowns. "It looks like you got caught in a rope. You okay?"

I nod, wiping the water from my face. "Shit, it really felt like something grabbed me," I mutter on the edge of hysteria, so I laugh. "I'm just tired. Sorry, man. Come on, let's go explore that other tunnel."

I feel him watching me cautiously as we swim back to the channel we came up from. I don't blame him since divers have been known to go crazy down in the caves. Tiredness is an ass kicker, and you can go insane, plus the darkness and water makes you loopy, but I'm not going crazy, I know that. It was just a weird moment; he can trust me.

When we reach the dive spot, we ready ourselves and go back under, swimming downwards, our lights piercing the dark. As we move farther away from the cave, I settle down. It was just a rope, nothing else. Fuck, I almost laugh at myself.

"Riggs, heading to the next turn," Tyler calls behind me as I use the line to pull myself down and ensure we don't get lost.

"Got it, be safe," he replies, his voice crackling through the speaker.

"Aw, you missing us?" I mock, making him chuckle.

"Shut up, asshole, just find us something good."

"Pfft, we all know I will, 'cause I'm the dive god." I laugh, causing even Tyler to snigger.

We head to the other tunnel, and this time, I go first, excitement racing through me. Tyler cautions me to be careful, which he always does. He thinks I'm too reckless and take too many risks. I just love the feeling of adrenaline pumping through me.

This passageway tightens, and we have to work to get through it without damaging the equipment. It's slow going, and when we're through to the other side, I whoop. It's a dry area. It's too tight to have an advanced base camp, but we found something! I climb from the water and leave my equipment as I rush to explore, Tyler calling after me.

It's uphill and leads to a wall we would have to climb, but the rocks have green shrubs growing in them, which means there's probably surface access somewhere. I don't climb it, but I move around it, searching for any ways out. "I found something!" I shout as I shine my light into the opening at head height. It looks like it goes somewhere.

Tyler joins me, and with a grin, I leap up to grab the edge, pull myself in, and start to crawl as he swears. "Fuck, Fin, be careful. We need to head back soon."

"Yeah, yeah, I just wanna see where it goes."

It gets tight, and I have to belly crawl through it, but then I stop when it turns upwards sharply. Shining my light up as I crane my neck, I grin at what I find. "Well, shit."

"What?" Tyler calls, his voice echoing.

"It goes up, but it's tight. Probably not our best way. Looks like we need to climb those walls to see where they go first." I sigh and then start scooting backwards. I move carefully, rocks crunching underfoot, until I'm finally back out and Tyler slaps my back.

"Oh well, next time."

I groan. "Fuck, you're going to let Kalen and Pey climb it, aren't you?"

"She's the best." He shrugs, and I swear as he grins. "If you're good, I'll let you cover the gap for us. You can free-climb across the ceiling and make a ladder."

"Fuck yeah." I chuckle as we head back for our equipment, help each other into it, and slip back into the water. Just as I am descending, I hear a screeching noise, but I blame it on interference in my mic . . . right?

When we return, I'm tired, and Kalen and Peyton are eating with Michael, laughing and joking and preparing for their next dive. Tyler heads their way, and I follow as he outlines his desire for them to climb that wall and what they will need, adding a reminder to be careful in the water.

They share a disappointed look. They both wanted to explore the right-side tunnel they found. But hey, at least they get to do something cool, as long as no more ropes wrap around anyone . . .

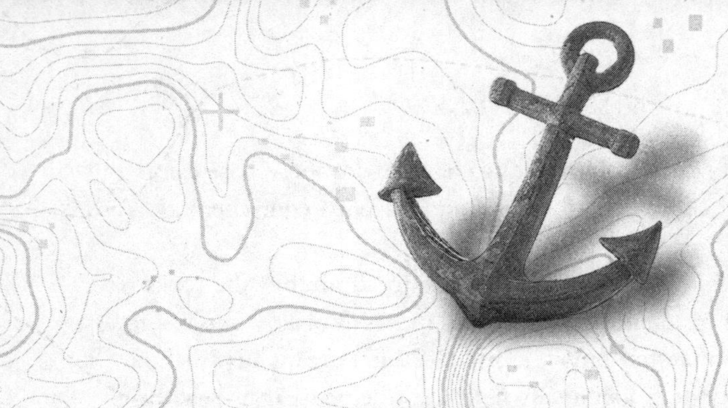

TWENTY-ONE

Peyton

Tyler and Fin seem disgruntled as they sit down to eat. Once I'm done, I use the bathroom and go to prepare for another dive. My body is tired, but we still have plenty of days to go, and I can rest when I'm dead.

Michael helps me into my gear and looks around to make sure no one is close to us. "You okay, kid? I saw you yesterday. Looked like you'd been crying."

"Fine," I reply and smile. "Really, just a misunderstanding. How are you feeling?"

"Wishing I could be down there with you, Minnow." He sighs, gazing at the water, and the smile drops from my face. I know that. Fuck, I wish he could be with me. I can't imagine never being able to dive again, but it's not worth risking his life. His lungs could pop, and I can't lose this man. He's my family.

My friend.

"I do too, old man, but I feel safer knowing you have my back up here." He smiles as he checks my air and equipment. Kalen comes over shirtless, his wet suit unzipped to his waist. My eyes drag down his impressive chest without even meaning to.

He's all golden skin and tattoos with his eight-pack on display and that delicious V leading down. He's the epitome of fitness, we all have to be down here, but Jesus, he's the biggest of the guys, and his chest and arms were always my favourite. I almost drool, my eyes caught on his pecs and the bunching of his arms as he lifts his equipment and begins the checks.

It's a good job this is a wet suit . . .

"Minnow, eyes on me." Michael laughs, and I jerk my head back to him and narrow my eyes. "Perv," he teases.

"Shut up, I'm just appreciating his good-quality wet suit." I grin.

We quieten when Kalen looks up at us in confusion. I turn away with a muffled laugh and sit down at the water's edge, ready for today. We are going to set up the climbing gear and see how far we can get, but from Tyler's description, we may not be able to do it all in one go. There is a truce in the air, at least between Ty and me. Kalen is still pissed and won't talk to me.

The next dive is almost a failure. We swim through the tunnel Ty specified to climb, but it takes so long to get there that by the time we arrange the equipment, I only manage to get a quarter of the way up, so we leave the gear in place for Riggs to try. He's up next, so we can take a break. Unfortunately, we don't get time to explore the one we wanted to the day before. When we get back to camp, it's time to eat and sleep again, but my mind isn't tired.

Kalen is sitting alone with his back to me. I sigh and head his way, passing him a water bottle. He takes it with a nod but downs his food and leaves me sitting on the rock. The asshole. I eat by myself and then leave to have a quick wash before getting a few hours of sleep. I tread towards the toilet and water system, which is rigged up behind some rock outcropping for privacy, and strip down to my panties and bra.

The water is cold as I splash it on my face and across my chest. My body is sluggish and tired, but I may not have time when I wake up, so I force myself to do it now.

Shivering, I quickly rinse my legs and the rest of my body when a noise makes me spin. My eyes widen as I meet the hungry blue orbs locked on me. I ignite under his regard as his eyes roam down my face to my chest, where my nipples are hard in my bra, thanks to the cold water. They dip farther down to my panties and legs before drifting up to meet my gaze. In those depths, I see a hunger so deep that I actually gasp, clamping my legs together as I remember the way he felt between my thighs.

Tyler steps into the rock outcropping, and I struggle to speak. "Sorry, I didn't realise anyone else was here . . ." I trail off, my voice soft and breathy. He swallows, and I watch his Adam's apple bob. His hands are fisted, and I see him fighting his own desire.

His cock tents his shorts, and I lick my lips as I stare, remembering how good he felt inside me, the way his hands would grip me, and how he owned me.

He steps closer again, his body almost touching mine. Almost. I shiver from his warmth, wanting to close the distance between us. My pussy clenches as I battle my own need, knowing it won't do us any good.

We could never fight what was between us.

When I open my mouth again, he loses control, bursting into action. He covers my mouth with his hand as he leans down, his dark, angry eyes meeting mine again. "Don't fucking talk."

I gasp against his hand as I'm spun. He pushes me, and I stumble forward, catching myself on the rocks before my face meets it, not that he cares.

He presses against my back, and I groan as his rigid cock nestles between my ass cheeks. My face rubs along the rough rock as he kicks open my legs before gripping my pussy through my panties as he leans in. His deep, hungry voice causes me to tremble, even as I feel his anger wash over me.

"I fucking hate that I still want you, that with one fucking look at you, I'm back to a being weak fucking man, aching to be inside you. I can't help myself with you, never could. I don't want this. I don't want to feel your wet pussy in my hand, and I don't want to hear your moans or feel your pleasure knowing I'm responsible. I want to hurt you for it, I want you to feel the same fucking pain I'm feeling right now as I try to stop myself from bending you over and fucking you right here."

I push into his hand. "Then do it," I whisper and clear my throat. "Make me feel it all. We both know we aren't walking away right now, we never could."

His head rests on my shoulder, and his breathing is ragged as he struggles to maintain control. Tyler's hand clenches on my pussy, so I rub myself against it. We shouldn't do this. He will hate me more later, and I'll hate myself too, but right now, I don't care.

Not with his hand slipping past my panties, his fingers gliding along my wet centre, and not when his lips meet my skin, tracing across my shoulder. He places possessive, open-mouthed kisses along my skin before he licks over my pounding pulse to my ear. "I fucking hate you right now."

"I do too," I rasp, widening my stance. "Why not show me how much?"

His deft fingers find my clit, rubbing it hard. He wrenches the pleasure from me with each harsh flick, and I almost scream. I press against the rocks, trying to hold back my moans as I push into his touch, aching for more.

"You like that?" he whispers into my ear. "You like the fact that anyone could find us right now? Walk around this corner and see me burying my fingers in your tight little cunt?" I groan when he does just that, pushing two thick digits inside me.

"Ty," I beg.

His other hand slides up my chest and grips my throat, squeezing it hard. "Don't fucking say my name like that," he snarls, punishing me by adding another finger and fucking me hard and fast, forcing my pleasure higher. I'm helpless to resist. "I hate you. I hate you so fucking much. Why do I still want you? Why am I so tempted to drop to my knees right here and see if you taste as good as I remember? To fuck you in front of them so they know you're mine?"

Panting, shaking, and a wet fucking mess, I fight my impending orgasm, but years of being together means he knows exactly where to touch. He flicks my clit with his thumb, curling his fingers expertly inside me and dragging them along those nerves that have a scream erupting from my throat. He cuts it off with a squeeze of his hand, fucking me through it with his fingers as I shake and whimper.

Finally, he pulls them free, and I slump into the rock, trying to catch my breath as I feel the slight sting of my panties slipping back into place. He pulls away from my ear slightly, but I still hear him sucking his fingers clean.

"Fuck," he mutters. "You taste better than I remember. My fingers are fucking drenched, baby."

His statement is hardened and rough, and I gasp, loving it.

His lips meet my ear again. "You want my cock, Peyton Andrews? The way we used to when we were younger? When those sweet little innocent eyes watched me so hungrily? You begged for it so beautifully, like the first time I fucked you and took your innocence. I hurt you, and yet you cried for more," he taunts.

I start to get angry and try to turn, but he slams me into the rock, effortlessly holding me in place. "Fuck you, Tyler. You were the one begging and working your ass off to get into my pants." I smirk, not that he can see. "Like the first time I sucked your cock and you begged me for it."

"Stop," he snarls, clenching his fingers around my neck.

"Why? We both know it's true. You used to get hard just from looking at me. Do you still? I think you do. You're hard right now, aren't you? Remember the way I used to ride you—"

His teeth clamp down on my ear, cutting me off with a gasp, and my pussy clenches from the pain. He rips my panties aside again, and then I hear a zip and feel his hard cock pressed against my entrance. I freeze, not wanting to move in case he's just teasing. I'm dripping for him, imagining him slamming into me right here, fucking all that hate into me.

My nipples brush against the rock, and I whimper, making him groan as the head of his cock pushes into my channel. This is it, the moment we implode and give in, using each other's bodies to get out all these feelings inside us.

I can't wait.

"Tyler?" comes Riggs's call.

We both freeze like cold water is thrown over us. He swears and rips himself away from me in disgust. I barely have time to turn to see him shaking his head as he runs away like he's being chased.

I pant, leaning back against the rocks. I'm shivering from aftershocks, my skin branded by his touch and hate, and I almost groan at the sensation of him being between my thighs again.

Fuck, fuck, fuck.

Closing my eyes, I remain there for a moment before washing up again and getting dressed. One thing is clear though—Tyler still has complete control over my body, and this new, dominant, hateful side of him has me wilder than ever.

I won't be able to look at him again without remembering his dirty threats and his fingers in my pussy, forcing my orgasm from me.

When I wake up, Riggs is going in.

"I'll help man your computer," I remark, grinning as he and Tyler head back down. It's risky, but Tyler can handle it. He hasn't so much as glanced at me after what happened, but I can't help but stare. I watch the way his body moves as he walks, remembering those fingers inside me, and if we hadn't been interrupted, his cock. It's clear he wants to pretend it didn't happen, so I let him. For now.

Fin, Kalen, Michael, and I relax and watch them on the screens. We really don't have to do much, with the equipment recording at all times and the map seeming to build itself as we go.

Fin and I talk, but Kalen doesn't join in. He seems to be ignoring us and even angrier now. Does he really hate me so much, he can't deal with us getting along? Surely, he would want that since it makes the dive easier, but the partial conversations we were having have stopped completely, and now it's just awkward.

Fin notices and tries to encourage him to speak, but as soon as Tyler and Riggs return, he helps them out of their gear and then disappears with Tyler. Sighing, I check the equipment over, trying to be helpful while we all have some downtime.

A few hours later, we give Steve a call to relay our progress. We're all gathered around the comms unit, nervously waiting for him to answer. We aren't as far as we had hoped to be, but we are making headway, which is good. We decided Kalen and I would go back in after the call, and we are determined to get to the top of the wall so Fin can free-climb across to make a ladder.

When he answers, I let Tyler begin. "Hi, Steve, how's everything up top?"

"Good, looks like there's a storm on the horizon though. How's everyone doing?" he asks, his voice crackly.

"We're all good, still excited and in good spirits," Tyler replies, and we all add a chorus of, "Yep!"

"That's great! How's the dive going?" he questions, and we hesitate to answer. "Tyler? Peyton?" Steve prompts.

I clear my throat. "Slower than we thought," I hedge, ignoring everyone's glare. "But we have found promising tunnels. The system is bigger than we ever thought, so don't lose hope. This is a good thing, I promise."

There's silence for a moment. "I trust you," he says with a sigh. "Okay, keep up the good work and let me know if you need anything." With this, he cuts off the call.

"Why the fuck would you tell him that?" Tyler snarls.

"Steve expects honesty. Lie to him, and he will never employ you again," I retort sharply, and he blinks in shock. "Yes, I did it for you. Don't act so surprised!" I huff before standing. "Now let's get back in the water and find something for him."

I hear a chuckle as I storm away. "She's hot when she's bossy," Fin teases, and then there's the sound of a smack. I don't bother hiding my grin as I go get ready.

We need to make this cave our bitch and fast, or it's over for us. This dive is for more than just my job, it's for my life.

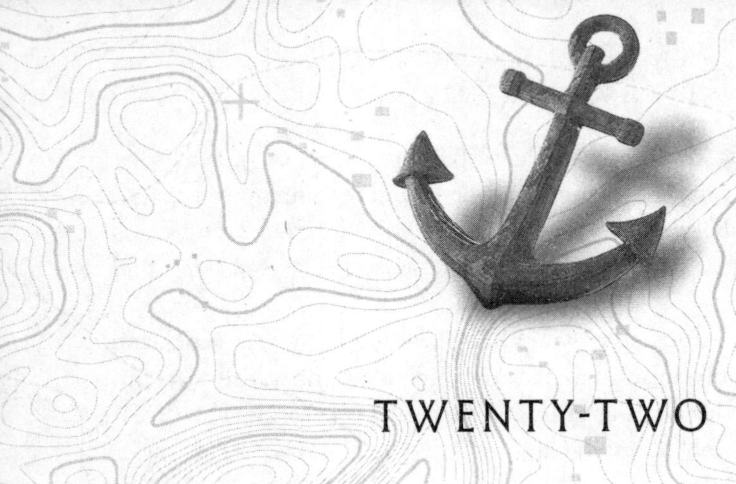

TWENTY-TWO

The dive is going well, and then it suddenly goes to hell.

It begins as a typical dive. We're swimming, using the guideline to lead us to the new tunnels, when it happens.

Down here, anything can occur, and you have to be prepared. One split second is all it takes. Luckily, we react quickly. The guideline breaks, throwing us backwards, nearly lobbing us into a tunnel wall. In fact, I hit it. My back slams into the jagged rock and knocks my breath from my lungs as I sink farther into the tunnel before grabbing the wall to hold on. Kalen manages not to impact it, but he grabs on beside me until we can recover from the panic and breathe properly again. When Kalen grasps the line that leads us farther down, we notice it looks like it's been gnawed on, which is impossible and shouldn't have snapped it. But it has.

That, however, is not the worst problem. I hear a noise from my equipment, the hissing of escaping air, probably from when I smashed into the wall. "Kalen," I yell. "Something's wrong!"

He turns and swears, and I see the bubbles rising. My computer chimes, alerting me to the fact I'm getting low on air. I'm underwater and losing it fast. I have to get to air quickly before I drown. His eyes turn hard, and he grabs my hands and squeezes, looking around hurriedly.

"Move!" he shouts and pushes me forward, the rope forgotten. We swim as fast as we can to the closest overwater section, which happens to be the first cavern we ever found. My computer chimes again, but I don't look, not wanting to see how close I am to running out of air. I can already feel the effects. I surface and drag myself up onto the ledge that goes around it, and yank off my equipment and gulp air to try to steady my heart. Fuck, fuck, fuck. Kalen surfaces and climbs up onto the ledge next to me, instinctively reaching for me.

"Fuck, what happened?" He looks me over in panic. "You okay?"

I hear Tyler shouting, but we're too busy gasping for breath as I spot the kink and the small hole in my line. "Fuck," I mutter. There's no way I can go back down with that. It would kill me. I would run out of air before I got back to base.

"Shit," Kalen swears, sitting next to me. "Ty, we have a problem. The guideline snapped, and the recoil slammed Pey into the wall and broke her air hose."

"Okay, we'll bring—" Tyler starts, but I interject.

"I can free-dive back. I can hold my breath that long," I say, trying to think of the quickest, easiest way to get back. We can't afford this delay. I'll swim back, get some new equipment, and dive again.

"You're fucking not!" Tyler argues.

"Can we buddy breathe?" Kalen inquires, thinking of a way around this as he checks my back where I hit the wall. "You sure you're okay?"

Just as I'm about to answer, we hear a rumbling, a telltale sign of the impending sliding of rocks, and our eyes widen as we turn to stare in horror at the cavern's opening. The rocks at the entrance come crashing down. Kalen throws himself over me, protecting me as we fall backwards onto the ledge and out of the water. I dig my hands into his suit and wait it out. The ledge under us is shaking with the force, and if it collapses, we're dead.

My heart slams, and the air in my lungs freezes as I wait for it to come down on us, but it doesn't. The noise of thunderous rocks eventually slows and then stops, and when Kalen lifts slightly, I see the damage. The whole tunnel is blocked. Kalen swears and gets to his knees, frantically looking me over and running his hands across my body.

"Are you okay?"

"Kal, Kal!" I call, grabbing his hands. "I'm fine, are you?"

He nods, and I get to my feet, seeing some small cuts on his back, but nothing major. He sighs and glances at the water. "Fuck. Let me check if it goes all the way down. Stay here and tell Tyler we're okay."

I nod and watch as he slips into the water before I grab the comms. "Tyler, we're okay. Looks like a rockslide. Kalen is checking if it's blocked the entire entrance. Neither of us is hurt."

"Fuck. Are you sure you're okay, baby?" he asks, his voice threaded with panic.

"We're fine," I assure him, but then Kalen breaks the surface, and from the downward curve of his lips and the shake of his head, I know. I close my eyes for a moment as utter panic blinds me before I breathe through it. It's okay, we can sort this, stay calm. Panicking helps no one. "The entrance is blocked, Tyler, and we're down to one rebreather . . . We're trapped." I stare at Kalen as I talk, both of us knowing what this means. The likelihood of us surviving . . . For one moment, nothing else exists between us. No past, no pain, no anger. Just the shared knowledge that we are probably going to die in here.

There's a minute of silence, and then Tyler comes back, breathing heavily. "We're coming in. We'll check from our side. Stay there." He knows even better than us what this means, but Tyler will never give up. If anyone can find us a way out, it's him. "Baby, I swear we'll get to you, okay? You have your rations, just stay there. We'll find a way."

"We're coming, darling," Fin adds. "I bet you did this so I would rescue you, didn't you?" he comments, making me laugh, the sound breathy and scared. Kalen heaves himself out next to me, sitting on the edge and rubbing at his head.

"Always. Kalen is here in his princess dress, waiting for you," I counter, trying to feign being okay so they don't worry about us.

They all laugh, and Kalen snorts.

"Kalen, watch her back. We are coming, brother," Tyler orders.

They cut off then, and I slide closer to Kalen and check the nicks on his back. I slide my hand down his suit, feeling the slices in the fabric from falling rocks. He got them for me. My heart flips at that. Even when he hates me, he's still willing to risk his life for me. He flinches away before realising it's me and then becomes motionless. "Thank you, Kal, for protecting me," I whisper.

"Don't get fucking sappy. I did it so Tyler wouldn't murder me," he mutters as he gets to his feet and looks around, straight at the other tunnel out of here. "If they can't find a way in, we may have to take that and hope it joins up somewhere. At least we have rations and air."

"I guess," I murmur, scooting back and leaning against the wall. "Until then, I guess we wait."

Waiting is boring.

Kalen is annoying me, pacing around the edge of the ledge. I'm sitting here patiently, sipping my water and ordering him to let me clean his back. He does, but as soon as it's done, he's back on his feet.

I watch him for a while before it starts to make me dizzy, and then I close my eyes. We can hear the others on the opposite side of the rocks, and then the comms turn on. "It's blocked, baby. We'll find a way, okay? None of us is going to sleep or rest until we do, I promise, just stay calm. We'll get to you both." The fact he keeps calling me *baby* doesn't bode well. If he's stressed enough to forget he doesn't still love me, then it's bad. "I will get you both," he vows.

But will he?

"Okay," I mutter, licking my lips. "Don't let Michael in the water. Promise me," I say, knowing the old man will try.

"Got it. Check in every hour or so. Try to get some sleep, baby," he tells me softly.

Sleep, right. Like I can sleep now. But it's better than just sitting here thinking of all the ways we could die.

I unpack the blanket and some snacks and try to force Kalen to eat while he paces before putting them away to ration them. Who knows how long we're going to be down here? I try not to let the panic take hold. We have the other tunnel we can use if need be, even though there is no guarantee it would take us anywhere.

Think, Peyton. Use logic, ignore the screaming in your head. Strength doesn't come from your body, it comes from your heart.

I let my dad's words fill my head until I can push back my fear and think through the situation. It all happened so fast, but now I have nothing but time to review and consider solutions.

First, we need to give them a chance to get through to us, and that means behaving so they can concentrate . . . and if they can't get through, then I will find us a way out of here. I'm not dying in some fucking cave. More settled now, I decide to actually try to sleep. We need to conserve energy as much as we can.

I lie down but can't fall asleep. Eventually, Kalen sits beside me, and as I'm staring at the ceiling, I realise now is the perfect time to get answers. He can't run away from me. Yeah, it may get awkward, but we have nothing else to do, and this not-talking bullshit is annoying. Plus, it may offer a distraction from what's happening.

"So, why do you hate me so much?" I inquire, sitting up and crossing my legs as I stare at him.

He whirls around with wide eyes before they narrow. "We're not doing this," he snaps.

"Yeah, we are. It's now or never, and let's face it, all we have is time, so why do you hate me so much? Is it really just because I left?" I press, tilting my head. Tyler hinted that his brother loved me and so did Fin. Is that true?

Or do I just want it to be? I'm a selfish bitch who wants them all.

He sighs and stays silent. I don't think he will answer, but then he finally does. "I don't hate you, Peyton. I hate what you did to my family . . . to me."

I flinch, but I asked so I stay quiet and let him carry on, knowing if I interrupt, he will clam up again. I miss my best friend, my dive buddy, and if him ranting and getting all his shit out on me is how we do it, fine.

"And I worry about what you will do to my family this time around. They are all I have; they are everything. I would die to protect them." He lifts his head, showing me his vulnerability for a moment. "When I got back, I was messed up. You know that. They brought me back from the edge then and every day since. I promised myself I would protect them. It gave me a purpose, but I couldn't protect them from you. You broke their hearts, and we had to pick up the pieces. And now you're back, and everything is getting messed up again. Tyler is lost, Fin is clinging to you like nothing happened, Riggs is scared, and me? I'm fucking terrified of what you could do. I don't think we could survive it again."

I wince and glance away for a moment, but he was honest with me, so he deserves the same. "I am too. I'm scared. I was back then; that's why I left."

"I know." He sighs. "Even if I hate that, I know you left to try to protect Tyler from the truth."

"But you told him anyway . . . about that night," I hedge, and he snorts.

"I had to," he murmurs. "Want to know the worst bit? I knew you were drunk, but I couldn't stop myself. I wasn't the least bit drunk, and I still kissed you back because I'd been imagining it for so long."

My heart skips a beat. "Kalen . . . I wasn't drunk." I sigh too. I guess it's all coming out now. When he frowns, I smile sadly. "I was tipsy, not drunk. I knew what I was doing. I just used it as an excuse to kiss you. Something I'd wanted to do for a while. I was hurting and lost, and you were my buoy among it all. Tall, dark, and strong, holding me so tightly, I felt like I could breathe for the first time since I heard the news about my dad. I wanted to do it again, still do, and that makes me hate myself, because it would kill Tyler. I left so I wouldn't break you both, so I didn't sever your relationship. I left because I was scared about how deeply I cared for all of you."

He stares at me, and I stare back, both of us unsure what to say. We basically just admitted we wanted each other . . . and still do.

"So where do we go from here?" he questions hesitantly.

"We can be friends?" I suggest.

He laughs harshly. "No, we can't."

"Wait, why?" I ask. "We were before."

"We were never just friends, Peyton, and that was before I knew what you tasted like. I don't want to be friends." Those hungry dark eyes lock on me. "I want to fuck you, always did," he states bluntly.

I inhale in shock. Two minutes ago, he couldn't look at me, and now he's admitting he wants me? It throws me, but happiness fills me from knowing he wants me just as much as I want him. I can't help but lick my lips as I stare at him, my pussy throbbing for a moment as I imagine him doing just that—fucking me. "So where does that leave us? You still hate me, Kal."

His eyes run across me, lust filling his gaze like a light in the dark that I can't help but lean into, and I shiver from the force. "Maybe I do. I can still hate you and want to kiss the fuck out of you."

My heart slams as my stomach clenches. We stare at each other, both knowing we shouldn't but unable to help ourselves. The same electricity and lust still arc between us, stronger than ever before. We know the consequences of wanting each other, but it doesn't stop us. We're like ships in a storm, bound to crash. This world always brings me back to Kalen, and I fought it for so long, so fucking long. I lied to myself, saying I didn't want him, but staring into his dark eyes, I can't lie. I can't fight it.

I need him.

For a moment, I want to be weak. I'm scared, locked away in a cave we may not get out of. Maybe we'll die soon . . . and I can't die without tasting him again, without feeling all that hunger and anger filling me, without tasting it on his lips and feeling it in his hands.

I throw myself at him, and he catches me so I don't hurt myself, but I refuse to be pushed away this time. He can't say shit like that, looking at me like he's never wanted anything as much as he wants me, and then push me away. Not ever again. Straddling his lap, I grab his face and fumble until my lips find his. He freezes, not even breathing for a moment, before he groans. He clutches the back of my hair, using it to deepen the kiss. He dominates my mouth. There's an edge of pain, of darkness, just like the first time, and it's addictive.

It has me pressing my body closer to his. He's so different from Tyler and Fin, all equally amazing. He obviously feels the same and is being fuelled by the need we have fought for so long, because he flips us and pins me on the ledge. His huge frame looms above me, holding me down as his mouth crashes back onto mine. He nips and bites, owning it, owning me.

It's just like that night, with the kiss I could never forget from the man I should never have fallen in love with.

I moan into his mouth, and he swallows the sound, grabbing the zip of my suit and yanking it down until my breasts, only bound in a sports bra, are revealed. He tugs that down as well, and his fingers instantly pluck and twist my nipples as if punishing me for how much he wants me. I arch into the sting of his touch as my pussy becomes embarrassingly wet, throbbing in time with my heart.

I wrap my legs around his waist, feeling his hardness pressed against me, even through the suit. He squeezes and grips my breasts until I'm crying into his mouth again. He groans, the sound so masculine and deep, I shiver as he grinds his cock into me. Kalen rips his mouth away, and I pant, tilting my head back as he kisses down my throat. We know if we stop or hesitate for a moment, the spell will break, our own guilt and past getting between us, but neither of us wants that this time. It's frantic, his lips never leave my skin, and each kiss leaves a brand on me that I feel down to my very core. He trails his lips down until he meets my chest, and his dark eyes clash with mine as he sucks my nipple into his mouth.

The dirty sight makes me tremble as I hold him to me, desperate for this. We are losing ourselves in each other, forgetting everything else—the others, the cave. It's just us and the hunger that has always existed between us. Rubbing myself against his hardness, I beg him with my body to fuck me, to take me like he hates me and unleash all that power across my skin until I can't breathe. I want him to wash away this heartache and sadness until all that's left is the love I have for this man.

The comms crackle. "Are you both okay?"

We freeze at Tyler's voice, guilt instantly assaulting us both. It fills me as swiftly as my lust did, and tears fill my eyes. What the fuck am I doing? Haven't I ruined these relationships enough? Kalen falls backwards, rushing to get away from me, his lips bruised from our kiss. I sit up and quickly pull my bra into place and zip up my suit, his eyes watching the movement with hunger and shame. Swallowing, I look away, blinking back my tears as my mind rages at me, throwing insults for giving in yet again.

I grab the comms. "Yeah, fine." I cough, clearing my throat from the hoarse quality it has. "How's it going out there?"

My eyes dart to Kalen, and I see he's having the same internal war I am. I can't drag my gaze away from him. Even though Tyler's voice comes on again, even though we feel guilty and hate that we want each other, we can't stop ourselves. We constantly gravitate towards one another. My pussy is still wet and pulsing, and my lips ache from his devastating touch.

I want more.

"We're looking at getting some equipment down to dig you out. It's slow going, but I swear, baby, we are trying, okay? So hang in there, both of you." Even now, the man I should be trying to win back, the man I still love, is trying to save me, and here I am thinking about how good it would feel to fuck his brother.

Yep, okay . . . I'll hang in here, with his brother's hands and mouth on my body. Fuck, I'm twisted.

"Okay, stay safe," I offer distractedly, my tongue licking my stinging lips to recapture his taste as I put the comms down. Our breathing is heavy, and his lips are taut as we both stare, unsure what to do.

"We should get some sleep," he murmurs, his timbre dark and rough. It sends a shiver through me, and he notices, his eyes fluttering shut for a moment. "Fuck, princess, stop looking at me like that."

"Like what?" I retort with a naughty smile.

"Like you want me to bend you over and fuck you right here, damn the consequences, even while my brother is fighting to get to us," he growls out, and his eyes narrow on me when I don't speak. "Sleep, we need to sleep," he grumbles, but is he talking to me or himself?

I nod and grab the blanket, lying down and trying to get comfortable, but it's difficult and my back still hurts from hitting the wall. With a curse, Kalen scoots in behind me, pressing his hard body along the length of mine, and he slides his arm under my head like a pillow while his other arm crosses my middle, holding me to him. "Only because there's one blanket, you hear me, Andrews? Now sleep."

I'm back to Andrews. I wonder if that happened before or after he sucked on my breasts.

I close my eyes and try to sleep, but the notion of being trapped in here has my mind running a million miles a minute, not to mention remembering the way Kalen's mouth felt against mine and how he watched me as he sucked my nipple. Plus, feeling his hard body against my back isn't helping me calm down at all. Sighing, I twist on the hard ground, until Kalen growls, "Stop fucking pushing your ass into my dick."

"I wasn't. I was trying to get comfy—" My words cut off in a gasp as his hand comes down right on my pussy. The fucker just spanked my goddamn pussy—what the fuck?

"Stop," he demands.

I huff and still for a moment. "Seriously, I'm just—" I yelp as I'm abruptly flipped, and my forehead connects with his hard chest. He grins, trapping my legs and wrapping his arms around me as he forces me to lie on him.

"There, you're warm and not on the hard ground, and I can stop you from fucking pressing into me," he mutters.

"Oh yeah, this is a lot better," I tease as I lift my head and meet his dark eyes.

"Princess, I swear I'll throw you into the water to cool down if you don't stop," he warns, his eyes closing as he lies back. Huffing, I get comfortable and rest my head on his hard chest, listening to the rapid beat of his heart. Both of us try to ignore the clear evidence of his arousal.

It's quiet, other than the shifting rocks and the slow lap of the water against it. "Kal?" I murmur softly.

"What?" he snarls.

I hesitate, but I have to ask. "We are going to get out of this, right?" It's hard to admit I'm afraid. I don't fear much, but this . . . this is pretty fucking bleak. I know the odds, and this is one of the worst things that could happen. We might make it through the other tunnel, we might not. There might be water, and we only have one lot of gear.

So many things could go wrong, so lying in his arms seems to be the only thing holding me together right now, and I need him to tell me it's going to be okay.

"Lie to me," I whisper when he's silent for too long.

"Never," he murmurs, tightening his hold as his lips press against my head. "We'll make it out, princess. You never gave up before, so don't start now. This is just a bump in the road, another adventure."

Another adventure. Fuck, I hope he's right.

TWENTY-THREE

Tyler

We have to get them out of there. Panic consumes me, but everyone is looking at me to lead to make sure we get Peyton and Kalen out of the cave. My heart stopped when I heard it through the mic. I thought I'd lost them both.

For a split second, everything seemed so stupid, all the arguments and resistance, because for one moment, they were gone, and all I could think about was that nothing mattered but them being in my life. Not the past, not the fact that she wants my brother too and he wants her. All that mattered was them.

My love for them.

That I can't live without them . . . without her.

I want to tell her I forgive her, to ask her to stay and come back to us, but I can't over the mic. It needs to be said in person. It gives me more motivation to get them out and her back into my arms, and then I'll never let her go again. I'll fucking chain her to me if I have to, and she can earn her way on her knees and back with my cock buried in her.

Until then, I won't stop, I won't give up.

There's always a possibility something could go wrong, but until it does, you never expect it will happen to you. Now it has, and we have to find our way through this and keep my family safe. Those up top, namely Steve, are fighting to get some equipment here that could free them, but it could take too long, and we don't know what the stability of that section is. It appears fairly good, and the rockslide seems to have occurred from a large force hitting it, although we can't figure out what.

We are running out of time and ideas.

Grabbing my hair and yanking, I lower my head to think. "I don't know," I mutter to Riggs. "I don't fucking know."

"Hey, look at me!" he demands. "Tyler, fucking look at me!"

It's the harsh tone that has me raising my head and meeting his gaze as he crouches next to me. "You are the best, and so are they. If anyone can do this, it's you. Figure it out and fast, because we are not fucking losing them, you hear me? Get over your shit, your guilt and worries, and focus on the job," he snaps.

Fin stands behind him, his mouth hanging open at Riggs's outburst. I'm gaping too. That's not like Riggs, but the fact they are trapped is wearing on us, and Riggs has mostly been the one doing the check-ins, trying to keep them updated and upbeat. It's clear it's hurting him.

"Okay, okay, so we can't move the rocks. The other tunnel . . . Can they get through it?" I ask, thinking logically.

Riggs frowns. "Maybe. We haven't explored it yet, but from a guess on the map, it could lead back to the submerged cavern . . . which leaves us with the issue that Peyton has no rebreather. They would have to buddy breathe to the second open cavern, or we would have to time it perfectly to be there with some equipment, which offers its own risk with getting her into it underwater."

"Fuck, okay." I stand up. "I think we should plan to meet her there. They can buddy breathe if we're late. She's experienced enough to swap over, and then we get them to the second open cavern and set up a temporary base for them there while they rest before they come back here."

"It's all hinging on whether my calculations on that tunnel are correct, or whether the system wants to be a bitch." Riggs sighs.

"They can do it; we have to trust in them. All they can do is try, but they are going to be exhausted, hungry, and cold. Luckily, they have water and food rations, but we know that won't last too long. The sooner we get them moving, the better. We need to be here supporting them. You too, Tyler. She needs your voice," Fin advises.

"No, I'm going to meet her—"

He narrows his eyes. "No you're fucking not. I will. I can get there and wait, but she needs you, bro. She needs your strength. You're the only one who can get her to listen, okay? You need to channel that now. Stay here, I know you'll hate it, but you have to trust us to bring her back."

"Fine, let's do this," I mutter as we start to get everything in place. We'll let them sleep for now, they are going to need it.

TWENTY-FOUR

Kalen

I wake up with my hands on her ass and my cock aching from the fierce hunger I have for the woman in my arms. My brother's girl . . . but she isn't anymore, is she? Yes, he still wants her, but they aren't together.

I bite my lip as my fingers twitch on the plumpness. It's wrong. I shouldn't. He might hate me if I do. He forgave me for kissing her, but if I cross this line with her, I'm staking my claim—unashamedly, unapologetically declaring her mine.

Would he forgive me? At this point, do I even care?

With her in my arms, her curves pressed against my hard frame, and the taste of her on my lips, I'm finding maybe I don't. That no matter what happens, I want to have Peyton Andrews to myself, for her to be mine just once. We might die here, we might not.

But I can't die without ever having her.

She's still asleep, snoring softly in my arms, and I find the sight addicting. I've never let myself be this close to her, even though it's all I've ever wanted. Dragging my hands up her back, I stroke along her spine, and she grumbles and flips over, rolling off me. I catch her before she falls, the fucking heavy sleeper. Her arm tosses over her face as she lies next to me. She only gets like this when she's had a really hard, long day.

She's tired. I should let her sleep.

But I won't.

Can't.

I want her—no, I *need* her.

Propping up on my side next to her, I run my eyes down her body, the body I've had fantasies about a million times. Fuck, I even used to wank off to the sound of her screams through my wall like a sick fucker, knowing that was as close as I would ever get to her. Yet here I am, about to claim Peyton Andrews.

About to fuck her and make her scream for me. Watch her writhe beneath me as I pound my cock into her again and again, and do all the dirty, depraved things I have always wanted to do to her. All I keep seeing are those little string bikinis she used to wear, the fabric cupping her pert full arse and breasts so full, they used to spill free, her nipples pressing against the wet material as the sun beamed down on us and our boat. Peyton is every man's wet dream. She's sugar, spice, and everything nice . . . until she's not. Until she's a fucking hellcat, a troublemaker in a beautifully strong package. She's all curves and muscle, with a filthy fucking mouth and an even better mind. I can still feel the way her breasts filled my hands and hear her moans in my ears.

If I had given in, if Tyler hadn't interrupted us, would she have let me fuck her? If I'd felt under her suit, would she have been wet? Rolling my lip into my mouth, I reach out and softly pull down the zipper of her suit, exposing her skin. She shivers, but she doesn't wake. I go slow, my eyes catching on every piece of skin I unveil until the fabric parts over her toned, bronze stomach. Her breasts push against the fabric of her sports bra, her nipples puckering in the cool air.

Fuck, she's perfect. I can't help but tug on the bra's front zip. Her breasts spring free, begging for my lips, so I lean down and suck a nipple into my mouth. She moans but remains half asleep as I drag the zipper on her wet suit the rest of the way down, enough so I can slip my hand inside her panties and cup her wet heat.

She's fucking soaked for me already.

Her pussy drips into my palm as she whimpers and pushes into the pressure, rubbing herself on my hand as I suck and lick her breasts. I watch as her arm moves and her eyes blink open in confusion before she looks down at me. It takes a minute for her to catch up, and when she does, her eyes widen farther before simmering with desire. She stills beneath my touch, but I don't stop. I cup her pussy hard, possessively, showing her exactly whom it belongs to. I don't want hesitation or words, and I don't want to restrain myself this time. I want her pleasure, and I want it now. I bite her nipple, forcing a gasp from her lips. The sound seems to wake her that last ounce.

"Kal— What?" she mumbles.

I pop her nipple free from my mouth and lick my lips as I smirk at her. "I'm done fighting it, princess. Every single fucking day, I want you even more, and I can't take it anymore. I want you. I have to have you." She swallows, her pink tongue darting out and licking her lips, making me groan. With my other hand, I cup her throat and narrow my eyes, trying to remain in control, even when I just want to flip her over, bury myself in her tight pussy, and fuck her until neither of us can think of anything but release. "Fuck, Andrews, don't make me come before I even get inside you."

"Then better get to it, asshole," she growls out, making me laugh as I kiss down the length of her body.

"Not until I taste you. I've imagined fucking you for seven years. Seven hard, long years, princess, with nothing but my hand to satisfy these urges. So you will shut that goddamn mouth for once and lie back like a good girl and take what I have to offer." I yank down her suit and throw it behind me, then I remove her knickers so she's bare before me.

She shivers again, but not from the cold. Her cheeks and chest flush with excitement as she parts those curvy, strong thighs without an ounce of embarrassment, showing me her wet, pink pussy. Grunting, I reach down and part her lips, tracing my fingers down her centre before sucking them into my mouth. As soon as her taste hits my tongue, I lose it. I drop to my belly between her legs and force her thighs open to accommodate my wide shoulders.

She throws her legs over them, sweeping her fingers into my hair and tugging me closer as I stare at her from just inches away. I watch her pussy clench for me. "So fucking pretty, and look how wet, princess. Did our fight get you all turned on?"

"Hell yes," she mutters, yanking harder now, nearly pulling my hair from its roots.

"Does it always? I remember the way you used to watch me when we fought . . . your heaving chest and hungry eyes. Did you go find my brother after to satisfy your desire?" I murmur as I drag my fingers down her pussy and dip them inside her. I watch as her channel clamps greedily around them before pulling them free, then I twist and shove them back in. She cries out, arching into me, her clit engorged and begging for my touch.

I turn my attention to it, laving my tongue over it again and again before I flatten it and drag it down her core, circling her hole before moving back up. She groans my name, *my* fucking name. No one else's, mine, and it sounds so sweet on her lips.

So I reward her.

Lashing her clit, I observe her as she plunges over that edge, exploding around my fingers and tongue. Her pussy clenches around me as she cries out and arches up, moving her hips desperately as she fucks herself on me. I lick her through her orgasm, cleaning around her hole, trying to taste every single drop of cream.

She tastes like the fucking ocean, all sweet and fresh, and I can't get enough. Pulling my fingers free, I rear up and suck them into my mouth as she watches me with a dazed, slack expression. She pants heavily, her hips dropping down and legs spread wide. Grinning, I press my fingers to her slightly parted lips.

My dirty little girl sucks them hungrily, hollowing her cheeks. She keeps her eyes on me as she swirls her tongue around them, tasting us both. Fuck, why is that so hot? I want to see her lips wrapped around my cock; I always have. So many times, I debated putting her on her knees and shoving my cock in her mouth just to shut her up during our arguments. Her eyes glint now like she knows.

It's the same glint she used to get.

Damn, I'm screwed. Now that I've tasted her, I will never be able to go back, never be able to not need her. One taste and I'm lost. I'm hers.

"Problem, princess? Not what you're used to? Expecting loving words? Well, tough shit, I'm crude and fucking hard, so get over it. Now get on your hands and knees and spread those thighs so I can fuck you until you scream loud enough for them to hear."

Her eyes narrow as she opens her lips and frees my fingers. I twirl them in a *bend over* gesture, and she huffs. "No," she snaps. "Now fuck me and shut up, you cocky asshole."

She's fighting me on purpose.

I arch an eyebrow in warning. I'm not feeling real anger, more like lust for our verbal sparring, for the hate and darkness it lets me express. I can be as vile as I want with her, and she will take it all. She will take all my demons as I fuck her, own her, decimate her.

If she walks away this time, it will be with the knowledge that no other will compare to me. For the rest of her life, she will remember my cock deep inside her, wringing orgasm after orgasm from her body. Whenever she looks at me and tries to fight me, she will recall how I'm going to force my hard length down her throat to shut her up, and she'll get wet.

I can't fucking wait.

"Andrews, on your knees now," I order, giving her an out. Of course my girl doesn't take it.

She sits up and grabs my cock through my suit. "Make. Me."

Two words.

Two fucking words.

A challenge, a dare. So be it.

I grab her hair, wrap it around my hand, and yank her head back painfully until tears enter her eyes and her mouth parts on a whimper. Standing, I drag her to her knees as she reaches up to scratch at my hand. "Kal!" she protests, even as she leans into me, wanting more.

"Shut the fuck up, Andrews. Take my cock out," I demand.

She chafes under the command, but I smirk.

"If you want my cock, take it out and do as you're told, or I'll leave you wet and wanting, and make sure none of the others will help you. It's me or none, Andrews. I won't ask again."

She huffs and drops her hand to my suit, unzipping it until it slides to my feet. I shimmy out and kick it free, then she yanks down my boxers. She's angry now, her eyes narrowed and mouth twisted. Fuck, I love her anger. "Problem, princess?" I taunt, fanning the flames.

"No," she snarls as she frees my cock. When the hard length springs free, she inhales sharply, staring at it with hungry eyes. Fuck.

"Wrap your hand around it," I order.

She swallows but does as she's told, rubbing her thumb on my piercing before she squeezes the base of my dick, making me jerk in her hand. She grins triumphantly. "Did I tell you to do that, Andrews?" I growl out. "For that, you will take it and like it." I tap her chin. "Open and suck me down. All the way. Now."

She goes to protest, probably just for the fight alone, but when her lips open, I shove my cock inside. She gags at the sudden entrance before blinking back her tears and swallowing me down, but she stops before I make it balls deep. So with a hard thrust, I slam all the way in. Her eyes tear up again as she holds on, but as soon as she has a handle on it, she's fine. "That's it, princess, take all of me, I know you can. Suck me real good. Show me that mouth is good for more than just talking."

Her eyes narrow in determination. I know Peyton too well, and if she can't talk, she will fight with her mouth, and won't that be something fucking incredible?

My eyes close as I widen my stance and pull out before slamming back in. She takes it, dragging her tongue along my cock, and as I pull out again, she flicks and plays with my piercing with her tongue.

The sudden arc of pleasure slams through me and joins the already building release at the base of my spine. I won't last long in her mouth, but I needed to see her on her knees before I buried myself in that sweet little pussy. She starts to hum around my cock, and I can't take anymore. I pull free so suddenly, she falls back to her ass, her lips puffy and breasts jiggling from the movement.

"Knees," I demand roughly, fighting my impending release. When I feel more in control, I narrow my eyes. "Now, Andrews."

"No," she snaps and flips her hair back with a smile. "When you fuck me, you're going to look at me, Kalen, so you can't distance yourself. If I have to look at your brother with the knowledge of how you feel deep inside me, so do you. I want to ride your cock, so get on your fucking back . . . princess."

Well, fuck. I want to fight her, to be in charge, but honestly, the idea of her riding my cock with those magnificent tits swaying above me has me nearly cross-eyed. So for once, I relent. I drop to my knees and get onto my back, ignoring the stabs of pain from the small cuts. She crawls up my legs before sitting across my abs, grinding her pussy against them. I groan as I reach out and grab her hips, rubbing her back and forth. I watch as her eyes close and she shivers. Fuck, she's truly beautiful. Her golden skin gleams from the reflection of the water and the lights, and she's all long blond hair, swollen lips, and toned muscle.

Her confidence in herself is so fucking sexy. She owns her body, loves it, embraces it. She knows just how much of a fucking weapon it is against a guy like me, and she wields it, still fighting me for control like always.

My fucking warrior princess.

She won't be mine forever, but for now, she is.

"Get that pussy around my cock, Andrews," I demand, and she smirks at me as she slips down my body, scraping her nails across my chest as she lifts herself and settles above my cock. She lingers over it, teasing me like always.

"So demanding. You're such a needy fucking asshole," she mutters, and then drops onto my cock, working down my length. I grunt as I refrain from thrusting up and slamming through her snug, wet heat. Fuck, she's too tight, too fucking wet. The sensation of her wrapped around my cock like silk is driving me wild.

"You gotta move, princess," I rasp, blinking hard as I stop myself from taking over. She tests my control, wrecks it, but right now, I'm helpless beneath her. I don't want to move, I don't want to disturb her. Her magnificent body is on display above me, and when she starts to ride me, twisting and winding her hips before she uses her knees for leverage, I'm lost in her.

I dig my fingers into her hips and help her, lifting and slamming her down, watching the wet slide of my cock pounding in and out of her entrance with a groan. Fuck, this is so wrong, so dirty, and I couldn't stop even if I wanted to.

She's my everything, and in this moment, I forget all the reasons why I can't love her and have her. Her body sways as if moving to music, a fucking siren's call to a sailor like me. I thought it couldn't possibly be as good as I imagined.

It's better.

I'm fighting my release, wanting this to last forever. If this is the only time I get to have her, I want it to be amazing. Reaching down, I spank her clit, and she gasps, clenching around my cock. Glaring at me, she leans down and places her lips on mine, moaning into our kiss as I flick her pussy again.

"Come on me, princess. Let me feel this tight cunt milk me," I command against her lips, and flick her again, hard. She whimpers as I move her hips faster, sliding her down my long cock until she cries out. Her pussy clamps around me, trying to draw my release from my cock. With a roar, I flip us.

I push her to her knees before me. Pulling from her pulsing cunt, I weave my hand into her hair and shove her down, then I yank her ass up and slam into her fluttering channel. My fingers dig into her plump skin along the shark bite scar. My fucking princess is a fighter.

Her round ass is addictive, and I can't stop watching it as I slam into her, watching my thick cock disappear into heaven itself.

"Goddamn," I growl, my grip denting her hips as I speed up. "You should see you taking my cock. It's fucking hot watching you surrender and take all of me, princess."

Her back bows as she cries out. Leaning down, I wrap my hand around her throat and squeeze, cutting it off as I continue to fuck her—hard, fast, and uncaring about holding back anymore.

"Kalen, please, fuck, please," she begs, pushing back to take my cock, her cream dripping down my dick from how many times she's come.

I can't wait to see her red, raw pussy dripping with my cum.

"Please what, Andrews?" I snarl, fighting my release, even as my balls tighten and my back arches.

"I-I need—" She whimpers and turns her head, pressing it to the stone floor. There's no inch of air between us, our slick bodies moving together faster and faster.

"Need what?" I grit out. My hand flexes on her throat, and I love seeing my tattooed knuckles clenched possessively around it.

"Fuck, Kal!" she yells and slams back, twisting her hips as her pussy clamps around me again with her release.

I can't hold back this time. I try to fight her tight channel, but with a roar, my release bursts from me. Hips stuttering, I slam into her again, burying myself as deep as I can as my cock jerks and fills her with my seed.

She slumps forward as I keep my cock in her until I'm spent. When I pull free, I lean back and watch my cum spill from her raw pussy as she lies there, breathing heavily. "Shit, that's so hot, but you can't get rid of me that easily, princess." Scooping up my dripping release, I push my fingers back inside her. She cries out, writhing as I fuck her quickly with my digits, forcing my cum back inside her before pulling free.

Exhausted, I collapse next to her, my chest heaving and sweat covering every inch of my body. I turn my head and meet her eyes as they flicker open, and I can't help but smile, a response she returns.

I pull her into my arms, letting myself be weak for once. I imagine she's my girl and the rest of the world doesn't exist, including my brother. If I'm going to die down here, it's with the knowledge of Peyton Andrews being mine, even if just for a moment.

I know the stress is weighing on her. She doesn't like to sit still, so after washing, dressing, and eating, we get up and begin to look for another way out. Being astute and resourceful was drilled into us in the army, and I've been in some bad situations overseas where I was pinned down by enemy fire, but this . . . this is different.

This is Mother Nature, and she's unpredictable and violent.

I can't shoot my way out of this one, but I will never give up. We won't die down here, not ever. My princess will get out of this and go on to break more world records. This fucking cave, or Mother Nature, none of it will stop me when I'm intent on saving my girl.

"I think our only way is the tunnel up top." She huffs and props her hands on her hips as she stares up at the wall. I move behind her, pressing my body to hers—it's the only time I ever will. I love her reaction, love the feeling of her pressed against me. I wrap my arms around her waist and brush my lips over her ear. She shivers before leaning back into me, making me smirk.

I want to scream, to roar in approval, and to show Tyler she's mine too. Petty.

"You think so, princess? You don't think the love of your life will come and rescue you?" I mock harshly, my thoughts of Tyler conjuring my guilt and anger. I'm taking it out on her, like always.

She turns, eyes narrowed, and the sight instantly makes my cock hard as we wait for the fight to start. Her hands press against my chest and push, but I don't budge. My smirk grows, and her lips compress in irritation, even as her eyes flare with hunger.

Andrews loves our fights, that much is clear. In fact, I'm betting if I reached inside her suit, she would already be dripping for me, remembering the way I punished her hot little mouth with my cock.

The thought makes me groan, and I back her into the wall, bracing my arm above her head as her soft body presses against mine. She tilts her chin up, unafraid and refusing to back down, even in her vulnerable position. Fuck, I love that about her. "Don't act like a fucking jealous prick," she snaps.

"Me? Jealous? Princess, please. I could bend you over and fuck you right now. I'm betting he couldn't." I laugh.

She goes to push me again, but I capture her hand with mine and drag it down my body to my stiff cock. She inhales, and her pupils blow wide with lust, even as she keeps up the fight. "Fuck you, Kalen. You're such a fucking asshole," she snarls. "It was a mistake to sleep with you. God, I'm an idiot."

I don't let it show just how much that hurts. I don't reveal that her words just stabbed through my heart and soul like a fucking bullet. She regrets it. The best thing to ever happen to me, the thing I have been dreaming about for years . . . and she regrets it.

"Yeah? Well, you're about to regret a whole lot more, princess," I sneer, and then I yank down her suit. She struggles, trying to get me off her, but not really.

Her nipples are tight and hard, pressing against the material of her sports bra. Her lips are parted on a moan, and her body rubs against me, even as her mouth spouts off insults.

"You fucking asshole! I hate you, I hate you, I fucking hate you!" she yells as I drop to my knees, pulling the suit with me. In one quick move, I tug her leg free, rip her panties aside, and flick her engorged clit with my tongue. She groans and pushes her pussy into my face, and like I assumed, she's already wet as hell for me. It drips down her pretty pink pussy, and I can't help myself.

I need to show her that she may hate me, regret being with me, but she still wants me all the fucking time. Like I do her. This is toxic, but I don't care.

I eat her like an animal, imprinting her taste in my mouth and on my tongue as she screams obscenities about how much she hates me. "Keep talking, princess. You'll be screaming for another reason in a moment, and we both know it."

I bury my tongue in her tight hole, and she stops her rant to moan, threading her fingers in my hair and dragging me closer. She presses her pussy to my face until I can barely breathe. Who fucking cares? Who needs air when I have her?

I attack her like I normally do, but this time with my fingers and tongue instead of words. In no time, she's riding my face, grinding her pussy onto my tongue as I lash her clit. I slide one finger inside her at first before I spear two more into her, stretching her as she writhes and yells.

"Fuck you, Kalen!" she shouts.

Pulling my mouth away, I meet her eyes, my lips coated in her cream as I smile. "Nah, but I'll fuck you, princess. Now shut up and come on my tongue—let me feel just how much you don't hate me."

She shakes her head, even as her body starts to quake, and I know she's close. Laughing at her stubbornness, I suck her clit into my mouth, and then with a cruel twist, I bite down on it. She screams, jerking in my grip as her pussy clamps on my fingers as she comes. I lick and suck her through it until she tries to push me away. Sitting back on my heels, I look at her shivering, sweat-coated body and lick my lips clean of her sweet taste.

Her eyes flicker open to watch me, hazy with pleasure. "Still hate me, princess?" I taunt.

"Yes . . . maybe not as much. Keep that up, and I might even start to like you." She huffs, reaching down and getting back into her suit before zipping up. Grinning, I get to my feet. She reaches for my obviously hard cock, but I pull away.

"That wasn't about me getting my rocks off, Andrews. That was about proving just how good of a liar you are . . . even to yourself," I murmur as I lean in and kiss her, bruising her lips before I turn away.

She swears and stomps off, muttering about assholes, and my grin widens. Fuck, I've missed this—the teasing, taunting, and getting her riled up for me—but watching her explode around me makes it all worthwhile, even if my brother hates me for it.

Just then, our mics crackle, and I grab mine as I sip some water. "Pey?" comes Tyler's frantic voice.

"Sorry, brother, just me," I snark.

He sighs. "Sorry, man. You both okay?"

"We're fine. How's it going? I'm getting restless," I tell him as Peyton crowds next to me to hear what they have to say, but I have a bad feeling.

It goes quiet, and that only enhances my suspicions. "We're working our hardest, but we can't get the equipment here for five days due to a tropical storm. I need to know your supply count so we can create a different plan. Fin and Riggs are already scouting for different routes through—"

Peyton swears and grabs the mic. "Ty."

He goes silent, and she brushes her hair back, looking at me for a moment. "We might have a way out, that high-up tunnel. I don't know where it leads, but it's better than sitting here and waiting to die."

"We have a plan. We need you to listen carefully. Your lives depend on it going right," Tyler orders, his voice hard.

"We have no choice," she retorts. "We have to try!" I glare at the tunnel she wants to try to get through, and her voice softens then. "Ty, please, babe, I can't—I can't sit here and wait for it to just happen." I flinch at her use of *babe*, and she presses against my side without a word or a glance. Jealousy roars through me, but I don't move away, even not wanting to break contact with her. "I need to keep fighting. I have to keep moving. If there is a chance, even a remote chance that it leads to somewhere, I have to take it, and I need your help to do it. We both do. Trust in us. I know it's hard for you to relinquish control, but you need to right now."

It becomes quiet, and I think she's pushed too hard, so I glare down at her as she stares sadly at the comms, but she's still determined. Nothing will stop her from going through that tunnel. I know her well enough to understand that, and so does Tyler.

"Fine, but there are conditions. One, you communicate with us at all times. Two, if you get into it and it doesn't seem safe or like it will go anywhere, you will go back and wait for us to get you out with no complaints," he grumbles.

"What? No three?" She laughs.

"Three . . . you do not fucking die, either of you. You keep yourselves alive no matter what you have to do, is that understood?"

She smiles and winks at me. "Got it, boss man. Okay, we'll pack up and get started soon."

She goes to move away when another crackle comes. It's Fin this time. "Darling, stay safe and come back to us."

She freezes, and our eyes meet as there's a fumble followed by another voice. "He's right. I'll monitor from here . . . but please, Peyton, don't do anything stupid. I couldn't bear to lose you again," Riggs whispers.

I close my eyes for a moment, pushing back my own issues when I see the pain on her face.

She swallows, staring at me helplessly, so I grab the comms. "What? No drawn-out demands for me?" I ask with a scoff, even as I lean down and kiss her forehead, comforting her, though I don't know why.

"Shut up, it includes you," Riggs huffs as Fin laughs.

"Want me to come kiss you better, Kal?" Fin taunts.

"Fuck you guys." I chuckle as another voice joins the fray.

"Minnow?"

She grabs the comms, and I let her. "I'm here, old man."

"Less of the 'old.'" He laughs. "Minnow, fuck, just be careful, okay? I know you can do this, but don't fucking mess up. I need you, kid. Who's going to kick my ass and drag me back to life if you're not there?"

"Save me a bottle, I'll be there soon," she promises and turns away, but not before I see the sheen of tears in her eyes. I watch her go, confusion growing within me. I'm still angry, I still hate her, but seeing her vulnerable and watching her struggle is hurting my heart.

All these years, I thought I wanted to make her pay, to hurt her like she hurt us . . . But now I'm not so sure, because seeing her in pain, even if she deserves it, only hurts me more.

Putting down the comm, I head over to her as she's packing her bag. I drop my hands to her hips from behind her, and she stills. "Look at me, Andrews."

She sniffs but doesn't turn, so I force her to, and her eyes drop to my chest, but I refuse to let her hide from me. I tip her chin back with my finger, and her watery eyes meet mine. "Princess." I sigh and then pull her into my arms and just hold her. "We're getting out of here, I promise you that. I won't stop until I get you back to them."

She rests her head on my chest, and I just embrace her for a moment as she gathers herself back together again. I hear her suck in some breaths before she pulls away slightly, brushing away her tears. I cup her cheek as she looks at me, searching my eyes. "Why are you being nice to me?" she rasps.

Leaning down, I kiss each eye and then her lips, lingering there as I taste the saltiness of her tears. "I can be nice, princess, you just usually prefer me mean."

"Nice? I've never seen you be nice," she teases, making me grin.

"Only for you. Don't tell anyone, I have a rep to maintain," I counter, and she laughs and pulls away again. Scrubbing her face, she sighs and stands taller.

"Okay, asshole, let's do this shit." She turns with renewed vigour to get ready, and I do the same, smiling at the fact she let me comfort her. Usually, only Riggs can do that, so it sends a weird bolt of pleasure through me. Everyone needs to break sometimes, to lean on someone, but Andrews never usually lets anyone, always wanting to be so strong—apart from the night she kissed me when her dad died.

She had been weak, alone, and lost in a whirlwind of emotions, looking to feel anything, and I couldn't help myself. I still regret that it was our first kiss—it haunts me—but we don't have time to waste dwelling on the past. All we have is now.

Down in the dark, anything can happen.

We still have a job to do. We will make it out of here, then finish exploring the cave . . . and then what? Break apart again? I don't know if I can let her walk away a second time.

Once we are ready to go, unsure what to expect, we press our foreheads together, the usual adrenaline starting to surge through us. "We've done this a thousand times. What's one more, princess?"

"Hell yes. See if you can keep up, asshole." She grins and then unexpectedly leans in and kisses me before ripping herself away and rushing to the wall, taking a running jump up onto it.

I stare after her, my lips still parted, and with a laugh, I chase her. She's already halfway up the wall when I begin to climb. My reach is longer than hers, so I easily catch up as she approaches the tunnel entrance and perches there, shining her light into it. "Here we go," she murmurs, and then she moves into the unknown.

TWENTY-FIVE

Riggs

I watch them on the cameras, although visibility is low, even with the lights. Nerves fill me, as does exhaustion, and I haven't slept or left my computers since they were trapped, needing to assure myself she's okay at all times.

I even saw when they fucked—not that I said anything.

I think they thought they turned the cameras off . . . but they didn't. Luckily, I was the only one here. Tyler was arguing with the equipment manager, and Fin was shouting commands and doing dive after dive to try to find a way through, almost frantic . . . reckless.

We are killing ourselves, but it doesn't matter as long as we get them back. We are family to the end, no matter what's happened and the mistakes we have made. Right now, our family is fractured, and we need to put it back together again. When they're safe—when, not if—I'm going to do what I've wanted since the moment I laid eyes on Peyton Andrews.

I'm going to kiss her.

I know Fin has, and now Kalen has fucked her, so it seems all bets are off. If they can take what they want, then so can I, and what I want more than anything is Peyton. Always have.

The others are gathered around me, watching the progress. Fin is bouncing on the spot from nerves. Tyler is stoic, viewing them, but I can hear the pounding of his heart against my side.

He loves her, I know that, and of course he loves his brother too. He can't lose them, none of us can. But what we said is true—if anyone can make it through, it's those two. We have to trust them now more than ever and send up a prayer that they do.

"The equipment is ready to be brought through to meet them if you're right, Riggs," Tyler mutters.

"Good. Who's doing it?"

"Fin and I. We need you here to monitor everything and keep us updated. I know you're tired—"

I turn, and for once, I narrow my eyes in irritation. "I love them too," I snap. "I'm fine. Do what you need to do; let's get them back."

I turn to the monitors. I feel their eyes on me, but I don't look, I'm too busy watching my girl and my brother trying to find their way back to me—to us.

Fuck, please let them make it, please let them come home to me. I swear I'll never let them go again. I promise I'll love them until my last days if they survive this.

Fin

It all seems so stupid now, all the reasons why I held myself back from her. Knowing I could lose her is making me frantic with the need to kiss her, hold her, and tell her how I feel.

Peyton is the love of my life, always has been, even when I didn't believe in it, and if she comes back—no, *when* she does—I'll tell her. I'll lay myself bare for her, no jokes, no flirting. I'll tell her how I feel and hope she feels the same.

Tyler will have to deal with it. I'm tired of tiptoeing around his feelings, and with us almost losing the two of them, the concern is stupid. There is so much more in life to worry about, and being in love shouldn't be one of those things. Peyton was made to be loved, and not just by him—she needs us all. I can share, I can do whatever the fuck she wants as long as I get to have her too.

I know Riggs feels the same, and Tyler will probably punch us, but I've decided I can live with that. What I can't live with, however, is never having loved Peyton Andrews properly.

I watch over Riggs's shoulder as Peyton and Kalen begin to crawl through the tunnel. Fuck, I wish I were there with them. I wish I could be there to help, to comfort her, to get her out. I have to trust in my brother, and so does Tyler, and if he can trust Kalen to save his girl, then he can trust him to love her as well.

Kalen loves her, and he has never loved before, never let anyone else close other than us. If he loses her again, we may just lose him forever. This is about more than my own selfish feelings; I can't let my family break apart again. I meet Tyler's eyes like he can hear my thoughts, or maybe it's just Riggs's declaration. I saw the fire in his eyes. He didn't just mean he loved her like a friend or a sister, he was telling Tyler he's *in* love with Peyton, and in Tyler's gaze, I see the truth.

He knows.

Maybe he always did.

A noise has us both spinning back to the monitor. These feelings, all these lies and suppressed truths can wait. For now, it's about them. We can do nothing but watch and wait.

Either they make it through, or we all die down here, because I'm never leaving her again, not to save myself or my family. She's trapped, I'm trapped. She dies, I die.

Together.

After all, she's this diver's heart.

TWENTY-SIX

Peyton

The tunnel is big enough to crawl through. Our breathing is loud in the silence, and my light shines steadily ahead, but it only penetrates the darkness just in front of me. Every now and again, Kalen reaches out and squeezes my ankle to comfort me and let me know he's still right behind me.

He held me while I cried. I never thought I'd see the day. Riggs? Hell yes. Fin? Maybe, though he would feel my ass. Tyler? Of course. But never Kalen. In his eyes, there was a softness I didn't know he had in him, and the worst part? It made my heart pound, and I almost admitted that I loved him once.

That I still do.

It was on the tip of my tongue and almost slipped free, but I couldn't let it out, because those are words I can't take back, and I know once we gain our freedom, he'll return to being cold and distant, to hating me for what I did to him and his brothers. He will go back to pretending he's never tasted me, never felt my body lock around him in the throes of passion, never kissed me so deeply that I thought I couldn't breathe without him anymore.

Part of me aches, wishing we could stay in this bubble for just a moment longer, but it's time to move, it's time to get free, even though it cracks my already fragile, shattered heart.

"How're you doing, Pey?" Riggs asks sweetly.

"Oh, you know, the usual. Cold and wet, and not in a good way." I hear a few laughs as I smile and crawl through the dark tunnel. "Also craving a big, fat burger."

"I'll have one waiting for you when you get out," he replies, laughter in his tone.

"Yeah? Extra cheese?"

"Of course, and a beer, maybe even some fluffy socks if you're quick enough."

I smile, even though I know he's doing this for my benefit to try to keep my spirits high and hopeful. "What about a foot rub?"

"Now you're pushing it, darling," Fin chimes in, making me snigger.

"Anything yet?" Tyler questions, interrupting our banter, and we become silent for a moment.

"Nothing, still going. It's heading down, I think," I murmur.

"Good, that's good . . . I'll rub your feet if you hurry up, baby," he offers.

"Well, damn, consider me speedy." I grin as I pick up my pace.

Kalen laughs behind me, and I yelp when he spanks me. "Don't be reckless."

"Or what?" I tease as I crawl. The conversation is keeping the fear and worry at bay like they knew it would.

"Or you'll be back on your knees again," he warns, and I freeze as I realise they can hear what Kalen just said. No one comments, so I carry on crawling like nothing's wrong. Like he didn't just joke about me sucking his cock in front of his brother, my ex, and our whole team.

The tunnel starts to tilt down, and I close my mouth and focus on what we're doing. After the trouble we have already been through, I'm not risking one little mistake. This beast of a cave system requires our entire focus.

"We're going down. I think it's widening too."

"That's what she said," Fin quips.

I snort but carry on, and in about another three or four metres, I know I'm right—the tunnel is opening. I don't feel the rocks scraping on my sides or along my pack, which is good. It means it may actually lead to somewhere.

"Good, keep going!" Riggs urges, and I know he's feeling hopeful too.

"You okay back there, Kay?" I ask as I maintain my speed—fast enough to cover good ground, but slow enough not to cut myself or accidentally fall into any sudden crevices or holes.

"Just great, got a nice view of your ass," he remarks, the bastard.

"Yeah? Angle your head up, brother, I want to look too," Fin teases.

"You're all giant pervs," I mutter, even as I smile.

We keep going, and I listen to them banter back and forth, laughing along, until I stop.

"Wait!" I call as Kalen nearly bumps into me. "Fuck," I exclaim as I stare. "We have a problem."

The end of the tunnel is wide enough to sit up in and probably large enough to get Kalen next to me as well, but I'm frozen, staring in shock.

"What?" Riggs shouts. "Fucking camera cut out. Okay, it's coming back—Holy shit!"

"Yep," I mutter, gaping at the cavern the tunnel opens into. Only, we are at the top, almost close enough to reach the ceiling, and it's a straight vertical drop to the water below.

"What?" Kalen snaps.

"Vertical drop, too high to fall into the water below. We're near the ceiling in a cavern, and there's only one way across," I mumble.

"Which is?" he prompts, sounding worried.

"Free-climb across the ceiling to the opening I see on the other side, while placing cams and rope along the way."

I hear swearing as he sidles up behind me and looks over my shoulder. "That has to be twenty metres away. That will kill our arms, and we're already exhausted."

"We have no choice; we can't go back." I sigh and pull off my bag and start to drag out my equipment as I turn to the side. Kalen slips into place beside me, grabs my hands, and squeezes.

"Wait, I'll go."

"No. You're heavier and slower. I can get across faster, and I'm a better climber," I reason without looking at him, but when he doesn't reply, I glance up.

He swallows nervously and looks out. "Fuck, Andrews, this is dangerous as hell."

I laugh softly and squeeze his hand. "Everything we do is dangerous. This is no different, so don't start getting all caveman on me now, asshole. Your one good quality is your ability to trust my skills."

"Skills?" Fin teases.

"Mad skills, babe, you know it." I laugh and wink into Kalen's camera. "I can do this. If I didn't think I could, I wouldn't try," I admit.

As Kalen pulls his hands away, I hear the others arguing, but I'm too busy getting ready to really listen. I clip on a rope for Kalen to hold as backup in case I fall, although it won't really stop me from hitting the wall. I add my helmet and climbing gear to my hip before taking a drink and loosening my arms.

I can do this . . . I can do this . . .

I lied—I don't know if I can do it. My body is tired, really tired, and this is a hard climb, even for an experienced, fresh climber. There is no guarantee I will make it across—the ceiling could crumble, my ropes could snap, anything could happen—but I have no choice. I have to get us out of here. I'm the smartest, best option, and everyone knows it.

"Be safe," Kalen murmurs, then hesitates, obviously wanting to add more, but he knows everyone is watching. "Ah, fuck it," he growls and grabs the back of my head and turns my body, dragging me closer and sealing his lips to mine.

I gasp in shock, and he swallows it down, his tongue twining with mine. The kiss is hard and fast, and then he pulls back slightly. "You get across there, princess, and I'll give you all the orgasms you want," he murmurs against my lips.

"You've got yourself a deal." I laugh as I turn away, trying not to show how flustered and turned on I am just from one bloody kiss. This man is lethal to my heart and panties, and now I know how well he fucks, how he feels inside me, and I'm craving it. Being trapped in a small space with him doesn't help.

I chalk my hands, and then Tyler's voice cracks through the speaker, stilted and angry, though he doesn't mention the fact he just saw his brother kiss me like his life depended on it. I don't say anything, unsure what I would say anyway. "You've got this, Peyton. Focus. See it in your mind," he orders, and then his tone softens. "Nothing is impossible, not if you're willing to do anything to make it happen. So make it happen," he says, echoing my father's words.

"I've got this," I mutter.

"Yeah you do, darling. Show us why you're the fucking best," Fin adds.

"Peyton, there's an optimum path if you go to the left. I've calculated a ninety percent chance of success if you use that route," Riggs informs me, offering comfort the only way he knows how—with numbers.

"Ninety percent?" Kalen snarls.

"Ninety percent is good enough." I smirk, and then I reach out and grab the ceiling, digging my fingers into the rocks before swinging my body forward and out of the tunnel. The sudden weight pulls on me, but I grunt and begin to climb, knowing I need to move fast before my muscles give out.

It's all in my mind. All in my mind, I repeat. A body can sustain so much, but usually, the mind breaks first. Mine won't.

I will get across and save us both.

I grit my teeth, keeping my eyes on my path with guidance from Riggs. Everyone else is quiet as they watch, not wanting to distract me, and the small tug of Kalen's rope reminds me he's still there. I stop and add a cam, swinging from one arm before grunting and carrying on. Shit, this is hard. I've barely made it a quarter of the way across, and sweat is already beading on my forehead and my arms are screaming.

"Get your ass moving, Andrews. Is this the best you've got?" Kalen goads, and his taunting makes me grind my teeth together and burst forward. I know he's doing it on purpose, but it works. "That's it, Andrews, keep fucking moving. I don't know how you broke those records, you're too fucking slow to think you're the best."

"Fuck you, asshole," I hiss as I swing and add another cam.

"If you can talk, you can climb faster, come on!" he yells.

With a scream, I swing myself across a big opening and place a cam there, but my hands seize and my arms ache, making me groan.

"Peyton? You okay?" Tyler asks worriedly.

"Fucking peachy. I just thought I would hang for a bit," I joke.

My arms start to cramp, so I dig my hands in and flip upside down, pressing my legs through the hole to take some weight off them for just a moment as I pant. Fuck, this is hard. I want lots of orgasms for this.

"Andrews, get the fuck up," Kalen shouts. I close my eyes and control my breathing as he carries on berating me. "Don't fucking make me come out there and save your ass like some fucking damsel; that's not who you are. Get your ass across this ceiling now."

"All right, all right. Fucking asshole," I mutter and uncoil before continuing. They all urge me on as I climb, and I'm nearly to the other side now. Adrenaline pumps through me until I barely feel anything at all.

"That's it, princess, so close! That's my girl!" I hear him holler, and it makes warmth pool in my belly as I roll into the tunnel and lie there, panting for a moment before getting to my knees. I hear the cheers of the others as I secure the rope for Kalen to cross.

"Yes, darling!" Fin screams.

"Are you okay?" Riggs questions.

"Well done, baby, I knew you could do it!" Tyler praises.

Wiping my face on the back of my arm, I call, "Your turn, asshole, now that I've paved the way and made it easy for you."

He laughs as he climbs out, and with my bag and his, he starts to climb across the ceiling. He moves slowly but surely, using the rope I set, his legs dangling below him.

Something catches my eye on the wall, and I lean out to see better. It looks like the rock is shifting. The others are still laughing and teasing Kalen, but I can't look away from the greyish black blob. Then I realise . . .

It's moving upwards.

Climbing the wall.

It's not rock, it's alive . . . It's a creature, a monster, something my eyes can't seem to make sense of. "Kalen," I start, but he's too busy climbing. I keep my eyes on it, but then flicker them up to check on his progress when I notice the whole wall seems to move.

There's more than one, and they are all heading towards him. I haven't a clue what they are, but I have a bad feeling. "Kalen!"

"What?" he grunts.

"Move faster," I warn.

He looks up, meets my eyes, and then spins to follow my gaze to the wall. I watch him squint and stare for a moment. "What's wrong, princess?" Then he sees it. "What the fuck is that?" he shouts.

"I don't know. Keep moving, just get across, okay?" I yell, trying to stay calm.

With a swear, he moves faster as I speak into the comms. "Something is moving on the wall, lots of somethings, can you see them?"

"We see them. What are they?" Tyler asks.

"Not a clue. Kalen is halfway across."

"Tell him to fucking move faster," Tyler snaps.

"Kay, move your ass!" I bellow, and he groans as he speeds up, tiring from carrying the weight of our equipment.

I keep my eyes on the wall, but they reach the top quickly, and I gulp as I finally get a good look at one—*creature* was right. I've never seen anything like it before, ever. It looks like it's adapted to live down here. It has no eyes, but when it turns its grey, scaly head, I see large holes for the ears. It looks like a bat. It's small, the size of my leg, but still a big son of a bitch. Its body is black and grey, nearly blending with the wall, and it has wings on its back. It has long claws on its spindly hands, bones sticking out from its side, and bowed, bent legs that propel it forward. Its face is pointy, with little lips and a tiny nose.

Honestly, it's terrifying, something out of a horror film. It's more than adapted . . . This is interspecies breeding. How the fuck did it even survive down here? I have a moment where I think maybe it's just curious when it does nothing but hang there, but then it screeches, emitting a sound that has me covering my ears . . .

And it flies.

Right at Kalen.

"Duck!" I scream. He presses against the wall, and the creature barely misses him, landing on the ceiling between him and me. It hangs upside down with its taloned feet digging into the rock, its long claws lashing out at a swinging Kalen. He yells when its claw slices through his arm. When I see the spurt of blood, I panic and look around for anything to help.

I spot a few loose rocks and grab them, then I fling them at the creature. It turns its attention to me with a screech as I keep tossing stones. One knocks it loose, and it tumbles into the darkness below. But when I look back at Kalen, he's fighting off three more. He's managed to get his knife out, and he's stabbing at them as they attack. Fuck.

He won't make it across like this. Even now, I hear the groan of the rope rubbing against the rocks. I grab more rocks and start flinging, making noise. They all turn to me, even as he shouts for me to stay quiet.

Fuck that.

"Hey, you fugly assholes! Come this way. You don't want him; I've got more meat! Come on, motherfuckers, it's feeding time at the fucking zoo!" I scream as I make as much of a racket as I can.

They turn and flock towards me. I duck and curl in on myself to protect my eyes and organs before grabbing my knife and swinging wildly as they beat against my back. I hear a scream, and the assault lets up. Lifting my head, I watch as Kalen goes berserk, and creature after creature drops dead to the water below. When he's done, panting and swearing, they circle him with chattering noises.

"Move now!" I scream.

He throws himself forward, moving faster than I have ever seen him as I keep an eye on the creatures.

"Peyton, answer us now!" the guys shout, but I'm focusing entirely on these weird, motherfucking creatures to protect my man.

Then I see it.

It scuttles towards him.

"Kalen!" I scream, my arm outstretched, but he's too far. He's not going to make it. I have a split second to think on what to do. He doesn't see it yet, and it will rip him down and kill him.

There is no other choice.

I won't lose him again.

He looks up and meets my eyes. In that split second, I see the dawning horror on his face as he realises what I'm going to do. He tries to reach for me, to stop me, but it's too late.

"Love you!" I yell as I lunge forward, feeling his hand catch in my hair as I pass. I connect with the creature with a resounding thud, the force of my leap sending us spiralling down.

TWENTY-SEVEN

Kalen

All it took was one second, but it felt like a lifetime as I stared into those green eyes I know better than my own. She dived towards the creature so easily, so selflessly, without thought.

And then she fell.

I reach the tunnel and stare down at the water, waiting for her to resurface, unable to answer the panicked screams and yells of the others. "Come on, princess," I hiss, my heart cracking, my body quivering in fear.

I thought I knew terror when I faced my enemies. I thought I knew dread when I came back home and nothing was the same and I couldn't fit in—or when I lost her. But it all pales in comparison to this as I wait for her to resurface. This is fear, terror, and it freezes me completely.

I wait.

And wait.

"Kalen, answer me right fucking now!" comes Tyler's frantic cry.

"She's gone," I whisper. "She—she fell."

"What?" he yells, and I hear the others as well.

"She fell, she fell." I keep repeating it, and when I see the water below turning red, I gag. No, no—not a fucking chance! I get ready to dive in, but Tyler stops me.

"No! Look, the current! She'll be pulled elsewhere. Your best shot is to go down the tunnel now! Find her!" he shouts. "Kalen, you have to move. They're coming again, brother. I know—I know, but you need to move."

"I can't leave her!" I argue, my heart breaking. My mind is torn between what I know I need to do—what she would want me to do—and what I want to do.

"You have to, okay? I need you to keep moving so you can find her again. If you dive down there, you might die, and then we'll lose you both. You're the only one there, brother, the only one who can save her. I-I'm trusting you to save our girl."

I hesitate, but a screech has me looking up. Tyler is right—they are coming for me again. I glance back at the water, which is red with blood, but I don't know if it's hers or the creatures', and he's correct. The flow is going the way the tunnel is, so they have to meet up. They have to.

"I'm coming, princess! Hold on!" I bellow before turning and crawling down the tunnel, my heart pounding. The sound of wings is loud behind me, but they seem to be hesitant about going through the shaft.

"I'm coming, I'm coming," I chant to keep myself moving. She's not dead. She can't be. Peyton Andrews does not fucking die.

She's a bitch, she's reckless and stupid, and sometimes she's selfish, but she isn't that easy to kill.

"Brother," Tyler rasps brokenly. "Please, please bring her back."

I know it's the only weakness he will allow himself. It must be killing him that he can't be here. To save her. To protect her. There's only me. It's all on me. I can't say anything, I can't . . . He loves her. He's always loved her, and they are supposed to be together.

So where do I come into this?

She said she loves me right before she fell. I heard it . . . Did he? What does this even mean?

Nothing, I realise, if I can't get her back. I speed up, uncaring about the reckless way I'm moving through the tunnel. She is all that matters. Even if I have to tear up this whole fucking place, I will find her.

Right into the abyss.

TWENTY-EIGHT

Peyton

I wake up cold, wet, and bleeding. Brilliant.

What the hell happened? My head is fuzzy, and luckily, the water I'm lying in is shallow and keeping me afloat. With a sigh, I sit up, but I wince at the abrupt movement and shut my eyes as I hold my head. The pounding is horrendous, causing me to groan in pain. Son of a bitch, this is worse than that time Fin made home-brewed vodka.

As soon as the pain recedes to something manageable and I can open my eyes, I get to my knees and look around. My shoulder twinges, and I look down to see it hanging at a weird angle.

Fuck.

My arm is dislocated. There is no one here but me, half of my equipment is missing or smashed, and I can't swim or climb like this. Closing my eyes for a moment, I prepare myself for what I have to do next. I grip my arm, hold it out, and then with a sharp tug, I align it back into place and pop it in. I bite my lip so hard from the pain that I taste blood, but once it dissipates, it feels better. Wiggling my fingers, I test my range of motion. It twinges a little, but not enough to stop me. I've had worse.

I check the rest of my body, moving toes and fingers. I have some bumps and scrapes, my head being the worst, but I'm lucky I didn't break anything.

That was a hell of a fall.

I find my bag floating next to me. I must have knocked it off the rope when I fell. After grabbing a torch, I slip the bag on. A lot has survived inside, thank fuck, but I've got no real diving gear, only my spare air tank. I can breathe from it in an emergency, but other than that, nothing. My thoughts instantly turn to my dive partner.

I hope Kalen is all right. I look up, but the ceiling is black. It looks like the water drained into another section of the cave and took me with it. Here's hoping those bat monsters aren't in here. Just to be safe, I slide my knife from my side and kneel higher, quietly, in the water. The waves move away from me, and I frown when I hear a plop.

Like something falling into water . . .

It could be a stone, but it could also be one of those creatures. Hell, I probably saw them before when I was diving. How long have they been living down here? What do they even feed— Fuck, the skeleton!

Nope, please tell me these creepy flying fuckers didn't eat somebody.

The plop sounds again, louder this time, and I slow my breathing, trying not to make any noise. They hunt on sound, that much is obvious, maybe even smell. Something swims by me, and I watch it with wide eyes, my torch shining on the dark shape in the water.

I stay motionless until it passes, and then I let a shallow breath escape. *Think, Andrews.* Kalen's voice echoes in my head, making my heart hurt. Fuck, I really hope he's okay. I didn't even think about it before I leapt; I just saw him in trouble and needed to help. Regardless of how much he hates me, he's still my family, and I would do anything for him.

Even die.

But now I'm alone, surrounded by monstrous creatures in the underbelly of the earth. What a shit show. Keeping still in case it's still close, I sweep my light around, catching on a low rock formation farther in the section I'm in—maybe some dry land?

Okay, time to move, Andrews.

Swallowing my nerves, I keep my knife close and eyes alert as I slowly start to wade to the rock, but nearly halfway there, I hear the screech a moment before one of those creatures dive-bombs me from the ceiling. I'm flung underwater, my light slipping from my hand. Trying to keep my breathing calm, I turn my head and block its sharp teeth and claws with my arm, but I almost scream when I feel its talons rake down my side.

Fuck.

Motherfucker. I swipe out with my knife wildly, unable to see in the dark water, but we sink deeper and deeper, its weight pulling us down into the black void. I stab and slice, and I hear it cry before its talons suddenly release me.

I waste no time.

I push upwards, kicking my legs and using my arms as I feel my blood polluting the water. I see a light farther up, my lungs screaming because I didn't get to take a full breath before I went under.

I kick harder, breaking the surface just as I feel like my lungs are going to pop. Dragging in lungfuls of air, I look around. I don't see any others, so maybe it was just one? I spot my light near the rocks, and I dive under the water to swim to it, knowing it will be quieter, unless they are lurking down here. I have the horrible feeling something is under me, but I don't look, I stay focused and keep swimming until I reach my light. I grab it, and the water is shallow enough for me to sit again.

Licking my lips, breathing heavily, I shine it onto the rocks. I can't see much from down here, so being brave, I pull myself up onto an outcropping, crouching at the edge before I freeze. It's wide, stretching across the space up to the cave wall at the back—and filled with the creatures.

Fuck, this is their goddamn sleeping area. There has to be hundreds of them curled up and slumbering as they release small, screeching snores. I gape, unsure what the hell to do. I can take one, maybe two, but this many? They would rip me apart in seconds. I debate going back into the water and diving to find another way when I see it.

A tunnel.

It's right behind them, of fucking course. It looks like my only way out. Okay, I can do this. I give myself a quick pep talk before slowly pulling my bag around. I bind my cuts to stifle the scent of my blood before resealing my bag and slipping it back onto my shoulders, eyeing the creatures the whole time.

Okay, I have to be quiet.

Getting to my feet, I attempt to find the best path to the tunnel. I pick up my foot, shining the light on my path as I lightly set it back down. It's slow going as I avoid the sleeping creatures, but when I put it down the next time, the stones under it crunch. I halt, my eyes wide as they begin to stir.

Fuck!

I rush to the edge of the rock and dive swiftly into the water, not wanting to risk it. I hear them screeching and flying, but I stay under, keeping my eyes open, the light shining, and knife poised. They don't seem to know where I am, however, and I know I can stay down for at least eleven minutes, so I relax and wait.

Slowly, the screeching stops. I hear flapping wings, and just when I start running out of air, it goes quiet. I wait a bit longer before swimming up. Barely breaking the surface, I peer around to see where they all are. When nothing happens, I head over to the rock and silently climb up. That tunnel is my way out, and I will get to it.

The rock is half empty now. I don't know where the others went, but it's better for me. I crouch lower this time and nearly slide my feet along the rock, taking long steps, almost lunging across. The quicker the better. I dare not tie my torch to my side in case it scrapes on the rock, and I have to make sure to grab my air tank so it doesn't either. The whole time, I'm aware of how vulnerable I am, causing my heart to hammer so loudly, I'm surprised they can't hear it.

I try to avoid getting too close to them so they can't smell my blood, but when I somehow manage to make it across to the channel, I spot a big fucker right in front of the exit.

Of course.

Rolling my lips inwards, I hold my breath as I lift my leg and place it on the other side of his body, but he's large so I have to hop over him. I land on the other side and teeter forward, swinging my arms as I almost hit the wall. I manage to recover and freeze, but nothing happens, so I duck into the tunnel and begin to crawl hurriedly, finally letting my breath out.

Never thought I would say this, but I hate this fucking cave.

I come to a curve in the tunnel about two hours later. Feeling safe, I place the light on a small shelf in the rock and pull my bag open, sipping some water before I uncover my side and inspect the wound. It's still oozing blood from the three long talon cuts. Well, I guess it's just more scars to prove I survived. I almost laugh at that.

No, I'm not fucking losing it.

I have something small to eat and cover the wound again, binding it tight with a hiss. As I'm packing my bag, a noise reaches me, so I freeze and turn my head. I spot it almost too late. One of the creatures is crawling from the direction I was going. I press back against the wall and hold my breath as it practically stops in front of me, scraping its talons along the floor. Keeping my eyes on the monster, I glance down to try to find my knife.

Fuck, I put it down next to my light. I inch towards it, but it sniffs the air, so I stop. It lifts its head, its nostrils flaring, and turns its head as if to see me. Fuck, the blood! On the floor is a strip of cloth I used to clean my wound, and it has blood on it.

It screeches and dives at it in a flurry of wings and talons, and I have no choice but to scrunch closer to the wall and wait it out. It's only a couple minutes, but it feels like forever before it finally moves on. I let out a sigh but wait to move in case it's nearby.

A few minutes later, I grab my bag, light, and knife and get moving. I need to find the others. There has to be a tunnel leading to one we explored. I bet they think something horrible has happened; I just hope they aren't losing their shit.

TWENTY-NINE

Riggs

"I'm going, and that's the fucking end of it," I snarl, squaring off with Tyler.

His eyes narrow, and I duck the punch he aims my way. Fin gets between us, grabbing both our shirts as we pant and fume. "You two fucking quit it! We have more important things than this. Our girl is out there, maybe hurt, probably scared, so get it to-fucking-gether. We're all going. We're going to get our brother and find our girl and get the hell out of this stupid fucking cave system, and then I'll spend at least two weeks in bed with her. Anyone got a fucking problem with that? I'm not above dick punches!" he warns, glaring.

Tyler scowls at him, ready to begin yelling again when Michael shouts. "Will you all cut it out? The only family I have is missing, and the caves we're in are filled with man-eating creatures. Get your fucking act together and start acting like a goddamn leader!" he bellows at Tyler, his voice booming around us. "We'll stay; you guys go. You find my minnow and you bring her back. Work together and get this shit done. Anybody got a fucking problem with that?" he roars, looking us over.

I rip out of Fin's arms and stuff things into my bag, fuming, but under that anger is fear. Fear we won't find Pey, that she's not alive. That she died alone and scared. I hate myself. I should have been with her. I should have kissed her, told her I loved her, and forgave her instead of being a shy fucking asshole. Statistics keep running through my head, and none of them are comforting, so I ignore them and focus on counting my supplies and double-checking everything.

Everyone is silent as we all pack, ready to go after them. Michael is watching Kalen and keeping him updated, but we have to go in after them, especially Pey. I don't give a fuck about some bat creatures. With how I'm feeling, I'll kill all of them.

"Riggs." Tyler sighs and steps up next to me. I grind my teeth but look up to see his expression is lost and resigned. He swallows and glances away. "I-I can't lose her," he whispers.

"I know," I reply, but for once, I finish the sentence I never dared to before. "None of us can, can't you see that? Stop being so selfish. We all love her, and right now, we're all scared, but arguing among ourselves won't help. We need to work fast and hard, and then we might just stand a chance of finding her. Michael's right—get it together. You're our leader, so lead," I snap before grabbing my mask and storming away.

Fin falls in step next to me, whistling. "Goddamn. Welcome to the party, Riggs, here is your man card."

I roll my eyes, even as a smile curls my lips. "We . . . we'll find her, won't we?" he asks as we reach the pool. I swallow and look up at him.

"We have to," I answer, not mentioning the likelihood of us never finding her. We haven't explored even half of this system. She could be anywhere. And that fall . . . Not to mention the attack.

If she is alive, it's a miracle, but I will never give up on her. I'll find her and then never let her go again. "Riggs," Fin calls and grabs my shoulder, looking into my eyes.

"She knows," he murmurs.

"She does?" I question. "How?"

He chuckles. "Not everyone is as bad as you are at peopling. She knows we love her; it's why she left, but she's back now, okay? What's a few man- and woman-eating creatures to deal with?" He winks, and then we both become silent as Tyler heads over, ready to dive.

Before we get into the water, he turns to us, his expression controlled, and it seems he's back in control of himself. Thank fuck. Kalen is the only drama queen we need. "I'm sorry," he offers. "I shouldn't have attacked you like that. I know we're all worried."

"Ty, man, we get it. You don't have to say sorry. Family forever," Fin says, and Tyler smiles.

Tyler goes to walk away but stills. "We'll have to talk about . . . the other thing later."

"You mean the fact we're all in love with the same woman?" Fin laughs. "I don't see the issue. Peyton is too much for one person anyway."

"Fin's right, and honestly, we were all pretty much in a relationship back then, just without the . . . physical aspects. You have to see that, Ty," I reason.

He nods but scrubs at his face. "Fuck, I thought it was bad enough that my brother loved her, but you two assholes as well? Shit, this is so weird. Okay, let's find her first, and then we can deal with this."

"But . . . you don't hate us?" I inquire, worry lacing my tone.

He looks at me and smiles. "Brother, I could never hate you, and I guess I always knew deep down. It's weird, I will give you that, and I might be a jealous prick, but honestly? It doesn't bother me as much as I thought it would." He turns away, and Fin and I share a look.

Did Tyler just give us permission to be in love with his girl?

Kalen

The screeches stopped about a mile back when they couldn't get through this section of the tunnel, but I keep moving, not giving myself time to think. My conditioning from the army is coming in handy. I still hear Peyton's scream echoing in my mind, but I use it, letting it fuel me and push me forward. I'm intent on finding her. My legs and feet are bleeding from their talons, and the pain surges through me with each step, but I don't give a fuck.

I've had worse—not physically but emotionally, when I lost my princess the first time. I won't lose her again; this is nothing in comparison.

"You still there, asshole?" Michael asks.

"Yes," I snap.

"Good, don't die. I would hate to have to tell Peyton it was me who killed you." He laughs, and I roll my eyes. I get why she likes him, hell, I can even appreciate his honesty. "Your friends have just gone in. They are going to go slow and see if they can find her, so just keep moving. I'm here with you."

"Comforting," I mutter, making him chuckle again.

"Does that attitude really make Peyton like you?" he inquires curiously.

"She doesn't care; she likes arguing with me," I tell him, unsure why.

"I bet. That girl loves a good fight, but here's an idea, slick, maybe try being nice to her for once," he suggests.

"Shut up, old man," I scoff as I round a corner.

"Just saying, kid, you wanna keep your girl? Get her some flowers, call her pretty, buy snacks, and rub her back once in a while. She might like the whole asshole thing, but that doesn't mean she wants it all the time."

"Oh God, how the fuck do I shut you up?"

"Also, if you hurt her again, you don't have to worry about those little fuckers in there with you. I will rip you apart myself, understood?"

I hang my head, groaning. "Fuck, talk about something else, like how you two met," I say desperately, trying to stop him from diving into Peyton's and my relationship.

"She found me drunk and passed out, offered me a job. Told me if I wanted it, to get sober and be at the docks the next morning. I turned up, don't know why, but I never looked back since," he shares, love evident in his voice. "She saved me."

"Yeah, she has a way of doing that," I mutter. I almost stop myself from asking, but no one else is really there to hear me. "Did she ever talk about us?"

"Nah, I think it hurt her too much," he replies.

My heart twinges at that as I scramble over a rubble section and keep crawling, ignoring the pain and exhaustion. "But she was okay, right?"

"Honestly, kid? She was heartbroken. She was just surviving, moving from dive to dive and looking for a thrill so she didn't have to feel. I know what heartbreak looks like—why do you think I started drinking? She was so fucking broken. She did good though, kept going and made a life for herself, but I don't want her hurt again. She's finally started to smile and laugh, so don't fucking hurt her."

I swallow and close my eyes for a moment. "I don't want to," I admit.

"Did she ever tell you my story?" he asks.

"No," I grunt.

"My family was killed in an accident, a stupid fucking car crash. It took my little girl and my wife at the same time. She was pregnant with our second child. I was so fucking excited to be a daddy again, and then they were just gone. I couldn't function, couldn't breathe. I even tried to kill myself, but I couldn't go through with it. So I tried drinking myself to death. I've seen a lot in this world, and I know the depths of darkness you can sink to, but if you give that girl half a chance, she will shine light into that gloom and save you. My advice? Don't let her go again. If there was anything I could do to hold my girls again, even just for a second . . . to see their faces, their smiles, there is nothing I wouldn't do. Nothing. Don't let her get away, or you'll regret it for the rest of your life and end up like me—an old, washed-up, drunk sailor."

I hear a noise and swear, moving faster. I let his words resonate in my head. I don't think I could let her walk away again anyway, but is he right? Can she save me from the demons in my soul? From the blood on my hands? The nightmares that plague me? And if she did, wouldn't I just be ruining her with all that darkness?

Do I care?

No, because Peyton Andrews is the love of my life, and even if it's selfish and wrong, I will never go without her again, even to save her from me.

It makes me redouble my efforts to get out of this fucking tunnel and find her. Turning my head, I spot one of the little assholes behind me. Fuck this. I see a light up ahead and throw myself out of the tunnel, landing hard on the rocks below. Flipping, I grab my knife, and as the creature flies from the tunnel with a screech, I throw myself up and hit it midair, slicing across its throat. Blood spurts on my face as we fall to the ground. Panting, I get to my feet, glare down at the little bastard, and spit.

"Not so tough now, are you?" I laugh before looking around.

I'm in some kind of cavern. It's small and circular and leads down to what looks like a submerged area. Fuck. I search for any other way out, but when I hear the screeching coming from the tunnel I emerged from, I stop at the water.

Here's hoping Pey is down there. I dive in, put my mask on underwater, and turn on the lights, keeping my knife in hand as I dive deeper and deeper, swimming around stalagmites. It's not just a passage, it's a whole underwater cavern.

I swim close to the floor so nothing can attack me from below. The ceiling is high, I can see it from here, and the room twists and turns as I keep swimming. I hear something enter the water with me and turn to look. They cut easily through the water, heading straight for me. Obviously, they hear my regulator.

There are three of them. If I keep swimming, they will surround me and attack me from behind. No, I need to kill them, then there will be less of these fuckers to hurt my girl.

I have no choice. I glance around and quickly form a plan. I duck behind stalagmites, using them like a shield. They split up, and I swim out, stabbing one before sliding around the rock and chasing another. It spins, slashing at me, and I have to lurch back, but I catch its wing and rip it to pieces. When I turn around, the third is on me. His beaked face smashes into my mask, cracking it. I struggle, stirring the water around us, and the silt makes it hard to see as we fight.

I grunt when it stabs its claw into my shoulder, but I manage to get my knife between us, impaling the creature. It recoils with a screech, and blood clouds the water, making it impossible to see. I swim away and wait, but nothing comes after me, so I turn and continue in the direction I was going.

"You okay?" Michael asks.

"Fine. Anything from the guys or Peyton?" I grumble, ignoring the pain in my shoulder.

"Nothing from Peyton. The men are working through the first tunnel, checking everything. Just keep going," Michael replies.

I do, my only thought of my girl. I may be surrounded by enemies, I may not know where I am, and I may be facing death, but none of it matters as long as I get to her.

Hoo-fucking-rah.

THIRTY

Peyton

This cave system is bigger than we could have ever imagined. Normally, that would be a good thing, but when you're cut off and searching for the rest of your dive team, not so much. Or when you are being chased by weird cave-dwelling creatures that want to eat you, and not in a good way.

It feels like it's been days, when in fact it has only been hours, but my body is exhausted, and I'm weary from blood loss. My arms hurt, my shoulder aches like a son of a bitch, my legs too, but I keep going, holding my knife ready in case any of them jump out at me. I can't lose hope; I have to get back to my guys, and we need to get out of here.

Some places should never be explored, and this is one of them.

I thought this dive was going to be for my life; how right I was. I'm willing to risk it all to save them—my heart, my sanity, and my life. But first, I need to find Kalen before the creatures do. I stay quiet and work fast, adapting easily, just like them. They may be hunting me, but I'm hunting them too.

I come to a break in the tunnel, and the only way is up, so I grip my knife in my teeth and start to climb without any gear on. Teeth clenched, arms straining, I haul myself up, not letting the pain settle in. I think only of my family somewhere in this cave, probably searching for me. It gets me to the top and the tunnel there. Panting, I stare down at the forty-metre climb.

"Easy-peasy," I mutter with a snort.

These creatures may have been down here for years, but they have never met Peyton fucking Andrews.

Shining my light into the tunnel, I rush into the cave and the awaiting monsters in search of my men.

* * *

Pizza, burgers, beer, beds . . .

I'm mentally listing all the things I miss. It keeps me going, even as fatigue settles in. The dive already took a lot out of me, never mind climbing and surviving. I want to stop, to sleep, but I can't, not alone. The creatures could find me, and there's no way I'm being that dumb bitch in a horror movie who just waits to be killed.

Head hanging down, mouth moving on silent words, I push forward through the never-ending tunnel until it begins to slope upwards. I stop and lean back against the wall and just take a minute, sipping my water and having a little break as I shine my light up. It's completely vertical, but where does it go? I guess there is only one way to find out, and there's no way I'm going back.

I force myself to start moving, knowing if I sit for too long, it gives them more time to find me as well as sends my legs and body into spasms.

Keep moving, one more climb. One more tunnel. One more breath. One more fucking minute closer to them.

Pushing my back against the wall, I press my hands to the opposite side and pull and shuffle my way up, propelling with my legs. It's slow going, but I just keep looking up, not down, and keep on fucking moving.

I think of everything I want to tell them, everything I wish I'd told them. Maybe if I had been honest from the start, we wouldn't be here. It's not my fault I fell in love with all of them. The human heart is made to love, and it's big enough for more than one person. Is it really so wrong? Why does it matter whom I love? Man, woman, fluid? As long as it makes me happy, why should anyone else fucking care?

It's how I keep myself distracted, thinking over what it means to love four men. If I do find them again, I'm telling them all the truth. If they can't handle it, then fine, but I'm done lying. I'm finished breaking my own heart just to save theirs.

I did it when I left. I thought I was doing it to protect them, but having grown up and thought it through, I realise maybe I did it out of fear. Like they said, I was scared of what I felt and having to face the music. Maybe it was a bit of both, but I can't change what happened. I just need to learn from it and do better in the future.

In this kind of relationship, we have to be open and honest. Honesty is so fucking important, and I'm tired of my soul being weighed down by lies. I have to make myself weak, vulnerable, and open to them. Pressing my forehead to the wall, I take a deep breath, trying to fight past the tiredness in my body.

Come on, princess. I hear Kalen calling to me, and it almost brings tears to my eyes.

Get moving, baby.

You heard him, Pey, Fin teases.

Sixty percent chance of survival on your rations right now, so get moving before they run out, Riggs adds in my mind.

I'm independent, I love being alone, and I've faced the unknown by myself for so long. But right now, I would do anything to have them here with me.

For a moment, I just let the thoughts of them fill me until I can feel their presence—Tyler's laugh, Kalen's snark, Fin's flirting, and Riggs's comfort.

It gives me the motivation I need to keep going.

I push and pull, the rhythm of the movements lulling me into a trance, and before I know it, I'm at the top. There are tunnels to the left and right. Fuck, which one?

Pick, Andrews.

The left one looks smaller, while the right one seems to curve back down . . . maybe to a cavern, back to where I came from, or to some hideous creature, but who knows? I choose, and I go right. Dragging myself up and over, I groan in pain when rocks drag against the cuts on my stomach. I grind my teeth, pull my knife free, and start to crawl again. A sudden burst of energy comes over me, and I'm covering ground in half the time I was before.

The tunnel does curve down, and I keep going, gripping and pulling myself through the shaft at this point. I feel air on my face, and that should be my first warning, but I blame my exhaustion. All it takes is one mistake.

And I make it.

The tunnel doesn't just swerve, it drops off right into a pit of water. I slip to the end, flipping to grasp the edge with my fingers.

It's too late. I try to hold on, but the walls are slippery, so to avoid hurting myself or breaking fingers attempting to cling on, I pinch my nose with one hand and let myself fall feet first into the water. I plunge into it with a splash, and it swirls around me before I kick to the surface, breaking into the air with a gasp and looking around quickly.

The water here is freezing, really fucking cold, and going from dry to wet is sending my body into shock. I'm shivering, which isn't a good sign. I need to get out of the water and get warm for a while. Hypothermia down here would be fatal. I duck under the water and swim, searching for a way out, and I find it at the very edge of the bottom. It's deep, so I go back to the surface and suck in some breaths.

It could go underwater for a long time, and I have no gear other than a tank, so it looks like I'm going to have to hold my breath for that and hope for the fucking best. It has its risks, but it's my only choice, and with my body preparing to shut down, it's now or never.

Taking a deep inhale, I dive down, trying to hold my breath without the tank for as long as I can. I swim fast into the tunnel and what feels like a maze. I manoeuvre around rocks, holes, and chasms, and about fifty metres in, I have to start using my tank. I know it won't last forever, but I stay calm and search for another tunnel or cave.

I swim.

And swim.

And swim.

Until I find one just as the tank is nearly empty. It's about sixty feet in front of me with light shining into it. I take one last suck of the tank, draining it, and let it fall to the sandy floor below. Using my arms, I propel myself forward, my lungs screaming and body hurting. My eyes water, and I'm nearly unable to see, but I keep swimming right into the light.

And out of the other side.

THIRTY-ONE

Tyler

We go slow through the tunnels, even though we have been through them before. We know something is lurking here now, and we also have to check every crack and entrance to see if we can spot Peyton or any other signs of life. It takes us hours just to make it through to the fully submerged cavern, and once there, we split up, searching some of the tunnels.

That's when it comes down the mic, and my heart leaps.

"Come to the cavern we ruled out as an advanced base! Now!" Fin yells.

I rush there, swimming as fast as I can, and I beat Riggs, who is right behind me. Ripping off my mask, I stand and pull myself out of the water, but my heart sinks when I see Kalen. I instantly feel guilty. I'm happy we found him, but that also means he didn't find Peyton, and now she's out there all alone . . . if at all.

"Don't look too happy, you fuckers," Kalen snarls, making us all laugh. "I know I'm not as pretty, but damn." Fin crouches at his side, and I head over to see him dressing a wound on Kalen's shoulder.

"You okay, bro?" I ask.

He nods, looking behind me, his face falling. "No Peyton?"

I shake my head, and his eyes close for a moment. I know he's blaming himself, so I crouch down, and Fin moves away. I grip his uninjured shoulder and force his eyes to meet mine. "No one can stop Peyton from doing something she wants to do. We would have all done the same thing in her shoes. Trust in her. She will find us, and we won't stop looking. Don't give up on her, not now."

He sighs. "You're right . . . but fuck, I'm sorry, Ty."

I lean closer and press my forehead to his like we used to do as children, before he enlisted and went away, back when we had no worries. "Don't apologise, you did the best you could, and it was better than anything we could have done. I'm just glad you're okay."

"Who thought this is what we would become?" He chuckles bitterly. "Both of us are in love with the same woman. If Mum and Dad could see us now."

I laugh. "The old bastard would have hated her, and Mum would have followed what he said, you know that."

He grins at that. Our parents aren't in our lives, and that's our own choice. Kalen enlisted to escape them while I found work that took me away and into the ocean so we would never have to go back and I'd have a job waiting for him when he got out.

They aren't our family, not anymore, Peyton is. She's *our* family, not just mine. I need to stop being selfish and hurting my family. I need to face the cold, hard truth laid in front of me. He's suffering, looking for my forgiveness and acceptance without even realising it. Can I give him that? It seems like there's no better time for honesty than now.

"I wouldn't want it any other way. I can't think of a better man to protect my"—I suck in a breath as jealousy flares, but I push past it—"our girl."

He swallows, and I see guilt in his eyes . . . and hope. "I love her, Ty. I tried not to, I tried so fucking hard, but she's the only person who makes me feel alive, who makes me feel anything but this fucking anger."

I nod. "I know. I was selfish and stupid not to see it. When she left, I thought that was the end, that we wouldn't have to deal with it. I didn't even consider how you would feel. But she's back, brother, she's here."

"What if she leaves again?" he questions, his voice rough.

"We won't let her." I smirk. "I don't know what the future holds, or if we can do this"—I gesture to the others and lift my head to see them—"but if it takes all of us to keep her, so be it. We'll figure it out, we always do."

"You finally fucking realised you want her to stay." Fin grins.

"Oh, I'm still pissed at her." I laugh, and they all laugh too.

"Take it out on her in bed; bet she would love it," Fin teases, wiggling his eyebrows.

Kalen snorts. "Shut the fuck up, man."

Riggs blushes but looks at me with consideration. "Does she like to be dominated?"

I groan and close my eyes. "Bro, I'm not talking to you about this. Just because I'm not killing you for loving my girl doesn't mean I won't punch you for talking about her in that way."

He blinks and looks at Kalen. "She liked you ordering her around. Do I need to do that, or can I go further?"

Kalen, Fin, and I share a look and burst into laughter, desperate, wild laughter—it's either that, or sobs. I don't even want to ask what he's talking about. Who fucking knew? Four men all in love with the same woman. I don't know if it will work, it's weird as hell for sure, but . . . but it also feels right. She was always the heart of our family, and their relationships with her were always more than basic friendships, I just didn't want to see it.

"Fucking hell, we need ground rules," Kalen mutters when he can talk again.

"So . . . we are really doing this?" Fin inquires, watching us. "I'm cool with it. Hell, I might even let one of you fuckers help me with her." He wiggles his brows again, and I scowl. "I don't mean sword crossing, but it could be fun." He smiles unabashedly, and I get to my feet and point my finger at him.

"Run," I growl.

He laughs and steps back. "But are we? Are we agreeing to share Peyton?"

Share her . . . Fuck.

Is this really the only way I get to keep my brothers and my girl?

If so . . . can I really do this?

It seems I have no choice.

"If that's what she wants," Riggs inserts, frowning.

"Oh, fuck it. I share everything else with you fuckers anyway," Kalen grumbles. "But if one of you pervs even so much as tries to touch my pork sword, I'm out."

They all look at me. It's hard to agree, it is, but I know this is the only way I'll get Peyton again. She was never just mine, she was ours, and this just makes it official. "We share her." I nod my assent, the words strange on my tongue. "If she wants to. But first, we have to find her and get the fuck out of these caves."

"I wonder if there is a name for this kind of relationship," Fin asks Riggs.

"Well, in ancient and royal dynasties, the kings had harems, which were large groups of women, or concubines."

"I'm not being a fucking concubine," Kalen snarls.

"So a harem it is?" Fin laughs. "I like it, Peyton's Harem. We could get shirts with funny names, like Captain Cock, First Cock, Second Cock."

"Please stop," I grouse.

We hear a splash and all turn, the mood turning sober as we remember just where we are. "Okay, Kalen, are you good to move?" He gets to his feet and nods. "Good, we need to find Peyton. It's time we got our girl back."

"Aye-aye, Captain Cock," Fin retorts.

I'm going to kill them.

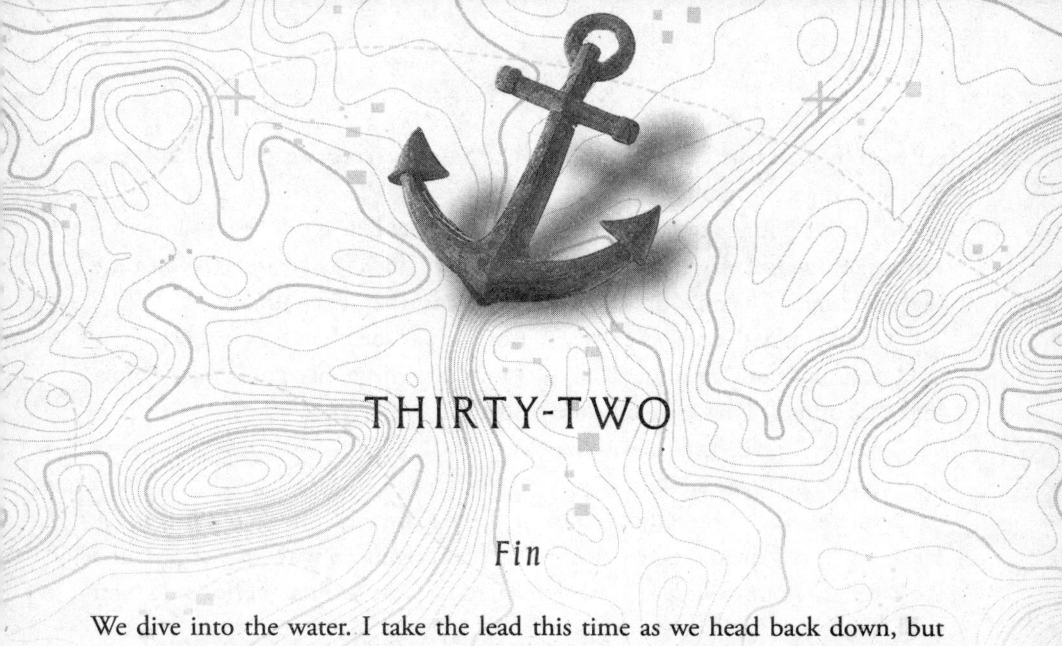

THIRTY-TWO

Fin

We dive into the water. I take the lead this time as we head back down, but when we reach the submerged section, we look at each other. Peyton could be anywhere, so we need to split up.

But that's a dumb move.

Do we do it anyway?

Yes.

Because it increases our chances of finding her, and I will do anything to find her. I gesture to the fourth tunnel, and they nod, each picking their own channel to investigate. With one last look at my team, I head straight into the narrow cavern in search of my girl.

I pray she's okay. I don't believe in a higher power, but right now, I'll pray, whatever it takes to ensure she's alive. I was a fucking idiot to hold back, to tell her no when we were alone. It all seems like such senseless reasoning now. When faced with her death, it's clear there is enough of Peyton to share, and we will share, because none of us will give her up.

She's ours, she just doesn't know it yet.

I keep swimming, slowly kicking along as I shine my torch around. I hold my knife at the ready in case any of those bat-like motherfuckers pop up. I will kill them for hurting my family. We still try to reach her over the comms, but it's obvious it's either damaged or . . . No.

Just damaged.

Nothing else.

I refuse to accept she's dead, my girl can survive anything. She's a fucking beast, and she will make this cave her bitch and come back to us. When she does, I'll show her just how fucking much I love her, and I'll never let her go again.

The tunnel narrows, and I basically have to crawl. Usually, I would turn back at Tyler's orders, not wanting to burst my equipment, but he's not here to tell me off, so in true Fin style, I push on. I hear the scrape against my tank and grin as I wiggle through.

My heart pounds from fear and adrenaline, the best type. That's what Peyton makes me feel as well, only ten times better. She's my greatest risk and my biggest reward. The only time I truly feel alive is when I'm with her.

"Come on, darling, answer me," I mutter. "Let me know you're there."

I wait, but nothing comes back. Refusing to believe she's gone, I keep moving. "Anything?" Tyler asks, his tone desperate.

"Not yet," Kalen snarls. "Keep looking."

"Nothing," Riggs says.

"Not yet. She's here, guys, I know it. Keep searching. She would never give up on us," I tell them. "Like that time Kalen got tangled with an octopus, and she dived for hours trying to unhook him, all because he thought he could fight it," I tease.

They all laugh. "I would have won too," he mutters.

"Bro, you lost to an octopussy," I taunt as I keep swimming.

"I'll give you pussy," he snarls.

"I think you already had the pussy," Riggs quips, making us all freeze and then howl in laughter. Oh God, did he actually just say that?

"Fuck, I can't believe you said that!" I laugh so hard I have to stop and regulate my breathing.

"Oops," he replies, but I hear the smile in his voice. Riggs is finally stepping into the game. It's about time, especially after I used to have to listen to how much he loved that girl. Apparently, he's decided he's not holding back anymore.

I just don't think she'll be ready for what he was hiding from her.

He's going to destroy that girl, and she will love it.

"Concentrate," Tyler snaps, his tone filled with jealousy. It's going to be hard for him to share, but it all pales in comparison to the situation we're in now.

Hell, we could have a chart, like a reward chart for pussy, I think as I swim, the tunnel angling down slightly.

It starts to open up, and I hesitate for a moment before diving forward in case those bitches are waiting to pounce. I stop at the edge of the tunnel, popping my head up, when I realise the water is draining and I can breathe without my mask. I stare into the opening with a whistle.

"Found an opening," I call, slipping to the edge before I dive down, holding my mask as I plunge into the water. With a kick, I reach the surface and head towards the raised rock, which protrudes above the water. I drag myself up and out, tugging off my fins as I stand and stretch.

There is a whole bloody cavern in here. The pool is only a fraction of the area. Above are pinpricks of light from bioluminescent bugs in the ceiling, the floor is rocky but smooths out, and there is a flat area to rest on. There are no other entrances over this way, so I relax. It's not likely the bats can get in here.

"Nothing here," I murmur. There isn't a bag, blood, or any other sign of Peyton ever having come through here.

It's just another dead end.

Just then I hear a splash. I spin, raising my knife as I step back, searching the water for those creepy little bats. I want to kill some of those bastards for hurting my brother and my girl. Instead, I see bubbles fizzing to the surface of the water. Frowning, I hesitantly step closer to the edge, peering into the depths below. The water is clear enough that I can see straight down.

Straight at Peyton.

THIRTY-THREE

She's desperately struggling to get to the top.

One second is all it takes. My heart skips a beat, and my entire body lights up with excitement that she's alive, but then I notice her movements are turning sluggish. She needs help, she needs air.

She's alive, but not for long if we can't get her to the surface. She doesn't even have a tank on.

Forgetting the knife, I dive in and swim right for her. Peyton's eyes catch on mine as she punches through the water, trying to reach me. I extend my hand as she slows further.

No, fuck that.

I didn't just find her to lose her again.

With a grunt and a huge kick, I manage to grasp her hand and drag her to me. We flip in the water, and I start to kick to the surface. Her legs wrap around me, but her eyes are panicked, darting from side to side as she shakes her head. She's telling me she won't make it.

Fuck.

I don't hesitate, don't wait. I will give her every breath in my lungs if that's what it takes. And so I do. I seal my lips to hers and blow air into her mouth and lungs. She pulls herself closer as I carry on swimming to the surface, sharing air with her. Even when my own lungs start to scream and she tries to pull away, I refuse to stop. I thread my fingers into her hair, holding her to me.

I will never lose her again, not ever.

She can take it all.

My air, my heart, my body.

Whatever she needs.

We break through the surface, and she tears herself away as I gulp in air. My heart is racing so fast, it feels like it may just break through my chest, but it isn't just from the lack of oxygen. It's because my girl is back in my arms.

"Fin," she whispers, her voice cracking.

Uncaring about anything else, I draw her closer and smash my lips to hers. She groans into my mouth, climbing higher on my body as I hold her. I pull away to breathe, pressing my forehead to hers, and she shakes in my arms.

"I didn't think I would see you again," she whispers brokenly.

"I never doubted you for a moment, darling. Not one fucking moment. Do you hear me?" I demand, and she nods, opening her eyes, which pierce straight to my soul. "I always knew you would come home to us."

We both know I'm referring to more than just today.

She swallows and looks around. "There aren't any of them here. I don't think they could get through," I assure her, and she settles a bit. "Are you hurt?" I ask, noticing there are cuts on her cheek and head.

"My shoulder was dislocated, but I popped it back in. It's just my head, really, and some cuts on my side." I flip her, holding tight, as I begin to swim us to the rocks so she can rest her body. Who knows how long she's been swimming? She must be exhausted.

When we reach the raised area, I help her out, and she stumbles across it to the flat section and drops to her ass. "Fuck, that was not fun," she comments as I crouch in front of her, searching for injuries. I run my hands over her, desperate to touch her and reassure myself she's really here.

"I want you to tell me everything, but we might as well wait for the others." I sigh and reach for the comms to let them know.

Staring into those tired eyes, I press the button, my voice coming out as a croak. "I've got her."

There's a moment of silence, and then they all talk at once. I wait for them to slow down before I speak. "She's okay, I promise. We're going to rest here for a bit before we come back. She's exhausted, and I need to dress a cut on her side. We'll meet you in three hours at forward base, I promise."

"I can come through—" Kalen starts.

"You won't fit, no offence. I promise she's here. Darling, talk to them before they bust through the cave," I murmur.

She leans against me, snuggling into my chest. "I'm okay, guys."

Again, there is a moment of complete silence, and then Kalen's broken voice comes through. "Promise me, baby?"

"I promise," she replies.

"Pey?" Tyler whispers.

"I know. I'll see you soon, okay? Get some food ready, and let Michael know," she says and then hangs up as she leans into me, closing her eyes.

"Darling, I need to look at your side," I murmur as I lay her down and pull my bag closer.

"Do it, undress me, I don't fucking care. Just don't ask me to move," she whines, making me chuckle and pop her on the thigh.

"Stop whining, that's not my Pey," I admonish, and she rewards me with a grin.

"Fin, look after me," she whispers, pouting.

"Always," I vow, and kiss her softly before peeling away the bandage she made. I don't need to take her suit off. Luckily, there is a huge hole around the slashes themselves. The wound looks clean but harsh—three long, deep furrows from claws. I glance up at her, but I think she's asleep. What the fuck happened down there?

We are lucky she's alive. No, luck had nothing to do with it.

Peyton Andrews is a goddamn monster-killing badass.

I clean the wound, causing her to wince before she settles—we don't want her getting an infection—and then I dry and redress it before lying down next to her and pulling her against my chest, ready to protect her while she rests.

My heart has never been so full. She's back in my arms, nothing else matters.

I will never let her out of my sight again.

I wake her an hour later to drink something and take in some nutrients. Straight after, she curls back into my arms and sighs. "Fuck, I missed this," I murmur, kissing her head.

"Yeah? Didn't replace me right away?" she teases.

"Darling, I could never replace you, you know that," I murmur. Even though she was teasing, I need her to know that. "No one could ever compare to you, not ever. Not in a million lifetimes. Peyton Andrews, you own me, always have. I never should have fallen for you, but I did," I confess.

She lifts her head and meets my gaze. "We both tried not to," she replies, and I nod, stroking along her cheek.

"You just made it too damn easy to love you." I give her a teasing grin.

Her smile grows as she stares at me. "So was that kiss an 'I'm glad you're alive,' one-time thing?" she murmurs, dropping her eyes to my lips. "Because I have to admit, feeling you pressed against me has me thinking of just how alive I really am."

"You need to rest," I rasp helplessly, staring at her lips as I groan and try to restrain myself. "Rest." I grunt. "Yup, rest."

"I don't want to rest," she whispers, her expression determined. "We could die in an hour, today, or tomorrow. I told myself if I made it through, I would tell you how I feel. I love you; I love you all. I do love you, Fin." She searches my eyes, my resolve lessening with every word. "I've wanted you since the moment I met you, and I'm tired of fighting it. Fuck rest. I've spent enough years without you, I refuse to spend a moment more."

"Pey," I groan, pressing my head to hers, trying to ignore my rapidly hardening cock. It's been too long since I fucked anything but my hand, years actually. Way before she ever left, I couldn't bring myself to be with anyone else, even when I knew I would never be with her. I couldn't stomach the idea of touching another, of her knowing I did and causing her pain.

I've always loved her, and I always will. And right now, my girl is right—we may not make it through, and this may be the only time I ever get to have the woman I love. Am I really going to ignore that chance?

"You're offering me everything I've ever wanted. I always imagined our first time together to be perfect. Special. Not like this." I look around. "I was going to spend hours exploring you, touching you, and teasing every inch of skin I dreamed about for years. I wanted to show you just how fucking much I always wanted you, how goddamn much it hurt every time I had to pull away, to leave our cuddles for a cold shower and my hand because you drove me crazy, Peyton," I admit, opening my eyes as I whisper her name.

"Even now, when I'm wet, bloody, and unwashed?" she teases.

Grinning, I press my lips to hers. "Even more, because this is real. And my Peyton is a goddamn badass bitch who survived on her own in a cave full of monsters to get back to me . . . So of course even now. Fuck, Pey," I mutter before finally . . .

Finally giving in to desire.

"Thank fuck," she whispers before I slam my lips onto hers. Swallowing her moan, I roll us so she's on her back and I'm between her thighs. I prop myself up on one arm and grip her chin as I turn her for the kiss. I show her with each stroke of my lips, my tongue, just how fucking much I want her.

Have always wanted her. Will always want her.

She moans, biting my lip before I lick along hers and slip inside, tangling my tongue with hers. Slowly, I lower myself and search along the rocky ground until I find her hand, stroking up along her arm to her wrist. I twine my fingers with hers and press it above her head before doing the same with the other, gripping them both in one of my hands as the kiss turns darker.

Deeper, hungrier.

Each of us fights for control as we try to hold out for as long as we can. I know as soon as I strip her, I'll be lost, and I want to remember every single last detail of this moment.

"Fin," she begs against my lips before pulling away. She turns her head as she pants, her hands clinging to mine. Chuckling softly, I glide my nose across her cheek to her ear before licking and nibbling the lobe, making her gasp.

"I can't tell you how many times I imagined hearing your voice like that, all breathy and pleading." I groan into her ear, grinding my cock against her stomach to show her how wild with lust she makes me. "Fuck, I had so many fantasies about the way you would cry and scream for me."

"Yeah? Show me," she challenges, flicking her eyes back to mine as her parted lips curve up in a grin.

"You're on, babe," I growl before dragging my tongue and lips down her throat, tasting the water from the caves, but it only adds to Peyton. She comes with water, with earth, and I have so many fantasies of fucking her in the ocean, of watching her come up from a dive, strip for me, and then ride me right there on the boat in the middle of nowhere.

Fuck.

I reach her chest, clench the zipper between my teeth, and start to tug it down, having to work it across her breasts. I end just above her pussy, placing a teasing kiss over the drying material. She groans and lifts her hips, but I ignore her body's plea and move up. I unfasten her sports bra, freeing her breasts, and I take my time staring at them. I saw them a couple of times before. It's not exactly easy to live on a boat and not see each other naked, but those moments pale in comparison to now. Her nipples are hard, begging for my mouth, and her chest is flushed with excitement.

Raising my gaze, I lean down and suck her nipple into my mouth as she watches. Her head falls back, and her eyes close as she arches her chest higher, pushing her breast deeper into my mouth. Chuckling, I pull back, licking around her nipple before flicking it with my tongue. I lap at her flesh, teasing her before sucking it between my lips again, making her cry out before I add the sting of my teeth.

I turn and give the other the same treatment, laving it with my tongue, coaxing it into a harder point. Her hips keep rolling against me, begging for more, and her muffled cries reach my ears, urging me on. She clenches her hand, squeezing mine as she holds on for whatever I have planned for her.

Releasing her nipple, I free her hands after squeezing in warning. "Keep them there. This is my time to explore, to touch you," I order, then sit back and look over her heaving chest, her swollen lips, and her wild, lust-filled eyes. Wrapping my fingers around the zip, I decide to tease her.

"Want me to pull this down?"

She nods and then licks her lips. "Do it."

"No going back then, darling."

"There never was for us, so fuck me already," she purrs.

"So demanding, Peyton. Did you kiss Tyler with that mouth?" I tease as I yank the zipper down. Working together, we get her out of the suit. I sit back and take in her curvy body before leaning down and kissing the shark bite scar. I remember that—it was one of the scariest days of my life until now. We thought she had been seriously hurt, but she just laughed it off and downed a beer while we dressed the wound. I run my lips across the slight scar on her kneecap, which she got when the guideline snapped on a dive in the Caribbean.

Working my way up her body, I kiss near her wound where her latest batch of scars will be before finding the one on her shoulder from debris in a blowhole. I kiss each one, worshipping their beauty, because they make Peyton who she is. Each holds a story of us falling in love, of our life together, and I have never been so thankful for them as I am now.

"Strip," she demands, but stays put like a good girl.

I shift back so she can watch, and then I yank down my own suit and remove it. I place a knife near her head for protection, in case any of those creepy bat fuckers come while I'm taking my girl. Though I'm betting it's not the type of protection most concern themselves with in these situations.

Her eyes run down my body, leaving heat like an actual caress, lighting each nerve on fire with just one look as she lies splayed on the ground before me. When she meets my eyes again, she smirks and parts her thighs teasingly, making my hard cock bob against my stomach.

I wrap my hand around my hard length and stroke once, then twice, as she watches. She groans, sinking her teeth into her lower lip. "Shit, Fin."

"Yes, Pey?" I grin. "Like what you see?" She nods as I pump my hand down my cock again. "Hmm, what, no words? Does my big cock make you speechless?"

She grins, giggling softly as I smile. "Such a corny line. We aren't in a porno, so get your fine ass back down here."

Moving to my knees, I kiss along her leg. "So demanding," I whisper against her skin before dragging my tongue up her thigh to her pussy. "What if I have other plans, like tasting this pussy that's whipped both Kalen and Tyler?"

"I'm all for that," she rasps, widening her thighs and exposing her pink, wet sex for me. Licking my lips, I stare, unable to help myself. It's such a pretty pussy, and if she tastes half as good as I think, it's no wonder they follow her around like she's a dog in heat.

Groaning, I drop to my belly and bring my hands to her thighs, massaging the muscular flesh before pulling them over my shoulders to give me better access. I drag my fingers along the length of her wetness, part her lips, and stare greedily at her cunt, watching her hole pulse. She reaches down, and I snap my eyes back to hers. "Hands up, Peyton," I demand, and she complies with a huff. In reward, I flick her clit with my tongue.

She moans and pushes her pussy closer to my face. Chuckling, I run my tongue down her core and back up before flicking her clit again. I lash her, over and over, until she's moaning continually and lifting her hips to fuck her pussy against my face.

And goddamn, her taste.

She tastes like the ocean, fresh and so sweet, and I can't help but dip my tongue inside, searching for more of her cream.

Her eyes stay locked on mine as I gaze up her body. I can hardly believe this is happening. I've been waiting for this for so long, and now she's here. She's mine. Her pussy drips under my mouth, and her body is almost thrashing from her desire. My cock begs me to fuck her, claim her, and make her scream my name like she has my brothers'. But not yet. I want to watch her come all over my tongue first.

Then my fingers.

Only then will I take what she's offering.

Her pussy tastes like heaven, and I would die a happy man between her thighs. A roaring satisfaction fills me from knowing she wants this, wants me, even if she wants my brothers too. All these years of build-up, of teasing, has led to this moment, and I will burn every single fucking second into my brain. I will have her coming so hard that whenever she looks at me again, she won't see Fin, her best friend.

She'll see the man whose face she came all over.

Whose fingers she rode.

And whose cock fucked her so thoroughly, she could barely walk.

Her hips lift, grinding her pussy into my face. "That's it, darling, ride it. Let those bastards see your cream all over me."

That has her moaning as her head rolls from side to side, her thighs quivering on either side of me. She's close already. I can feel it. I can see the cream dripping from her tight little cunt. Her clit pulses as I wrap my lips around it and suck. I pull back before she can come, wanting to drag this out.

She whimpers as her pussy clenches. I don't stop, lashing her clit over and over before dragging my tongue down her wet heat and dipping it briefly inside her. When I feel her pussy flutter, I nip her clit, finally letting her come. She screams her release, clamps her thighs around my head, and grinds her pussy into my mouth, smearing her cream across my face.

Fuck yes.

I lap at her, licking up her release. She tastes so fucking good. When she collapses, I lift my head and meet her eyes. "Orgasm one. You came so fucking prettily, Pey." I trail my fingers down her raw pussy, and she whimpers as I circle her hole. "Now you're going to do that again around my fingers. Let me feel that tight cunt clamped around them. I want to hear my new favourite sound—your screams."

She shakes her head. "Fin."

"Nope." I pop her thigh with my other hand. "I've waited years for this, darling, so be a good girl and come around my fingers."

"Such a hardship," she mutters. "Better make me, then."

Smirking, I press two fingers against her hole, and when her eyes meet mine, I thrust them inside. She groans as I turn them, rubbing along her front wall until she gasps. "You were saying, darling?" I tease as I pull out and slam back in, fucking her with my fingers. "I wonder if Tyler fucks you like this . . . or Kalen. Did they, darling? Did you come all over their fingers for them?" She gulps, averting her gaze for a moment. "Nope, don't look away," I snap, and punish her by pulling out and spanking her pussy, making her cry out.

"Want to know what I think?" She looks back at me then. "I think you want all of us to fuck you, always did. You love the idea." She opens her mouth to talk, but I plunge my fingers back inside of her, three this time, stretching her. "You can't lie to me, Pey, not with my fingers in your cunt. It's clamping around them so tightly from the thought."

She purses her lips, remaining silent as she tries to resist me while I fuck her with them. We agreed to share, and she needs to know it's coming. I need her to accept her own feelings and not be ashamed of them before we get back. I don't care if she wants to fuck my brothers—hell, it's kinda hot—but she needs to feel the same. I need her to understand it's okay, to stop worrying what we think and take what she wants.

"Is that what you want, Peyton? For all of us to fuck you? What about at the same time?" I tease as she gasps. "Oh yeah, you like that idea. Your body can't lie to me. Want to know a secret? I have fantasies about fucking this sweet little pussy while Riggs fucks your ass. We even talked about it once." I chuckle as her eyes flare wide. "Oh yes, little innocent Riggs. He has such dirty things he wants to do to you. You thought he was so nice, but as soon as you left the room, his hand was on his cock or he was describing his fantasies about you. All the naughty, depraved things." Her pussy clenches around my fingers with my declaration. I lean down and kiss her clit.

"Fuck, you love that. Knowing that after your innocent, friendly cuddles and interactions, he fucks himself? Yeah, you thought I was going to be the one to wreck your body, but baby, Riggs is going to ruin you. All those years of pent-up desire? He's going to make you feel every second of it, and I will be there to watch you come apart for him, for us, again and again. You have no idea what you have unleashed, Peyton Andrews. You created possessive, lust-filled monsters in all of us."

I slam my fingers into her on the last word, and she cries out, lifting her hips to meet each thrust. Her tight channel clamps around them, trying to keep them inside of her as I kiss her clit. Her cream drips from her hole, and my cock throbs at the sight, wanting to be buried inside her, but I want to feel her come on my fingers first.

"Yes, okay!" she finally admits when I don't stop. "I want to fuck all of you. I want to ride you knowing they're watching. I want to see if Riggs is as restrained when we fuck. I want Tyler to watch me fuck his friends before I fuck him." Her eyes meet mine. "I want each and every single one of you, and I will have you."

"About fucking time," I mutter and then grin as I teasingly lick her clit. Pulling my fingers free, I spank her pussy again. "Next time you see them, you tell them that," I order as I lift my cream-covered fingers into the air, studying her as I suck them clean. My eyes close on a groan as her taste explodes across my tongue again. "Fuck, no wonder you and Tyler were always fucking. I bet he couldn't get enough of this pussy. I haven't even had you yet, and I'm addicted."

She finally raises her hands from the ground, then trails them down her body to her pussy, framing it as she teasingly strokes herself. "Then stop fucking talking. I want to come, so get your fucking fingers back inside of me before I do it myself."

"Yes, darling, as you command." I grin as I lie as flat as I can, pressing my fingers back into her pussy. Her hand twines in my hair, yanking me closer. I lick her clit while I fuck her, speeding up until she comes all over my hand. Her tight cunt clamps so hard, I can't pull free. Her legs wrap around my head, holding me there as she grinds into my face.

When the aftershocks roll through her body, she releases me, and I sit back on my heels. I grab her shaking thighs and yank them up so her bare feet are pressed against my shoulders. Her eyes are closed, and her mouth is slack in pleasure, but when I press my cock to her pussy and slide it up and down her raw sex, coating it in her cream, they flicker open and clash with mine.

I see the anticipation there, the desire, the love. Leaning down, I kiss her softly. "I love you too, Pey," I whisper before I kiss her again, sealing my lips to hers as I notch the head of my dick at her entrance. In one smooth thrust, I bury my length inside her. I swallow her gasp as I force myself through her tight channel until I bottom out. It's my turn to groan then as a shiver moves through me. She's so fucking tight, wet, and hot.

Shit.

How the fuck am I supposed to last when her pussy is heaven?

It's never felt like this, as if every sensation is enhanced. I break our kiss, trying to control my breathing as I pull out and slam back in. I attempt to go slow, I really do, but she doesn't allow it. She lifts her hips to meet my thrusts, urging me on. Her hands cup her swaying breasts and squeeze as she tweaks her nipples. The sight makes me wild.

"Fuck, Pey," I growl, closing my eyes as I start to pound into her. She takes every thrust and begs for more. "You're going to have me coming like a fucking virgin," I rasp.

She laughs, but the sound tapers off into a moan as I spank her pussy. She clenches around me from the action, so I do it again and again until she's crying out continuously. "Fuck, fuck, fuck," she whispers raggedly. "Fin. Oh God, please."

"Now who sounds like a porn star?" I grit out through clenched teeth, trying to ignore the pleasure surging through me, wanting it to last.

"Harder," she demands.

Fuck this.

I pull out, and uncaring about everything else, I flip her. She lands on her hands and knees, her pert ass in the air. *Later*, I remind myself as I yank her hips back and slam home. She screams, clawing at the rock as she pushes back to meet my brutal thrusts. Years of desire come out through each and every one. Branding myself across her skin, I dig my hands into her hips so hard, she'll have bruises.

Good, let them see.

Bringing my hand down on her ass, I watch her jolt and cry out. Her skin reddens, and I resist doing it again. After all, we're trapped in a cave, so there isn't much time for aftercare. Instead, I part her ass cheeks and slip my finger down her crevice, never once stopping my thrusts. "Next time, I get your tight little ass. I want to watch my cum drip from it while you ride Riggs," I rumble, my voice rough and low.

"Fuck yes," she cries out. "Do it."

Not even my brothers could stop me now. Or those bat motherfuckers. I would happily die buried in her pussy with her curves in my hands and my name on her lips.

My rhythm falters as I imagine doing just as I said I would. I can barely breathe now, the pleasure is too much, and I know I'm going to come, but not without her. Reaching down, I flick her clit once, twice, three times. She comes with a scream, her pussy milking my cock. And with my own roar, I slam into her, plunging as far as I can go as my orgasm explodes from me. The pleasure is so great, I almost black out.

Panting, I lean against her sweaty back, unable to move or speak. She whimpers, her pussy pulsing around my softening cock as I slide free. "Shit, Pey," I mutter before I drop a kiss on her spine. "You're going to kill me. Kill us."

"Death by pussy," she teases as she slumps forward and turns over. I lie next to her, pulling her into my arms. She meets my eyes as I stroke her cheek and kiss her softly. "You okay? I didn't rip your wound?"

"I'm fine, Fin." She grins as she leans up and pecks me on the lips. "I love you too."

I swallow, searching her eyes as my heart skips a beat. "You mean it?"

"Always have," she whispers. "Always will."

"Always is a long time, darling. I should warn you not to promise someone your forever," I hedge, trying to protect her, to give her an out. "But I can't. I don't know how to live without you, I don't know how long our lives are going to be, and I don't know if we'll get out of here, but the one thing I'm certain about, Peyton Andrews, is you. Always you. So whether it's a day, a month, or fifty years, I'm here. I'm forever."

Tears fill her eyes, and her lips tilt up. "Look who's a secret romantic," she teases. "I feel the same, Fin. You have always been my family. It's always been us against the world, and I missed you all so much. I know one thing for certain, I don't want to live without any of you again. Not ever." She leans up and kisses me. "I'm going to tell them you're a soppy bastard."

I narrow my eyes, sliding my hands down her back to cup her ass. "You do, and I'll bend you over and fuck you right in front of them," I promise.

"Sounds good to me," she whispers.

To me too.

Here, in the beast of a cave system, I finally find what I have always been looking for—the love that was right in front of us for so long. Only this time, we are strong enough to reach for it.

True love isn't just a myth or a chemical reaction . . . it's everything.

It's her smile. It's her laugh. It's her bad days. It's her good days. It's her support, her passion, her strength. It's her brain and her beauty. It's her.

Always has been.

Always will be.

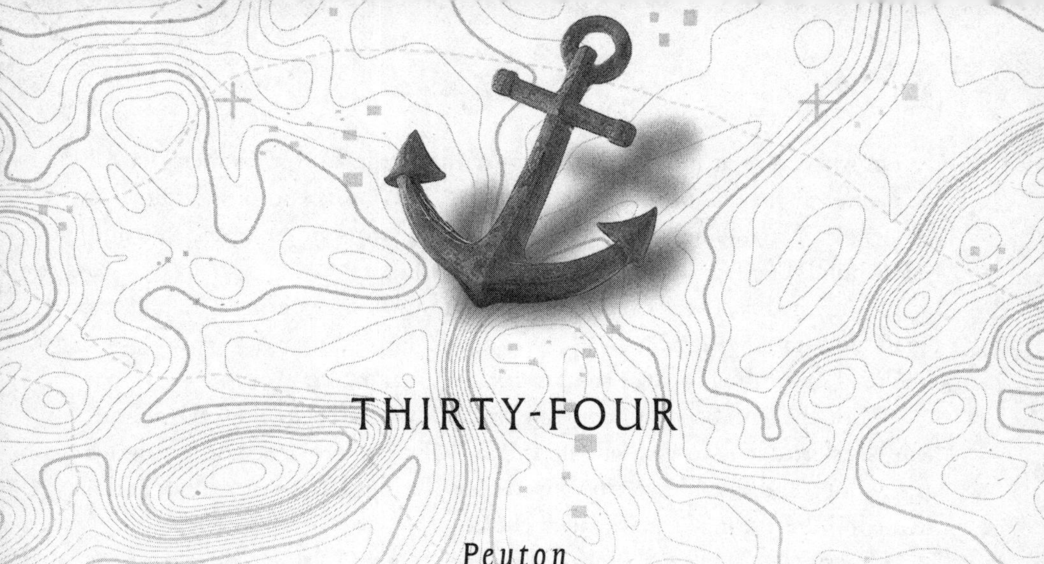

THIRTY-FOUR

Peyton

I can't stop touching him to assure myself he's really here. More than that, he's okay . . . and he loves me. I know we need to get back, the others must be worried sick, and we have monsters to fight off, but for a moment, I just lie in his arms and close my eyes. For the first time since I jumped to save Kalen, I relax, knowing I'm safe in Fin's embrace. His lips brush across my head, and his arms are wrapped around me so tightly, it's like he'll never let me go again. That's okay with me, I don't ever want to be free of him.

Of all of them.

The radio crackles to life then, and I smirk. "I'm surprised they left us this long," I murmur, making him chuckle as he drops a kiss on my head, then another on my upturned lips.

"I am too. We better get back to them before they tear these caves down looking for you," he whispers.

Sighing, I get to my knees, wincing at my sore body—not from Fin, but from swimming, climbing, and surviving. When all of this is over, I need a spa day . . . Okay, that's a fucking lie. Knowing me, I will be diving the next day. Fin gets to his knees too, and checks my side, which he bandaged before. With a happy nod, he grips my chin and kisses me firmly, his soft lips harsh against mine in a claiming caress.

I can hold my breath for eleven minutes, yet these men steal that ability from me. They leave me breathless in a way no ocean or cave ever could.

"Remember that when we get back." He grins before grabbing the comms. "Yes?"

"Are you okay . . . Both of you?" Riggs asks nervously, making me smirk.

"Yes, we're fine. We're coming back now," Fin replies, then grouses, "So needy."

"Shut up, asshole. Bring our girl back," Tyler orders, and I raise my eyebrows at his word choice.

Fin winks over at me. "Oh yeah, you're in for a few surprises there, babe." He glances at the equipment, then meets my gaze. "The end of the tunnel is submerged. We're going to the advanced base we set up in the cavern you and Kalen found, but you don't have a tank or a mask."

Licking my lips, I look over the equipment, my mind whirling with plans as I grab the comms. "Riggs?"

"Yes, beautiful?" His voice sounds instantly, making me grin.

"Work the numbers for me. Can we buddy breathe to the cavern from here?" I ask and look to Fin, who nods. He's willing to give it a shot. It's always a risky thing and should never be done unless it's your last resort . . . but at the moment, I don't think we have much choice.

"One sec," he murmurs, already distracted. Fin and I wait, and a moment later, he comes back. "Yes, it's possible . . . But, Pey, it's dangerous."

"I know." I sigh and look at Fin. "It's your choice."

"Share air with you, sexy? No choice." He smirks and stands. "Let's do this. Riggs, we're coming back."

"Understood—"

"Princess, don't do any stupid shit. Leave his ass if you need to," Kalen jokes.

Fin's mouth drops open as I laugh. "I see how it is. It's the vagina, isn't it? Or is it the boobs?" He glances over as he speaks. "Definitely the boobs, though I think you might be an ass man—"

"Stop," Tyler barks. "Christ, he looks ready to murder you. Get your asses back here, both of you, safe and sound, or you won't have to worry about the monsters—I'll kill you myself." There is a moment of silence. "Kalen is meeting you in the junction before the cavern we're in to watch your backs. Peyton"—he sucks in a breath—"see you soon," he finishes lamely, and we all know that wasn't what he wanted to say.

Tyler is struggling with his anger towards me right now, so I can understand where he's at. Maybe he just needs to fuck it all out. Sounds like good therapy to me. Climbing to my feet, I face Fin, who helps me back into my suit, and we test the tanks and his mask. My suit is ripped, but we don't have far to go, and it's better than being half naked in the cold water. "Okay, it's only towards the end. Until then, we can breathe without masks," he explains as he straps us together just in case a monster or draft pulls us apart while breathing. It's loose enough so we can swim side by side or behind each other.

"We get through fast and meet them." He cups my cheeks. "Stay close. One breath each?"

"We've got this," I state with a grin as I grab my knife. "Just in case we see those bat motherfuckers."

He groans and leans in and kisses me. "So fucking hot. Come on, then, darling, let's get you back to your other men."

As he puts on his flippers, I climb into the water first. Fin follows after, turning on his torch as he takes the lead. Each kick of my leg pulls on my aching side, but it's not going to get any better, so I ignore it.

He guides me through an entrance to a tunnel. It's easy to get through for a while, and then it starts to get tighter and tighter. Luckily, we get through, and when we reach the end, I suck in a breath as we reach the junction into the underwater section. We swim hard through that part, and I hold my breath the entire time, not wanting to risk passing the tank back until it breaks into a bigger area. When we reach the entrance to the junction, Fin takes in air and passes the tank back, and I draw a big breath as I look around, the torch illuminating the underwater area.

It's the place Kalen and I found at the beginning. We float there, kicking, not connecting to the guideline for a moment. I try to pass the tank back, but Fin turns, ignoring me, and begins to lead the way. Rolling my eyes, I follow after him, tank in one hand, knife in the other. I watch his back and mine as he watches our fronts. They could still come from below and above, and that has us on edge as we cross the giant cavern. We pass the tank back and forth after I insist, and each and every disturbance of the water has me turning around, wanting to kill some monsters.

The swim must only take a few minutes, but it feels like a lifetime before I spot the other torch shining from somewhere in front of us. We head that way, closer and closer, until I can finally make out Kalen. His legs are kicking slowly, a line connecting him, anchoring him, and his eyes are narrowed as he watches us approach. His gaze darts behind and around us constantly, looking for danger.

I draw from the tank, pass it back to Fin, and then speed past him to Kalen. He grabs me with one arm, pressing his mask-covered face to mine for a moment. The dark water around us is still and quiet apart from the sound of the tanks and machines. I kiss his mask, and his lips quirk up as I pull away. He pushes me past him towards the advanced base, and I go willingly. Fin follows behind me with Kalen taking up the rear.

I only take one more draw from the tank before passing it back to Fin, not wanting to risk his lungs. I kick hard, my arms cutting through the water. Nerves and excitement fill me, each movement bringing me one stroke closer to my men. My family.

I'm almost there.

I never thought I would see them again, and now only this bit of water separates us. I'm desperate to hold them, to kiss them and never leave their sides again. That urgency fills me until I break through the water with a gasp, and there, waiting at the edge, are my men.

Tyler and Riggs.

Their expressions are worried, they have bags under their eyes, and their hands are clenched into fists.

Standing side by side, they're waiting for me.

Always.

THIRTY-FIVE

I'm pulled from the water and drawn into waiting arms. Both men surround me, their lips running across my face and cheeks. Their hands trail across my body in worry, their voices mixing as they speak, and a moment later, Kalen joins us. Tears fill my eyes, and my body shakes from exhaustion, fear, and happiness, until Fin's voice breaks us apart.

"I'm okay too," he jokes.

Laughing, I pull back and wipe my eyes.

Kalen cradles my jaw and searches my face. "You sure you're okay, babe? I was so fucking scared when I saw you—" He stops, sucking in a breath, and I nod in his grip.

"I'm okay."

He swallows hard, leans in, and kisses me so softly I start to cry. When he pulls away, his eyes turn dark and angry again, his lips thinning. "You pull a stunt like that again, Andrews, and I'll kill you myself. You hear me?" he snaps.

Grinning, I lean into his touch. "I hear ya."

"Good," he mutters and then kisses me again. "Fucking brat," he murmurs as he pulls away, and I'm turned towards Riggs, who opens his arms. I rush into them, accepting the hug. This time, he holds me tighter than he has before, his lips pressing to my wet hair repeatedly like he can't believe I'm here.

"I'm so glad you're okay," he whispers as I fist his suit and hold on to him.

"Me too," I murmur, and then I pull away to see Tyler watching us. He has a strange expression on his face, a mixture of hope, pain, and jealousy.

"You need to rest," he barks, crossing his arms, and I slump. I guess I shouldn't have expected a warm welcome, but still . . . I suppose almost dying doesn't earn my forgiveness. He looks me over then, and his eyes soften for a moment. "You're shivering. Are you cold?"

"Freezing." I nod. "I've been in and out of the water since I fell, not to mention shock and blood loss." Years of telling the truth in stressful situations comes into play. It's not for sympathy; it's so they know the full extent of my body's pressure and how to plan around it.

"Kalen, get a fire started. Riggs, grab the thermals and blanket. Fin, help her from her suit; she needs to warm up and get as dry as possible." He points his finger in my face, stepping closer. "No shit or attitude. You're going to rest, understood?"

"Understood." I grin. "Thank you for coming for me," I tell him softly as the others move away on his orders and to give us privacy. For a moment, all those emotions drop from his eyes and before me is my Tyler.

"Always, you know that," he replies softly, his hand coming up as if to cup my face before he drops it and sighs. "I don't know how to do this."

"Do what?" I ask in confusion as I step closer, taking a chance while he seems to have let his guard down.

"Be with you again." He glances away, scrubbing at his black hair. "I want to— I promised myself if we found you again, I would never let you go. But then I look at you, and I'm still so angry . . ."

"I get that," I reply, and he looks back at me in shock. "I do, Tyler. I just hope you find a way around it because I miss you. I really miss you, and when I thought I might die, all I could think about was telling you I love you. Always have and always will. It's always been you, Tyler, since I was a goddamn snot-nosed teenager following you around. But it's them as well." I look over to see my other men. "I didn't mean to fall in love with them, it just happened." I meet Ty's azure eyes again. "I can't change that, and I wouldn't if I could. I just hope I'm worthy enough for you to fight for. Maybe it's the time the past died. In this cave, we found the light, a new future." When I finish speaking, I leave him to his thoughts.

Only he can decide what he wants to do. In his eyes, I saw what he wanted—me, this. Yet his own fear—the fear I put there—of being hurt and rejected again is stopping him, and my own heart cracks at that. It's not easy, and I should stop pushing, but I can't. I want him, I love him, and one way or another, we're leaving this cave together. Even if I have to take a million of his punishments and bear the brunt of his anger.

Kalen has the fire structure sorted, so I head over. Riggs is close by, helping set up the aluminium blankets and dry clothes. Fin's just waiting, his eyes sliding to Tyler, then back to me. "Keep pushing, babe, he needs it. You should have seen him when we thought—" He sucks in a breath. "Well, you should have seen him. That man still loves you; he's just confused." He winces and then nods at me. "Let's get those damp clothes off. He's right—we need to get you dry and warm before you get hypothermia."

I nod and try to unzip my suit, but my hands are numb and my body is trembling. It seems finding them again has caused all the adrenaline fuelling me to stop, and I suddenly feel like I might collapse. Fin notices, as does Kalen, who lights the fire before coming over and standing behind me. He props me up as Fin unzips my suit and starts to tug it down. Kalen helps him get it over my chest, and then he drops to his knees to slide it over my ass and off each leg. Fin is on his knees too, his eyes on mine as he drags it off my toes before cupping them to warm them up as Kalen wraps his arms around me.

"She's freezing. We can't let her get too warm too fast or it will stop her heart. Get your asses over here," Kalen demands.

They rush over to help, but I can't stop shivering now. My bra and panties are taken away so I'm nude. Kalen strips from his suit, as does Fin, and they help me into the blanket. Kalen pulls me into his arms, and Fin steps to my other side, but Tyler jerks his head. Fin wraps around my legs instead, his head above my pussy. "I prefer being here anyway," he teases as I close my eyes and clench my teeth to stop the chattering. Tyler pulls off his shirt and lies down next to me, wrapping around my other side. Riggs closes the blanket around us and sits behind me, propping me up with my head on his chest.

"That's it, baby, let us warm you," Kalen murmurs, stroking my skin. Their bodies feel like they are blazing, but I know they are just a normal temperature. Fin runs his hands up and down my legs and to my toes.

Tyler clutches my hands, blows on them, and rubs them together before holding them between his as I lie there in a huddle. I'm still shivering, and I try not to complain, but my brain is running through all the negative scenarios. Getting hypothermia down here would be a death sentence, and my men wouldn't leave me, even Tyler. So I have to be strong, which means I need to stop imagining things that may never happen.

"Distract me," I beg, my voice weak.

"Like with my cock?" Fin teases, and Tyler kicks him, making me giggle as he lets out a fake cry.

"There's an eighty percent—" Riggs starts, and Tyler hits him too.

"You are both idiots." He sighs, and I grin as I snuggle closer to Tyler. He traps my hands between us, and they catch on the ring still hanging around his neck. My eyes open, and I look up to see his blue gaze glancing from me to the jewellery. Something passes across his features, and his lips twist down for a moment before he shakes his head.

"I wear it still . . ."

I close my eyes, hearing the pain and longing in his voice. "Ty," I whisper, pressing closer, "you don't need to."

"I do," he murmurs and holds me closer. His eyes flick between mine. "I need you to know . . . I can't hold it all in anymore. I wear it to remind me how easy it is to lose those I love, to lose the best thing to ever happen to me." His voice catches, and I feel like crying as his lips tip up unhappily. His pain is evident, filling those blue depths. I could swim in his fucking tears, tears I put there.

"I thought it was to remind you how much you hate me," I reply, my words choked by my own regrets and longing. To be this close to him, to see that love there in his eyes, fills me with hope.

"I did at the beginning. It's a reminder to never be so blind again, to not be so oblivious to what's right in front of me." His gaze goes to the others. Does he mean what I think he does? He looks back at me sadly and cups my cheek. "To never be so selfish again. I lost you once, Peyton Andrews, and no matter what's happened or my own messed up feelings, there's one thing I know—I want this, I want our family to be whole again, and if that means I finally have to accept what was there all along, then I will."

"That is?" I press, feeling the others wanting to ask also, but they remain quiet.

"Our love. Not just yours and mine. Kalen's and yours. Fin's and yours. Riggs's and yours. I love you all, I do, so why shouldn't you feel the same?" He winces. "I'm not saying I'll be okay all the time, I'm still struggling, but I want to be. I want to be okay. I don't ever want to be the reason any of you are unhappy. I'm over that. Maybe we needed to break apart to come back together again so it could heal in a way it never could before. So I could see our future clearly. All of ours." He gives me a tender, lingering kiss, and I taste the truth on his lips.

Tyler is still mine. Always has been, always will be. And right now, he's regifting me with that broken heart of his, trusting me with it once again. This time, however, he knows my hands are filled with the others' hearts as well.

Can I be woman enough to juggle them all?

"When we get free of this hellhole, we start again," he whispers against my lips.

"Just five apex predators," I tease, and he grins, his lips curving against mine.

"You know it, Peyton. Now rest, that's an order," he murmurs before kissing me again.

I close my eyes, and for the first time in three years, my heart is full.

Healed.

Loved.

"I swear to fuck, Riggs, that better be your ice pick," Kalen snarls, and we all laugh, the loud sound of happiness startling us.

I listen to their banter and laughter as I drift off to sleep in their arms with a smile on my lips. I missed this—friendship and family. I could never leave them again. Tyler may be right—maybe I had to leave so I could find what I really wanted, and when I came back, we were all ready.

To be together.

To be one.

Because this diver's heart is owned by every single man surrounding me.

Forever.

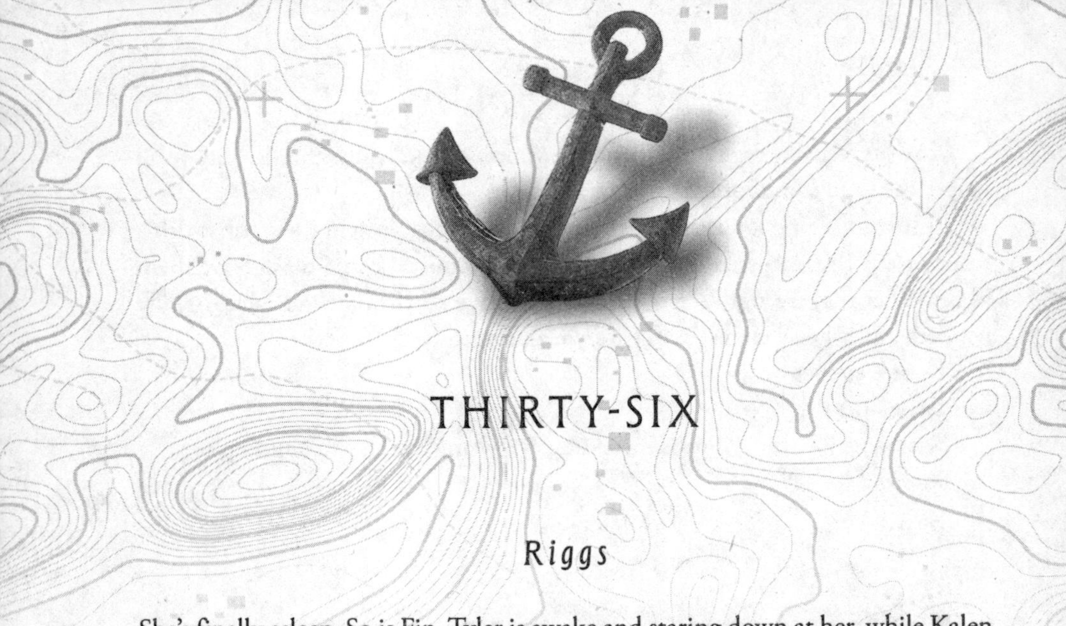

THIRTY-SIX

Riggs

She's finally asleep. So is Fin. Tyler is awake and staring down at her, while Kalen refuses to let her go, holding her so tight, like a teddy bear, it has to hurt—not that she complained. She stopped shivering thirty minutes ago, which is good. I think she's out of danger of having hypothermia.

I slip from behind her, causing her to grumble, and then I move silently away and whisper through the radio, giving the others an update, before walking away, needing to piss.

Taking a torch with me, I head behind the rock we found. It's more like another cave section, apart from the fact there is only one entrance and a hole in the back, with a running stream trickling into it, that we're using for the toilet. The same bugs light up the ceiling, making it look like stars scattered in the night sky, as I place the torch onto a rock and shine it up so I can see. It's still dark but not pitch black at least. After pissing, I'm washing my hands when I hear footsteps.

I turn, and a moment later Peyton enters the cave. She's fully awake now and still naked, though she doesn't seem to notice or care. "You okay, Pey?" I ask worriedly, shaking my hands to get rid of the water as I step closer.

She nods. "Fine, I promise, but I woke up and you were gone."

"Sorry, I needed the bathroom," I say as I stop before her. She tilts her head back and smiles at me, and I can't help but smile back and reach out to cup her cheek, knowing I can now—especially after Tyler's confession. She sighs and leans into my touch, shivering, so I wrap my arms around her and kiss her head as she stands in my arms.

"I missed you," I whisper.

"I missed you too," she replies, kissing my shoulder as she moves closer, pressing every inch of her beautiful body against mine. Holding back my groan, I close my eyes and try to behave, even as my cock hardens. All the dirty things I have ever wanted to do to her flash through my head. She leans back, enough to meet my gaze as I watch her. "I'm glad everything is finally out." She swallows. "I didn't expect this though, I've always felt so guilty for wanting all of you," she confesses, slipping into her old habit of always telling me her innermost fears and secrets.

"You deserve all the love, Peyton, you always did. One man would never be enough for you. How could he be? You deserve love deeper than any stream. You deserve an ocean, and we're going to give it to you. No more running. No more hesitating. We're all in this time, and if we never get free from this cave, you will know just how fucking loved you are. We live, we die, we explore together always," I tell her, and her lips tip up in a slow grin before she leans up for a kiss. I tilt my head down and softly press my lips to hers.

At the first taste of her, I groan and pull back. "If I kiss you, Pey, I won't stop," I admit, and with a slight blush and a smirk, I step away, dropping my arms. "Not with you naked and offering me everything I have ever wanted and dreamed of. And you need to rest—"

"Fuck rest," she snarls. "I've been away for three years, and you're telling me you don't want to do anything? You want to put me back to bed?" She arches her eyebrow, and I narrow my eyes. "I'm disappointed, I have to admit. Fin promised me you'd do all these dirty things." She shrugs. "Okay, then." She turns away, and I know she's pushing me on purpose.

And it's working.

I catch her before she leaves, wrapping my hand around her neck from behind, and then I pull her back until that pert fucking ass presses against my hard cock and her body is plastered to mine. She's all soft curves and hard muscles. "Don't tempt me, Peyton. I've been imagining all the ways I would fuck you for years, but I know we have the rest of our lives for that. I just want to make sure you're okay *now*. Your well-being and wants always come before my own desires or needs."

"I'm sick of that. I love how you look after me, I do, Riggs, but take what you want for once. Stop being so worried about what everyone else thinks." She turns to face me, meeting my eyes. "What do you want?"

I'm nearly vibrating with the desire I can't contain anymore. Not with her looking at me like that. "You," I growl and drag her closer, smashing my lips to hers. She groans into my mouth, grabbing my shirt as she goes up on her toes and presses closer. Her tongue tangles with mine, but I don't let her lead. No, I make her play catch-up as I dominate her mouth. I may be sweet, I may love her deeply and be her best friend, but Peyton never knew the extent of my obsession with her, or all the things I wanted to do with this body of hers.

She's unaware of the naughty, depraved thoughts I had about her—still have about her—and now she's giving me permission to do whatever the fuck I want. She may live to regret that when she can't walk, never mind swim, tomorrow.

She's right, however, I'm tired of holding back. I push away all the numbers crowding my mind and lose myself in the taste of her. The taste of my girl. My fucking girl. Even thinking of my claim on her sends desire surging through me.

She's mine now, and it's time she experienced what that means.

Releasing her neck, I slide my hand down her back and cup her ass, squeezing it before lifting her effortlessly. She gasps into my mouth, and I swallow it as I turn and press her into the closest wall, her legs wrapping around my waist.

She bites my lower lip, and I grip her hip tighter until she releases it as I pull back. "Want to play like that, baby?" I murmur, gripping her chin. I turn her head to the side as I lick and kiss her neck before scraping my teeth down to her pounding pulse, and then I bite. It's soft at first before I slowly apply more pressure. She cries out from the pain, even as her hips rub against me, wanting more.

"Riggs," she moans, the sound breathy and going straight to my rock-hard cock. I imagine her making that noise around my length as I force it down her throat.

"I'm going to fuck you hard, princess, but not before your cream covers my face like a goddamn shower, you understand me? All over my fucking tongue and face." I squeeze her throat until her eyes lock on me, and she bites down on her lip.

She nods, and I nip her ear hard, punishing her. "Peyton . . ."

"Yes," she hisses as I run my hand up her thigh to her wet pussy.

Her eyes squeeze shut, so I strengthen my hold on her throat until they open again and meet mine. She will watch me as I touch her, taste her, and take her for the first time. She will view my every move while we experience this together. "Eyes on me, baby, so you know who's touching you, tasting you, and making you scream your release until your legs give out."

She groans and arches into my touch, rubbing her pussy on my hand to try to get me to move. Chuckling, I spank her pussy in reprimand, and when she cries out, I drag my fingers down her lips, parting them before sliding them across her wetness and flicking her clit in reward.

"I've been imagining touching this cunt for years," I tell her as I feel her heartbeat thumping against my hand around her throat. I slowly rub her clit as I speak calmly, honestly. It's the only other time outside of numbers I ever do—with her. "Tasting it, watching it turn pink from my tongue, that pretty little hole pulsing as I fuck it . . ."

"Riggs," she breathes, arching higher into my touch as she tries to grind herself against my hand. I pull away slightly, stroking around her clit until she sags, and then I return to rubbing her methodically—slow enough to build her up, but not fast enough to send her over the edge. I keep her there, caught between pleasure and frustration. Her eyes flash in defiance, but she doesn't try to stop me.

"I carefully planned each moment," I carry on. "Visualising every possible way I could touch you, imagining how your cunt would taste." Trailing my fingers down, I dip them inside her and fuck her with them twice, stretching her around them as she whimpers before I suddenly pull them out and she growls in frustration. I raise my hand to my mouth and suck my fingers clean, and now it's my turn to groan. My eyes close in bliss—she tastes like freedom, like that feeling when a dive goes perfect, or when the numbers match up.

She tastes like perfection.

Opening my eyes, I slam her harder into the wall, careful of her injuries. "Don't fucking move," I demand as I drop to my knees and rip open her thighs. I'm wild with the need to taste more of her, to feel her cream drip across my tongue and lips. I stare at her pretty pink pussy, the light allowing me to see it, and her throbbing clit. Her pulsing, pretty little hole, which I'm going to fill, glistens, clearly showing me her desire.

She buries her fingers in my hair, trying to pull me closer, but I resist. The slight tug of pain makes my grip tighten until I know it will bruise. When she stops trying to control me, I lean in and lick a long line from the top of her pussy to her ass, tasting every inch of her. I do it again and again before dipping my tongue inside of her, seeking more of her delicious nectar.

She whispers my name, rolling her hips as she tries to find her release, but she will only get it when I'm good and ready, and I'm not yet. Circling her clit, I tease her with my tongue before flattening it and dragging it over her nub, back and forth, and then I suck it into my mouth and hum. She jerks in my grip, crying out as I suck it hard before popping it free and blowing my breath across it.

"Oh God, please!" she begs.

Grinning, I lap at her clit as I trail my fingers up her thigh to her cunt and dip them into her, holding them there while I consume her. She clenches around my digits, and I know she's close, so I curl my fingers, stroking her walls as I lash her clit, forcing her to reach her orgasm.

"Come for me," I murmur against her intimate flesh. "Let it coat my fingers and tongue."

She tugs at my hair, moving her hips, then she suddenly cries out as her pussy clamps on my fingers, trying to keep them inside of her as she rides through her release. I lick her gently, softly, until she slumps away from me, and then I pull my fingers free and suck them clean before licking her hole, tasting her release, before I sit back and stare up at her.

Her chest is flushed, cheeks too, and her mouth is parted as she pants. She stares down at me like she's never seen me before. "First of many, babe. We have years to make up for."

"Hell yes," she mumbles and strokes my face, cupping my cheek as her thumb rubs my wet lips. "Fuck me, Riggs, like we've always wanted. I'm tired of waiting. I want you."

It's all she has to say. I surge to my feet and kiss her, letting her taste herself on my lips and tongue as I back her into the wall again. I capture her hands and raise them, twining our fingers together as we kiss deeply.

I want to look into her eyes the first time I thrust into her though, so I pull away, breathing heavily myself, as she hooks a leg around my waist, opening her pussy to me. I reach down and stroke my hard cock before pressing it to her entrance. Her eyes tighten slightly, her lips curling up. "I love you," she whispers, and I slam into her with one smooth thrust, burying myself in her tight cunt.

Both of us groan, and my eyes nearly cross. She's so fucking tight, so wet and hot. She feels like a silken glove around my cock, and when she moans, it vibrates through her, going straight to my balls until I have to move. I have to, or I'll explode from one thrust like a virgin. I pull out and push back in, slowly at first before speeding up, aware the others could wake at any time and come find us.

Let them. Let them watch me fuck my girl.

She may be theirs, but she's mine right now. She's taking my cock, kissing my mouth, and caressing my skin.

Mine.

She gasps against my lips and tightens her hands around mine as we move together. Years of repressed desire explode through us, and we can't get enough. Our kiss is sloppy as our skin rubs together, and the sound of our slapping bodies is loud in the little cavern.

"More," she demands, and what my girl wants, she gets.

Pulling from her pussy, I quickly turn her and press her chest into the wall. I kick open her legs and lean down to whisper in her ear. "Don't move or I stop, do you understand?"

She nods as I pull her ass out, grip her hips, and slam into her again. I hammer into her from behind, angling my cock so it hits that spot that has her moaning continually as her hands scratch at the walls and she pushes her ass back to meet my thrusts.

She's a fucking sight to behold. Her tight, perky ass. All those muscles, that strength, yet such softness, such submission and heat. It has my balls drawing up and my spine nearly bowing as I hold back my release, wanting to feel hers around my dick first.

"Riggs—" Her breath hitches as I slam into her. "I'm so close—please—I need—" Her plea ends in a scream as I pinch her clit, sending her over that edge once more.

Her tight pussy clamps around me like a vise as I struggle to pull out and push back in, pulling my release from me. I explode inside of her, filling her with my cum as I plaster myself to her back, feeling her body quiver as I fight to stay upright. We're both spent and panting as I lean into her back, kissing her shoulder, unable to move.

"I love you too, Peyton," I murmur. "You're the perfect equation."

Her head turns slightly, and I see her smile, even as her eyes remain closed, and for a stolen moment, we just stand here, connected and in love.

"Oi, fuckers. Captain Cock is waking up, so you might wanna hurry up and get dressed. I have a feeling he won't be as kind about seeing the whole sharing thing." Fin laughs, and then I hear him wander away.

"How long was he standing there?" Peyton asks with a snigger.

"Who knows? He's always been a pervert." I grin as I pull out of her body and tuck my cock away before turning her. I cup her cheeks as I kiss her soundly, and then I kiss her eyes and cheeks too. "Come on, beautiful, let's get you back in there and find something to eat and drink. You need the energy."

I help her wash in the stream, and hand in hand, we head back to the others.

THIRTY-SEVEN

Peyton

I'm naked. Everyone turns to me as I walk out holding hands with Riggs. Kalen's eyes narrow before running down me. Fin whistles and fake slaps my ass. Tyler . . . Tyler's eyes flash with jealousy before he turns away, hunching over the fire he's starting. I frown and share a look with Riggs. We communicate through that one action, and then he nods, lifts my hand, and kisses my knuckles before letting go. My heart flutters from the gesture. Smiling, I head over to Tyler and stroke my hand down his shoulder. "Can we talk?"

"Kinda busy, baby," he grumbles, the endearment slipping free before he sighs.

"Please?" I ask sweetly, knowing he's pissed.

"Kay, come do the fire so Tyler can stop ignoring me," I request. Kalen snorts but comes over, relieving Tyler, who stands back. He continues to ignore me before he rounds his shoulders, looks at me, nods his head to the side, and then storms away. I follow, sharing a look with Fin, who shoots me a thumbs-up for good luck.

We walk past the stalagmites and rocks in the corner, and then Tyler leans back against them.

"What, Andrews?" he snaps. Okay, so we're back to using my last name. He's mad. I get it. I fucked Riggs, and he knows that.

"You can be mad, it's okay," I tell him as I step closer. He flinches when I lay my hands on his chest, grinding his jaw as he usually does when he's trying to bite his tongue. "I fucked him." He flinches again like I slapped him, and I smile but refuse to soften the blow. If this is going to work, he needs to know what's going to happen. If he can't handle it now . . . I need to know. I don't know if I can step back from loving the others when I'm this close to having what I've always wanted, but I also can't hurt Tyler again.

"I did," I murmur. "It doesn't mean I don't love you or don't want you." I allow myself to be vulnerable, knowing it's the only way for him to see the truth.

We can't dance around this. "It means I love him too. I need to know if you can handle it. I know you all decided to . . . share me"—I stumble over the words—"but the reality is a little different. I need to know, Tyler."

"Will it make a difference if it hurts me . . . or if I can't handle it?" he asks with a scoff.

"Yes," I answer seriously, "because I hurt you once, and I refuse to do it again, even if it means losing them. Even if it means I'm miserable for the rest of my life. I will never—" I step forward, pressing myself against him and holding my eyes steady on his blue ones I know better than my own. "I will never hurt you again. I can live without all of you, it killed me before, but I can do it. Yet I can't live with breaking your heart again."

He stares down at me, and gradually, his face softens. "Baby," he whispers before wrapping his arms around me and pulling me close. I shiver, and he sighs, kissing the top of my head and holding me close like he used to. "I don't know. It hurt to see, I'll admit, but I don't want you to be in pain either. You love them, I love you, I agreed to try it. It doesn't mean I won't get jealous or walk away for a while to cool down. There's going to be a learning curve, but I also don't want you to hide it because it's a relationship with them as well, and they deserve more than sneaking around to protect my delicate sensibilities."

Fuck, how can one man be so amazing?

"I love you," is all I can say in response. "I'm sorry it hurt you to see us together."

"I can think of a way to make it better." He smiles slowly as his eyes darken, giving me a smouldering look as his hands slide down my back to my ass, squeezing it.

"Yeah?" I purr as he pulls me closer. I feel the beads of the bracelets scrape along my skin as he softly spanks my ass. Closing my eyes, I tip my head back as his lips descend, brushing along my cheek and neck. "I can't believe you still wear your bracelets."

"Of course I do. Even when I hated you, I still loved you," he murmurs against my pulse. "I'll always love you. I wore them to carry a piece of you with me at all times, so we could explore the world together like we always promised."

"You big fucking softie," I whisper, rubbing my breasts against him.

"I'll show you just how hard I can be, baby," he retorts, biting my neck.

"They're going to hear us," I murmur breathlessly, and his blue gaze turns down, locking on me intently. The love of my life, one of them, is offering me what I want, again.

"So?" he whispers. "Let them. It's nothing they haven't heard before, baby, and I've been waiting three years to fuck our problems out . . . Unless you don't want to?" he teases.

I narrow my eyes and throw myself at him. He catches me with a laugh as my legs wrap around his waist and backs me into the rock, his hand going to my hair and his mouth descending on mine.

"Fuck me," I demand against his mouth.

"That's the plan, baby. Fuck you so hard you can't ever walk away from us again," he mutters.

Hell yes.

Pressing my back against the rock, he holds me in place as he cups my breast, kneading the plump flesh as he kisses me. His skilled fingers tweak my nipple just the way I like it, bordering on the edge of pain, but then he twists it again, forcing the ache through my body until I moan loudly, and he grins against my lips. Oh, so that's the game we're playing, is it?

He wants them to hear, wants to make me scream while they listen.

I hear their conversations halt for a moment before Fin laughs and they carry on, no doubt trying to ignore the obvious noises leaving my lips. "Ty—" I whimper when he releases my nipple before tweaking the other one and pinching it into a hard point. He pulls his mouth from mine and lowers his head, sucking one into his mouth. Leaning against the rock, I close my eyes as pleasure sparks through me, arcing from my nipple to my clit. I'm still sore from Riggs, but I wouldn't stop this for anything in the world. I've been imagining this for three years—being back in his arms, feeling him touch me, kiss me . . . sliding his cock inside me.

Like he knows the direction of my thoughts, his hand slowly strokes across my belly, along that spot he knows relaxes me to jelly before he caresses lower. He slowly rubs along my pussy lips, teasing me tenderly, even as his teeth tug at my nipple.

"Please," I whisper pleadingly, though I don't know what I'm asking for. But Tyler always does, because he knows my body better than me. He knows exactly what to stroke, pinch, flick, and rub. He knows how hard and when. Ty's a master at stoking my pleasure, always has been after spending years learning every dip and curve, but it's clear he's intent on learning them again, wiping away those years between us.

His fingers part my lips and drag down my wet pussy before stroking back and slowly circling my throbbing clit. "Please what, baby?" he rasps, releasing my nipple and kissing along my chest as his eyes meet mine. "Fuck you? Taste you?"

"All of it." I groan and arch up as he kisses my nipples, trying to press them into his mouth.

"I have three years to make up for, Peyton. You're not rushing me," he states dominantly. My strong, sure boyfriend is back, the one who used to taste me and touch me for hours without letting me come until he was good and ready.

"We need to get out of here, out of the caves," I start, and his head comes up. He grips my chin to the point of pain as he forces me to look into his eyes.

"That's nothing that can't wait. Now stop making excuses, or I'll fuck your pussy until I come and leave you wet and wanting. Understand, baby?" he snarls, making me shiver at the strength in his tone. He smiles, knowing I love it when he gets all controlling as his other hand finally moves lower, and he pushes one finger inside me, then another. His eyes never leave mine as he stretches me. My mouth opens on a pant, and my eyes try to close in pleasure, but his grip won't let me.

"I missed this pussy," he growls, licking his lips as he watches me.

"Yeah?" I groan. "Then show me how much."

With a chuckle, he leans in and kisses me again as his fingers curl within me, stroking my walls before pulling out and pushing back in, slowly, ever so fucking slowly. He keeps me on a precipice as his tongue tangles with mine.

I lift my hips, urging him on, and he pulls back, banding his arm around my waist. "Grab the rock," he instructs. I do, just in time for him to let go and drop to his knees. He parts my thighs, grabbing them meanly as he stares at my pussy with hungry eyes, and just when I'm about to snap, he leans in and sucks on my clit. The suddenness of it causes me to jerk, and I nearly fall before I dig my fingers in and hold myself up, draping my legs over his shoulders as he attacks my pussy.

He eats it just how I like it—fast and messy.

His tongue drags down my core before dipping inside me. He spears me with it before sliding up and flicking my clit over and over, until I'm on the verge of coming, but then he pulls back and grins at me, his chin and lips glistening with my cream. "Still so predictable," he murmurs as he sucks his fingers clean. "The first time you come with me again will be around my cock, Peyton Andrews, where you can stare into my eyes and remember just how fucking good we were together."

Getting to his feet, he grips my hips and leans in to kiss me once again. I taste my cream on his lips as he reaches down, frees his hard cock, and presses it to my pussy. He guides my hips back and forth across it, coating it in my cream as I groan into his mouth and bite him in punishment for not letting me come.

"Peyton," he snaps as he pulls away. "Behave, or you won't come at all," he threatens, and then like he promised, he presses the head of his cock to my pussy and rams into me in one smooth thrust, making me scream. I hear a groan from one of the other guys as I dig my nails into Tyler's shoulders, holding on as he pulls out and slams back in. I have no way to escape his huge cock as he fucks me hard and fast. It's a punishment for testing him.

He pushes me into the rock, rubbing me against it to the point of pain. His fingers pinch my clit, sending me over the edge, and then I'm coming around his cock with a cry. He groans and fights through my contracting channel, fucking me through the orgasm until the pleasure crests and then starts to rise again, forcing me back up without even letting me come down. "One." He grins. "How many can I take from you before they come to check if we're killing or fucking each other back here?" he wonders out loud.

"God, I hope three at least," I reply huskily, clawing my nails down his back to cup his ass. "Move faster; fuck me like you hate me."

With a groan, he anchors his hand around my neck, squeezing it as he pummels into me. He doesn't care if it hurts or if I enjoy it, he just pounds his cock in and out of my tight hole. The slapping of our bodies is loud in the cavern, and my cream drips from my pussy and down his cock as I close my eyes and gasp for air.

The pleasure is too much, like ecstasy shooting through my veins.

For someone who can hold their breath for eleven minutes, Tyler never fails to take it away from me. He's pulling another orgasm from me, demanding it, dragging me along. His thumb presses into the side of my neck, and the pleasure and pain race through me, creating an electrical storm until, with one more spark, I detonate.

"Count," he orders through gritted teeth, knowing I'm close. Meanly, he pinches my clit, and I scream my release. He fucks me through it, only slowing slightly before I remember I was supposed to count.

"Two," I say, and then my breathing hitches as he pulls out.

With a grin, he turns me around and bends me against the rock as he rubs his wet cock along my ass.

"Think we can get another two from fucking your ass?" he questions as he parts my cheeks and circles his finger around my hole. "I think we can. What was our highest?"

"Seven," I gasp out, pushing back.

"Seven? Shit, I need to up my game again." He groans and leans forward, trailing his tongue down my spine as goose bumps erupt on my skin and his fingers massage my cheeks.

"You do," I taunt, pushing back, urging him to take my ass. I need to come again already. I'm a greedy fucking bitch, and I don't care.

"Shit, did I ever eat this ass? 'Cause I'm so fucking tempted," he mutters.

"Later," I pant. "I need your cock."

His hand slaps my back as he presses the head of his dripping cock against my hole. "So fucking demanding, Peyton, nothing has changed."

"Some things have," I mutter, and he freezes before fisting my hair and tilting my head back.

"What was that?" he asks slowly, angrily.

"I said some things have. You tease more; you're more patient to get your cock in me," I whisper.

"I have three years of practice," he snarls, "of waiting and being needy." He pushes his cock in, starting slow and forcing me to relax before pulling back and pushing in again. The angle makes him spear me so deeply, and I'm stretched so much, it's almost painful. He's showing me he's still pissed about me leaving and is taking it out on me, but our love has always been like that. "Three years of wanting you. Remembering the heat of your body, the sound of your cries. Three fucking years, baby, makes me a patient fucking man. Especially when it comes to your pussy and pleasure."

He stops talking and starts fucking. Each thrust is faster and harder than the one before, almost splitting me open around his fat cock. He fucks me like he hates me, just like I asked.

He pins me in place with his hand gripping mine, the other digging into my hip. He uses my body, takes it, but this time when I come, I want him to as well. I want to feel it dripping from me, to know he wants this as much as I do, so I push back, meeting his thrusts and urging him on. He groans, the sound strangled as he fights through my tight ass.

"Fuck, baby," he growls, and his hips stutter in a familiar way. I grin, knowing he's close, no matter how hard he tries to fight it. Unwilling to come without me, he slams his fingers into my pussy, just holding them there as his thumb rubs my clit, throwing me into my third orgasm with a silent scream.

He yells as he drives into my ass once more, and then I feel his release fill me as he grips my hip harder. A moment later, his head presses against my back, and his ragged breathing blows over my sweaty skin as he holds me up—good thing, since my legs are trembling. I close my eyes as fatigue hits me and bask in the afterglow.

"Tell me you're done," Fin calls, his voice pained. "I'm hard as hell from listening to you two, and Kalen is basically holding his head underwater."

We both laugh, and Tyler kisses along my spine. "Even after all these years, baby, each time still feels like the first."

"You mean when we were fumbling, idiot teenagers?" I tease.

"That too, but when we first got to experience the depth of the emotions between us. It never changes. I love you so fucking much," he whispers.

"I love you too, Tyler," I reply. "Even if I love others, you will always be the first man to hold my heart."

It's true, I love the others, but Tyler . . . Tyler was my first love, and I know he will be my last too. It just so happens now that that love has changed, matured, and grown with us.

Like it should.

THIRTY-EIGHT

Kalen

Ignoring the sounds coming from behind the rock, I update Michael and the ground base on what's happening. He's relieved Peyton is okay and demands to speak to her, but I have to brush him off without telling him she's currently fucking my brother's brains out. Both envy and lust rage through me from the sounds she's making.

I also start to pack up some gear. We're going to stay here for one more night to ensure Peyton is fully rested and okay before we begin the dive back to forward base. This way she can keep up and fight off any attacks. Not that she will need to; I don't plan on leaving her side ever again.

I start cooking food after that, knowing she's going to need it to recover from her ordeal and all the fucking. Fin helps me while Riggs charts a map, looking for possible attack paths and the best exits. We are getting out of this fucking cave as soon as Peyton can move.

Just before the food is done, she and Tyler return, hand in hand. I raise my eyebrow at the wide smile covering his face. I haven't seen him look so happy since before she left. It helps dull my anger and jealousy, and when she lifts her eyes and they meet mine, her gaze is filled with that same love and happiness—not just for him—but for me too. I settle and offer her a small smile in response, which only makes hers grow.

Tyler helps her dress in new thermals and a suit to keep her warm, and then we all sit down to eat. Fin, of course, has to break the silence.

"So . . . who was better?"

I throw my skewer at him, and he ducks and laughs.

"What? I was just curious! We should get like a chart system with stars for who gave her the best orgasm that day," he teases, grinning as he leans back opposite me.

Peyton giggles on my left as she leans into me without even second-guessing herself, her other hand on Tyler's leg. "They would both get stars," she says.

Fin leans closer, wiggling his brows at her. "Yeah? Spill the deets, babe. Was it the hands—"

This time Tyler throws something at him. "Shut the fuck up, Fin."

"Or next time it will be my fist," I grumble.

Unafraid, he laughs and winks at Peyton. "He's just mad he hasn't had your pussy today."

"That's it." I start to get to my feet, careful not to disturb Peyton, ready to kick his ass. She laughs and grabs me, yanking me back down before plopping onto my lap. I blink, unable to move in case I hurt or jar her. Glaring over her head at Fin, I wrap my arms around her and pull her into my chest, keeping her warm, and Fin begins to howl.

"She stopped your attack so easily," he teases. "The big bad Kalen was undone by a girl on his knee."

"Baby girl, warn your boyfriend to stop before I kill him," I whisper in her ear, inhaling her scent as she relaxes into my hold, which has a smile curling my lips. I have no doubt she feels it against her skin.

"Fin, if you don't stop, I won't suck your dick ever," she tells him.

He freezes, his eyes wide. "Babe, don't threaten shit like that." He looks down at his cock. "She didn't mean it. I promise, little fella."

"Jesus, I'm going to kill him before we get out of these caves," Tyler murmurs.

"I'll join you," I offer, meeting his eyes. He smiles at me before his gaze flickers down to his girl on my lap—my girl too—and he softens, unable to pull his eyes away from her. I know the feeling.

I wonder if he will give her the ring, or if this will calm him down. Maybe it will even soothe Fin and alleviate Riggs's anxiety. She has a way of helping all of us. Peyton sighs and snuggles closer, oblivious to my thoughts. "So what's the plan, boys?"

"We rest here today. Base is packing up, so as soon as we get there tomorrow, we'll move quickly but safely through the tunnels we took to get in, and then we'll get the fuck out. It's going to be reported as an unsafe environment," Tyler explains seriously.

"We can go today—"

I lift and turn her so she's straddling my lap, and then I grab her chin, forcing her to look into my eyes. "Don't fucking finish that sentence. Let us look after you for once. Today, you're going to rest." I narrow my eyes. "I mean *rest*, not fuck, and then tomorrow, we'll leave. Got it, baby girl?"

She leans in and kisses me, startling me, and then leans back with a chuckle, knowing she won still because she is only giving in because she wants to. "Fine."

"That was too easy," Riggs comments. "We need to remember how he did that."

She rolls her eyes and goes to say something when we all hear a noise. Frowning, I set her to the side as I stand and look around. Years of training kick in, causing me to react instantly. They try to talk, but I lift my hand to silence them, scanning the surrounding area for any threats to my family and girl.

Just then, a scream splits the air—a familiar crying caw.

My head jerks up, and I grab my knife as I shove Peyton behind me. "Fuck," I mutter.

"That's them," she snarls.

"Shit, you mean those monster motherfuckers are coming?" Fin yells, leaping to his feet.

"Not coming; they're here," I murmur, watching them crawl from a small crevice near the top of the cavern that we missed.

"Shit!" Tyler yells.

Pretty much.

THIRTY-NINE

Peyton

I grab a stick from the fire, with one end aflame, and clench my knife. Fuck these monsters. They don't get to hurt my family. I watch, standing half behind Kalen, whose body is vibrating with barely leashed violence, as they crawl from the opening above us before bursting into the air. They fly around blindly, seeking us. We all go quiet, filled with tension as we wait. I can feel Kalen's concentration, unlike the nervousness that fills the rest of us.

He's used to this, used to being ready for an attack at any moment. From going relaxed to defensive. We all just stare, putting our backs towards each other as the creatures circle above us, trying to remain silent since that's how they hunt.

The fire is still hissing though, and they focus on that, their screams increasing as they descend. Fuck. Moving closer, I start to slowly stamp it out, darting my gaze back to them every few seconds until the fire is out, and then I move away again, back to Kalen's side as the cave is plunged into darkness. I reluctantly put out my stick too, not wanting the crackle of the fire to give us away. Instead, I hold my knife closer. Our lamps are still on but are casting shadows. I watch as they land on rocks and the walls around us, their heads tilting as they listen and bide their time.

They can undoubtedly wait us out.

I look at Kalen to see what I should do. He's watching them, seemingly unconcerned. The seconds drag into minutes as my heart hammers and adrenaline pounds through me, my muscles bunching with tension as I try not to shift from foot to foot.

Suddenly, there's the sound of sliding rocks. My eyes widen, and I whirl around to see an open-mouthed Fin gaping down at his feet before the monsters scream and dive at us. I prepare myself, focusing on their descent. One comes close, so I stab at it, and he caws and dives backwards as another's claws dig into my arm, but I continue to slash and stab, fighting back and going wild.

I feel the others fighting around me, but someone cries out in pain, and our intent to drive them back doubles for what feels like hours. My arms grow heavy, and I'm starting to slow when a loud crash comes and they instantly fly away.

Panting, I look around and spot Riggs moving back from the edge of the plunge pool where he just tossed a rock. He presses his fingers to his lips, and we all freeze, barely breathing. The monsters fly straight into it, swimming down towards the noise. We all remain still and silent, and as the minutes pass, we begin to relax.

"They could come back at any time; we need to move," I whisper.

"We can't," Tyler mumbles. "You're bleeding, and so is Fin."

I spin in panic to see him weakly smiling at me with claw marks across his face. Fuck, they aren't too deep, but they're still deep enough to have blood running down his face in rivulets. "Kalen, Riggs, keep watch. Peyton, get the bag and help me clean it." I rush to follow orders as Fin sits. I pass him water and hold his hand as Tyler starts to clean his wounds and unpack the bag. I ignore my bleeding arm, knowing it isn't as bad.

"Babe, you're bleeding again. Ty, do her first," Fin insists, but I narrow my eyes.

"Shut up, you big baby. The faster he cleans and dresses that, the faster he can get to me," I retort before softening my voice as I kiss his other cheek and then his lips. "Please?"

"Fuck," he mutters. "Fine, but be quick; I hate that she's bleeding."

I distract him by talking softly of nothing and everything. I regale him with stories of stingrays I swam with and the island that had pigs in the water while Tyler dresses the wounds. Once he's done, they both clean my arm and dress that as well. I know it's not too deep, so we're okay, and once it's dressed, I barely even feel it.

Done, we look around, knowing we aren't safe here, but we can't go into the water yet in case they are still there, and Fin and I need to rest. The blood loss might not be much, but there is plenty of adrenaline and fear in our bodies so we need to calm down, otherwise the worst could happen during the dive.

We all settle in to rest for a while.

We barely sleep. We keep our weapons in hand all night, trying to stay silent. Fin naps, and I do as well, knowing we need the energy, but after a few hours of rest, Tyler gives up and agrees we can head back. We aren't safe here.

Nervous but overjoyed, we start to pack up the remaining bits. It goes smoothly and quickly because we're all used to this. This is routine, normal, and when we function best, even at the worst of times. Just as we're strapping on our flippers, the radio crackles, and screams and yells come through it.

"Base—attacked." It cuts off. "Don't come back!" Michael shouts.

I grab the mic. "Michael?" I yell in panic.

"Minnow, don't come—" He cuts out and then comes back panting. "Don't come back here. It's a massacre. Minnow, stay there!" The static is loud in the silent cave. I stare at the mic, my eyes wide as fear winds through me.

I try to get their attention again, swapping channels and yelling, but Tyler pries it from my clammy fingers and tilts my chin up. "He'll be okay. Trust in him like he did you. But he's right—if they're there, we can't go back."

"So what do we do?"

Tyler growls, yanking at his hair in frustration as I stare at Kalen. I feel my heart cracking, and fear causes me to shake. I can't lose Michael . . . but that's also our only way out.

We are trapped.

"We survive," he murmurs. "It's the only thing we can do."

Oh God, Michael, please be okay.

FORTY

Tyler

They are all looking to me for a plan. They don't outright say it, but the panic I see written on their faces is enough to tell me their thoughts. I can't afford to lose it; I have to stay calm. I have Riggs doing inventory of what we have left. Kalen is checking the gear and setting up a warning system at the water entrance in case they come back. Fin is resting, and Peyton is checking the gear with Kalen. Me? I'm staring down at the virtual map Riggs has drawn up so far, looking for anything—another way in, another way . . . but deep down, I know.

We have to keep going; there isn't another way yet. This system is unmapped, but it has ocean water, which means it has to have another exit somewhere. We just have to find it before those fucking monsters find us. And I'm the one leading them. One wrong move, and my family dies. That means every fucking decision has to be calculated and thought out, because I'm not losing any of them.

Not now, not ever.

I tell myself this is just another cave dive, another obstacle to overcome. We've been in cave-ins before, and we've been surrounded by predators and threats—not together—but just as we did then, we will survive this. They are animals, that's all, and we are the fucking intelligent beings. We are going to get out of this. We have done it before; we can do it again.

Tightening my grip on the computer, I sigh and close my eyes. If we keep going, we need to head back through the tunnel those creatures flew into. But as cruel as it sounds, they are clearly busy at the other base at the moment. That gives us a window of time to get through and out.

Peyton moves closer, leaning into my arm. She knows I need her without asking, allowing me to continue with my calm, complacent demeanour. "What's the plan?" She's not inquiring to rush me, she's asking so she can help. She's good, smart; she might see a better way. It's an old tradition to work together, and it brings me a twinge of sadness before I look up into those bright, loving eyes. We might have done it before, but everything has changed now, and we're starting fresh. That means letting her back in.

One step at a time.

"We can't go back; I think we need to go deeper. I know that sounds—"

"Smart," she interrupts, throwing me a smile before it drops and she concentrates on the screen. She turns the map, her lip caught in her teeth like it usually is when she's concentrating. I swallow, feeling my heart flip, and I try to push back the sudden burst of love. "I think we do too. There has to be another exit." She looks up, blinking when she finds me staring at her. Clearing my throat, I look down at the map, but I catch her smile.

"My thoughts also. They should still be . . . back at base. We need to move quickly but watch each other. We need to find another exit. We won't make it until rescue comes." I sigh.

"Nope, we only have two more days' worth of rations," Riggs says, coming over. "So we need to move now."

"It looks like it, especially before we start getting tired and hungry. That would be bad," I mutter, spinning the map again before trailing my finger along a line. "We take this one; we follow it. We stay quiet. Our suits make noise, but hopefully, the tide and rocks down there cover it. We swim for as long as we can, stopping only when necessary. It's going to be exhausting." I look up to see Fin and Kalen have joined us. "But it's our only way. We're getting out of here, and we're doing it now." I shut the map. "Any objections?"

"None from me, boss man." Fin salutes.

Kalen shakes his head. "Let's get the fuck out of here, then I want to drink and sleep," he grumbles.

"I'll join you," Peyton teases and then winks at me.

"Come on, then, baby, let's suit up." I lean in and kiss her. Part of it is to prove to them I can, but the other part is that she's just too fucking cute to resist. Pulling back, I smile at her when we suddenly hear a splash.

Something is in the dive pool.

Kalen is instantly there, knife in hand, while the rest of us freeze, staying silent. We wait anxiously as the noise becomes louder. The water bubbles, and I pull Peyton behind me, even as she tries to remain by my side. I throw her a *behave* look and ignore her simmering anger as Kalen moves closer to the edge, ready to stop them as soon as they surface.

But the head that pokes through the water isn't of a beast.

It's human.

FORTY-ONE

Peyton

My breath catches as the mask-covered head pops through the water, and in an instant, I know who it is. I fight free of Tyler's hold and race across the ground, my heart leaping as Michael whips off his mask.

"Michael!" I scream and rush towards him as he pulls himself over the ledge, coughing and sputtering as I fling myself into his arms. He catches me with a shocked laugh.

"Hey, Minnow!" he murmurs, embracing me tighter for a moment.

I feel tears dripping down my face as I look at him. "I thought I'd lost you," I whisper.

"Nah, I'm too stubborn to die. Bit like you, kid." He chuckles.

I can't help but grin as I pull back and look him over. "How you doing, old man? What happened?"

"Let me get out, and I'll tell ya," he replies. I pull back with a wince, and then I notice the huge gash running the length of his arm.

"Tyler, first aid kit!" I yell as I prop my arm under Michael's and help him sit with his back to a stalagmite. His face is pale, and his eyes are slightly bloodshot, but other than that, he looks okay. He shouldn't be diving, but when I press my head to his chest, I don't hear anything unusual. It was only a short dive, so hopefully, it was all right. I lean back as Tyler and the others surround us. My hands are shaking, so Riggs takes over and begins to clean and dress Michael's wound.

"Did anyone else make it?" I ask. His frown tells me everything.

"No. The fuckers hit us out of nowhere; we didn't stand a chance." He grunts. "I tried to save them—"

"I know." I squeeze his hand. If there was a way to save them, he would have. Michael isn't the type to leave anyone behind. I'm just glad he's alive, even if my heart breaks for all those we lost. They were down here for us, after all.

"Minnow, we didn't even see them coming. One second, we were packing up and checking the monitors, and the next, they were there, attacking from the water, from above. There were so many of them, we could barely see. I fought as many as I could, but we were overrun. The others were grabbing gear to dive, and I ran to them, but they were dragged down into the water, and it turned red. I knew I had no choice. I grabbed the gear and went under, killing the creatures waiting for me, and slipped into the gear. I waited and poked my head out, but . . . there was no one alive." His breath hitches, and I hate the vulnerability I see in his eyes. This man has been through so much, and now this is another horror to add to his list. "I swam right here, hoping you hadn't left yet."

He looks from me to Tyler. "We can't go back that way; there were too many."

"We agree, we have to push forward. As soon as you have rested and—" Tyler starts.

"Fuck rest, I'm fine. We need to move before they come for us." His narrowed eyes move to me. "I may be old, but I can keep up. We need to swim quickly and beat those bastards to an exit."

"Old man," I begin, but he narrows his eyes farther, giving me that *don't mess with me* look.

"I'm not dying down here. If I'm gonna die, it's going to be with a fucking vodka bottle in my hand at my family's grave. And you're not dying down here either, Minnow, so stop worrying about me, okay?" He squeezes my hand. "Ya forget why ya hired me? I'm a fucking machine. Let's get going, so we can get away from those winged fuckers and back to the surface."

I run my eyes over his face. I feel the others staring, knowing this is my decision. "Okay, if you say you're fine, but you will tell me if or when you need breaks, or I'll force them, got it?" I snap in my bossy voice.

"Got it," he agrees.

I look up at Tyler. "Then let's get moving and get the fuck out of this place."

He nods and glances to the others. "Get suited up, we're leaving."

I gaze back at Michael, and we share a look that only those who have spent a lot of time together can. I'm silently asking if he's okay, and he's replying that he is, all without words. "Okay, then." I squeeze his hand and stand. "Let's see if those swim records you boast about are real."

"You're on, Minnow. I'll show you kids how to really dive," he teases as he gets to his feet with my help.

I smile, even as nerves fill me. He shouldn't be diving, but we don't have much of a choice. Hopefully, the exit isn't too far. We'll find it, we'll get out of here.

We won't lose anyone else.

We are the fucking apex divers, not those bastards.

Bring it.

FORTY-TWO

Fin

We waste no time getting in the water. If Michael says he's okay, then we have to believe him. As a diver, he knows the importance of being honest, even if it's not good news. Every diver understands the significance of telling the truth and knowing their body's limit, so if he says he can, we have to trust that.

We suit up quickly, buddying up to check each other's equipment. Before Peyton puts her mask on, I steal a quick kiss, which makes her grin. Michael glares at me. Laughing, I back up with my hands held out, winking at the old man. I like him. He's protective of her, and I want him to like me too. He's important to her, that's for sure.

He's family, like we are.

Once we are all ready, we form a circle at the pool as Tyler gives out orders. "I'll go first, with Kalen bringing up the rear. After me, it's Fin, Riggs, then Michael and Peyton, understood?"

I almost balk at him putting Peyton near the back, but it makes sense. She's the fastest and strongest swimmer, so if anything goes wrong, she and Kalen will be okay. We know that, and he's showing he trusts her.

Tyler goes in first, and we wait, staying silent, not wanting to draw the attention of those creatures. As bad as it sounds, they may be resting after . . . feasting. Even that word nearly makes me gag, but breaking down and getting worked up won't change what happened to our team, and right now, I need a clear head. I push my feelings aside, ready to deal with them when we aren't in a life-or-death situation.

When we are all in the water, we clip ourselves to the guideline and start to swim. We sweep our torches around, each holding a knife in our hand. The water is murky now, and it makes it hard to see, so we have to go slow. Tyler heads to the tunnel we chose, the only one we haven't explored. It's risky, but we know where the others go, not this one.

We have one shot; I just hope he's right.

The tunnel starts out wide and then tightens. He places a rope as we go for the others to clip onto, and we keep each other aware of our position by tugging on it, not wanting to speak in case we draw their attention. Our regulators make enough noise as it is, but without them, we would die, so we don't have much choice.

We swim for what feels like hours but must only be about forty or fifty minutes. We manoeuvre around twists and turns, pikes where we can almost stand, and tight tunnels we have to take our equipment off to move through, staying silent the entire time.

Ready, prepared.

We won't lose another member of our team. We are getting out of here, and when we do, we'll be a family again and make Peyton ours forever.

Tyler rapidly tugs twice to indicate we're reaching the end of the tunnel. I slow to give him room if he needs to retreat or turn, my torch shining on his back and ass as he keeps swimming. Light is beginning to filter in . . . Is that an exit? It can be tricky down here, so I don't get my hopes up as he reaches the end and sticks his head out. A moment later, he turns and gestures for me to stay. I give him the *okay* symbol, and he starts to swim. All I can see is water as he floats up, and we all wait nervously for his return. Minutes pass, and I start to become worried, even though I haven't heard anything. Suddenly, his face pops into the exit, and he gestures for us to follow.

I do, and once I'm in the open water, he points upwards, telling me it's okay. I swim up, glancing back to see him ensuring everyone gets out safely. The light grows stronger and stronger, and when I break the surface, I pull off my mask and look around.

Holy fuck.

We might have found a way out, but it's going to be fucking difficult to use it.

Why is nothing in this cave system easy?

FORTY-THREE

Peyton

I break the surface, floating next to the others, and whistle. *Fucking hell.* Before us, stretching up to the top of the cave, is a fucking towering wall. And with no other exit, it looks like we're going up. The rock glitters, and I almost grin.

This is what I'm good at, what I excel at. I can do this. Fuck monsters, fuck cave-ins, we're getting out of here, and it starts by climbing that.

There's a sloping bit of land leading from the water to the rock, so we swim there and quickly get out. Noiselessly, we all begin to lose the gear we don't need, putting it away and switching over to our climbing equipment. I hook on my crampons, rope, and picks before putting on my hat, gloves, and harness. We won't have time to fully secure everything, so it's going to be a risky climb, but we are professionals.

We've got this.

Tyler comes over and presses his head to mine, his bright eyes locked on me, speaking a million things, even though his mouth doesn't move. He's telling me to be safe, to be smart, to follow, listen, and know my limits. He's telling me he loves me.

I smile and kiss him.

"Minnow, really?" Michael coughs, and when I pull back with a soft laugh and look over, I freeze when I see him. He's pale, really pale, and he's trembling. I rush over, and he tries to bat me away. "I'm fine," he wheezes, even as he tries to suppress his coughs, which seem to echo around the cavern. The guys circle us, their knives drawn in case it attracts the monsters, but I'm focused on him.

He's too pale and sweaty, and his coughs rattle. They sound deep, like his lungs are in trouble. I push his hands away and press my ear to his chest, trying to listen. There's a definite crackle. I pull back to speak, but he turns away and coughs so hard that blood splatters across the rocks.

Bright, fresh red blood.

"Michael," I whisper. He shouldn't have been diving, I knew it. Why did I let him? We should have found another way out.

"I'm fine," he rasps, wiping his mouth and smiling weakly. "Nothing a good climb can't fix."

It's a lie. He knows that. I know that. He's dying. His lips are tinted blue, there is a rash on his hands, and his body is quivering from exhaustion. How long was he hiding this? I knew the risk, so why did I let him? He suffered pulmonary barotrauma years ago and never should have dived again.

Fuck!

"We need to get him on some oxygen," I almost yell.

"Minnow." Michael sighs, grabs my hand, and squeezes. His eyes are dim, but he smiles. "It won't help; we know that. Give me some water and five minutes, and then let's get going."

"But—"

"The best way to help me is to get out of here," he reasons. I know what he's doing, but he's right. I understand that, even as my heart pounds and bile rises in my throat at the thought of leaving him to suffer.

I sit with him, helping him sip water as he gets his breathing under control. The others prepare everything, but a few minutes later, Kalen lays his hand on my shoulder. "Fin wants your help looking for the best route up. I'll stay with him, baby."

I swallow hard, smiling feebly at Michael, and stand. I throw Kalen a look, and he nods, letting me know he'll get me if anything changes. I relax a little at that and head over to Fin, who's waiting with Riggs, staring up at the wall.

Calculating the best route, no doubt.

I look upwards, propping my hands on my hips as I try to get my head back into the game. I can't afford to be distracted. All it would take is one mistake, and we could all die. They are relying on me—Michael too. I hear him cough again and flinch. Closing my eyes for a moment, I breathe and ground myself, and when I open them again, I'm back in the zone. Fin and Riggs are watching me worriedly, but I smile and scan the wall.

"There," I murmur. "See how it zigzags? It's not too solid to get the pick through and hard enough we can rope into it. We go one at a time. I'll go first and set the rope."

"You sure?" Riggs asks, looking concerned. I lean closer and kiss his lips.

"I've got this."

"Hell yes you do, baby cakes!" Fin calls and spanks me. "Show that wall who's boss."

I pull away, grinning, but his eyes twinkle, and I know he did it for that reason. "All right, then, let's get going."

* * *

I was right—it's the best route. I manage to get my pick into the rock and pull myself up. Finding a crack, I reach down, grab a cam, wedge it in, and tug to make sure it's secure. Once I'm certain it is, I keep going at a fast but safe pace. The others are a ways below me, tied to the rope and working their way up. Michael is directly below me to ensure they can keep an eye on him, but I hear him coughing and look down mid-climb to see his face pressed against the wall, his hands gripping the rock as he coughs.

He's choking on the fluid and lack of air.

I wait until he lifts his head and gives me the *okay* symbol before I start to climb again, moving faster now. I need to get him out of here. I lift, pull, and place, over and over, making my way up the eighty-foot wall. I put a nice lead between the guys and me, giving them rope to climb with and ensuring the way is safe.

About three-quarters of the way up, I encounter a problem. The rock isn't secure, and I can't place the cams here. Climbing it would mean suicide. It would crumble, and we would fall. I glance to the left and right, knowing we need to move diagonally now to reach the top. The left seems too soft as well, but I test it by reaching out, and the rock breaks under my touch, so I swing back to my position.

Right it is, I guess.

Looking down, I whistle and point right, and they nod in understanding. Riggs checks it over from below before giving me the okay, which means he thinks it's possible. That's always good, since I trust his judgement more than my own.

I begin moving right, slowly dragging across the rock face. I slip and lose my footing, but my fingers catch the sharp edges, making me hiss as I dangle before I pull myself up and keep going. I place some more lines, focused on the next moment, the next movement . . . but then I stop. There, tilted inwards so we would have never seen it from the ground, is a crevice.

Not just a crevice, a fucking chasm, running all the way up. It's at least ten feet to the opposite wall. Fuck. I look upwards, and though I'm not sure the rock will hold, I reach and pull, digging my pick in, but it jams and the wall crumbles around it. I try to pull it free, wiggling and yanking, but it's caught on something.

Fuck, fuck, fuck.

I know better than to panic. My heart rate actually slows, and my mind hyper-focuses like it does in these situations as I analyse and think about my next move. I could finish the climb without an axe, I could use my body as leverage to pull it out—

A screech sounds.

My heart stops as I gaze out across the open cavern, just as the monsters start to fly out of the water. Fuck! I look down and press my finger to my lips. Everyone flattens themselves against the wall silently.

We can't hang here forever. Even now, my fingers and arms ache, and my legs are quaking slightly from the fatigue of the dive, but we have no choice. If I try to move and make a noise, it will mean our deaths.

The minutes tick by as they circle the cavern, screeching and attacking each other. The sounds grate my ears like nails on a chalkboard as they crash midair and fight. Just then, I hear a muffled noise, and I glance down to see Michael's panicked face pressing against the wall, his body shaking as he tries to stop the cough.

Time freezes as the sound bursts free from him, stopping all the screeches. I look up to see them all turn mid-flight and start to soar towards us, ready to attack, drawn by the noise. Michael looks at me, his eyes wide, and in his gaze I see acceptance. He knows they are coming for him. His lips tilt in a slight smile as he reaches for his hook on the rope.

I shake my head, searching for another option. Any option, anything.

The others begin climbing, racing up the wall to reach us. Me? I grab my axe, and with a strength I didn't know I had, I yank. It slides out, and I turn and start to climb down. Michael attempts to stop me, but I ignore him. When I reach him, I swipe at the creatures as they come near us, but they land on him, and a scream leaves his throat.

The guys have nearly joined us now, and I see Riggs being attacked, trying to climb as he soundlessly fends them off. His face is locked in concentration as he tries to get to me, to help, even when he's being assaulted. One almost pulls him off the wall, so I make a split-second decision.

I throw my axe.

It sails through the air, and Riggs ducks into the ice as it hits the monster and sends it flying. He looks up, his eyes meeting mine. He knows I just sacrificed my weapon to save him.

I have to climb a bit to escape one's claws, but then I look down at Michael. Everything's happening so fast, it's chaos. He meets my gaze as yet more converge on him. There are too many to fight. My heart clenches. My usually calm, collected mind can't see a way out of this.

I don't know how to help, but he does.

He holds my gaze, and again I see the acceptance in his eyes, the love and understanding. He nods at me, smiling widely for a moment, and my lips part, trying to stop whatever he's going to do.

He opens his mouth and screams.

The guys quickly climb around him, racing past me, and try to drag me away, but I stay in place, even as they search for a way forward. I stare as all the monsters converge on him, covering him, and he still screams, drawing as many as he can. He's giving us a way out, a chance.

Tears drip down my face, my own screams and shouts trapped in my throat as I hear them ripping into him. A muffled cry escapes me, and one of them lifts its head before it starts to climb towards me. My eyes widen as I look up, but then it's there, clawing into my ankle just above Michael.

I kick at it, trying to stay on the wall. For a moment, I see Michael's bloodied, cut up face appear in the mass, and then his hand shoots out and grabs the monster.

His eyes connect with mine.

"I love you, Minnow! Let me save you the way I couldn't save my family. Go! Get out of here! I love you!" His bellow is filled with agony, and then he unclips and throws himself backwards.

"No!" I whisper.

My hand goes out as my own choked scream catches in my throat. I watch brokenly as he falls through the air, his body weightless and covered in monsters. He doesn't fight, he doesn't try to stop his descent, he just takes as many with him as he can.

He knew he was dying, he knew he was going to slow us down, and he knew we needed a way out. So Michael did what he always does best—he protected me. I turn, unable to watch any more as I hear them ripping him to pieces, seeing the blood mist in the air. I press my face against the wall, stifling my sobs, my vision blurred from tears as my heart shatters and plummets with him.

I want to scream, to kill them, but I'm trapped here.

I hear a splash as Michael hits the water.

"Climb!" someone hisses, and I look up to see them all waiting for me. Kalen is about to come back down, so I get my ass moving. My heart is broken, my body is shaking, and my throat is clogged with pain, but I won't dishonour his sacrifice by remaining frozen.

I climb, even when I can't feel or see, until a hand grips mine and pulls me over the edge and into their waiting arms. I sob into their chests until I can't take it anymore. I can't breathe, can't think. We sit there, listening to the water and the screeches, and when I can inhale, I lift my head.

I peer over the edge at the bloodied, swirling water.

He's gone.

Michael's dead.

FORTY-FOUR

Kalen

I watch Peyton. She's trembling from her sobs, and her eyes are overflowing with tears. She stares down at the water as it bubbles, but I pull her back, turn her head, and rest it against my chest.

I meet Tyler's eyes over her head. He's unsure, hurt, and worried for her, but I know loss, I know grief—maybe that's why Peyton and I were always drawn to each other—so he lets me handle it, even as he leans in and kisses her shoulder.

"I love you, baby. I'm going to find a way out; take as long as you need," he whispers, staying quiet in case the creatures hear us. He takes Fin, whose lips are tilted down. He hugs Peyton before following after Tyler.

Riggs moves closer, stroking her back and shoulders as her hands fist my suit. Her face is pressed against my chest to muffle her sobs. Even now in her pain, she's conscious of her surroundings, trying to protect us.

"Shh, princess," I whisper into her hair, holding her close. "I've got you; let it out."

So she does. We sit there silently as she weeps. Riggs holds her too, and she breaks between us. My eyes go from her to our surroundings, guarding her. Eventually, she lifts her head. Her eyes are red and still leaking, her nose is pink, and her lips are parted.

I lean in and cup her cheeks before resting my forehead against hers. I wish I could make it better, that I could change what happened and take it back. I want to give her the words she needs, but I'm not Fin or Tyler. She smiles sadly and closes her eyes.

"We need to get moving," she murmurs brokenly.

"It can wait," Riggs says.

"No," she whispers and winces at how loud it was. "He told us to survive, and he's right. I'll have time to grieve when we get out of here. I'm not letting him . . . die"—she stumbles over the word—"for nothing. We need to get out of here."

Tyler and Fin return just then, kneeling next to her. Fin brushes back her hair and tells her he loves her, while Tyler looks her over and then kisses her. "I'm sorry, baby, but you're right—we have a way out. Can you move?"

She nods and begins to get to her feet, so we all jump up and help her. She scrubs at her face, pushes her hair back, and straightens her shoulders, but there's a fractured way to how she carries herself. "Let's go."

We share a look, knowing we all need to keep an eye on her. There is no point escaping this place if our girl isn't okay. She is all that matters, always.

We silently help pack her gear as well as ours and force her to drink some water. I look her over as we go. Her ankle has some scrapes, but other than that, she's okay, thank fuck. I keep her hand in mine as Tyler goes first, then us, then Riggs and Fin. They protect our backs, their knives out as she holds on to me. Her expression is stern and strong, but her hand trembles slightly in mine. I squeeze it, giving her my own strength.

Giving her whatever she needs.

She glances back, swallows, and mouths, *Thank you.*

I love you, I mouth in response, and she smiles faintly before turning forward and following Tyler through the narrow passage he found—guiding us away from Michael and the memory of his death that she will never forget.

My girl has lost so much—her mum, her dad, and then the man who took her in and made her family—but she will never lose us, not ever again.

We are apex predators for life, and she is our queen.

FORTY-FIVE

Peyton

I can't even fathom my life without Michael. Just thinking his name makes my breath hitch. I want to break down, to fall to my knees and rage at how unfair it all is, to scream and let it all out, but I can't, so I trap my grief in my throat to protect us.

So I don't lose anyone else I love.

It rots me from the inside out until my breaths are short and sharp, and each step forward is a struggle. The only thing keeping me going is those behind and in front of me. My men, my family. I have to survive and hold it together for them. Once we are free of this nightmare, of this fucking dive, I can break. Until then, I have to push Mi—him to the back of my mind. I have to focus on the next moment, the next breath, the next step until it becomes slightly easier.

The tunnel twists and turns and seems to be going back down. I can feel their worry that it's just a maze taking us around in circles, but we've come this far. We can't go back, we've lost too much, we have to keep moving until we find a way out. Tyler doesn't stop, he keeps going even as we grow increasingly tired and begin to lose hope.

We have to break for water and food, and we stay silent the whole time. Kalen watches the way we came while Tyler guards the way we are going. If we don't get free soon, we'll run out of supplies. Our situation is getting more and more dire by the hour. I know they will be working to get us out from up top, but we are too deep. By the time they got through the collapse and network of tunnels—if they survived the monsters—we would be dead.

Part of me hopes they don't come. I can't stand the idea of them burrowing into this cave and finding what we did. There would just be more death.

"Ready?" Fin whispers, and I nod, packing my bag up. When I stand, I stumble, feeling cold and weary, not to mention the shock and grief are taking their toll. I need rest, but we don't have time. He watches me with concern, but I wave him off.

"I'm okay, let's keep going," I mumble. When I look up after donning my equipment, they are all staring at me, so I narrow my eyes in irritation. "I'm not lying, move," I order.

Tyler nods but sends a look over my head, and I know he's telling them to keep an eye on me. It annoys me, so I push past him and take point. I don't need babysitting, even if they are just trying to look after me. I just want to get out of this fucking cave.

I keep moving, even as he catches up and lets me lead, probably realising I need to or I might lose my mind.

We walk for another few hours, barely speaking, until I hear screeching. We can't go back, but if we go forward, the monsters will be there. Tyler passes me a knife, and with a determined clench of my teeth, I slowly step forward, lifting my feet and setting them down softly.

After another few minutes, the tunnel ends in another cavern, but this one is different. It's huge. I can barely see the ceiling, there's no wall or water that I can see from here, and it's filled with those bastards and their kills.

Skeletons litter the floor as some of them hang from the ceiling and stalactites while others are nesting on the ground and outcroppings. They cover nearly every inch of the space, and where they don't, old, grey dirty bones stick up. Whether they're from animals or people, I don't know.

I just stare, unsure what to do or where to go.

Then I see it.

Light.

FORTY-SIX

Riggs

I stop, wide-eyed, as I scan the room. Numbers pop into my head as I estimate the size, height, diameter, and even the amount of kills it must have taken to fill a cavern like this. None of that's helpful though. Peyton turns slightly, careful not to move or scrape the rocks underfoot, and points. I follow her finger and see the spark of light in the back right corner. It could be a trick—it happens sometimes in caves—but we can't risk that it's not. That could be our only chance out of here.

Everyone is watching me, waiting to see if I'll have a solution.

How do we get across the floor? It will make too much noise. There isn't a path at all. So if we can't take the floor . . . we take the walls. The ceiling is filled with them, but the walls aren't. Along the sharp outcropping and walls, however, are foot- and handholds. If we can somehow climb as quietly as possible, we have a chance to reach that opening and get out of this monster-ridden cave.

There's a soft sound of dripping of water to the left, and a slow-moving stream coming in from another opening. The tinkle and noise from those should cover our breathing and some movements, so as long as we remain as quiet as possible and use hand gestures, we may *just* make it.

It's a long shot, even for me, but we have no other choice. Numbers and statistics are good for evaluating, but even I know that sometimes with diving and cave exploring, you have to throw the odds to the wind and just go for it.

Movement is life.

I turn my head and start to mouth the plan to them, gesturing. Peyton frowns, even Kalen seems against it, but I narrow my eyes on them. *It's the only way*, I mouth. *Floor is death, ceiling is death.*

Peyton looks across the room, but her eyes harden, and then she turns back to me with a nod, clearly seeing what I'm going for. She slowly reaches down and into her pocket to dust her hands, but Fin stops her and sluggishly moves past her, clearly intent on going first to protect her, to protect us.

He's fast and quiet, but Peyton is the better climber—except we all know she isn't going first again after what just happened. Instead, she goes second, Tyler goes third, then me, and finally Kalen. He's the biggest and most likely to pull off any loose rock, so although it's brutal, he knows he has to give us as much time in front as we can get.

Everyone is nervous. Me? I'm afraid, but being a diver, I know how to conquer that and use it to help me. Fear can stop you if you let it, but when you channel it, you become unstoppable. It's something we learned early on, and right now, we all need to remember it.

Knowing this could be the end, we huddle with our heads close together and our hands out, like we did on our first dive. Back then, the biggest thing we had to worry about was standing out as a new company, about having enough work for our expenses, but now it's about our lives, about survival. Any misstep, any mistake, and we could die.

But we do what we always do: work smart, fast, and together to get the job done.

The thing that comes with being reckless, with fearlessness, is that it makes you beyond powerful. Fin has that, and as we break away, he doesn't hesitate to step out onto the ledge and press to the wall. The tiny bits of rock used as footholds drop a bit but not much. He doesn't spare them a glance, his demeanour calm but determined. He's always been that way; there was nothing he couldn't face, not until Peyton anyway. She showed him what true fear was, love too, and now he stays alive by reducing his risks to ensure he will be there for her forever.

Now though, we need the man who swung one-handed over the edge of a sixty-foot drop. Who swam with great white sharks without a cage. Who once fought a croc and dived into eel-infested waters to retrieve a necklace Peyton had dropped. We need that version of him, and I see him emerging in his eyes as he reaches across the darkened wall for the next handhold.

Peyton steps to the edge and waits until he swings his leg forward, perching on a tiny little ledge with one hand gripping the rock as he searches for the next step. Giving us a smile, she moves out onto the wall, and they slowly start to move across it, stopping every now and then to make sure they are on the right path as she silently points sections out. By the time Kalen is on the wall, they are at least four moves ahead of us. At one point, they have to hang from just a handhold using only their fingers and inch across to another foothold. We have to go up diagonally to avoid slippery areas and loud places. All the while, my back burns from having it towards those creatures, knowing they could swoop in at any given moment.

We are exposed.

Peyton stops, and I watch as she glances at us. She taps Fin on the shoulder, leans in, whispers something to him, and then takes a step back. Fin leaps across an opening, hitting the wall with a soft thud to grab on to the next hold. We all freeze, looking over our shoulders to see if they heard, but the noise of the water covered it, thank fuck.

With a deep breath, she does the same, and again, we wait.

It's slow going, and when I'm across, we hear a tiny squeak. We stop, waiting until they settle down again while Fin climbs higher, too close to the ceiling, but it's the only other ledge. Peyton follows and then descends again. I do the same, and Tyler waits until we are across to make a move, not wanting to spook or dislodge them. He hits the leap and quickly climbs up and down next to her. Kalen is next. His thud is the loudest, and he freezes, his hand going to his knife while I shake my head.

There's some flapping of wings, but they don't seem to know we are here. We keep moving, listening to the sounds of water dripping and their quiet squawks. Eventually, we make it about halfway around the room, and we're settling into a rhythm, thinking we have got this.

You can prepare for everything, think through every possibility, and come up with solutions . . . but something can still go wrong.

And with our luck, it does.

Tyler reaches up for a hold to swing onto the gap between the tiny ledges, but the rock rips from the wall. His hand drops, and he catches himself before he falls into the water, but he can't stop the rock, which plunges into the water with an audible smack.

We all freeze, pressing against the wall as we hold our breaths.

Then they wake up.

FORTY-SEVEN

Peyton

Kalen turns, hanging one-handed as we watch them flap their wings, flying into the air. Some drop, landing on the rocks and water with shrieks, searching for the source of the sound. Tyler looks over at me sadly.

Go, he mouths as they soar straight for him, following the echo. Holding my gaze, he lets go and drops back, flipping to land on the rock below and pulling a knife. He holds it with the blade angled across his hand and crouches, waiting for them. Fin tries to grab me, to drag me with him, but I'm having none of it. I won't leave someone else behind—no one else fucking dies.

Not now, not when we are so close.

Tyler is mine, my love, and I'm not abandoning him. If we die, we die together. I drop and land on my feet, stumbling slightly from the force. Tyler hears it, of course, and turns to glare at me. "Run! Go! Now!" he screams, ordering me around as he ducks and slashes up at the creature circling him, toying with him.

"Like fucking hell I will!" I yell back and run, sliding across the floor to get to his side as they dive-bomb me too. "I'm not fucking leaving you!" I snarl when I reach him, pressing my back to his as I stab and kick at them. "Not ever again, so get the fuck over it!"

One is crawling towards me, so I kick it in the face, the other creatures circling overhead. He turns and meets my eyes, panting.

"Live or die together, remember?" I rasp.

He smiles before shaking his head, his eyes sad. Tyler knows he's lost this fight. I won't leave him, which means we have to win or we all die here. Kalen drops next to me, and Fin rushes over, Riggs too, until we create a circle.

All of us share a look, an understanding. It's our final showdown, us versus them. Either we all make it out, or none of us do. There's no more walking away, no more hiding or running.

No more.

Michael's death weighs heavily on me, and the idea of any of my men dying . . . No. It's unthinkable. I wouldn't survive their deaths, even if I got free. So instead, we ready ourselves. Kalen pulls a flare and throws it, Fin does also, lighting the room with a reddish glow as they swoop closer to us.

"Apex predators, bitch!" I scream at the mass approaching us, their talons stretched wide and beaks parted to swallow us whole. Tyler drags me down when they dive, missing us with a squeak as some hit the wall and others flap to reach the ceiling and circle again.

"What's the plan?" Kalen snarls. "'Cause standing here and dying doesn't work for me." He throws his pick, hits one emerging from the water separating the rocks—which we didn't notice before—and knocks it back in as blood fills the once-dark liquid.

"Move together towards the light," I snap. "Let's get the fuck out of here and kill as many as we can on the way."

One flies right at my face, and Kalen leaps in front of me, stabbing as he does and taking it down into the water. I watch him go, wide-eyed, but I don't have time to panic as another flies at us. I have to concentrate on keeping it back with my knife. A second later, I hear a quiet gasp, and Kalen breaks through the water and climbs back to us, dripping wet and snarling and covered in blood. His or theirs, I can't tell.

"Move," he barks.

Sounds like a good idea to me. Keeping low, we race across the rocks, leaping over sections of water. We move as fast as we can, slipping and ducking and weaving to avoid them, stabbing out to kill as many as we can.

One hits Riggs, taking him down to the rock as he fights it off, trying to protect his throat from its beak. I kick it as hard as I can, sending it sailing away as I reach down and help him up. He's panting but nods that he's okay, and hand in hand, we follow after Fin, who's setting the pace and path towards the light.

Our end goal.

I'm running so fast, I don't see the dark water clearly, the red glow of the flares barely illuminating it. I leap and miss the ledge, and my foot plunges into the water. Grunting, Riggs pulls me free as Tyler and Kalen watch our backs, but just as my foot leaves the water, claws grab it. My eyes widen, meeting Riggs's frightened gaze as I'm jerked from his grip and pulled under. I have a second to take a deep breath as everything goes dark.

The water is almost pitch black with hints of red as I sink farther down. I kick at the claws as it releases me and then spin, turning slowly to try to find the creature responsible as I grip my knife. A slash swipes across my back, and I wince as pain flares through my body. I feel it trying to crawl up my back, so I turn and stab until it lets go again.

The red refracts through the water, giving everything an eerie ambiance as I turn, waiting. If I swim up, it will get me.

Come on, you little fucker, let's end this.

I see it a moment later, swimming right towards me. I brace, and just as it's about to reach me, I lift my legs, trap it, and stab downwards again and again. Blood swirls in the churning water, its screech loud, even down here. Bubbles escape it as I stab and hack, and when it finally stills, I let go and watch as it floats away.

Take that, winged bitch.

Looking around, I try to determine which way is up—everything can get so confusing in the dark water—but then I spot the fading flares. Holding the knife tightly, I cut through the water, swimming for the light. I break through the surface with a gasp, accepting an outstretched hand, and then I'm yanked up onto the rock with Kalen, who quickly checks me over. Slicking back my hair, I feel something thicker than water drip down my face, and I notice my hands are pink with watered-down blood, but I ignore it.

Tyler, Kalen, and I work together to push them back far enough to jump the distance again and catch up to Fin and Riggs. Fin waves us on. "It's a tunnel. We have to crawl through!" he yells over the sound of the screeching.

Just then Tyler shouts, and I turn to see him on the ground with at least eight of the creatures on him as he bucks and fights. Kalen gets there first, stabbing and kicking, but I'm right behind him. I try to get one off his side, but as I pull it, it digs its claws in, ripping his skin. Blood pours from the wound, but Tyler gets to his feet before stumbling. I look at Kalen in panic, knowing he can't walk like that.

"I can't carry him!"

"Shit!" he hollers, putting his arm around Tyler and dragging him backwards as I slowly move before them, watching their backs as we go. I panic, wondering how badly he's hurt, but I can't check, not until we reach the tunnel. Fin goes through as soon as we're there, Riggs slips in next, and I look Tyler over as they circle closer. He's bleeding pretty badly, but he'll make it.

"It's going to hurt like a bitch, but you need to crawl, baby!" I yell. He nods and grits his teeth as Kalen starts to lower him to the floor. With each second that ticks away, my heart races faster, and I glance back to check on the monsters.

They are almost on us, so I step away, swiping at as many as I can. One knocks the knife from my hand, and I hear Kalen yell my name, and then I see what he's so terrified of.

There are more streaming into the fucking chamber from every nook and cranny, and I'm still being dive-bombed. I look back to see Tyler on the ground waiting for me.

We don't stand a chance. They will follow us in there, and Tyler won't have an opportunity to escape. He's hurt. I look back to see them. Kalen is determined, and Fin and Riggs are shouting my name, wondering what's happening. They are through, at least, but I've got to give Tyler a head start. Kalen too. If I don't, we are all dead. They will block that tunnel, and we won't have room to run or fight.

I can't let them die here, not when I just found them again. They gave me back my heart, my life. I ruined theirs for so long, they deserve a chance, a chance at a better life.

I meet Kalen's gaze. He knows. His eyes widen as he reaches out to stop me, but I glare, silently making him promise to save them, to protect them the way I never could.

"Go!" I scream, and then without waiting so they can't stop me, I run towards the mass, snatching up a pick one of them must have dropped.

I hear them shout, but I trust Kalen to get them out. He'll come back for me, but he'll get them out first.

Even though there will be nothing left to come back to.

FORTY-EIGHT

I hold them back as long as I can, and when I glance away, I get scratched and bitten, but I see Kalen making his way through the tunnel. I know he's planning to get Tyler through, then come back for me, but I also know I won't be alive when he does. More and more creatures spill into the cavern, brought by the scent of blood and the sounds of screams.

I need to protect my men.

I turn and sprint to the tunnel, trusting them to handle the ones that already crawled through, and with all my strength, I shove against a rock, rolling it. My muscles strain as I hold back a scream, my teeth clenching as they attack my back, scratching and kicking as I manage to position the boulder at the entrance, blocking it. As soon as it's done and they are safe, I drop to the ground and crawl to avoid the monsters as much as I can, trying to find a way out. Just because I stayed behind doesn't mean I plan on dying. Not if I can help it. I'm not the type to curl into a ball and give up. I'll fight to my last fucking breath, and if there is no other way . . . then I'll take as many as I can with me.

FORTY-NINE

Kalen

I kick at the monsters behind me. My heart is screaming, my head too, telling me to go back, but I have to trust her, and I have to get my brother through. I manage to kill the creatures and push Tyler forward, urging him on. The faster he gets to the other side, the faster I can go back.

We break out into the cave on the other side of the tunnel. Riggs and Fin look past me, searching for her as they call her name, and as soon as Tyler is propped up, I dive back into the tunnel, crawling as fast as I can. I cut my arms, face, legs, and sides on the rock, but I don't care. Each second that passes is a second I could lose her. I can barely breathe through my panic. I know why she did it, but that doesn't matter. I won't be okay until I reach her side. Going back means I'll probably die with her, but I don't give a fuck.

I clamber over the creatures' corpses with my heart in my throat. As I draw closer, I hear her scream, and my heart shatters. With a roar, I leap forward . . . and hit a wall.

Blinking in surprise, I start pounding my fists against the rock that wasn't there before. It's too perfect of a fit for it to have fallen, and it's blocking off the tunnel from her side. That means she did it. She put it here.

To stop us from coming back.

To stop us from saving her so she could save us.

I stare, wide-eyed, as my heart freezes in my chest. No, no, no!

Not her!

Anyone but her. No, I can't lose her. I ram my fists into the boulder again and again, splitting open my skin. It's not working. I turn and use my legs, putting all my strength into each thrust.

"Peyton!" I roar over and over again.

I won't lose her, I can't!

She's the love of my life.

She promised me forever. She doesn't get to leave me this way.

"Don't you fucking dare! Do you hear me? You left us once! Never again! Get your ass over here, baby, and move this rock. Don't you dare fucking do this to us, you selfish fucking bitch! Fuck, Peyton!" I breathe heavily, panicking as tears form in my eyes. "Baby," I whisper. "Baby, please, don't do this." A sob racks my chest as I continue to kick, my vision becoming blurry. "Please don't fucking leave me. I can't do this without you. I can't live without you. You're my whole fucking world. Please, baby, move the rock, that's all you gotta do, I'll do the rest. Come on, baby, please!" I beg, the words flowing continuously. "I love you so much, I can't lose you again, please! I can save you, let me save you." I choke, the entreaties feeling like splinters against my already raw throat.

Never in all my life have I felt such terror.

I thought watching her walk away was bad.

I thought living without her was hard.

I thought seeing her again would wreck me.

I thought handing her my heart again was scary.

Those things have nothing on this moment. With each second that passes, the chance of me getting to her diminishes. Then it all quiets past the rock. No creatures . . . no Peyton.

I stare, wide-eyed, as motionless as a statue.

"Baby?" I whisper softly. "Baby, talk to me."

"Kalen, what's going on?" I hear the others shouting. "Fuck, they're trying to come through the walls. Kalen, bring her back, we gotta go!"

I turn to see the light at the end of the tunnel, but I want to stay right here, in the dark, waiting for her to save me again. But they need me, and I promised her.

So even though turning away makes me gag, I force my hands and feet to move as I crawl out of the tunnel. I stand and meet their worried eyes as they glance past me. Even Tyler struggles to his feet, his face pale as he watches me, his brow furrowed.

"She's gone," I rasp. "She blocked the tunnel. I can't get through. I heard her— Fuck!"

"There has to be a way back; we can find one!" Riggs snaps.

"Yeah, yeah, we gotta." Fin starts running around, searching for a way to get to her, but I just stare at Tyler. We know there isn't, and we know the likelihood of her still being alive is extremely low.

As I observe my brothers, my heart shatters. The broken, dark pieces of the organ she put back together and breathed life into.

All I can think is one thought—I failed her. She deserves more than to die alone.

Peyton Andrews deserved the world and then more. She lived exploring the darkest, farthest reaches of this earth, exploring the unknown, loving those too hardened to love, and saving those who needed it.

She left us again.

Tyler

"No," I whisper, staring at my brother's stricken face. He looks broken, more so than after the war, more so than after she first left us.

He looks . . . hopeless.

"No," I repeat louder, even as my brain latches on to the fact she's gone. If even Kalen has no hope . . .

"No!" I scream and hobble towards him. He lets me come and doesn't even try to stop me as I slam my fists into his chest. He takes it stoically with tears streaming down his face. Kalen thinks he deserves it, he's blaming himself, tearing himself down.

I know he thinks he lost the woman he loved, but I can't stop. I can't. "No!" I howl, and he finally wraps his arms around me as I start to fall from my wound. He holds me up as I press my face against his chest and sob.

My heart cracks with the force of my pain, and I'm unable to catch my breath without her. The ring around my neck burns against my skin. It belongs to her, just like I do. Always. I can't lose her.

I can't.

I sob harder as he helps me down, rocking me back and forth as he cries too. Her name is on both our lips and stamped across our hearts. Our love for her is deeper than any ocean, any cave.

Fin and Riggs keep searching until I hear them start to cry, realising there is no way. Their arms wrap around us, and we huddle together, sniffing, sobbing . . . broken.

Unable to move. Unable to think.

We're shattered messes without our heart.

Without our girl.

We hear the creatures coming for us then.

Let them kill us. At least in the next life, I will be with my love again.

FIFTY

Peyton

I manage to rush away from the rock, trying to lead the creatures away, but one hits me from behind, sending me sprawling into the water. I sink under the surface as they dive in, chasing me. The water churns around us as they attack, but I twist and swim away, hardly able to see.

Some latch on to my legs as I paddle up and up and up, hitting a rock as I surface.

I grab on to the rough edge, kick at the creatures clinging to my legs, and finally dislodge them. I drag myself from the water, gasping for air as I heave myself onto the slippery ledge, smacking something sharp and solid with my left hand.

Then they grab me again.

I don't scream as I'm ripped back under, no, I take a deep breath and clutch the object. I take it with me, seeing it before I'm pulled down . . . It's the sharp end of a bone.

I sink lower and lower, being attacked from every angle. My blood pollutes the water as I stab and slash, refusing to give up. I use every ounce of strength and energy I have. If I can, I'm getting back to my men, and if I can't, I'm taking as many of these fuckers with me as possible. One grabs on to my hair, nearly making me scream as it rips out strands, yanking me with it.

It's swimming up.

Fuck.

We break the surface, and its wings flap, lifting us into the air. We rise higher and higher as I twist, reaching up to grip its taloned foot to reduce the pain as tears stream down my face. Others circle us, screeching, as it flies across the cavern, heading for a large patch of rock filled with skeletons. My arm with the bone dangles in the air, and I grip it tighter, despite my fatigue and pain.

Fuck that.

I swing my weapon up, screaming as loud as I can, and I manage to pierce its leg. It releases me immediately as it careens through the air, only we aren't over the rock yet, so I plunge into a different section of water, sinking . . .

Down I go.

My eyes flare wide as I look for another monster, preparing for an attack.

As I search, my gaze catches on a dark hole, a possible cave entrance with a water current filtering through it. Fuck this. Uncaring about the noise, I swim down as hard as I can. My lungs hurt and my body aches, and black spots dot my vision from blood loss, exhaustion, or lack of air, I don't know which, but I keep going. My complete focus is on that dark fucking entrance. I swim until I get near it . . .

And then I'm sucked inside.

I don't know how much later I wake up, but I'm alive . . . I think.

I'm floating in a pool of shallow water with my arms to the sides, my legs spread, and my hair floating behind me. The ceiling has speckles of light across it, and the soft splash of the water entering the room is loud as I'm pushed and pulled across the cavern.

I need to move, to find a way out, a way back to them, but I'm so tired.

My body hurts so badly, and black still spots my vision, letting me know I'm more injured than I thought. Moving will be agony, surviving even worse. I look down as far as I can to see my blood clouding the water around me, making me wince as I lay my head back down, trying to gather my strength.

Come on, Peyton.

They need you; get fucking moving.

But it's no use. All of me, from my feet to the top of my head, hurts, and I'm so tired . . . so very fucking tired. Of fighting, of being in pain. The water laps next to my ears peacefully, trying to lull me into the darkness with its promise of peace. Of rest. Of numbness.

As I lie there, drifting in a pool of my own blood, all I can think about are my men. Their lips, their smiles, their love, and the things that made me fall in love with them in the first place.

I would gladly die for them, but the thought of their pain, of being the reason they grieve and hurt once more makes me fight. I scream internally as I force myself to move. Gritting my teeth, I get to my knees, hanging my head as I breathe heavily. My body is screaming at me, telling me to let go, that this is enough. But I can't give up.

I have to fight for them.

For me.

Dying is easy, living is harder.

I clench my jaw, tasting blood as I stumble to my feet. My vision blurs from the pain, and I squint to avoid the dizziness spinning through me before I pick up one foot and put it down, then the other. Over and over. I focus on the next step, the next breath, the next moment. I hear their cheers in my head, spurring me on, knowing their hearts are with me, demanding I return to them.

One step.

Kalen.

One step.

Tyler.

One step.

Riggs.

One step.

Fin.

I repeat their names again and again to remember why I'm still going, why I'm always fighting. For the way they make me laugh. For the way they make me feel safe and excited at the same time. For the way they love me, trust me, push me, and help me.

I reach the wall and slump against it, just trying to catch my breath.

Come on, Minnow, Michael urges, his voice filling my head like he's right here with me. I shake my head, dislodging my tears at the pure, rough sound.

"I'm so fucking tired," I whisper, admitting my weakness to him.

I know, kid, but it ain't ever stopped you before. When you're at your weakest, it's when you have the greatest opportunity to be your strongest. Rock bottom, kid, and there is only one way to go. Don't you dare give up. You never did for me, like I never will on you. Those men need you. Now get your ass in gear!

With a quiet yell, I push away from the wall and turn, searching for a way out. There's a tunnel to my left, so I move slowly towards it. Once inside, my hand drags along the rock. I don't know where it's leading me, but I keep going forward with determination in each step.

That's it, Minnow, fucking move. You've got this, I'm with you every step of the way. You aren't alone, I'm right here.

I know he's not real, but it helps to hear him cheering me on like always. His voice gives me the strength I need to keep moving. My breath heaves out of my tight lungs, and I feel my blood dripping from my cuts, leaving a path across the rock as I walk. I duck when the passage tightens and then opens up into a junction with three tunnels. I pick one at random, stumbling through the dark space. It only grows darker and darker, and I have to hold my hands out in front of me to guide me forward.

Don't fear the dark, Minnow. You find out what you're made of in oblivion.

My breathing is loud in the silence, and my heart races as I wonder if one of those creatures is right in front of me, but I still keep going. Although I'm scared, I walk on and on, never stopping, even when my body tries to fall.

Then I hear the voices.

With a cry, I fling myself forward in the dark and drop through a hole, tumbling down . . . down . . . and right into someone. We crash to the ground with a grunt. I force my eyes open and stare down at the wide, bloodshot, puffy eyes of Riggs.

"Hi," I croak, and promptly pass out.

FIFTY-ONE

Riggs

"Pey?" I whisper, not totally comprehending that the warm, bleeding body on top of me is my love until her eyes close. "Peyton!" I shout as I grab her and sit up, cradling her in my arms as the others crowd around me. They're all talking and running their hands across her, checking her over. Kalen even slaps her to try to wake her up, his panic in full force.

We thought we had lost her.

Fuck, I'm getting too old for this shit.

My heart can't take it as I hold her against my chest. "Fuck," I mutter, shaking. I thought I'd lost her, truly lost her. I could survive knowing she was somewhere in this world if it was her choice . . . but when I thought she died, left this world entirely so we could never see her again . . . I could barely hold it together. I knew I had to for my family, and the only way I could was by counting numbers. Fin and I dragged Tyler and Kalen from that room, saving them like she would have wanted us to, even as we crumpled.

We were barely able to put one foot in front of the other, our minds caught on the last moment we saw her. "Princess?" Kalan pleads as Tyler twists and turns her body to inspect her.

"Fin?" I snap, wanting answers.

"Cuts and scrapes, some deep but not in need of stitches. It's more the quantity of them, and she's reopened her side wound. I'll clean and cover that, and disinfect as many as possible," he replies instantly. "Please put her on her back." I lower her softly, stroking her hair from her face, needing to touch her as he gets to work. As I peer down at her slack, pale face, I can't help but smile.

"I knew you couldn't be dead," I whisper. "No matter what the numbers said, you are too fucking strong. You hear that, Pey? And when we get out of here, we're going to relax for so long, you'll start to get bored."

"And get drunk," Fin adds with a grin, "and feel you up, babe."

"And be together," Tyler vows with a trembling smile.

"There's no escaping us now, princess," Kalen comments, kissing the back of her hand and pressing it to his cheek.

"You hear that, Peyton Andrews? You're ours, so wake your ass up and kick us into gear."

We hold her as Fin works, talking to her the entire time, sharing stories of our past—some after she left. We laugh, we cry, and through it all, I feel my heart starting to heal. When those eyes blink open and stare at me, that last piece falls into place.

Peyton Andrews controls my heart, and she always has. Without her, there's no me anymore.

"Hey," she rasps. "Did I hear something about Fin trying to wrestle a crocodile?"

I laugh so hard I cry. Fin sits back, his hands covered in her blood, but I've never seen him smile so wide nor look so relieved. "You know it, babe, and when this is over, I'll wrestle you too."

"Romantic," she teases and looks down. "Oh, look, I'm not dead."

"You, princess? Never. You're too strong for that," Kalen murmurs, and she grins at him.

"Don't you ever fucking do that again," Tyler snarls, crawling around me and getting in her face. "You fucking hear me? Don't you ever sacrifice yourself for us again. Live or die together, remember?"

"I love you too," she whispers, and he shudders as he leans down and kisses her softly.

"Never again," he murmurs as he pulls away.

"Can we get the fuck out of here now?" she grumbles as she tries to sit up. I quickly press my arm behind her, as does Tyler, and she goes to lean into him, but he winces when it hurts his wound, so she leans into me instead. I happily wrap my arms around her.

I need to feel her close, need to feel her alive. Safe. With us.

"Yeah, babe, sounds like a good plan to me."

"Have you found a way out?" she asks.

"Maybe, we, erm . . . got distracted." Fin coughs awkwardly.

Her eyebrow arches, and she looks around as we all avert our gazes. "Riggs," she demands, focusing on my face since it's the closest, so I sigh. I'm unable to lie to her.

"We might have lost it when we couldn't get back to you and haven't looked for an exit—yet."

I expect her to be mad, disappointed even, but instead she cups my cheeks until I meet her eyes and kisses me tenderly. "I love you," she whispers before looking at the others. "All of you. I'm sorry I stayed behind. I thought it was the only way, but we've gotta keep moving. I'm not dying here, and neither are you, so put the emotional shit away for later and let's go."

"There she is." Kalen smirks. "My fucking bitch Andrews."

"You know it, Kay." She winks. "Now help me the fuck up and let's blow this cave."

"You heard her." Tyler laughs.

"Hell yes, time to go," Fin agrees.

"Together," I add.

Fin

Peyton's right. As much as I want to throw her into a wall and fuck her raw in both punishment and pleasure for her leaving us and still being alive, we don't have time. We need to move before they figure out a way to get to us. The two that already did are lying dead in the corner.

There's no more time to mess around. Tyler is hurt, and so is our girl. It's only a matter of time before they struggle to go on or another one of us gets hurt, then we'll be screwed. Determined to get the hell out of here, we check the equipment we have left, since some of it was dropped when we escaped the other cavern.

When we realise how little we have left, we share a sad look, but it won't stop us. We have three tanks of air, two masks, one rope, one pick, two knives, and some water and food. It's meagre, but we have to use it and hope it's enough.

We switch as much as we can over to Kalen's, Riggs's, and my bags before we set off. Tyler is being held up by Riggs, while I'm at the front with Peyton behind me, and Kalen brings up the rear. I know she hates letting me go first, but she's hurt, and we are not letting her get attacked again. Her wounds may be small, but if we don't get her out, they could get worse or become infected.

There is only one tunnel out of the section we find ourselves in. We have to bend our heads, but we manage to get through. It twists and turns, and at one point, we have to move sideways with Peyton helping Tyler from one end and Riggs the other.

Even when exhausted with sweat pouring down his face, Ty doesn't utter a single complaint. He keeps moving, keeps going. As does our girl. Both of them are fucking survivors, and they're so fucking strong, it makes me want to do better, be better, to find us a way out of here so they don't have to be in pain anymore.

That's why I push myself to move faster, to stay ahead so that if I run into any issues, they have enough time to escape while I deal with it. My recklessness may come in handy right about now, because if it saves my girl's life, my family members' lives, then so fucking be it. We can't count on anyone but ourselves—never could and never will—and down here, our luck can change quickly. But if anyone can get the fuck out of this cave, it's us.

Apex predators all day, baby.

We keep walking, only breaking for water and to check on Tyler's wound. Luckily, the bleeding has stopped. It didn't hit anything too important, but he lost a lot of blood, plus who knows what was in their claws or the water. He's pale and sweaty but determined, and Peyton ignores our concerns and promises she's okay.

Once I'm sure, we push on. The tunnel leads upwards, and we have to struggle up the incline. Tyler grunts with the effort, and Peyton pants but forces herself forward. When we're at the top, I freeze and stare down.

You have got to be fucking kidding me.

FIFTY-TWO

Peyton

The entrance is big enough for us to stand in side by side, so we do, and then we gape.

Fuck, why is nothing in this cave easy?

I know they say life only throws you stuff you can handle, but holy shit, I'm reaching my limit.

Below us is a pool, and from here, we can see the way out. Light is filtering into the water, bright sunlight. It's a submerged tunnel leading out of the cave. It's our exit, but it's also at least thirty feet below and filled with water, and who knows how long the passage is. We only have three tanks and one rope, not to mention Tyler's injuries.

I share a look with Kalen, and Tyler narrows his eyes on me. "Don't," he snaps. "We're getting out of here. We are problem solvers, we've got this."

"Okay." I bite my lip, debating our options, and come to the same realisation they probably have. "Fuck, I have a plan, but it's insane."

"The best ones are," Fin remarks, making Riggs grin.

"Okay, someone dives down there with the rope, tying it off at the bottom for us to climb down. We need somebody before and after Tyler if he can manage t—"

"I can manage it." He nods solemnly.

"Then we buddy breathe through the tunnel."

"Fuck," Kalen grumbles.

Pretty much. Buddy breathing alone is dangerous, but heading into an unknown tunnel *and* buddy breathing? It's fucking suicide, but we have no choice, especially when we hear the squawk of the monsters not too far away.

"Okay, so I'll share with Peyton—" Kalen starts, and I shake my head.

"No, you need to protect our rear, which means the slowest ones need more air. You need a tank," I tell him. "Fin needs to go first, since he's the fastest after me, but I'm too hurt to go too fast. He needs a tank, and he can buddy breathe with Riggs." They nod, and I share a look with Tyler. "We're the most injured, the most likely to fail, so we need to share air."

"Babe," he groans, and I grip his head and press my forehead to his.

"You know I'm right. It's our decision for our team. If we fail, then we only kill each other, and we're already hurt. We share air, my love."

"You've always been my air anyway," he replies, even as Fin fake gags. "You're right."

We both know sacrifice, the weight of leadership. We can't kill our team for our weaknesses. We're wounded, meaning we're more likely to panic or run out of air and suffocate. We share to ensure we don't hurt the healthy ones on our team. With our eyes locked, we nod our agreement, knowing if one of us suffers, dies, then the other does too. We accept that.

"Don't go being all dramatic on us. We all get out," Kalen snarls.

"Exactly. No matter the distance, we dive it." Riggs nods. "It works, and we can see the light, so it can't be too far. No panicking, slow breathing. Two and two."

"Two and two." Fin nods. "Get to the surface and find help, then sleep forever, and after, all the sex." It makes us laugh, even as I pass over the rope, our hands sliding together.

"You get us out of here, love, and you've got yourself a deal." I wink.

"Fuck yes. Now watch this, babe. You'll be wet as hell at my impressive skills," he teases with a smirk. With the rope tied around his waist, Fin dives over the edge, plunging into the water below. He hits it clean, and within a moment, he resurfaces and grins up at me. *Wet,* he mouths, making me shake my head with a laugh.

"Okay, Riggs first to help Tyler," I instruct. He goes to protest, but I narrow my eyes. "Riggs, you, me, Kalen. Don't fucking argue. We can still dive down if needed, you can't. Now, get your sexy ass down there. You owe me orgasms, and when we get out of here, I plan on claiming them."

He kisses me hard. "That's a promise, my love."

We work together to get him hooked on to the rope below me. I lean against the side of the jagged wall and help him from behind as Riggs assists from below, holding as much of his weight as he can on the rope. Kalen and I help Tyler down, walking backwards. I can see how much he hates this, but we have all been there, and the only thing that matters is that we're alive and still together.

"You've got this," I say as Kalen turns to watch our backs. I hold the rope at the top, kneeling as I observe him slowly climb down with Riggs's help. He's breathing heavily, and his teeth are clenched, but he manages it and softly drops into the water, going under before resurfacing as Riggs stays by his side.

They nod at me to come down, so I glance at Kalen and get to my feet. He looks back, his dark eyes stealing my breath as usual. Standing on my tiptoes, I kiss him hard. "I know you came back for me, and I love you for it. Thank you for saving them," I whisper, trying to pull away, but he palms the back of my head as he deepens the kiss.

"If you ever try to leave me again, I'll chain you to my side," he snarls against my lips, nipping them in warning as I shiver in desire.

"Yes, Kay." I giggle. "Be right behind me."

"Always," he promises as I pull away and grab the rope.

I back to the edge and step over, slowly descending as I ignore the aches in my body. We are almost there, I know it, and adrenaline pumps through me, pushing the exhaustion and pain away, giving me enough energy to finish this.

I reach the bottom and let go, slipping under and resurfacing next to the others as Kalen unties the rope with a wince—his hands are a bit torn up, but he's dressed them—and throws it down to us in case we need it. Riggs reels it up and ties it as Kalen dives, hitting the water next to us smoothly. We swim closer as he breaks the surface, forming a circle as we tread water.

"Okay, are we ready for this? Everyone know the plan?" They nod. Our tanks are already distributed, the levels checked. They are at 50 percent, but we ignore that, knowing we can drop them and push through free-diving if need be.

I let Tyler start with ours, and we share a look as we swim as close as we can. It's a ritual, one we haven't done in many years. "Why do we do this?"

"To explore the unknown," Fin answers automatically, knowing the drill. I taught them after my father died. It was tradition, and the fact we carried it on makes me feel that much closer to him.

"Why are we here?"

"To find ourselves," Riggs responds with a smile.

"What do we do?"

"Work together as a team," Kalen replies.

"Because who are we?"

"Apex predators," Tyler says, and we all close our eyes and press our fingers to the water to honour my father and all those we have lost. When I reopen them again, we are good to go.

We're ready to get out of this cave once and for all.

I share a look with Fin and Riggs. "I love you," I tell them, needing them to know.

"Don't say it like it's goodbye, Peyton." Fin wags his finger. "We have lots of sex and relaxing to do." With that, he winks, sucks in a breath, and dives under. Riggs blows me a kiss, takes a breath, and follows.

I share a look with Kalen. "No hero antics."

"Shut the fuck up and dive, baby girl." He rolls his eyes.

Tyler sucks in a breath and submerges, and I look at Kalen again. "If it's a choice between me or him, get him." Unwilling to give him time to become angry, knowing I'm asking the impossible, I take a deep breath and dive. Kalen waits a moment before following.

Luckily, we still have our torches, and as we move deeper, we flick them on. Tyler and I swim side by side, and he holds the tank in his hand in case he needs it. Fin and Riggs are before us, heading through some underground structures with holes. We twist through them and around the stalagmites coming up from the bottom before it narrows into a tunnel that seems to be heading straight.

I have a good feeling. The same feeling I get when we make a new find, when I see a cave I know is going to be incredible, life-changing. I have it now. This has to be the way out.

I just know it.

We follow behind them, and a little way into the tunnel, Tyler takes his first breath from the tank. I'm okay, so I don't reach to take it, letting him keep it instead as Riggs and Fin pass their tank. The bubbles blow into the water and float to the ceiling.

Tyler takes another breath and reaches over, giving it to me. Sealing my lips around it, I inhale and pass it back, knowing he needs it more. The farther we swim, the more the water heats, the light growing brighter. Excitement fills us as we speed up, swimming as fast as we can, even Tyler, but when I look back, he's trailing blood behind him. It makes me nervous, knowing those monsters can smell it, but there is nothing we can do about it now.

The water starts to have more of a current, and even Fin's and Riggs's kicking increases, knowing what that means. Tyler draws from the tank and passes it over to me. I take one just as we all come to a slow stop behind Fin and Riggs.

The tunnel ends.

Open water.

Freedom.

We did it.

We are at the edge of the tunnel with the sunlight right before us. The ocean stretches before us, promising us air and freedom . . . then I hear a grunt.

I turn to see Kalen fighting three of the monsters. I look back to Tyler, who's ready to help, but we both know he's in no shape to do so. I take a deep draw from the tank before I pass it to him, knowing he'll need it to get free. I nod my head to Fin and Riggs, and without a backwards glance, I spin and swim as fast as I can back to Kalen.

I trust Tyler to follow Fin and Riggs, but I refuse to leave Kalen down here in the dark. He sees me coming and shakes his head before they swarm him again, blocking my view. I see blood polluting the water and almost snarl as I make my body as streamlined as possible to reach him faster.

Fuck these monsters and their stupid cave. They will rot down here.

As soon as I reach him, I grab one around the neck and throw it off, kicking another so Kalen can deal with the third. The one I threw comes at me, scratching along my face, but I grab it, ducking to avoid its talons, and slam it into the wall.

Over and over again.

Eventually, it stops moving, and when I turn around, Kalen has his hand around one's back end as it snaps at me, trying to reach me as he effortlessly breaks the neck of the other. I'm left wide-eyed as he turns, reels the other in, breaks it in two, and lets go. It drifts to the floor in a bloody haze. I stare at him, and he grins before it falls away. His hands swipe through the water, and he looks back at me with panic as he gestures to his mouth.

The tank.

Fuck!

It must have gotten lost in the fight.

With no other option, he swims towards me, grabs me, and drags me after him as we fight to get out of the tunnel and into the air before we drown. We swim as fast as we can, but my lungs are starting to scream at me. Not just because of how long we've been down here, but because the fight made me lose valuable air time. I tap his hand, and he knows, probably struggling himself.

I search for a solution and find it above us.

I point, and he follows my gaze with a nod. We both swim up, up to the top of the tunnel. Hopefully the others are out by now, but we won't stop until we are as well.

There, on the surface of the ceiling, are air bubbles. Who knows how long they have been here, but it's either that or drown. We press our faces to the ceiling and suck down as many as we can before diving and swimming hard again.

We have one last try to get out.

He never once releases my hand until we break through the tunnel. Fin is there with his tank, just about to swim in. He passes it to me, but I hand it to Kalen, knowing he can't hold his breath as long as I can. The sun filters in, and I swim as hard as I can. My heart races so fast, it's all I can hear, and then I break through the surface.

Right into the open air and sunlight.

I suck in fresh air for the first time in weeks, my eyes watering as the sun hits my face, instantly warming it. The ocean laps at me, gently pulling my body with its current. Kalen surfaces next to me, Fin too, and I spin, looking for Tyler, but Fin stops me.

"No splashing; gentle movements," he warns softly.

"Wait, what?" I ask, still looking for Tyler. I find him nearby with Riggs, and I'm about to swim there, ignoring Fin's advice, when I see what he meant. Not too far away is a fin.

An unmistakable shark fin.

Fuck.

I dive under and search the water. There are none right around us, so I surface and gingerly swim over to them. "You're okay." Tyler sighs in relief, hugging me. I wrap my arms around him and hold him afloat, watching the blood in the water. I share a worried look with the others. Not only has he lost a lot, he looks bad . . . and now we have sharks.

In open water.

Fuck.

"At least we're out of the cave," he jokes as we swim in a circle, protecting him as we watch the fins. They aren't super close, but we all know how quickly that could change. And if we're in a feeding ground, we're fucked.

"Great whites, it looks like," Kalen observes, and I nod.

"Probably, it's their territory around here. Any boats? People? Anything?" I question.

Riggs shakes his head as we search the horizon. The ocean is pulling us farther out to sea and away from the cliff where the entrance to the cave was located. The island is there, but it's steep, and there is no way we could climb that, especially in Tyler's current condition.

"What do we do?" I worry as I hold him up. Unlike what most people believe, sharks don't attack unless threatened or if they think you are a seal . . . But in our wet suits, it's hard to tell.

"We wait. Someone has to be looking in the ocean for us. If we see no one in the next hour or so, Riggs or I will climb up and search for help," Kalen suggests.

"Good idea. Until then, let's stay quiet and swim softly. Keep an eye out in case they come closer."

We float on the water, heating from the sun. I never thought I'd be so grateful to be out of a cave as I am. The sharks circle near us, but none come too close. Tyler is getting weaker, his bloodied, wet fingers coming up and trying to grab the necklace around his neck.

The ring.

"It's going to be okay; stay with me," I murmur, kissing his salty hair.

"This is yours. Wear it," he slurs.

"No. When you're better, you can give it to me yourself," I retort, kicking my legs as I watch the fins around us. "Until then, you stay with me, you hear? We are so close, Ty, so fucking close."

"I need you to know I love you," he wheezes.

"I know you do. I know, babe, but please hold on, okay? We need you—I need you," I whisper.

The rumble of an engine sounds, cutting through my anxious pleas.

We scan the water desperately until we see the small fishing boat trolling the waters. We wait for it to draw closer and start screaming, shouting, and waving our hands, still trying not to splash. It stops close by, and Kalen, without an ounce of fear, dives under and swims right into the shark-infested water before it.

I watch, terrified, waiting for him to resurface. He does, right next to the boat, and climbs up, just as a shark lunges. I see him talking to a confused man and gesturing to us before pushing him out of the way and into the cabin of the boat. A moment later, it turns, roaring towards us, and I cry as the water splashes around us from the sharks.

One almost takes a bite, but the boat cuts past it and then idles next to us. Kalen comes to the side and reaches down, trying to get us out of the water as fast as he can. I push as he pulls, helping Tyler in. Kalen pulls me out next, then Riggs and Fin. I fall onto the stained bottom next to Tyler, Fin and Riggs drop to my other side, and Kalen sits at our feet as the man who owns the boat yells into a radio. I turn my head and feel water dripping down my face as the sun heats every bleeding exhausted inch of me. I meet Tyler's eyes and smile.

"We did it, baby, we're safe," I whisper, and using the last of my energy, I drag my hand across the wood and reach for his. He takes mine and tangles our fingers.

Smiling, I close my eyes and turn to face the sky again as I feel another hand grab my free one. A palm lands on my leg, Kalen's, and another on my side, Fin's or Riggs's. They all touch me as we remain silent.

We are free, but we have lost so much along the way.

FIFTY-THREE

Once on the boat, everything goes pretty fast. We are rushed to the island, where those from up top are gathered. There's excited chatter and so many questions, but we are all too worn and injured to answer much. I greet Steve and tell him what happened as we wait for a chopper to arrive. It's there in thirty minutes, and Tyler is airlifted away. I go with him since he's unwilling to let go of my hands. The others set out on a boat straight after to go to the mainland with the closest hospital where we're being airlifted to.

I lay my head on his chest on the way there as they put an IV in and check his stats while covering his wounds. They try to check me over, but I shake my head. He needs them, not me. When we arrive at the hospital, they take him for surgery, and I'm forced to be looked over. I have to get some jabs and will need to take antibiotics. They also have to sew some of the lesions from the monsters. When they asked what made them, I just look away, knowing the likelihood of them believing me is pretty low.

Two hours later, I'm in a bed and on a drip for dehydration when the others get there. We wait together for news on Tyler.

It feels strange to be out; I feel . . . nervous around them, as if unsure how to act. Are they still mine like they were down in the cave? Or are they giving up on me again in the sunlight? But then Kalen strolls over and takes my hand as easily as before, maybe even easier, as if it's made to be there. Fin scoots onto the bed next to me, cuddling into me as Riggs lays his head on my leg.

I start to cry for everything we have lost, but also for everything we have gained.

Michael . . . I can't even begin to grieve for him, but the exhaustion and pain overwhelm me, and I sob. They hold me the entire time, his name on my lips, and finally, my mind shuts down and I sleep.

I'm surrounded by those I love with my heart reaching out to the other who isn't with us, hoping that our luck changes and Tyler is okay.

That we left all of those bad times down there in the dark.

I'm woken by a doctor. My mind is foggy, and he kindly waits for me to take some water and fully fight through the haze before he sits and begins talking. He explains they had to operate on Tyler immediately to close the internal wound. Luckily, he had no damage to his organs, but he lost a lot of blood. He's had two transfusions, and all his other wounds have been treated. He's in recovery on an IV mixture like me, and we can see him if we want. I try to get to my feet, but the doctor sighs and helps me up so I can lean on the IV pole, and then he soon puts me in a wheelchair and wheels me to another floor and another room, my men following.

I see him through the glass, looking clean and almost smaller in the white bed with the bright lights above. He's so still with monitors beeping next to him. Kalen walks in, Fin too, but Riggs waits with me as I hesitate, wondering if he wants me in there.

When he wakes up . . . what if he goes back to hating me?

"You're family, Peyton. You are who he wants to see, to listen to, above all of us. He needs you now, Pey, more than ever. Don't hurt him again." He leans in and kisses me softly. "Get out of those doubts. We've had a hard few weeks, so let's just . . . be. All we're asking for right now is for you to stay, to be here for him . . . and us."

I nod and take his hand, getting up from the wheelchair and letting him lead me inside. Fin has pulled out a chair, and I sit stiffly with a wince, reaching out to take Ty's warm hand. Raising it, I kiss the back as I stare at him. "I'm here, Ty," I whisper before clearing my throat. "We are all here. You're okay, we're all okay. Just rest, and we'll be here when you wake up . . . I'll be here. I promise."

I kiss him again and watch the rise and fall of his chest, wondering if it's enough this time, wondering if I'm enough.

I don't want to hurt them ever again. Down in the cave, we found love, we found forever, but that's the easy part. The hard part is fighting for it, keeping it alive. But if anyone can, it's us.

Together.

FIFTY-FOUR

Fin

As soon as we are allowed to, we go into Tyler's room. We stay there all day and night, even when the doctors try to take Peyton back to her own room claiming she needs rest. I watch her light up as she stares them down, daring them to try and stating she will only rest with him next to her. They leave her alone after that.

We still haven't discussed what we're going to say happened down there—who will believe monsters attacked us—but if we don't give them something, someone will go back down and end up with the same problems we had. However, that's a problem for another day. Today, as the sun rises and starts to shine through the window of the hospital room, is a day for celebration.

Especially when Tyler opens his eyes.

It's only for a moment. He looks around, meeting our eyes and then Peyton's. A small smile curves up his lips. His mask was taken off late last night, and he's breathing for himself. "You stayed," he whispers before he passes out again.

I watch tears roll down her face as she kisses his hand. "I'm not going anywhere, Ty, you hear me? I'll be right here, just rest. I'll look after them for you."

"You can try," I tease. "We're a handful."

She laughs, wiping her tears away, and gives me a grateful smile for trying to cheer her up. I'd do anything for that smile, do anything to keep my girl happy . . . or should I say *our* girl. She will never be just mine, but I don't care. As long as I get a piece of her heart, as long as I get to be in her life, why would I care? Loving them doesn't stop her from loving me as well; love isn't restricted. It isn't a percentage you give out, it's endless and can stretch to fit anyone. We were all already in love, we just don't fight it anymore.

Maybe she had to leave so she could find her way back to us, so we would be ready for this, ready for her and the life we are going to live, because there is one thing I know for sure—Peyton Andrews is never getting away from us again. Wherever she goes, we go.

Family. Always.

Riggs

We stay by Tyler's side the entire time. Steve drops by to check on us, assuring us no one will touch the cave until we're ready to discuss it. He's blocked it from all investigations and is holding the police back as much as he can. He has also paid for private care and the best doctors, as well as a hotel suite for when we are ready to leave the hospital. He promises he will get anything we need or want, we just need to reach out.

His worry is genuine, his sadness too, and Peyton trusts him, assuring him it wasn't his fault. It makes my respect for him grow. It wasn't just a job for him. He's like us, an adventurer, and he clearly feels horrible about what occurred.

But how was he to know? How was anyone to know?

Once he leaves, we settle back down. Peyton is checked over by her doctor again and given the all clear, though she's told to rest and not dive for at least four months. You can see her sigh, but she accepts that even with what happened, none of us can ignore the call of the water—it's in our blood, it's who we are, and that cave won't stop us.

Tyler starts to wake up more often, becoming more lucid with each blink of his eyes before he goes back to sleep. He needs to rest, and what Peyton said is true—we will all be here when he wakes up.

Apex for life.

Kalen

Watching my brother in that hospital bed had me worried. He's the strongest man I know, and to see him in pain with nothing I can do is heartbreaking. My own worries surface, my own darkness, and I bury my head in my hands.

I know he's going to be okay, the doctor said so, but what will be the mental aftermath of what he's been through? What we all went through? I know the effects of PTSD; I've suffered them. I always wanted to protect my family from ever having to go through anything like that. And yet here we are, with my brother lying in a hospital bed, my other brothers cut up and exhausted, and my girl . . .

Fuck, the love of my life is hurt, tired, and drained.

We all need some time to heal, both physically and mentally, but that's not going to happen. We have things to do once we get out of here, like stopping anyone else from ever going down there. I wish I could shoulder all the burden for them, but they would never let me.

As if she knows my thoughts, Peyton lifts her head and smiles at me. Squeezing Tyler's hand, who's asleep again, she stands and heads my way. Riggs takes her spot and talks to Tyler about numbers and animals. One of us is always at his side so he knows he's not alone and that we are okay.

"Hey, babe," she murmurs as she climbs onto my knee. I sit back and hold her tight, burying my head in her shoulder and sucking in the scent that is my girl. How does she always know when I need her?

"Behave, Andrews, don't rip your stitches again," I warn.

"Shut up." She laughs and kisses my head, making me shiver as she holds me back, giving me the comfort I didn't know how to ask for.

"Whatever you say, princess," I promise and nuzzle closer, letting her warmth, her scent, and the feel of her in my arms settle me the way nothing else ever could.

"Just breathe," she whispers. "Take one moment at a time, one day at a time."

It's almost word for word what she used to say to me when I struggled before she left, when the memories of the tours were too much and overwhelming me. It helped then and it helps now. I breathe, letting the sound of her steady heartbeat guide me, anchor me, and bring me back to life like she always does.

"He'll be okay, Kay. We all will. You did so good. Without you, we wouldn't have made it," she murmurs and lifts her head, cupping my jaw and dragging it up until I meet her eyes. "I mean it, Kalen, you saved us." She leans down and kisses me softly, lovingly, telling me everything I need to know with her actions.

Just when I thought I couldn't love this woman any more, she steals that last broken part of my heart.

FIFTY-FIVE

Tyler

A masculine voice hisses, "I swear, if you don't stop putting your cock in my face—"

Groaning, I open my eyes, fighting through the fog and numbness. Pain instantly flares through me, but it's less than the last time I woke up, almost a dull ache. I blink, clearing my eyes as the bright lights shine down on me. Whoever is arguing is too busy to notice, so I sigh and try to lift my head, but I feel weak, so I drop it back.

I'm annoyed at my own body.

"No yelling at the hospital, people are trying to sleep," I chastise them with a croaky voice. There's silence, and then they all surround me, asking questions. I grin and look at Peyton who, with a shaky hand, helps lift my head so I can sip some water before she assists me with getting comfortable.

"Are you okay?" she asks worriedly, her big eyes staring right into my soul like always.

"I am now that I know you're here," I reply promptly, and she grins, even as Fin fake gags. In my drugged state, I panicked, anxious she would slip through my fingers again, that she would be gone when I woke up, but she's here. I see her flinch at the reminder, and I wince, wishing I could take it back. It's going to take time for us not to worry about her disappearing, but I didn't mean to throw it in her face and hurt her . . . even if she smiles at me to pretend it didn't.

"What did the doctors say about you?" I demand.

She rolls her eyes while Riggs recounts everything, making me frown at her. "Then you should be resting."

"I'm fine." She sighs.

"And the cave?" I demand, questions flowing from my mouth now that I'm awake. Fin laughs, and even Kalen joins in. "What?"

"Nothing, it's just good to have you back. It was almost too quiet for a moment there." Fin grins at me.

"Asshole," I mutter and relax back with a wince. I fucking hate being injured or ill, but it won't stop me. I plan on getting out of this bed as soon as possible and back out there with my family, with my girl, making sure those we lost are honoured, and their families are made aware—we need to come up with a plan to explain what happened.

But my body forces me to wait as pain flows through me. Peyton notices, of course, and presses the buzzer for more pain meds until I feel floaty again. Gripping her hand, I close my eyes once more. "Don't leave," I beg just before I pass out.

Five days later, I discharge myself, agreeing to rest at the hotel. My family needs to rest too. Spending every day at my bedside in cramped chairs is not helping, and they refuse to leave me. The other crew members have been by to see me as well, as have the police, who collected our reports before Steve ushered them away.

I'm even wheeled out of the back door to avoid the press and then taken with my family in a van with tinted windows to the hotel. I refuse the wheelchair on the other side though, taking Peyton's hand as we head to the top floor and our suite—kindly provided by Steve. Once there, she strips me and forces me into bed, and not for a fun reason.

She checks my wounds and then bustles around the room before I roll my eyes. "Fin," I bark.

He stops hitting Riggs with a pillow, looks at Peyton, and smiles. "Got it, boss," he calls and then rushes her, scooping her up despite her protests. She kicks and punches, defending herself as he laughs and passes her to Kalen, who glares down at her, making her stop. Gently, even with the dark expression, he lays her down next to me and takes painstaking care to tuck her in.

"You need to rest," he snaps. "Behave, Andrews." He walks to the sofa and collapses, going to sleep almost instantly.

I grab her hand and stop her from getting up. "Lie with me, baby," I murmur, knowing she will when she sighs and turns into me, resting her head on my shoulder.

"I just want to look—"

"I know," I murmur and stroke along her heartbreaking face. "But right now, you need to rest, and so do I, and I can't do it without you next to me. Close those beautiful fucking eyes and get your cute ass to sleep so we can all rest."

"Love you," she whispers, even as she huffs and settles down. Her eyes close, and I watch as she falls asleep almost immediately. Everyone is exhausted, their snores filling the room as I stare down at my girl.

"I love you too, Peyton Andrews," I whisper, pulling her closer. "We all do. Please don't break our hearts again . . . please don't break mine. It's yours, always has been." I kiss her parted lips softly.

Please be here when I wake up.

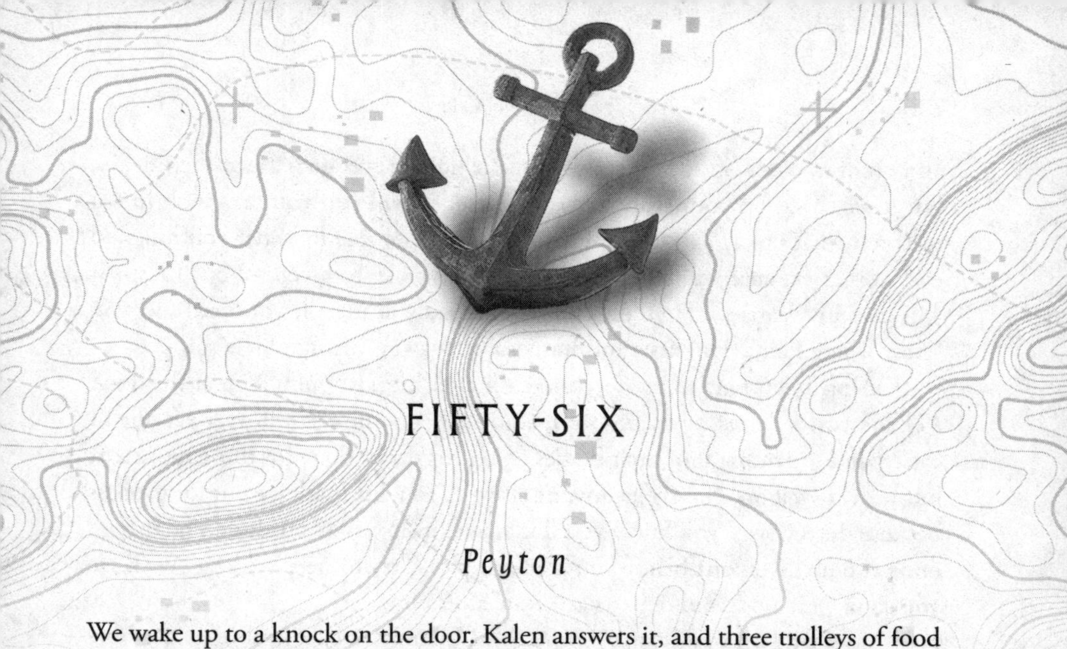

FIFTY-SIX

Peyton

We wake up to a knock on the door. Kalen answers it, and three trolleys of food roll in, all steaming hot and smelling delicious. We pile onto the bed and eat as we talk and laugh, reminiscing. We purposely don't bring up what happened, and we won't until Tyler is better. Once we've eaten, Tyler falls back to sleep, and I sit with Riggs and Fin, just relaxing . . . until a knock comes again.

It's Steve. He seems serious as he sits us all down. Tyler struggles over to the sofa, refusing to stay in bed no matter how much I glare. It hurts my heart how tired he appears. He kept waking during the night as if to check if I were still there. I sit next to him now, holding his hand as I look at my old friend.

"I wanted to take a moment to express my sincere apologies for what happened—"

"You never could have known," I interrupt, unwilling to let him blame himself. His shoulders are hunched, and he's pale and tired. I'm betting he's condemning himself and carrying the weight of all those deaths like we are.

"Still, I will never forgive myself for not protecting you. It was my dive, and I let you down. I need you to know those . . . those we lost down there will never be forgotten; I'll make sure of it. They will be called heroes. Their families will be provided for, for life, and their funerals will be paid for. It's the least I can do. It's not a lot but . . ." He scrubs at his face. "Michael . . ." He looks at me as I flinch. "I'm so sorry, Peyton. I know how much he meant to you."

"He died doing what he loved with family by his side. That's all a diver can ask for," I murmur, even as I swallow back tears.

He nods, probably realising I'm not ready to talk about it. "I have some other news. I don't know if you want to hear this, but you should know before anyone else." I nod, and he takes a deep breath before he continues, "We dived down to the exit you escaped from to check it out, and we found a few of . . . the monsters' bodies." He stumbles over the words. "We can use them for research and proof to block off the cave. I will ensure no one ever goes down there again, but it will back up your story and, of course, so will I, if you ever wish to tell it. If not, that's okay as well. You will all be paid double for what you did, and every other expense will be covered. I can't buy your forgiveness, but I hope it will ease any worries." He stands and smiles sadly at me. "If you need me, you know where I am." He turns and starts to walk away, his shoulders stooped.

Kissing Tyler, I get to my feet and rush after him, stopping him at the door. "Thank you for trusting us and for making sure no one else will ever get hurt. I can't stand the thought of their bodies being left down there for those monsters, but I . . ." I swallow. "I can't let anyone else die. You didn't ask for our forgiveness because deep down, you know you don't need it. It was a bad situation, and no one's at fault. We don't blame you at all, so please try to sleep and eat. We'll see you soon." He nods and departs as I stare after him.

It's the best of a bad situation. At least I know nobody will ever get hurt down there again. It doesn't make up for their deaths, their impact on this world, or their families' losses.

But maybe, just maybe, it will have to be enough.

After dinner, I help Tyler back to bed and go for a long bath. I showered quickly once we got back to get the blood and feel of the cave off me, but I had to be careful of my wounds. I shouldn't be having a bath now, but I need to soak, to get rid of that last layer of grime and the impression of what happened down there in the dark.

My stomach pulls as I bend over to turn on the tap. I give that dream up though, and with a sigh, I turn on the shower, letting it warm up as steam flows through the giant en suite. The shower takes up nearly the entire back wall, with three heads and a seat. Turning to the mirror, I strip and stare at myself.

I'm skinnier, and I have more scars . . . but it's my eyes. They look different. Filled with more pain, more ghosts. How can someone suffer so much, lose so much, and yet also find love again? My inside is a battle between grief for Michael and fear of what happened.

Yet I also feel true happiness about being back with my men, alive.

Annoyed with myself, I step into the cubicle and shut the glass door. Propping my hands on the tiled wall, I drop my head and let the water run across my body. My hair hangs down my back and shoulders as tears escape my eyes—tears I can't let them see. It would worry Tyler, and right now, he needs to focus on healing. But I lost someone I loved so deeply, there is a hole in my heart, and the grief finally pours out of me. Sobs catch in my throat and snot drips from my nose as I fall to the tiled floor and wrap my arms around myself. I bury my head in my arms, hoping it stifles the sound as I cry it all out.

Michael's face is in the forefront of my mind, his touch, his screams, even his jokes and snores. I miss him already, miss him more than I could even explain. It's like losing my father all over again. I was a mess then, thinking nothing could pull me from the pain. I survived it, but I lost a piece of myself. Will this be the same?

How much can a person endure and lose before there is just an empty shell? A husk where they should be?

Arms touch me, and I jump. I turn my head and meet Fin's sad eyes. One look into them, and I hiccup before throwing myself at him. I need him, need them to hold me while I break. I don't have to do it alone, and he reminds me of that as he holds me in his lap. He rubs my back, embracing me as he kisses my hair and whispers sweet nothings into my ear.

Fin promises me it's okay, I'm safe. He reminds me they are here, and that it's all right to mourn.

More arms wrap around me, and when I peek through my wet lashes, I see Riggs's concerned face. He smiles at me and kisses my shoulder as he helps Fin hold me. All of us sit in silence under the warm spray, my cries the only sound other than their heartbeats.

"It's okay to not be okay, Pey," Riggs whispers against my skin as they hold me together. "He might be gone, but he loved you so much."

"You gave him his life back, a purpose," Kalen murmurs, and I jerk my head up to see him crouched before us. His eyes are dark and sad, and his lips are tugged down as he takes me in. "He told me about his past. He told me how you saved him, how you made him want to live again. He died to save you, princess, to save the only person in this world he loved. He would be happy, and now he gets to be with his family again."

"But—but I'm his family," I sob. He leans in and cups my cheek.

"You are, and he'll be waiting on the other side, but it's not your time now. He knew you would be okay, that you had us, the rest of your family. You gave him such a good life, princess. I know, because you gave me mine back too. Cry it out, let it hurt, but don't you dare blame yourself. Michael was a great man, but he had ghosts. You saved him, my love, the way you saved us . . . saved me," he rasps and swallows hard. "He knew we needed you, and I will owe him forever for that. I can't live in a world without you. The only reason I survived before was because I knew you were out there, but there is no us without you, Andrews."

"What if I hurt you again? What if I'm not enough?" I whisper.

"Peyton fucking Andrews," he snarls. "Don't let that shit even cross your mind, you hear me? You are more than enough; no one else ever could be. You are everything, and even if you broke my heart again, smashed it to pieces, it would still be yours, I would still be yours, because some people are worth the pain, worth the fight, and you, baby girl? You are worth every inch we suffered."

"You won't hurt us again," Riggs whispers. "I know you won't. We trust you, babe."

"More than anyone. We can do this, we can figure it out, together this time. We promise not to lie and hold back our feelings, and you promise not to run," Fin adds.

"Always," Tyler calls, and I look up to see him leaning against the door—he's pale, but there. "I can't get my broken ass over there, otherwise I'd be spanking you raw for doubting yourself."

I laugh, I can't help it. It's a snort as I wipe away my tears and try to glare at him. "You should be in bed."

"Yeah, well, you should have been next to me," he snaps and narrows his eyes on all of us. "Get her washed and bandaged and back in bed." He turns and stumbles. "Fuck, one of you morons needs to help me."

Kalen rolls his eyes and kisses me softly before going to help his brother, leaving a wet trail behind him.

"We've got her," Riggs calls and helps me to my feet.

"You're both wet through," I tease.

"Easy fix." Fin winks and quickly sheds his clothes, tossing them in a wet puddle on the floor outside of the shower. Riggs nods seriously and does the same so they are both naked before me.

Fuck.

My pain quite literally explodes into lust, into a raging need to feel them. My breathing is still ragged from crying, but I'm panting for a whole other reason now as I watch them. Riggs is oblivious as he turns, his muscles bunching with the movements. His plump ass twists as he reaches to turn up the shower and grab some soap. My eyes drag down him greedily. Now that I'm allowed, now that we don't have the threat of death over us, I appreciate him. I stare, just drinking in the man I've been in love with for years.

I'm turned to meet Fin's sparkling eyes as he leans in, making me shiver as he whispers in my ear. His dark voice lights me up, my nipples harden, and my clit pulses. "Not going to check me out too, sweet cheeks? How rude."

I push him back as he pouts and purposely run my eyes down his body. It starts as a joke, but as my gaze slides across his abs and then over his half-mast cock, it turns serious. My teeth catch on my lip. I may be hurting, I may be sad, but I'm still alive, and two of the men I dreamed about for years are right here. Wanting me, loving me.

He groans. "Shit, babe, I was joking. Don't look at me like that when we're supposed to be looking after you." I watch his cock harden the longer I stare, and I throw Tyler's words out of the window. He's right—I need them, but not in the way he's thinking.

I need a reminder that we're alive, that we're safe and together, and what better way than by fucking their brains out? The very same dirty things they whispered about down in the cave?

We are about to see if they really can handle sharing me.

I know Fin will break the easiest. Riggs will run the numbers and determine it's not worth hurting me for it, even if his cock is hard and he's watching me with dark, hungry eyes. He always puts me first, even over his own needs. His head controls his emotions, but if I break Fin . . . Riggs will follow. I don't need his brains at the moment, I need his hands, mouth, and cock. Turning my gaze back to Fin, I step closer. He retreats, his eyes widening as his breathing picks up. He knows what I want but is still trying to play the good guy, to look after me, but that's not what I need.

"Babe," he warns as I stop before him. He's pressed against the tiled wall now in his retreat. I drag my hand down his slick chest as he trembles and wrap it around his stiff cock, squeezing as I stand on my tiptoes and run my lips across his.

I wonder if he can taste the desperation on my lips, since he doesn't protest anymore. He stands still as I kiss him, until I stroke my hand up his cock, and then he finally breaks. He groans into my mouth as he fists my hair and pulls me closer.

My wet body slams into his as he decimates my mouth, claiming it. He sweeps his tongue in, not teasing this time. No, he's reminding me that I'm here with him, keeping me grounded as his hands trail down my back and cup my ass.

Breaking the kiss, I drop to my knees, ignoring his protests, and suck the head of his cock into my mouth. His eyes shutter for a moment before his head drops forward, those mesmerizing eyes opening so he can watch me. Licking at the tip, I suck and release until he pushes me away, his chest heaving as pre-cum drips from the mushroom head. "You keep that up, and I'll be coming across your face before I even get a chance to get into your little cunt."

Smirking, I turn my head to see Riggs. He's watching us, his fists clenched at his sides. His cock pulses, but he doesn't move. Turning fully, I crawl across the shower floor to him. His Adam's apple jumps, and his eyes track me, but he doesn't move away as I stop before him. I slide my hands up his legs, and he flinches from the sudden touch.

"You need to rest," he mutters—whether he's reminding himself or me, I don't know.

"I can rest later. Right now, I want you both in every way Fin promised. I want to feel alive." I get to my knees, my breath blowing over his cock as I roll my eyes up to his. "Help me forget, Riggs, please," I beg.

"You never have to beg," he growls out as if annoyed, and then he bends over, hoists me up, and turns me. He presses me against the glass shower door as he cups my chin and meets my eyes. "You do exactly what we say. If you hurt yourself more, I'll be really fucking annoyed."

"Yes, sir," I tease, arching my chest to rub against him. I wrap my legs around his waist as I dig my heels into his ass to urge him on, but he ignores that, the dominant side of Riggs coming out to play. I'll only get his cock, only get to come when he says so. Not when I want to. I might have started this game, but he damn well is going to finish it when he's good and ready.

Fin is right—Riggs will destroy me . . . but in the best damn way.

I look past him to Fin and see him grinning. He has his hand wrapped around his cock as he watches the show. Riggs pinches my chin harder, bringing my gaze back to him. "Look at him when I tell you to. Until then, focus on me."

Without waiting for a reply, he swoops down and kisses me hard, our teeth crashing together as I whimper into his mouth. He sucks my tongue, taking control, and grips my thighs to keep me still as I rock and rub against him. His hard cock presses against my pussy and stomach, and I impatiently grind against him, my pussy dripping as I imagine it inside me while Fin watches.

He pulls away, leaving me breathless, and then turns me. Fin is there in an instant, pressing against my back. He slides his hands between us as I lean back into his chest. Fin drags his lips across my shoulder, his teeth catching on the skin as his hands glide up my stomach to cup and squeeze my swaying breasts hard.

"Harder," Riggs orders, frowning as he watches. "She wants it rough."

Fin chuckles into my skin as he clutches my breasts harder before tweaking my nipples. He plucks and twists to the point of pain, but that pain meets the numbness, the emotional agony inside of me, and explodes in a shower of desperate need.

For them, for this.

"Lean farther back," Riggs orders, and I do as I'm told. I relax back into Fin, trusting them to hold me up. "Good girl," he purrs, and for some reason, the praise makes my pussy clench as I visualise him saying that while he drives his huge cock into me.

"You want her first?" Riggs looks to Fin and then tilts his head, his eyes going distant for a moment as he thinks. "Or you could have her ass. I read a book once where one was in her mouth?"

"Fuck," Fin mutters. "Don't say shit like that. I'm close to coming as it is just from that fucking mouth."

"Then I'll have her mouth," Riggs decides. "I'll control her that way, stop her from hurting herself. You can have her pussy."

"Deal," Fin agrees, and the fact they are so casually discussing how they are going to fuck me makes me wild. I arch into Fin's touch, rubbing my pussy against Riggs's hard cock as I lick my lips.

"We taking bets on who will last the longest?" I tease, trying to remain in control as much as I can. "Because I reckon Fin will fill me with his cum before you do."

Fin shivers behind me, twisting my nipples so hard, I cry out, even as the pain heads straight to my pulsing clit. "You two are going to fucking kill me."

"Sixty percent chance? I'll take those odds. What does the winner get?" Riggs asks nonchalantly as he juggles me to one hand and drags the other up my thigh to my pussy. Finally, he touches me, gliding those long fingers down my centre, swirling them around my hole, and sliding back up again, doing the same to my clit. He caresses me with maddening circles as he watches me try to form words, frustration and the need to come warring within me.

"Whatever they want," I rasp, lifting my hips to try to get him where I need him, but he just grins at me. Patient, as always.

"Deal." His fingers finally flick my clit before he trails them back down and pushes the tip of one inside me. Fin still kisses and licks along my throat, tasting my thrumming pulse as I close my eyes and shiver, caught between them and loving every second.

Riggs slams two fingers into me, making me cry out. My eyes fly open to meet his as he starts to fuck me with them. He moves slowly at first, pulling out and pushing back in, each one ending with him curling inside of me to stroke along my walls. But as Fin speeds up his kisses, Riggs increases his thrusts, fucking me harder and faster, jiggling me between them from the force. Fin grins, slowing down, and so does Riggs.

They're taunting me, building me up so I'm almost coming, only to stop when I reach the edge of the abyss.

"Fucking assholes," I hiss, whimpering when Riggs grinds his palm into my clit.

"What was that?" Fin asks.

"I said—" My words end in a yell as Fin pinches my nipples at the same time Riggs pinches my clit. It throws me over the edge, the orgasm ripping through me with wave after wave of pleasure. I cry out and jerk between them, my body taut and legs shaking. When it passes, I slump, trusting them to keep me up.

My skin is slick with sweat and water from the shower, and my lips tremble as I open my eyes and meet Riggs's cocky gaze.

"Shit," is all I can whisper, and they both laugh.

Riggs releases my legs, and I dangle from Fin's hold. "On her back, we don't want to hurt her side," Fin instructs, and Riggs nods. I'm limp as they manoeuvre me how they want me. They could fuck me in the ass right now, and I wouldn't even care. I'm floating in such bliss . . . In fact, that sounds like a great idea.

Riggs grabs a towel and rolls it up as Fin gently lays me down on my back on the wet tiles. Riggs raises my head and places the towel under my neck to keep me comfortable.

Even in the throes of passion, as they unleash all of their pent-up desire, fear, and worry on me, they protect me, careful of my injuries. Fin holds me softly, so I don't injure myself further. They're always protecting me, always looking out for my best interests. Right now, that thought makes me want to cry. I've spent so long looking after myself, it's nice to be weak, but only ever with them, my loves.

Fin crouches and lifts my legs, which I wrap around his waist. Leaning down onto his elbows, he kisses me softly, doing a push-up to grin at me before he drops again and kisses me.

I smile.

"I'm winning that bet, and when I do, you have to be naked at all times," he murmurs.

"Now I kind of want you to win," Riggs comments.

"And if I win, I'm making Kalen walk around naked at all times," I tease, and they both groan in mock horror.

"Fuck her mouth already and shut her up, will you?" Fin mutters as he sits back on his heels, lifting my lower half into the air and just holding me there.

"With pleasure," Rigg replies, and I turn my head, watching as he gets to his knees beside me, cock in hand. Fin presses his cock to my pussy, rubbing it back and forth, teasing me.

In sync, Fin surges forward at the same time Riggs does. Riggs grips my mouth, opening it as his hard cock slides between my lips. Fin slams into me, making me cry out as he forces his huge cock through my tight, fluttering channel. Riggs pushes farther into my mouth, causing me to gag before I breathe through my nose. My fingers come up to grasp his base, so I have something to hold on to as he pulls out and slams back in, forcing his cock all the way down my throat. I suck but soon realise I just have to hold on as Fin pulls out and pushes in with hard, quick thrusts. He grips my ass as he lifts me higher, tilting my hips so that every time he pushes inside of me, his cock drags along my inner wall, making me cry out around Riggs's cock.

The sound is muffled as I skim my gaze up Riggs's wet, tanned muscles to meet his dark, narrowed eyes. His lips are tipped in a snarl as he fights his own desire, taking my mouth for as long as he can. He's intent on winning, but I want to break that control, so I swallow him deeper, right down to the base. He cries out, his cock throbbing in my mouth, and finally, that restraint breaks, and he slams into me mercilessly. Riggs takes my mouth so hard, I know I'll ache later.

Tightening my legs around Fin, I squeeze down on his cock. His thrusts stutter, and with a snarl, he fucks me harder too, pushing me down onto Riggs's cock from the force. Fin's fingers dig into my thighs, so I know I'll bruise, as he grinds into me after each thrust.

I feel well and truly fucking used, and I love it. They push every thought and every sensation from my mind but the taste of their skin and the feel of their desire until I can only just hang on and breathe. My own release builds within me, but then Fin rubs my clit hard and fast and throws me back over that precipice again.

I scream around Riggs's cock as I come, my pussy clenching Fin as he snarls and tries to fight it. Riggs doesn't; he comes with a grunt, slamming into my mouth and shooting down my throat. Fin thrusts once more and finally lets go, filling me with his cum like I asked.

All of us are sweaty and breathing hard when Riggs pulls from my mouth and, uncaring about his cum filling it, leans down and kisses me. Fin leans in and kisses my stomach as I lie here.

"I won," Fin murmurs, making me laugh as I swallow, still tasting Riggs.

"I'll beat you next time," Riggs retorts.

They lie here with me, holding me and stroking my skin as we come down from the high. I'm useless, remaining limp as they force themselves up. Fin washes my hair while Riggs washes my body. Each touch is soft and tender and brings tears to my eyes. They even help me out of the shower and dry every inch of me methodically before Fin checks my wounds, redresses them, and puts me in one of his oversized, comfy shirts, ignoring my protest. He won, after all, but with one look into those loving eyes, I know he will claim that prize later.

The caring, loving way they touch and watch me makes me weak again. But I'm sick of crying, so I let them pick me up and carry me back to the other room.

Back to my other men.

FIFTY-SEVEN

We spend a week in the hotel before we all start to go stir-crazy. There is only so much relaxing we can do, and for people who like to be on the go all the time, it's mind-numbing. Tyler is healing well and can walk now. I'm still not allowed to dive, but I'm feeling much better. We get up early with the sun and go for breakfast before deciding to search out Steve and close up the location and dive.

We all feel it—the need to leave this place.

My thoughts this week have been troubled. I blame grief and worry, but it's making me quieter than normal, and I know they are noticing. They try to make me laugh, to comfort me, to bring me out of my shell. Hell, last night, Kalen lost his shit with me and told me to fucking beat him up if I needed to and to stop withdrawing.

Is that what I'm doing?

It's like I have moments of pure clarity, and I'm there in the moment with them, but then I'm lost in the dark, filled with worries and pain again. I blame myself for taking Michael down there; it's that simple. His death is a weight on my shoulders. Everyone around me seems to die . . . How long before they do as well?

I know it's my own insecurities and fear talking, but I can't seem to escape those grim thoughts.

The worst part is knowing that I'm hurting them again, making them worry—the very thing I promised myself to never do again—but I can't help it. I'm pissed at my own head, annoyed at my own hurting heart. The fact they are hurting because of me only adds to that.

Steve greets us happily while I stand quietly. I still don't feel right, still don't feel like myself. Tyler tries to hold my hand, and I flinch, making him frown as he pulls away. My eyes go to the sea near the boat we're on, wondering if they are still out there, if Michael is floating down there.

"Come, this is what I wanted to show you," he tells us, leading us into the galley. We all follow, and I perch on the arm of a chair near Fin. He eyes me worriedly, but I ignore him and focus on Steve.

"Show us what?"

He licks his lips nervously and winces. "Please don't be scared or angry." He lifts a tarp from the table, and I leap to my feet, recoiling at the sight of one of the monsters lying there.

Its mouth is open, showing its fangs, and blood coats its leathery skin. It looks so . . . fucking small and harmless.

"It's dead, I promise. I mentioned we went to check the exit of the cave to make sure they couldn't get out and found some of them floating. We brought them back to study and to have evidence of your story. I promise it's a good thing; it means that the cave will never be touched again, I made sure of it. But you needed to know, and I needed to ensure . . . this is the creature, correct?"

I nod mutely, wrapping my arms around myself, wondering how such a terrifying thing from the caves can be here, being discussed so casually. "Yes," Tyler answers, even as Kalen stands and paces, continuously glancing at me as I drop my gaze to the floor.

"Okay." Steve covers it, and I sag with relief. "The crew has . . . expressed interest in having a funeral for the lost this afternoon. I understand if you can't be part of it, but we wished to honour them—"

"Michael too?" I ask, raising my eyes, my voice hoarse.

"Of course, Peyton," he says with a sad smile, and I nod.

"We'll be there."

"Peyton—" Fin starts, but I glare at him.

"It's Michael," I snap, and then look at Steve. "We'll be there."

"Okay, feel free to stay here if you wish, or you can explore for the next few hours while I prepare what I can." He stands. "I'm sorry, I wish there was more I could do. All I can do is offer you the knowledge that no one will ever go through what you went through again."

I stare after him as he disappears, the slow movement of the anchored yacht making me ache for my boat, for Michael's laugh. I expect him to turn the corner with a chuckle and a dirty joke. It's too much. I turn and rush from the boat as they call after me. They chase me, and when they catch up, I suck in a deep breath.

I try to push the darkness away as they all talk. "I'm fine," I snap, making them flinch. "Let's just explore," I say lamely.

They frown at me but agree, and Riggs wraps his arm around my shoulders, starting to walk slowly into the city on the cobbled streets. Fin strolls next to me, talking about everything and anything. Tyler is behind us with Kalen. I feel

Kalen's eyes, and when I glance back, they are narrowed and seeing through me, demanding the truth, so I look away.

I'm scared of the storm brewing inside me.

We explore all afternoon until it's time for the ceremony. It takes place at the beach. The whole crew is gathered, and there are some locals who knew some of the lost. It's a nice ceremony. The sun shines down on us, and we're close to the ocean as people tell stories, say goodbye, and honour those who died. Michael included. Steve asks if I want to talk, and I can't think of anything worse, but I do it. I step forward, owing the man who was my best friend for three years more than my silent pain.

I turn to face everyone, scanning the supportive sad faces of my men before I quickly look away. "Michael was a good man. He made mistakes in his past, but he was doing his best and fighting every day to be a better man. He found me when I had nothing and no one. He always said I saved him, gave him a home and a job, but it was the other way around. I was drifting, completely alone at sea until I met him. He made me laugh again, brought me back to life, and gave me the drive to be better. He taught me how to fall in love with myself, and I was able to be who I truly was inside. He trusted me, he believed in me, and most importantly . . . he loved me. Selflessly."

My breath hitches as I push back the tears.

"We explored this world together. Some of my favourite times were just floating on the ocean after a dive with a beer in my hand and his laughter surrounding me as we told stories to pass the time. We both lost family, yet we found another in each other." The tears drip from my eyes. I don't dash them away, knowing they need to fall, knowing each one is a memory of me and the man I loved. "He became my everything. I don't know how to go on without him, honestly." I laugh bitterly. "But he'd be kicking my ass right now." I smile. "Saying, 'Minnow, don't fucking cry, it's a waste of time. Have a beer in my name and get back in that water.'" Others laugh, knowing it's true. "He was a brave, forgiving, imperfect man, and this world is a darker place without him." I can't say anymore. My chest aches, and my sobs are caught in my throat, so I quickly rush across the sand. Tyler opens his arms, and I slip into them, letting him hold me.

The others grab my hands and hold me as we say a prayer and have a moment of silence. We all turn to the ocean. Like any diver, it's where I want to be . . . but right now, all I see is a place where I lost so much of myself and my family.

Even with my men around me, I feel completely alone.

Lost.

Adrift.

FIFTY-EIGHT

Kalen

I notice her pulling away, becoming quiet. I can't have that, not again. I've been nice, sweet Kalen to her while she heals. I've been loving, like we both needed, but I'm pissed at her, at me . . . but mostly her for making me angry again. For trying to get away from me.

Once back at the hotel, I throw her over my shoulder, ignoring her yell of surprise, and march to the bathroom for privacy because what I'm planning requires it. I kick the door shut behind me and drop her to her feet and back her into the wall. For a moment, I see a flash of my girl there, fighting me. "What the fuck, Kay?" she snaps before looking away, trying to create distance. Not happening. I saw this happen last time, and I won't stand idly by now.

My princess needs a reminder of just how much of an asshole I can be when it comes to her.

"Don't fucking look away from me, Andrews," I snarl and drag her gaze back using her chin. I pin her to the wall with my body, pressing forward until she feels every hard inch of me. The door opens, but we don't look away from each other.

"Kay, maybe now isn't such a good time," Riggs starts, always protecting her, even when it means hurting us. Well, fuck that. Can't they see she's struggling? She's pulling away, and we are going to lose her again.

As usual, it's up to me to fix it. None of them are willing to do what needs to be done to bring her back.

"Get the fuck out," I snarl.

"Kay . . ." He sighs, and I turn to him, scowling. This is my girl, my fucking love too. He knows I won't hurt her, but right now, she needs to be reminded that she's ours.

"Get. The. Fuck. Out."

He nods and shuts the door with a tiny bit of fear in his eyes.

Looking back down at my girl, I lean closer. "They won't save you now, princess," I taunt. "So that's it, huh? Not even going to fight me? Just going to shiver and stare at me all doe-eyed? You're useless. Where the fuck has my Peyton gone? You're just going to survive all that and let it ruin you?"

"Shut up," she whispers, her eyes wide and panicked. She doesn't get to act all innocent and hurt to escape this.

"No. Fuck that, you don't get to pull this shit again. I don't care if it fucking hurts or if it's hard. You don't get to hide because of that. Fucking fight," I demand.

"Shut the fuck up!" she yells.

"Make me, Andrews," I growl. "Because right now, I don't think you can. You're not the woman I love. You're nothing but an empty shell, hurting those you love most again."

"Fuck you!" she screams and pushes me back, but I don't budge. I do laugh though.

"That's all you've got, Andrews?"

I see the anger now, the life going back into her eyes and body. Thank fuck. I want to slump, but I don't. I continue to play my part, pissing her off. Part of me even enjoys it, like I always do when we fight. "Get the fuck off me!" she demands, pushing me harder until I nearly move.

"Or what?" I goad, licking my lips. She follows the movement, even though she's pissed at me. My hand snaps out and circles her throat, squeezing as I tilt her head back. "Going to cry? Run away? Pretend it's not happening? Because that solves everything, right, Andrews?" It's cruel—it's fucking mean. She's hurting and confused, but so are we. Add that to the fear we are losing our girl again and, well, my patience for her fucking snaps.

"Never," she snarls, fighting in my hold as I chuckle.

"Really?" I mutter. "Because I don't even recognise you anymore. Where's the girl who fought all those monsters to get to us? The girl who chased us until she got what she wanted? Where's the woman I fell in love with, who didn't just lie back and accept my shit? She called me on it, she fought until we exploded. She is the one I love."

"So I'm not allowed to be weak?" she fires back.

"You can always be weak, princess. Cry, scream, break . . . but just don't fucking give up like you are."

"I'm not," she argues softly. Even she knows it's a lie.

"Yes you are, and I won't let you, do you fucking hear me?" I squeeze her harder, getting in her face. "I lost you that day on the boat, I almost fucking lost you in those caves, but I'm not losing you here when we finally have a shot at being happy. So rage, hit me. Fucking use me. Whatever you need to do, whatever you can't show them or do to them because they don't know the darkness like us. Do it, but don't you dare fucking lie to my face. Don't you dare try to slip away from us again. If I leave you here with pretty lies on your lips, then you lose me too, you understand?"

"Kay," she whispers.

"I will always fight for us, even when you can't . . . but I won't force you to love me. To love us. Is this still what you want?" I demand as she swallows against my hand. "Answer me, Andrews."

"Yes," she hisses.

"Then fucking prove it," I order. "Stop being a weak-ass cunt and take it."

I see her coming back as she holds my gaze and almost sag in relief, but I don't let her see that.

I stay still, demanding, waiting.

But she's still holding back. Sneering in disgust, I let her go and step away, turning to leave.

"Don't you dare fucking walk away from me," she snaps, and I still. "I didn't fucking survive that shit show, I didn't put my heart out there, didn't lose you all once before just to lose you again. I'm hurting, okay? I'm struggling with the fucking darkness inside of me. My mind is turning on me, luring me into that oblivion. I'm not fighting monsters this time, I'm fighting myself. My own doubts, pain, and fear. I need you, don't you see that? I need you to be my light, all of you, to keep me here instead of tumbling deeper. I'm fucking scared, Kay." Her tirade finishes in a whisper, and I turn back to see tears in her eyes. Her lips are trembling, but her head is tilted defiantly.

"I'm fucking terrified every choice I make is wrong, and the worst part is I'm trying to protect you from that inky pain inside me, yet I'm only hurting you all more. I see it and can't do anything about it, like a fog surrounding me." She slams her hand into her chest. "Can't you see how much I'm struggling?"

"I see it," I snap, tilting my head down to meet her eyes as I step closer, standing toe-to-toe with her just like old times. "But I can't save you, princess—only you can do that. I believe in you, even when you don't. So do they. You can fight this, you can win this, but you don't have to do it alone. We are here, so use us. Talk to us."

"I don't know how," she whispers.

"Like this," I whisper and slam my lips to hers, reminding her she's here with me. With us. I let her feel my desperation, anger, and fear. I show my princess that I would fight in that darkness with her for the rest of my life. I'd fight all her demons. I'd plunge myself so far into that blackness she couldn't see me anymore if only she would stay. She gasps into my mouth, and I pull back just far enough so I can speak against her lips. "Fight, Andrews." I kiss her again before pulling away, leaving her chasing my lips. "Fucking fight."

Her hands grip mine, making me grin against her lips. "Good, that's it, princess," I purr and bite her lip until she slaps me hard. I groan as my head jerks away. Turning back, I see her chest heaving, her lip bleeding, and her eyes wild.

There's my princess.

Smirking, I slam her into the wall. Her legs wrap around my waist as her lips descend on mine, biting and kissing as I tear at her dress, yanking it up to expose her panty-clad pussy. I grip her over the fabric, groaning into her mouth when I feel how damp she is already. I turn her head and bite her ear before whispering into it. "You want to fuck while we fight, princess? I'll even argue with you like old times. I know how hot that gets you," I tease as I stroke down her pussy.

Her head falls back against the wall as she grinds into my hand, urging me on. "Argue about what?" she questions breathlessly.

"Anything you fucking want, Andrews."

"Either I'm your princess or call me fucking Peyton," she snarls, making me chuckle into her ear. She shivers against me as I push her underwear aside and part her pussy, flicking her clit in warning. She gasps, trembling in my arms as I pin her there.

"I'll call you whatever the fuck I want," I murmur and kiss down her throat, feeling her pulse jump under my tongue. "We both know I'll still have you coming and screaming my name in under five minutes."

"Cocky prick," she snaps.

"You fucking love it," I retort and nip her neck as she grinds into my touch. I drag my fingers through her cream to her pulsing hole and circle it, teasing her as she snarls and fights in my arms. When she gets bored of me teasing her, she leans down and bites my neck, making me snarl. I turn, drop her to her feet, push her down, and kick her legs apart. She almost falls but catches herself on the sink. She raises her gaze to look at me in the mirror behind her as I keep her there, pinned and bent over the sink.

"You want to act like a fucking animal? I'll fuck you like one," I growl out.

Twisting the back of her dress, I rip it away, leaving her in nothing but those tiny panties. I grab them and step back, dragging them off her body, leaving her pert ass in the air as she pants. I reach behind me, tug my shirt over my head, and toss it away before shedding my shorts, naked as she is. Her eyes widen with lust as they run across me. Her admiration of my body only makes my already rock-solid cock that much harder.

Moving forward, I dig my fingers into her hips to hold her there as I drag my tongue up her back, tasting the salt of her sweat. "Is that what you want, princess?" I mock when I reach her neck. Sliding my other hand down between her parted thighs, I spank her clit, eliciting a groan.

"Yes," she snaps. "Fuck me; make me feel."

That I can do.

Dipping back to her hole, I spear a finger inside her. She jerks and gasps my name as I quickly add another and start to fuck her with them. My other hand releases her hip and strokes up her back to her neck, squeezing as I hold her in place.

"I want you to scream so loudly, they'll hear you." I smirk. "So they'll know exactly what I'm doing to you in here." Her pussy clenches at my words, and I grin wider. "Dirty fucking bitch—you love that idea. Love the idea of them listening just like I used to listen to you moaning on our boat."

Her eyes close as she shivers, her hips coming back to meet my thrusting fingers, but it's not enough to make her come. I make sure of it, and she groans in frustration. "Kalen," she demands.

"Yes, princess?" I tease.

"Enough fucking talking, or I'll go out there and fuck your brother instead. Or Riggs or Fin or all bloody three."

I freeze and then give her exactly what she wants.

Me.

Adding another finger, I curl them inside her, stroking her inner wall as I drop to my knees, releasing her neck, and suck her clit into my mouth. She cries out loudly as I fuck her relentlessly with my fingers and add my teeth to her clit. It sends her over the edge, her cunt squeezing around me, her thighs too as she screams her release for them to hear. I yank my fingers out and stand, then I grab her neck with my other hand, dragging it up until her eyes open—only then do I suck my fingers clean, making her moan.

"You could try," I snap and kick her legs farther apart until she wobbles, until it's on the verge of hurting her. Until she can't escape me. "The only way you are leaving this room is with my cum dripping from that greedy cunt."

I squeeze her neck when she tries to talk, stopping whatever insult she would have thrown at me as I press my hard cock to her pussy. I let her feel the huge length, the same fucking length that will be inside of her bratty fucking body, reminding her exactly who she's messing with.

She rubs against me, spurring me on. I let her, my cock sliding between her pussy lips, getting it all nice and wet for me. The smell of her musk makes my nostrils flare, driving me wild.

Only when I've teased her enough do I let go of her neck, grab both hips, and lift her legs from the floor. She has to clutch the counter to hold on as I line up and slam inside of her tight little cunt. I fight through her channel as she cries out, jerking and struggling in my hold. I pull out and slam back in, again and again, until I'm balls deep.

Then, I show her what I'd been holding back. I ram into her over and over. The sound of our skin slapping together is loud, but not as loud as her moans. I fuck her like I own her, like every inch of her belongs to me, and I show her exactly why she should fight, why she should stay.

I show her how much I love her with each thrust.

Her pussy is so wet, it drips, the wet sound turning me on like nothing else, in a way only my princess can. I need her so much, I can't even catch my breath, like I will die without being inside her. I watch my huge cock spear in and out of her tight little hole, stretching around me. Her clit is engorged, begging for more.

She's taking everything I offer.

I meet her eyes in the mirror, a snarl on my lips as I watch her. "I want to watch your face while you come all over my dick."

She groans, licking her lips as I drag her hips higher, the new angle making her crazy and tossing her off that ledge. She screams her release, her eyes slamming closed in bliss as her cunt clamps down on me. I have to fight in and out of her pussy as she practically squirts across me.

"Kalen!" she hollers when I reach down and slap her clit.

Pulling out of her fluttering channel, I turn her, lift her, and force her to wrap her legs around me. Her eyes are still closed as I slam back into her, fighting through her cunt until I'm buried balls deep again. She cries out, the others no doubt hearing, but I don't give a fuck. I argue with her because I care, and now I get to reap the rewards. Her hands come up, holding my shoulders as I turn us and slam her into the wall and fuck her.

I'm getting all my anger, fear, and worry out in her body, forcing her to take it all. Her moans become louder and louder, her cream dripping on my cock and balls.

"Kay," she cries, her pussy squeezing me. Grunting, I try to hold back my release, wanting this to last, to stare into those dazed, lust-filled eyes with her tight cunt wrapped around me. But I can't, especially when she leans in and kisses me like she needs me to breathe.

It explodes out of me, dragging her with me. Her pussy clenches around me, milking my release as I grunt into her mouth. Cum splashes inside of her as I still, pressing my hand to the wall to hold us up as my legs shake from the force of my release.

We have to break apart to breathe, and she presses her parted lips to my sweaty shoulder, her body shaking as she holds me tight. "Don't give up on me," she begs.

"Never, princess," I reply breathlessly.

FIFTY-NINE

Tyler

They are finally quiet in the bathroom. Riggs and Fin left about ten minutes ago, unable to focus or be here with her screaming in the other room. I understand, I wanted to leave too. There is jealousy in me, sadness too, even though my cock is hard from the sounds she's making, but she needs me.

She needs him too, but when she comes out, red-faced, and looks at me, I'm ready with my arms open. She rushes into my embrace, climbing into the bed and hiding her face in my chest as I cover us both. I know Peyton better than I know myself, and right now, she's struggling. It's the same way she struggled after she lost her father. I saw her losing herself then, and I see it again now.

She has such a big heart that when it gets broken, it's hard for her to recover. It's the very reason I love her, but it also hurts her. I just hope she doesn't run away this time to try to fix it.

Kalen comes out and nods at me, and without a word, he leaves. I'm grateful. I love the bastard, but I want to smack him for making her cry. Although I know it was necessary—we were losing her again. He brought her back in a way none of us ever could by pushing her, so even though I'm jealous and annoyed, I relax and hold my girl. She might have fucked him, but she's in my arms right now, and that's enough.

"I've got you, baby. Always," I promise, kissing her head, and we fall asleep just like that, wrapped in each other's arms with her tears wetting my chest as she cries herself to sleep.

I wake up a few hours later, confused, warm, and hard. I pry my eyes open when I feel lips. They are pressing against my chest in soft, chaste kisses. I blink and meet Peyton's eyes as she rolls them up to mine. She's straddling my waist, and her bare pussy is pressed against my stomach. Her hair is dry and wavy, and she's naked as she rubs herself on me. I watch, half asleep and turned on as she kisses down my abs and pulls down my boxers, but then I stop her. I reach down and cup her cheek.

"Baby, we don't need to—" I start, my voice rough from sleep.

"I want to," she insists, and cuts me off by sucking my cock into her mouth, making me groan. My hips lift, even as I try to fight through the haze of lust I've woken up in thanks to her. She needs me right now. She needs reality, she needs healing and love, but her eyes dare me to stop her as she sucks me deeper, all the way to the back of her throat.

"Baby, I promise we're okay. Let's go back to sleep—" I groan as she pops her mouth free of my length, squeezing with her other hand as she continues to stroke me. My breathing picks up as I fight it.

"I don't want to sleep. Do you?" She arches a brow. "I want to forget, I want to fuck the man I love."

"Peyton."

"Do you want me?" she asks.

"Always." I frown as she squeezes me harder, making me gasp.

"Then what's the problem?"

I search her eyes, needing to know she's not doing this out of guilt, but all I see in her eyes is sadness, love, and desire. Rolling my lips inwards, I observe her before laying my head back. She grins, wiggling her ass as she curls between my legs and sucks my cock back into her mouth. I reach down, anchoring my hand in her hair and pulling her close as I thrust into that hot little mouth. She hums around me, bobbing her head as she sucks me off.

My heart slams as my body flushes with desire. My world narrows to her and that talented mouth. Popping free again, she licks down my length, teasing me until I've had enough. I drag her up by her hair and crush my lips to hers. She whimpers and grinds against my cock, rubbing herself on me. Running my hands down her curves, I trace every inch of her body, relearning her, making her gasp and groan. I flick her hard nipples, stroke her belly, and squeeze her ass before I stop her grinding.

"I love you," I mumble against her lips before I slam her down on my length.

She cries out, her head falling back. "I love you too!"

Working together, we make love. She rides my cock, grinding, lifting, and dropping while being careful of my injuries. I watch her incredible tits bounce with the force. Dragging my hand up her hip and across her belly, I grab one and squeeze, making her cunt clench around me as I tighten my hold. Thrusting up, I fuck her while I hold her.

It feels like old times, but only better. There are no unsaid secrets between us now, just life and a whole lot of desire and memories.

I watch her ride me, each roll of her hips, each bob of her breasts driving me crazy until I grab her throat and pull her down. I kiss her hard as we make love. The beauty of my girl steals my words like nothing else ever could. We come together like we can't bear to breathe without each other anymore. Our bodies are in sync, fitting together so perfectly, and our kisses are slow and drugging. We make promises with our bodies, our hearts healing. This isn't about pleasure or desperation, it's about love.

It's a slow orgasm that builds between us, the type that grows so softly, rolling like a gentle wave until it crests. We gasp as we come, swallowing each other's cries of pleasure and love until we lie in a sweaty, satisfied, tangled mess. I can't help but smile at the feel of her in my arms again, where she belongs.

That's how I fall asleep, filled with so much love and happiness, I can't imagine anything ever ruining it.

SIXTY

Peyton

I watch him sleep. Each steady rise of his chest makes my heart crack further. There's a small smile on his face as he holds me close. A tear drips onto his chest as I turn my head away.

He's in love with me, I know it. He's happy and content . . . while I'm struggling. When he's there with his eyes on me, I feel happy, I feel like I can breathe, but in the quiet of sleep, I have a hard time. It comes when I'm alone. That darkness returns. I hear Michael's screams in my ears, bringing back those demons Kalen dared me to fight.

I slip from Tyler's arms and pad to the window. Staring out at the ocean, I remember what happened. How Michael sacrificed himself for me. His cries and last words fill my head until it's too much. I close my eyes, but his face is there, wearing the expression he had when he fell. I struggle to breathe, to escape.

I can't. I need air.

I open my eyes, finding the window fogged. A tear escapes, dripping from my eye and rolling down my cheek as I quickly scribble in the fog before turning away.

I grab the first clothes I see and get dressed. I freeze at the door with my hand on the handle. I should stay, wake him . . . but this isn't his fight. Kalen is right—I need to do this alone. And right now, all I can think about is needing air and escaping those demons clambering through the darkness, not the love of my life sleeping peacefully in the mussed bed. I can't even think clearly—my only thought is that air will help.

I need it.

I rush from the room, shutting the door behind me. I don't bother waiting for the elevator, my heart is racing too fast. I take the stairs and hurry from the hotel.

Once outside in the early morning light, I swallow desperate gulps of air. My head is muddled, fuzzy. I know Tyler will wake and panic, and I know the others will be back from wherever they went and worry, but my world narrows to the need to escape, to evade my own memories, my own demons. I don't even consider where I'm going. I just start to walk, faster and faster, until I'm jogging and then sprinting.

I'm convinced if I can just go fast enough, I can escape it. But no matter how fast I run, I know deep down, it will never be far away. The only way to stop the darkness is to stay and fight.

But I can't, not yet . . . so I run.

I'm not running from my men, but from myself.

The streets blur, and the people watch me pass until I find myself at the dock, my heart racing and lungs tight. Even in my pain, in my darkest hour, I ran to the ocean. I find myself viewing the churning waves and needing to be on them, to feel them and the oblivion and peace they offer. I search the harbour for a small boat about to set out. On bare feet, I carefully tread down the docks and find a tourist boat. The man frowns at me as I quickly thrust some money at him from my pocket. He holds out his hand to help me on, but I ignore it and jump on, moving to the front. I lean against the rails as the engine starts, and we pull from the docks and into the ocean. I turn and look over my shoulder to see the shore and city getting smaller as we chug through the water.

Guilt fills me as the panic starts to subside. They will be so worried. Fuck! They will think I've left them again, and that was never my intention. I just needed air, I just needed to get away from the demons surging within me.

But it didn't help. I can't outrun my own mind. I can drown it in sound, the waves, music, and films. I can ignore it with booze and drugs. I can make it disappear for a time in my lovers' bodies, but eventually, it will catch up to me when I'm alone or weak. When I'm not distracting myself from it. I know that, yet I still have those emotions inside of me. Running won't fix it.

I fucked up.

I look back at the dock and see four figures there, and my heart breaks.

No.

Fuck.

I can't hurt them again. I wasn't thinking . . . but that's not an excuse. Just because I'm hurting, it doesn't give me the right to abandon others, to inflict pain on them.

I rush to the stern before turning to the man at the wheel. "I need to go back," I exclaim, my heart racing for another reason now.

He turns, frowns, and starts speaking another language. I gesture to the shore.

"Back, I need to go back," I demand quickly. I won't break their hearts again. Not ever.

He cuts the engine and faces me fully as I look between him and the shore, but when I glance back, they are gone.

No.

Fuck.

No!

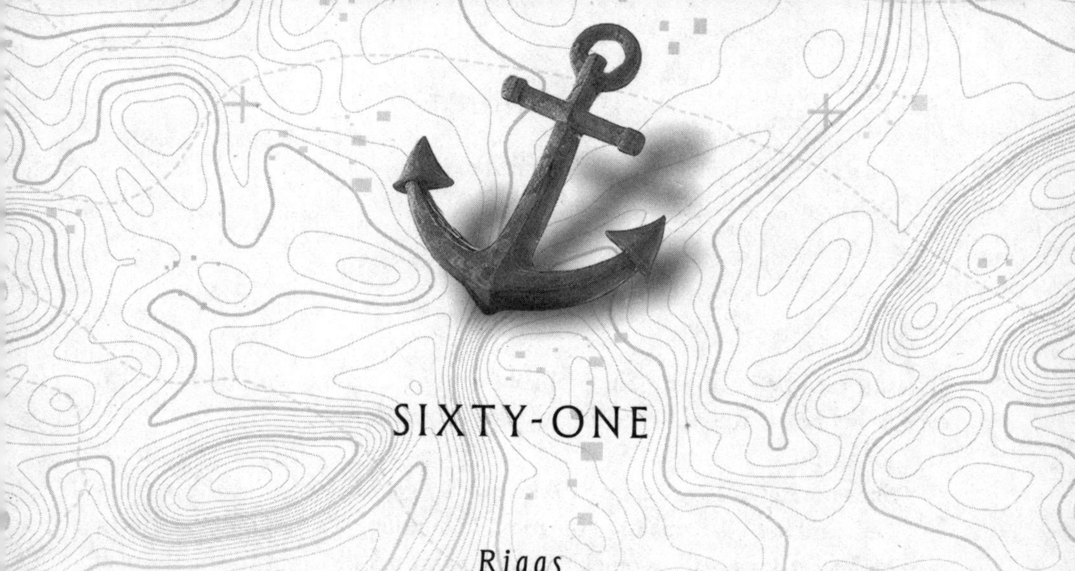

SIXTY-ONE

Riggs

After eating breakfast and sleeping on Steve's yacht, all three of us head back, laughing and joking, excited to see Peyton again. Even after being away from her for a few hours, I miss her. She needed Tyler last night, and they needed space, so we gave them that, but I can't wait to hold my girl again and promise her it's going to be okay. We've all seen her struggling the last few days, but I know it will pass. She will get better, she's too strong not to, and we will be there every step of the way as we discover our new life and set a new course for our future.

I'm excited at the thought of being together. We're not hurting anymore, and we're together, like old times. We can get a bigger boat and explore the ocean. We can heal together and create our own happiness.

We'll be a family once again.

When we get back to the hotel, we let ourselves into the room. Tyler is still asleep, but the bed next to him is crumpled and empty. I frown as Fin grabs a bottle of water. Kalen changes his shirt as I check the other rooms and bathroom, but they're all empty. Moving back to the other room, I search for a sign before spotting the slightly fogged window.

"What's up?" Fin calls, waking Tyler. "Yo, baby cakes, get your sweet ass out here and let me have my breakfast. It's you, by the way."

I don't speak, staring at the window and the word written there. My heart drops and shatters into a million pieces at the one simple word. It's only five letters, and yet they steal my breath and destroy the future I was just imagining.

"Princess?" Kalen calls with a frown, moving farther into the room.

On the window, *sorry* is hastily drawn.

Why does it feel like goodbye? As if we are trying to hold her to us, but the harder we grasp her, the more she slips away?

I'm losing my life again, and this time, I know if I let her go, she won't come back.

I turn to them, my heart cracking further.

"She's gone."

Fin

"No, she can't be." I frown. "She probably went for a walk or breakfast," I offer, even as my heart races at Riggs's heartbroken expression.

Not again.

"She's not here," Riggs snaps as Tyler quickly gets dressed.

"Let's find her." We are out of the room in minutes. We rush into the streets, searching faces as we walk as quickly as we can. We ask those we pass, and a man points to the docks, so we rush there and search the boats. How did we ever miss her? We were right here—

"The boat," Tyler whispers, pointing to a small boat on the ocean.

I shield my eyes and look out, spotting a lone female on the back of it, gazing at us.

Peyton.

The boat becomes smaller and smaller, and I have flashbacks of last time. Of watching her speed off into the ocean not to be seen again for years. She took my heart then, and she will now as well.

Only, I know this time she won't come back. We'll lose her to the depths forever. She was struggling, but I didn't think— Fuck, how could she do this? How could she leave us again? She promised! She knew how much it hurt. How could she?

"Fuck!" I scream and turn away, pacing as the others just stare. "Fuck!"

"No," Tyler murmurs.

"What?" I snap, whirling to face him. "Can't you see? She's leaving again!" I pull at my hair as he shakes his head.

"No, she's not leaving this time. I won't let her." He looks us over. "I don't know about you, but I regretted not going after her every day of my life. Not again." He dives into the harbour.

We stare before rushing to the edge. He surfaces and begins to swim, chasing her.

"He's right." Riggs nods and dives in after him.

"Fuck," Kalen growls and goes too, leaving me standing here alone.

I didn't believe in love, but she made me. Can I really go back to the empty pain? The numbness? To seeing my brothers hurting and destroying themselves?

No.

So I dive in also, deciding to fight for her, even when she won't fight for us.

SIXTY-TWO

Peyton

I'm arguing with the captain when I hear my name being shouted over the waves. I turn to the edge of the boat, grip the rail, and search the waves—then I spot all four of them swimming towards me.

They—they came after me.

They cut through the water, chasing me this time.

Kalen is the first to reach the boat. He drags himself out of the water, dripping wet and pissed. "What the fuck do you think you're doing, Andrews?" he demands.

"I wasn't running, I promise. I woke and I couldn't breathe, I needed air. I was coming—"

Tyler is next, and Kalen helps him up, and then Riggs and Fin follow. Tyler glares at me, but I see the hurt in his expression. Riggs looks devastated . . . and Fin? My easygoing Fin looks so angry.

"What the fuck, Peyton? Was leaving once not enough? What? That's it, no goodbye? Nothing? Just a fucking shag and then gone again?" he screams.

I stumble back, eyes wide, knowing I fucked up. "I didn't mean—" I start, but he ignores me, his face thunderous.

"No, you didn't mean; you never do! You broke our hearts once, you won't ever do that again! You promised!"

"I wasn't leaving!" I yell, but he doesn't give me the chance to continue.

"Sure the fuck you weren't."

I turn to Tyler, pleading. "I promise, I wasn't leaving, Ty. I couldn't breathe, I needed air. I didn't even notice until I was on the water, and then I panicked. I tried to come back, I tried, he doesn't speak English," I explain in a rush. Tyler steps forward, frowning.

"Do you love me?" he demands.

Tears fall as I nod. "Words," Kalen snaps.

"Yes, yes, I love you."

"Do you love Kalen?" he questions, stepping closer.

"Yes," I reply instantly.

"Do you love Fin?" he asks.

"Yes, yes." I nod.

"And Riggs—you love him?"

"Yes, I love you all!" I yell in worry, meeting their eyes. "I do, I love you all. I didn't mean to hurt you," I rasp, nearly sobbing. "I'm sorry."

Tyler stops before me, tilting my chin up to meet his eyes. "I watched you leave on a boat once before, and it destroyed me. I said never again. I woke, and you were gone; my heart broke." I shiver at the pain in his voice. "But I had to see, had to know. You say you love us . . . Do you want to be with us?"

"Yes," I reply instantly, knowing it's true. No matter how much I'm struggling, it's what I want. They are what I want. "More than anything."

"And you weren't leaving?"

"No," I murmur. "I promise."

"It wouldn't have mattered." I flinch at that as he smiles down at me.

"I watched you leave once, and I promised myself never again," he murmurs. "You are never getting away, Peyton. We will always come after you, even when you're lost, hurt, or angry. We will always follow."

"You're not mad?" I ask.

"Oh, I'm angry as hell, and you'll pay for it." I shiver at the dominance in his tone. "But if you're sure, if you're not running, then okay. But try that shit again, and I'll let Kalen loose on you."

"Not just Kalen," Fin snaps. "I'll chain you to me, understood?"

I nod, smiling through the tears. "I'm sorry. I didn't mean to hurt you," I tell him as he moves closer. Kalen sighs and steps over too, kissing my head.

"I'm sorry, I should have been there, princess."

I lift my head and see Riggs standing at the stern, his face turned down. I slip from their arms and stop before him. "Riggs, I'm sorry—"

He grabs me, pulls me closer, and kisses me hard, stealing my breath. When he moves back, his eyes are narrowed dangerously. "Leave one more time, and you will be locked up in my bed," he snarls, then softens as I suck in a breath. "I love you."

"I love you too," I whisper.

"Good, you better." He kisses my head and sighs. "God, you're a pain in the ass." He chuckles, making me laugh too.

He kisses me softly and turns me. I stumble into him when I see Tyler, Fin, and Kalen staring at me intently. "Help me?" Tyler asks them, and I frown as Kalen assists him to his knees before me. He pulls the ring from his neck and meets my eyes.

"Peyton Andrews, I asked once before, but you were right—it wasn't perfect then, but it is now. We were the right people, but it was the wrong time. Now, I know it's the right time. I love you more than anything in this world. You're my best friend. My family, my soul mate. Will you marry me?"

"Tyler," I whisper with wide eyes. Fin drops next.

"Yeah, babe, will you marry us?" he asks, and steals the ring to show me. Tyler chuckles and rolls his eyes. Kalen smacks Fin's head and moves over, getting to his knees before me, his dark eyes on mine.

"Princess, be mine?"

Riggs plucks it from his fingers and turns me, falling to his knees with a blushing grin. "Peyton Andrews, will you marry us? Tie yourself to us for the rest of our lives?"

"Yes . . . yes!" I shout, and then I'm surrounded by arms and hands and passed around and kissed until the ring is placed on my trembling finger.

"If you ever take this off, I'll superglue it on. It's always belonged to you, and so have we," Tyler swears as I laugh.

There, under the sun, my heart heals.

The darkness still circles in the background, but I know with them here at my back, loving me, that I can defeat it like always. I will come out stronger than ever with four men to love me unconditionally. Every broken, damaged, scarred piece of me.

We have to move forward. We can't dwell on what happened in the past, and holding on doesn't change a thing. Those memories hurt nobody but us. We have to learn to let go, heal, and move past it and into our future. Otherwise, we'll always be stuck in the same spot, caught halfway between our past and our future.

We can't give in to the doubts, anger, and pain. Being embarrassed, disgusted, or even hating who we were back then doesn't make us better people now. We have to learn from it, use it, and be the people we want to be. In this moment, with them, I realise it's time we all healed from it.

That cave might have been a place of true horror, but down there in the rubble and water, through the bloodshed and hopelessness, we found each other. We found the love we used to have, and now it's stronger than ever.

Maybe I disappeared last time because I knew I didn't deserve them back then. I bet they often asked why I left, but the truth is, I didn't, not really, not deep down. I was pulled away from them because I didn't deserve them yet.

I do now, and I will fight every day for the rest of my life.

This world is a wide, unexplored place. My love for them is the same, it's like the ocean. We can only see the very top of it, yet its depths run so much deeper. It makes up all of me, and it flows so deeply, I could drown in it, but they keep me aloft, like always.

Apex predators.

SIXTY-THREE

We manage to turn the boat around, and once onshore, I'm thrown over Fin's shoulder. He ignores my protests and spanks my ass when I wiggle. I expect this from Kalen, but it seems I hurt my usual, comical best friend, and he's taking it out on me. I'm okay with that; I'll take whatever he—or any of them—gives me as long as it means they forgive me for almost leaving them again.

I lift my head and the ring sparkles on my finger, making me grin as I meet Tyler's hungry eyes and Kalen's dark ones as they follow us. Riggs is by my side, talking softly to Fin. I catch some words, even though they are quiet, and what I hear makes me shiver with desire.

Ass. Tied up. Punishment.

Riggs has been taking it easy on me. Fin already warned me of his dominant side, and I've seen it firsthand, but now it seems like I've cracked that control. It's obvious I'm their prey today, and I'm perfectly fucking happy being so.

I barely notice the streets as we rush down them, this time with a different purpose—to come together, to reconnect for good this time, to remind me that I'm theirs and they are mine. My heart races, and all of my worries and panic are pushed away with their touches and the promises in their eyes. My pussy rouses with a vengeance, happy to let them heal me, hurt me, love me. My entire body comes alive in the way only they can make it.

Nothing else matters but being in their arms and showing them how much I love them.

By the time we reach the room, I'm almost panting, my breathing ragged with anticipation. I'm tossed on the bed, and as I bounce, I lock my eyes on them. I hear the lock being thrown on the door, and then they are there. All four of them stand at the edge of the bed, watching me. Fin smirks, Riggs grins, Tyler licks his lips, and Kalen runs his dark, hungry eyes along my body. Propping myself up on my arms, I tilt my head and smile at them.

"Well, what are you waiting for . . . fiancés?"

The hair on my arms rises as Fin steps forward, the move filled with power and purpose. I won't be in charge today, and honestly, I'm good with that. I need to be forced to let go, to concentrate on nothing but the pleasure they will give me as Kalen's hands flex and Tyler crosses his arms.

"You okay with me going first, boss man? I have some . . . things I need to remind our girl of," Fin growls out, reaching down and gripping the bedding. Veins pop on his hands from the force of his hold, the sight making me groan and wiggle as I imagine his fingers wrapped around my thigh or throat—fuck, even my pussy.

"I don't know, I think we all might have some . . . things"—Tyler smirks, the new, angry Tyler rearing his head, rather than my once soft lover—"to work out with *our* girl."

"Or you could stop talking and fuck me already," I taunt, parting my legs. Kalen inhales as Riggs's eyes drop to my parted thighs, his shoulders tightening.

"Strip her," Tyler orders, ignoring my comment, even though his voice is darker, more growly, not unaffected like he's trying to portray. He's attempting to remain in control, to stay in charge so he isn't weak before me. Not like last night when we made love and he gave me his heart. He's still hurting right now, even if he won't say it, and his way of dealing is pulling away. But I can't let that happen, not now, not when we're so close to getting everything we want.

So I do what Kalen did to me—I coax him out. I get to my knees and pull my shirt off and toss it away with my bra before I drop to my hands and crawl towards him. His eyes narrow, but he doesn't step back, even as I reach him and slide to the floor. I move my hands to his jeans and unbuckle them. He grunts as I wrap my hand around his hard cock and pull it free, blowing my breath across the leaking tip. My other hand slides up his thigh, which trembles under my touch, showing me he's not indifferent.

"Fuck me, Tyler," I murmur. "No orders, no remaining aloof, I want it all. You're mad, I know that. Use it, fuck it out, so we'll be free to start over," I whisper, my breath blowing across his cock with each word until he surges forward slightly, thrusting so his cock touches my lips.

"Peyton," he warns, and I chuckle as I lick his tip.

It breaks him. He reaches down, yanks me up, and tosses me onto the bed. He's on me in a moment, ripping away my shorts and panties until I'm naked, wet, and wanting. His fists come down on either side of my head as he holds himself above me. "You want to be fucked, baby girl? You better hold on, because we aren't stopping until you can't fucking run away again," he threatens before dropping slightly to kiss me. It's hard, and his teeth catch my lip, making pain shoot through me before his tongue slides past my parted mouth and tangles with mine. He pulls away, leaving me panting and dazed, staring up at him.

"Promises, promises," I murmur huskily.

"I get her first. If she can stay awake after . . . well, you three can have your fun." Tyler smirks, and I hear the others groan as he steps back and sheds his jeans.

"Guess we are watching for now," Fin mutters.

"I like watching," Riggs comments.

"I know you do, you sick bastard," Fin says with a scoff, but my full concentration is on Tyler as he crawls up the bed and my body. He stops above my quivering thighs and drops a kiss on each before moving higher. His tongue dips into my belly button and swirls around it before dragging up between my breasts. I whimper, unable to hold it back, and those hungry eyes roll up to mine as he turns his head and quickly bites the underside of my breast hard enough to leave a mark. He soothes it better with his tongue before sucking my nipple into his mouth. My eyes slide closed, and I thrust out my chest as he sucks and licks. Pleasure builds from his talented tongue, until suddenly, he pulls back and then does the same to my other breast, torturing me. When I huff, he bites again, this time at the side of my breast, nearly breaking the skin.

"Are you going to try to leave us again?" he demands when he lets go. I shake my head, licking my lips, but his eyes narrow.

"That's not good enough." His hand drags up my chest, wraps around my neck, and squeezes. "Will you try to leave us again?"

I gasp out my reply. "No."

"I still don't believe her, do you?" he asks the others, and there is a chorus of noes.

He smirks at me. "Guess I'll have to make her scream her answer over and over until we believe her."

Releasing my throat, he scrapes his teeth down my chest, belly, and pussy as he wedges his shoulders between my thighs. He forces them wider as he lies down, his eyes locked on my dripping cunt.

He wants me to scream? He'll have to work for it.

Like he knows my thoughts, his hands span my thighs, gripping them meanly. His fingers press into the tender skin until I gasp in pain, and only then does he lick a long line down my core as if he's praising me for the sound.

I make it again, and he rewards me by flicking my clit with his tongue, so I keep emitting noises. I let them slip free of my throat as his fingers dig deeper into my skin and his talented tongue flicks my clit and drags down my pussy, dipping inside of me until he tastes my cream. He repeats the same path repeatedly before he sucks my clit into his mouth, and I scream in ecstasy.

My release builds, and I'm so close when he pulls away. "I didn't hear your answer," he growls, his lips, chin, and cheeks coated in my cream. I slump, annoyed, and he chuckles, stroking his fingers down my pussy but avoiding my clit, and then he does it all over again. He builds my release once more, this time adding his fingers. He pushes them inside of me and fucks me with them hard and fast.

"Not leaving, not leaving," I chant as I grind into his face, gyrating my hips as I fuck myself against him. I need to come so badly, I'm unable to think or even see past the urge. The pleasure is too much, and the pain only adds to it.

"Not leaving!" I holler as he finally lets me come, nipping at my clit as he strokes along my front wall. I soar off the ledge, waiting for them to catch me.

He surges above me, nudging my thighs wider as I tremble and my pussy clenches from the aftershocks. He gives me no reprieve as his hard cock presses against my entrance, and in one smooth thrust, he buries himself in my pulsing cunt. He holds himself above me with his hands, his eyes wild as he pulls out and hammers back in. He fucks me hard and fast, giving me what I wanted now that I gave him my answer.

"Never again," he snarls, fighting my tight channel as I finally come back to life, wrapping my legs around his waist to urge him on. The pleasure, which was turning to a low simmer, begins to build back up again from his thick, hard cock sliding along the nerves inside me. Those dark eyes lock me in place, and the feeling of his firm, slick body moving above me makes me groan as I toss my head back but try to keep my eyes on him. I need to see him, to see the love and anger on his face as he takes it out on me. He doesn't relent, doesn't let me catch my breath. He uses his body to show how pissed he is, but also how much he loves me. Tyler drops his head and licks and nips along my jaw and throat, catching my jumping pulse between his teeth and digging in. The sharp pain makes me cry out as my eyes close, and I lift my hips, meeting his hard thrusts. I take it all, accepting everything he has and more. I need him to know I'm here and that I love him and will never leave them again.

"Never," I promise, my voice catching on the last syllable as another orgasm slams through me. He groans as I come around his cock, his hips stuttering as my pussy milks him, and with one final thrust, he grunts and fills me with his release.

He leans into me, breathing as hard as I am. My legs tighten around his waist as I come down from the high. I close my eyes, and a smile tips up my lips. Tyler kisses me softly before pulling out of my body and dropping next to me to keep from crushing me.

His cum drips from me, and my skin is marked and pink from his mouth and hands, and yet I still want more. I open my eyes when the bed dips, seeing

Fin moving towards me. I'm the main course, and they are fucking hungry. Even after watching Tyler fuck me and fill me, they are unbothered, wanting me just as much, and that rips away the last of my doubts.

"She's awake, you didn't do her well enough," Fin jokes. "Don't worry, there are three of us left, so she won't be able to walk when we're done. Will you, babe?"

"She won't even be able to move if we fuck each hole," Riggs muses. "Ass, pussy, mouth. Fill each one and fuck her hard, and she'll pass out filled with our cum without being able to leave."

"Fucking hell, Riggs," Kalen growls. "But shit, yeah, I like that idea. I had her pussy yesterday, so I want her tight little ass."

"Then I get her pussy." Riggs grins. "I want to feel her come around me and watch you both fuck her."

Bloody hell. I almost come from that visual alone, my breath hitching at the promise in his voice.

"That means I get her hot little mouth?" Fin teases, leaning down and kissing me softly. "This mouth? The one that spent years teasing me? Fucking deal."

"You ever had a cock in your ass, princess?" Kalen asks, and I shiver as I meet his eyes.

"Yes," I reply unashamedly. His eyes tighten with jealousy, and he shoots Tyler a glare. I turn to see Tyler leaning back against the pillows with a cocky grin on his face.

"Good, means I won't rip you with my huge cock," Kalen finishes and looks back at me. "On your knees."

I flip and get to my knees, tilting my head to watch Fin as he reclines next to me. I feel Riggs's eyes observing carefully as Kalen touches me finally, caressing my ass before his hard cock presses against my pussy. "I'm going to need you dripping down my dick, princess," he murmurs, nipping my shoulder. "So wet that I can slip into this ass without hurting you . . . too much."

"Then you better make me wet." I grin, wiggling my ass and pushing back to try to impale myself on his cock. He doesn't let me, gripping my hips and holding me still as he drags his cock up and down my pussy, coating it in my cream. He bumps my clit over and over until I'm sighing and pushing back as much as I can, trying to get him inside of me.

When I stop, he slams into me, making me scream as I'm shoved forward from the force. His cock stretches my already sore, wet channel. He forces himself deeper, his hips slapping my ass as he holds me still, pulling out and thrusting back in. He fucks me hard and quick without letting me move. The feeling is too much, his cock is too big, and the pleasure builds until I'm crying out and fisting the sheet as my nipples rub against the bedding. Then he's gone, pulling from my body as quickly as he thrust into it.

Leaving me cold and empty.

"You get to move when I say so, princess," he snaps, slapping my ass hard. I jerk from the pain, and then his big hand caresses it, rubbing the sting away before he parts my cheeks.

I feel his huge, wet tip pressed to my asshole, and I tense before forcing myself to relax, knowing how good it will feel. Tyler loves anal, but Kalen is bigger, so I drop my head and close my eyes as I try to regulate my breathing.

"Good girl, relax for me," he coos as he slowly pushes the head past the ring of muscles. He works in deeper before pulling out. The pain is sharp and sudden as he forces his cock deeper into my ass, stealing my breath and words. My lungs scream before he's finally settled in my ass. He stills and rains kisses along my back and shoulders as I relax farther around him. "Fuck, you should see how sexy you look taking my huge cock so deep in your ass."

His words make me whimper. The pain is too much, I need him to move, and Kalen, always knowing what I need, moves. He pulls out and pushes back in, slowly at first, changing that pain into a low, simmering desire. My pussy drips at the sound of his grunt as he fights his way into my tight asshole, his fingers clenching my hips to pull me back and push me forward.

I begin to meet his thrusts, and he speeds up. My clit throbs, and my pussy clenches at the smack of our bodies coming together, at his harsh breath, his hard cock, and nipping teeth.

He pounds into me, forcing his huge cock farther into my ass until I can barely breathe as I writhe below him.

He fucks me tirelessly with hard, quick thrusts. The pain of him filling my ass transforms to pure pleasure. It surges through me as he grunts into my ear. The slap of his balls is loud as he spanks my ass again and again. I cry out and buck against him, almost coming just from his cock before he suddenly slows. His thrusts turn almost gentle.

Measured.

"Lift her," Riggs orders, and Kalen wraps his arms around me and drags me to my knees. I'm held immobile on Kalen's huge cock, so I can do nothing but moan and wiggle, needing to move. Needing more and yet less. Needing everything they offer.

He lifts me, keeping me impaled as Riggs settles below me. He watches me as Kalen slowly fucks me before he nods at him over my shoulder. "Lower her, I want inside of her."

Kalen does, lowering me until my pussy is pressed against Riggs's hard cock. Kalen thrusts, pushing me over his cock as I drip down it, so wet it's almost embarrassing. Riggs groans, sliding his hands down my body to grab my pussy before he slaps it, slaps my clit, making me jerk.

"Stop while I get inside of her, I don't want her coming yet," he murmurs, and Kalen stills behind me. Riggs lines his cock up at my pussy, keeping his eyes on me as I whimper.

"Please," I rasp, and with a snarl, he slams into me, making me scream at the sensation.

I'm so full, too full, stretched between them as their cocks fill me like I've never been filled before.

"I can almost feel you stretching her," Riggs says calmly to Kalen. "She's so tight." His voice deepens then, and he blinks and meets my eyes. "It feels good. Move when I move, that way one of us is inside her at all times."

"Oh shit," I whimper, dropping my head forward as Kalen slowly pulls out and slams back in. Riggs just lies there for a moment until I realise he's analysing the best way to fuck me. Then he starts to move in when Kalen pulls out, thrusting up into my pussy and tilting me forward until he hits those nerves over and over. They fuck me hard and fast, and I explode again as a sudden orgasm rips through me, leaving me gushing and tightening around them as I cry out.

They still fuck me as I gulp in air . . . until another cock presses against my mouth, coating my lips in pre-cum.

"Swallow me, babe; no more talking, no more excuses. Let me fill that taunting mouth until I explode down your throat and all you can taste is me for days," Fin growls out.

My tongue darts out, dragging along his cock blindly, and with a groan, he pushes the tip into my mouth. I swallow him down before he gives up trying to be nice and soft and just slams into my mouth, forcing himself in deep before he pulls out and slams in all the way to my throat. I almost gag, my eyes watering and tears dripping down my cheeks to mix with my saliva dribbling from my wide-open mouth. I grip Riggs's chest, making him grunt as I dig my nails in while I swallow around Fin's cock.

Fin quickly falls into their rhythm until all of my holes are being fucked. I revel in the feel of it, knowing they are all in my body, sharing me, loving me. I finally let go, my eyes closed as bliss and pleasure flow through me.

I'm held between them, unable to move, unable to think or speak, as they pound into me, fucking me hard and fast like they promised. I won't be able to walk or think or run away from them ever again. Each thrust is a reminder that they are here, we are here, and we are alive.

Each touch, caress, and kiss is filled with love.

I'm anchored by them but missing a part . . . until Tyler reaches down and strokes across my shoulder, letting me know he's here with me. With us. When he moves closer and tweaks my nipples, I let go completely.

"Love you, princess," Kalen growls, each word punctuated with a thrust. Thrusts that send Riggs's cock deeper in my pussy and Fin's sliding into my throat and back out again as they work together to fuck me.

It's too much, and even though I didn't think it was possible, I come again. I scream around Fin's cock, and he yells, slamming deeper as he finds his own release, exploding down my throat like he promised. My pussy tightens on Riggs's cock, and he groans, fighting it, fighting his release to prolong my own. Kalen lets go, biting my shoulder as he snarls and slams into my ass until he's balls deep, and then he explodes inside of me, filling my ass with his cum.

Riggs fights to pull from my pussy and push back in, fucking me through my release until I clench around him again and he snarls. He stills as his own release bursts through him, his cum splashing inside of me.

I collapse. They hold me, since I'm unable to move—just like they promised.

I don't move as they pull from my body, but I wince. Fin chuckles and leans down, kissing me softly, uncaring about his cum coating my tongue. "Don't clean her, let her sleep with our release inside her."

Shit, the thought has me shivering all over again, and Kalen spanks my ass.

"No. Sleep before you kill us." He groans and drops next to me.

Riggs lifts me from his softening cock and lets me curl up on his chest, unbothered by the sweat and cum dripping from me. Tyler reaches down and strokes my hair.

"I love you," he murmurs, and I settle further, knowing he's okay with what just happened.

Fin cuddles into my left side, into Riggs as well, whereas Kalen grips my leg, holding it as he relaxes.

I smile as I curl into them with their arms and legs surrounding me, grounding me, protecting me from those demons that made me run in the first place. They will still be waiting for me tomorrow, but I know I can handle it. As long as my men are here for me, I've got this.

I'm not perfect, but I'm theirs. I'm not the seventeen-year-old girl who fell in love with four men. I'm older, I'm stronger, but I'm still learning. I'll hurt them again, no doubt, and they'll get angry, but we'll forgive each other because that's what true love is. It's forgiving, it's resilient, it's capable of growth and change and . . . it's true.

Through the best and darkest of times.

It's a beacon home.

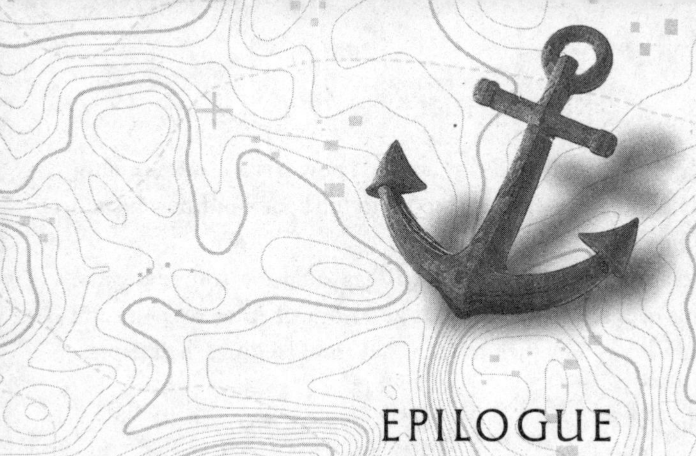

EPILOGUE

Three Months Later

The blue water is tranquil around me as I free-dive to the bottom. We finished the actual dive two days ago and decided to anchor near the bay to relax and explore. Steve paid us handsomely for this dive—the first one we have done since the cave.

Thank God it went smoothly. There were no undiscovered sea monsters there, just some old treasure lost in a ship's crossing.

The cave we found has been closed off and protected, like he promised. The news story went viral, and many disregarded it and said it was all lies, but some believe.

We don't care, we know the truth.

We went landside after for a couple months to heal. I buried Michael under a tree on a cliff overlooking the ocean so he can always be there when I go home, and he can keep watch for me. I also went to my father's and my mother's graves and showed them the ring I'm still wearing to this day.

We are a family.

I smile as I watch an octopus shoot past me, blazing with happiness as the sun shines through the water. The others went up a few minutes ago, but I'm staying down as long as I can.

I'm happy.

More so than I have ever been. Tyler was right—I left to be found again. Sometimes the people are right, but the timing is wrong. They were my people, but I had to find myself in the depths of this world and learn to love myself before I could love them completely.

Now I'm wholly theirs, and they are wholly mine. We never plan to stop. We are family, and we'll explore this world together until we physically can't anymore.

Turning in the water, I swim through the fish before I head to the surface. I break through with a grin, slicking back my hair, and then I see Tyler waiting at the stern of the boat with his hand held out for me. I grab it, and he pulls me out effortlessly. He's fully healed just with a few more scars now. Tyler kisses me automatically and holds my hand as we move farther onto the boat—our new boat.

We named her *Minnow*.

The others are there with food and drinks. Riggs laughs at something Fin said, and Kalen rolls his eyes at their antics, but he smiles when he sees me, and my heart flutters like always as they turn to me. They're all smiling, their expressions filled with love.

How did I get so lucky?

Life isn't always easy. I've struggled, I've had a lot of darkness, and I've lost many people I love, but in this moment, it's worth it. We may not be the richest people in terms of money, but money isn't everything. I'm rich in love and happiness, and here, on the sea with them, is where I belong.

It's where I am at home and happy—with them.

I will never leave or hurt them again, and they will always support me. We will grow together, and we will fall deeper in love with each passing day.

"We were listening to the radio, and we just heard about some sort of storm they rescued a few people from—it sounds crazy. A freak accident," Riggs says as I stop and sit on the towel, leaning into Fin's side.

Freak accident . . . That's what they called ours too. Let's hope they are okay.

"Really?" I ask, picking up an apple and biting into it.

"Yep, anyway, Steve messaged us and wants us for another dive whenever we're ready."

I nod and lean back in the sun, smiling as they talk and relax. I look up at the sky and smile wider, knowing my parents and Michael are looking down on us. They are proud and always watching.

Wherever we travel, they are with us.

My gaze drifts to my men. My heart always belonged to the ocean, but then they came along and stole it, and now it belongs to them too.

These men, these apex predators.

My loves.

Life is all about the little things. You may never be famous, you might never discover untold riches, but you don't need it to be happy. All you need is love. If life were easy, it wouldn't be life. It's a journey, and just like a boat on the ocean, sometimes you hit a rogue wave or a storm, but through the storm, you learn what you're capable of.

You find your strength.

Mine lies with them.

My family.

This is our story.

This is my diver's heart.

HAPPILY EVER AFTER . . .
DOWN BELOW

ONE

Peyton

"Peyton!" My name is being shouted throughout the villa we are renting to relax in after a difficult dive to map a new cave system for Steve. It paid well, but it was exhausting, hence the downtime in the sun with nothing but time to kill. My name is shouted again, and I hear it even from here, in the primary bedroom. Groaning, I lift my head, but Kalen's hand trails up my back and drags me back down so our lips meet once more.

"Pey?"

"Babe!"

"Peyton?"

"Ignore them, princess," Kalen murmurs against my lips, nipping my lower one as he thrusts up from below, filling me with his huge cock. My eyes close for a moment, our sweaty bodies locked together tightly.

"They will just keep shouting," I reply, even as I roll my hips and take him deeper.

"Let them," he growls as I sit up and spread my hands on his chest, my ring sparkling on my finger. I ride my fiancé, bouncing on his cock as his dark eyes watch my every move like a predator.

It's been six months since they asked me to marry them, six incredible months of us exploring the world together and settling into our new life. I will never forget what we survived to get here, and I'm still haunted by nightmares of what happened down in that cave, but with their help, I'm putting the pieces of myself back together.

"That's it, princess. Let me see you take me. Fuck, good girl, just like that. It drives me crazy when you ride me, seeing all this delicious, tanned skin above me, your sexy fucking hips, and your incredible tits bouncing for me." His dirty words make me cry out as I clench around him, my hips speeding up as I chase my release.

I'd woken to his mouth on my cunt, and honestly, what better way to wake up than that? The others were gone, probably shopping, reading, or swimming, so we took our time, but as he sits up, his cock inside me, his lips meet mine again as his pace turns feral.

Kalen's possessive hands grip me to the point of pain as he forces me onto his length. "Princess," he murmurs into my mouth, and it goes straight through me, making me shiver. My clit throbs as I quicken my hips, my release building inside me. "That's it. I can feel how close you are. Let go for me. Let me see you come. I want to watch you shatter for me. I want to feel it drench my cock."

My head falls back as he drags his lips down my throat and bites. The sharp pain is what sends me spiralling over the edge. Screaming his name, I come all over him just like he wanted. His groan is swallowed by my skin as he bottoms out inside my fluttering cunt, and I feel his hot release pump deep inside me.

We stay locked like that, panting and sweating, until he kisses up my neck to my lips, both of us smiling before he falls back, his eyes heavy-lidded as he stares at me. "I love you, princess."

I smirk teasingly. "Good job I love you too. Your brother won't if you keep leaving marks on me though."

"He started it," he mutters. Tyler marks me every chance he gets, and it's become something of a competition between them. I swear I constantly look like I've been attacked, but it's worth it.

It's not easy living with four possessive, overprotective males, not to mention the laundry and bathroom situation, but we make do, and we've never been happier.

Leaning down, I kiss him softly. "Yes, well, one of these days, I'm going to start biting back."

"Fuck, I wish you would, princess," he snarls as he kisses me again, deepening it just as I hear the bedroom door fling open.

"Peyton Andrews." The familiar, angry voice fills the air. Turning my head, I meet Kalen's brother's eyes. Tyler, my lover, sighs. "Really? You didn't hear me shouting your name?"

Riggs appears over his shoulder, looking confused as he glances from Tyler to me.

"Oh, I heard," I answer as I sit back, still astride his brother. "I was just a little busy."

"Busy. Is she—" Riggs's face blushes red, even as he grins. "Ah, busy."

"Shit, and I wasn't invited?" Fin whines as he elbows Riggs and Tyler aside and wiggles his eyebrows at me. "Looks like one hell of a party."

Rolling my eyes, I dismount Kalen, who groans, and then I pad over to the side table and open a bottle of water, chugging some down. "What's up?"

When I glance back, they are all busy gawking at my body, so with a pointed look, I bring their eyes up to my face. "Up here. What's wrong?"

"Absolutely not a damn thing," Fin says as he rips off his shirt and starts to head over to me.

Tyler sighs, pulling him back and tossing him into the hall. "Steve called. The locals have reached out, needing our help. A diver went missing during a routine fun dive. By the time their team gets there, he'll be out of air. They want our help. So, Peyton Andrews, are you ready to dive?"

"Always."

TWO

We don't waste any time, all of us knowing how time-sensitive a rescue mission such as this is. We don't do it often, but more than once, we have been called in too late and the rescue was turned into a retrieval. We hate those missions, so today, we are determined to have a good outcome as our boat, *Minnow*, bounces across the waves, shooting around the island to the south side where they instructed us to go.

Steve is on the ground, helping the locals and police, but it's up to us now. We have the experience and the equipment. It also just so happens that this is a dive spot we were planning on checking out, so we know some of the particulars about it. It's not a hard dive, but the water is choppy and dangerous, and if you're not careful, you could get caught in the tide.

Anything can go wrong when you're down below. It's something we know all too well.

By the time we reach the spot, the sun is high in the sky as we make anchor. Without speaking, we fall into a rhythm, checking and preparing the equipment as Tyler sorts out the boat, then radios in to let them know we are here.

We are their only hope, and that pressure weighs on us.

It all happens very quickly, and we are in our gear within ten minutes of arrival, looking over the pictures and maps we have been sent. "The most likely place for him to have gotten stuck is here. He probably ran out of air, so he took refuge in this little outcropping. Locals have confirmed there is air in it, but it could be old or running out, so we need to move quickly. The water is clear, but we can never be too safe. I want torches and constant communication. Everyone moves together, and we check the area as we go," Tyler explains.

Nodding, I worry on my lip as I listen to the plan. I know he's doing it to keep us safe, but it's not the most efficient method and he knows it. I say, "That wastes time though, time he might not have. We need to split up. Check as you lot go down, and I'll head right to the outcropping we expect him to be at. I'll bring an extra tank."

I'm the strongest diver, and I'm also the fastest, so it makes sense, but I know they hate it.

Tyler watches me carefully and glances at the others, finally relenting to my plan with a jerky nod. "Fine; Riggs and Fin together. Brother, you're with me. We check as we go. Peyton, head to the outcropping and check there. That is our meeting spot in case anything happens. If anything goes wrong, head back to the boat. Is that understood?"

"Yes, boss," we all answer.

"He's alive. I know it," I tell them. He has to be. We don't want another body.

Tyler nods, and I grab my mask. Riggs helps me into my gear and double-checks it while Fin kisses my head. "See you down there, babe."

I wink at him as I check my gauge and dive computer—old habits, something Micheal used to do with me. It's always better to be safe than sorry. Any diver is only as good as their equipment, and without it, I'd be dead. It's saved my life more than once, and I respect the brutal yet beautiful edge that the ocean has.

It doesn't care how many times you've dived or how much experience you have. Below the surface, there is only survival, and if you're lucky, you might see something beautiful while you're at it.

Tyler heads my way as I perch on the edge of the boat, all suited up and ready, and he doesn't stop until he reaches me. He checks over everything twice more before looking into my eyes.

His hand suddenly darts out, sliding up my neck, and he tugs me in for a brutal kiss. I gasp against his lips, lost in his taste. He pulls back, rubbing his thumb across my bottom lip. "You stick by me as we descend, and only then can you go. We'll follow. No antics this time, Pey. I mean it."

"Got it." I wink then I kiss him too, unable to help myself. "In and out, and then you can be in and out of me."

He groans, but his lips twitch. When he steps back, the smile drops, and he turns into our leader, not my lover. "Okay, he's probably scared and running low on air, so we need to be smart and save this man's life, then beer is on me."

Riggs and Fin high-five each other, and with a thumbs-up to us, they flip back into the water. Rolling my eyes, I step off the edge and plunge into the warm water after them. Splashes let me know Kalen and Tyler follow closely behind.

Kicking my fins, I yank my mask down and wait, bubbles surrounding me before the water clears, and then everyone swims over. We hit our watches in unison, timing this, and we won't make any mistakes.

I give Tyler the okay, and with the spare tank at my side, we start to descend. Tyler and Kalen will double-check areas to our left, while Riggs and Fin will swim to our right as we go, just to be sure and to check for a body.

I am aiming for that outcropping. It's my only focus.

He has to be there. It's a wish and a mantra running through my head. The ocean claims many lives, but it won't claim this one. I'll make sure of it.

The water becomes darker the deeper we go. We shouldn't need a compression stop at this depth, which is good because it would waste more time. When we are about ten metres deep, we turn on our torches and break apart. I feel their eyes on me, but I focus on swimming down, trusting them to do their jobs just as they trust me to do mine.

I know time is of the essence, so I don't take any detours or explore like I normally would. I just dive until I start to see the outcropping of rocks to my left, where we assume he is taking shelter. They stretch far off into the distance and extend down to the ocean floor. The locals said there is a gap in this dive spot where some divers relax.

Please let him be alive in there.

Something catches my eye as I head over. It's darker than the rocks and definitely not wildlife. I head straight for it. It's caught on the jagged rocks. "I've got something," I mutter into the mic, a bad feeling building low in my stomach.

"What is it?" Tyler asks.

"Give me a minute." When I reach it, I tug it free and flip it over, taking a good look before sweeping my gaze around once more, but there is nothing or nobody else. "It's a dive mask, cracked and hanging on some rocks. Looks like he panicked and got caught. If he was smart, he would have had enough air to get into the outcropping and wait."

That's my hope at least. The break in it has to be close. He made it. He had to because I don't see a body around.

"That's a lot of what-ifs. We are coming down," Tyler replies.

"No. Keep searching. I can't be certain. I'll check it out," I protest, hooking the mask at my side just to be sure. I follow the rocks down, careful of my tanks as I kick my fins.

I search the outcropping for the opening, wondering if I missed it, when I spy a dark opening about two feet down. Swimming hard, adrenaline pumping through me, I send up a prayer to Michael.

Please let the man be alive.

I can't handle any more deaths.

Please, for once, let us win.

Pushing through the opening, I kick up to the surface and tug off my mask. I turn in the water and freeze when I see the slumped shape hanging on to a rock, bobbing in the water. His back is to me, his suit wet and dark. His hands are on the rock, cut and bleeding, but otherwise, he seems okay.

He's not moving though.

Is he alive?

Swallowing hard, I hesitate before plucking up the courage and covering the short distance between us. There isn't much room in here, just enough for our shoulders. The air has a faint smell to it, which I know can't be good, but I need to deal with his body first.

I place my hand carefully on his shoulder and wait, then he suddenly sputters and jerks around. He blinks water from his eyes, his teeth chattering as he gapes at me. "You're not real. You're not real."

I slump in relief as I grab my mask.

"I've got him. He's alive!" I yell into my mic.

"Heading down now."

I drop my mask to my side after hearing that, then I grab my tank and lift it.

Venting the tank, I release some new, pure air into the hole, and he breathes deeply. "I'm real. My name is Peyton, and your name is Faro, right?"

He nods, sucking in air as he looks at me. "You're real?" he whispers. "You're really here? It's not my mind playing tricks on me again?"

I wince at that. He has probably imagined someone coming to save him a million times. It's normal in this situation.

Grasping his hand in the water, I squeeze it so he can feel how real I am.

"I'm real, and I'm here for you. Just breathe. That's it. My team will be here soon. You're going to be okay. We'll put a new mask on you and get you out—"

"I can't. I can't go back out there." He panics, his eyes wide. "My mask caught and snapped. I barely made it here. I can't go back out there. I'll drown. I'll die. I can't—"

I slap him hard, and he stills, blinking, but he's out of his hysteria. "You can and you will. Otherwise, you will die here, and I'll have to swim your body out to your family," I snap. Every diver knows and accepts the risk when they go down, but facing it is a different story. Right now, he's alive, but going back out there is another risk. We can't stay here though, so I need him on my side. I can't fight his big ass and swim him to the surface. It would put us all in danger if he panicked. "I know you're scared—I've been there, but you beat fear by facing it. You won't die down here. I won't allow it, okay? I won't allow anyone else to die when I can save them, so you're going to listen to me, put on that mask, and let me save your life. If not for you or your family, then do it for me. I cannot handle another death on my soul."

"I heard rumours about a dive team that got trapped. They said it was a tragedy. It was you guys, right?" he asks as he stares at me.

"Yes, and it was the worst and best time of my life. I lost someone I love very deeply down there, and I never thought I would see the surface again. You will. I promise you. You're a diver, and divers do not give up or back out. Can you do it? Either we go up together or we stay here and die together. It's your choice."

I let him see how serious I am. His decision doesn't just affect him. It's selfish and manipulative, but it's the kick in the ass he needs.

He watches me for a moment before nodding. "I'll try."

"Good. We'll be with you the entire time, okay? It will be the longest moments of your life, but then it will be over and you'll be up top. You want to know the hardest part?" I tease.

He nods again, watching me like I'm a lifeline. "Getting back into the water after."

"I always loved the water, but . . . but . . ."

"You're scared," I offer. "I thought I'd never be able to go back into a cave after what happened, but you know what I did? I got my ass into a cave the very next chance I got. I refused to let it win. I'm stronger than that, and so are you. You made it here. You're alive, and you are strong, Faro. Do not let fear win, okay?"

"Okay." He nods just as more bubbles reach us and Tyler breaks the surface next to me.

"Not enough room for all of us," he explains as he looks at Faro. "Glad you're alive, mate. Now how about we get you the fuck out of here and back home safely?"

"Yes, please," Faro replies, squeezing my hand again.

Tyler unhooks a spare mask we brought and hands it over. Faro struggles with the straps, his fingers pruned and clumsy, so I reach over and hook it on for him and help test it. "Can you see okay? Hear us? Breathe?"

"Yes," he answers shakily and peers at the water, fear in his gaze.

"Hey, want to hear a joke?" I say suddenly. "Why did the scuba diver cross the ocean? To get to the other tide!"

He snorts and shakes his head. "That's terrible," he says, but he rolls his shoulders back and looks between Tyler and me. "I can do this. I want to go home."

"Then let's get you there. Tyler, you go first."

Nodding, Tyler shoves his mask on and dives under. Keeping my eyes on Faro, I put my own back on.

"I'll be with you," I promise him. "Right next to you, okay? Just keep your eyes on me the entire time." I hold his hand as we sink into the water. He panics at first when we duck out into the open ocean, his fins kicking desperately.

"Breathe," I remind him, and he does. His breaths are fast at first, but they slow down as we circle him and wait, his training kicking in. "That's it. That was the hard part. Now it's the easy part. We just swim."

I keep one hand on him, and Tyler swims on his other side as we start our slow ascent to the top. I speak to him the entire time, distracting him and trying to keep him calm.

"Why don't clams give to charity? Because they're shellfish!" I giggle.

"That was bad," Fin remarks. "What does a dolphin say when he's confused? Can you please be more Pacific?"

We all groan, but the others eventually join in, even Kalen, though he sounds grumpy about it. We kick to the surface, the water turning clear around us, and before we know it, we are there.

When we break the surface, there are two more boats waiting. Riggs and Fin help Faro up onto one where police and rescue services wait.

Bobbing in the water, I tug off my mask as they huddle around him, but he looks at us. "Thank you, thank you. You saved my life."

"Thank me by getting back in the water. Remember, don't let fear win."

We watch as the boats take off, hurrying to get him back to land.

Looking at my men, I can't help but grin. "What did the diver say to her fiancés? I'm all wet."

They groan at my terrible joke, but I can't stop smiling.

He's alive. We did it.

THREE

It doesn't take us long to get back onto *Minnow*. We could linger or even dive ourselves, but it feels like testing fate after we got lucky finding him alive down there. No, there will be other days to swim and explore. Today is a win, and that's all I care about.

"I say we celebrate another successful dive," Riggs suggests.

"How?" I ask curiously as I unzip my suit and shimmy out of it, letting it fall to the deck with a splat.

"Let's get married," Tyler answers seriously, and we all turn to him, blinking. "What? We are going to anyway. Let's do it here, today, on our boat under the setting sun."

"It won't be legal," I caution. It's something we have discussed a lot, but they don't care.

They all want to marry me.

"So?" Fin replies. "When did we ever care about anyone else's rules, babe? I'm with Ty. Let's get married. I want to be able to call you my wife when I fuck you tonight."

I look around at them, and the hope in their eyes is my undoing. "You're serious."

"Princess, we are always serious when it comes to you. When will you realise that?" Kalen says with a narrow-eyed look.

I search all of their faces before throwing my hands into the air with a grin. If they want to marry me right here, right now, then who the hell am I to complain?

"Fuck it, let's get married."

They converge on me, and my laughter rings out across the water as hands and lips slide over me in excitement, tasting of the ocean.

I'm getting married.

My eyes drift over the water for a moment, tracing the blue waves that brought us all together. "Let's do it out here, where we fell in love, on the water," I murmur.

"Sounds perfect to me," Tyler replies as he kisses my head. "It's time to make you officially ours, Peyton Andrews."

We dock to make preparations, but then we are back on *Minnow* and racing out into the ocean before the sun starts to set. The locals were so thankful to us for helping Faro that they offered us everything we needed to make it happen. We owe them a debt of gratitude for that as we make anchor in the ocean. The island is behind us, and the sun is starting its descent towards the water, so I hurry to the cabins below, leaving them up top to finish setting up whatever it is they snuck off to get. Opening the box on the bed, I finger the ivory dress I bought.

Smiling brightly, I quickly undress and slip it over my head, then I add accessories before turning in the primary cabin and opening the door to see the mirror there.

I peer at my reflection, taking in the short, lacy boho dress I managed to find on the island. It runs to mid-thigh, with holes in the flowy woven material, has a low V-neckline, and is sleeveless. It's so beautiful. I knew it was the one when I laid eyes on it in the boutique after we had broken apart to get supplies. White and pink flowers are woven into my hair, which is loose and wavy from the water. I'm barefaced and barefooted, but I know that's how they like me.

I wish Michael were here.

I wish he were here to see this and give me away, but I know what he would say—this is just another adventure, and he is proud of me.

I ache to hear his thick voice rolling over the word *Minnow* as he smiles at me.

Tracing a petal on one of the flowers, I secure it better and take a deep breath.

"Are you ready, Peyton Andrews?" Tyler yells from above. "Don't make me chase you again."

Smiling, I lay my hand on the mirror and close my eyes. "I miss you, Michael." I drop my hand, turn around, and head to the stairs and my future.

My heart pounds faster than it ever has—not from fear, but from anticipation.

This is my biggest adventure to date, and I am so excited, so ready, to officially be theirs.

I have been in love with them since I was a teenager, and now, I finally get my happily ever after with them.

Our love might have started with a tragedy, but it's ending as one from legends.

Stepping onto the deck, I freeze at the transformation they managed.

Flowers in an array of bright spring colours are scattered across the deck, and a red carpet is rolled down to the railing where they stand. An arch of balloons and flowers frames the setting sun as they stand on either side of it, wearing white shirts.

Tyler's is tight and tucked into his shorts with a few buttons undone. Kalen's is fastened neatly to the top, Fin's is loose and only holding on by one button, and Riggs's is open to show a white tank underneath. Each is holding a flower and looking at me with so much love, it chokes me for a moment.

The setting sun casts everything in a beautiful golden glow that touches their exposed skin like a lover's caress.

"Peyton Andrews." Tyler holds out his hand. "I have been in love with you since the moment I met you. Will you marry me, marry us, and be ours forever?"

I nod, a grin blooming on my lips.

"Thank fuck. I was going to throw you over my shoulder if you got cold feet again." Kalen winks as Riggs hurries over, and after gathering the flowers from their hands, he gives them to me before kissing my cheek.

"You look beautiful, my love," he whispers before returning to their side.

Fin's eyes run down me, and when he meets my gaze, his expression darkens with hunger. "The moment you say *I do*, I'm ripping that dress off and fucking you under the stars."

Shaking my head, I step towards them when music suddenly starts to play. It's soft and gentle, blowing across the ocean, and I smile wider and walk faster, practically running to them. They catch me in their arms and surround me, turning me to the sun and the altar they made there.

"I love you all," I say, knowing it's out of order, but I don't care, and neither do they.

We never do anything the normal way.

"We love you too," they reply, holding me tightly as my ring sparkles in the light.

Here, under the setting sun, near a beautiful island in the Mediterranean, I say I do.

It might not be legal, but to us, it's perfect.

It's our vow of love to one another forever. No matter what adventures this world holds, we will face them together until the very end.

ABOUT THE AUTHOR

K.A. Knight is a *New York Times*–bestselling romance author from a small town in England. She has always enjoyed dreaming up crazy story ideas and characters who love more than one person. After all, #WhyChoose. Knight also loves her fur babies, coffee, a good book, and monster flicks.